DEADLY ALLIES II

DEADLY ALLIES II

PRIVATE EYE WRITERS
OF AMERICA
AND
SISTERS IN CRIME
COLLABORATIVE
ANTHOLOGY

EDITED BY
ROBERT J. RANDISI
AND
SUSAN DUNLAP

DOUBLEDAY
NEW YORK   LONDON   TORONTO   SYDNEY   AUCKLAND

PUBLISHED BY DOUBLEDAY
a division of Bantam Doubleday Dell Publishing Group, Inc.
1540 Broadway, New York, New York 10036

DOUBLEDAY and the portrayal of an anchor with a dolphin
are trademarks of Doubleday,
a division of Bantam Doubleday Dell Publishing Group, Inc.

Acknowledgment
From *The Prophet* by Kahlil Gibran.
Copyright 1923 by Kahlil Gibran and renewed 1951 by Administrators C.T.A. of
Kahlil Gibran Estate and Mary G. Gibran. Reprinted by permission of Alfred A.
Knopf, Inc.

Library of Congress Cataloging-in-Publication Data

Deadly allies II : Private Eye Writers of America/Sisters in Crime collaborative
    anthology / edited by Robert J. Randisi and Susan Dunlap. — 1st ed.
        p.   cm.
    1. Detective and mystery stories, American. I. Randisi, Robert J. II. Dunlap,
Susan. III. Private Eye Writers of America. IV. Sisters in Crime. V. Title:
Deadly allies 2. VI. Title: Deadly allies two.
    PS648.D4D39   1994   93-31344
    813'.087208—dc20   CIP

ISBN 0-385-42468-X

10 9 8 7 6 5 4 3 2

To
Marilyn Wallace,
the first Deadly Ally

CONTENTS

FOREWORD

Once again two of the foremost mystery writers' organizations have combined forces to produce a collection of first-rate crime short stories: *Deadly Allies II.*

With the publication of the first *Deadly Allies,* the Private Eye Writers of America and Sisters in Crime proclaimed their commitment to the common goal of producing the quality entertainment mystery readers love. Ben Schutz's "Mary, Mary, Shut the Door" from that volume won both the Mystery Writers of America's Edgar Awards, and PWA's Shamus Award. Two other stories (by Sue Grafton and Loren D. Estleman) were nominated for the Shamus and one (Max Allan Collins's) for the Edgar. How's that for succeeding?

For readers, the pleasures of an anthology are the finds: new stories by writers you love, and new writers whose stories you will love. For editors, one of the thrills is discovering new writers. And we are delighted to introduce our "find," Carolina law professor Cathy Pickens. She debuts with a witty, totally Southern story, "Uncommon Law" (and one that should dispel any thought that the life of a small-town South Carolina lawyer is uneventful).

And for writers, too, the short story is special. For the writer of a series the short story can be a vacation in an utterly different setting, with new characters unlike those to whom he is accustomed, and problems he normally does not tackle. Or it can be a chance to have his series detective tackle the "on you in a flash" type of problem for which short stories are known. Give a dozen writers the same topic and they will produce twelve stories, each one utterly different from the other eleven.

We haven't gone that far in *Deadly Allies II,* not a dozen writers per topic, only two. In the following pages you will see how uniquely pairs of writers—a Sister in Crime and a Private Eye Writer—deal with the same theme. Sometimes the results will surprise you, occasionally shock you, often show you the familiar in an unfamiliar light, and more than once make you laugh aloud. But we feel sure they will always entertain you.

Happy reading,

Robert J. Randisi
Susan Dunlap

DEADLY ALLIES II

"The play's the thing."

"The show must go on."

For entertainers, what matters is played out before an audience. That's where they sizzle. Or where they bomb. When the houselights come up, things are safe.

Or so they should be.

But as Los Angeles actor/P.I. Saxon and Chicago Kountry Klub Lounge singer Hank Benton discover in these taut, engrossing tales, it's not acting and singing that are the life or death issues.

LES ROBERTS

Les Roberts was the first winner of the St. Martin's Press/PWA Best First Private Eye Novel Contest with his novel *An Infinite Number of Moneys.* His newest and most ambitious novel to date is *The Cleveland Connection.*

Formerly a professional musician, formerly the producer of the original "Hollywood Squares" game show—"I'll take Paul Lynde to block"—Mr. Roberts presently chronicles the cases of two P.I.s, California's Saxon—who is also a part-time actor—and Cleveland's Milan Jacovitch. Roberts is presently the President of PWA.

In "The Pig Man" Saxon is being hounded by someone who is convinced that he is not what he seems. Isn't it usually the other way around for a P.I.?

THE PIG MAN

I make half my living involved with people you'd never ask to dinner. Punks, wise guys, skels, grifters, junkies, hookers, and the bigger, dirtier fish who feed off them. It can get sticky sometimes. Nevertheless, I don't consider myself a violent person. I cross the street to avoid confrontation, and when I do find myself hip-deep in hard guys and loaded guns, I keep kicking myself for not paying more attention to my second career, which is acting. It's why I came to Los Angeles in the first place, and while no one in their right mind would call show business a kindlier, gentler profession than being a private investigator, it's considerably less dangerous.

My agent had packed me off to Minnesota for a picture, which sounded okay until they had an early snow and fell behind schedule, and I wound up doing seven weeks in a town so bereft of anything to do that the locals think it's big time when they drive over to Duluth on a Saturday night and have supper at Denny's. Tends to lull one into a feeling of safety and security to spend so much time in a place where the most heinous crime they've ever heard of is crossing against the municipality's single red light.

So when I came home to Los Angeles I was ready for some excitement. I wasn't prepared for terror and sudden death.

Since my plane arrived in L.A. at nearly midnight on a Sunday, I hired a limo to ferry me from the airport to my rented house on one of the canals in Venice. Anyone who thinks you can't drive from LAX to Venice must be thinking of the city in Italy; we have one in Los Angeles, too, just a few blocks from the ocean, built as a tourist attraction near the turn of the century and now home to a colorful collection of yuppies, druggies, elderly home owners who've been there thirty years, and a counterculture stunning in its infinite variety. If you don't believe me, check out Ocean Front Walk some Sunday afternoon, where third runners-up in a Michael Jackson look-alike contest and turbaned evangelists and one-man bands on roller skates zoom past Small World Books and the endless line of stalls and shops selling sunglasses and T-shirts.

The limo was an indulgence I couldn't afford but felt I'd earned. The backseat, the well-stocked bar, and the wraparound sound system made me feel like a Sybarite. I like that word—like a warring tribe of ancient Judea. "And Samson rose up and slew the Sybarites . . ." Of course, Samson had not slain the Sybarites at all; they'd simply moved to Los Angeles, bought a BMW, and subscribed to *Daily Variety*.

I had invited my adopted son, Marvel, to join me in the wilds of Minnesota, but he'd turned his big brown eyes on me and said, "You got to be kidding!" So he went to stay with my best friend and my assistant, Jo Zeidler, and her husband Marsh. Jo spoils him and Marsh talks basketball to him more intelligently than I can, so Marvel didn't complain about the living arrangements.

I paid off the limo driver after we'd struggled into the bungalow together with seven weeks' worth of luggage, tipping him less lavishly than I'd planned when he observed that I must be carrying the baggage for the entire Yugoslavian army. Nobody likes a smart-ass.

It was good to get home after so long, to be surrounded by my own books and paintings and furniture. And my plants. Since my lifestyle doesn't allow for pets, I'm a plant freak. I have more than fifty in varicolored pots all over the living room and about eight in my bedroom, including a ficus I'd nursed back from near-extinction and moved from my last residence in Pacific Palisades. My house sometimes resembles the set of a Tarzan movie. My next-door neighbor, Stewart Channock, had graciously consented to come in and care for the greenery while I was gone, as well as pick up and forward my mail and start my car every few days so the battery wouldn't expire.

I refuse to eat airplane food, so after dumping my bags I checked the refrigerator. Not much after seven weeks of absence—a bottle of Chardonnay, a six-pack of Guinness Stout with one missing, and a forgotten wedge of cheese that had outlived its usefulness. Nothing you could make a meal out of. What I really wanted was the kind of fancy omelette Spenser always cooks before he makes love to Susan Silverman on the living room floor—but I was out of both eggs and Susan.

Sighing, I changed into a sweatshirt and jeans and went out to my car, which by prearrangement I park across the street in the lot of an apartment building. My destination was an all-night market four blocks away. Even in the dark I could see that someone had scrawled WASH ME in the dust on the trunk, a not unreasonable request after the car had sat out in the elements for seven weeks.

I was pleased that the engine started and made a mental note to buy Stewart a bottle of scotch for his trouble. I switched on the headlights. The windshield was smeared with an overlay of greasy California grit, in which someone had written with a wet finger: CIA. Damn kids, I thought as I Windexed the glass with a paper towel. It's not a bad area I live in, it just isn't a great one, but then unless you're in Beverly Hills or Bel Air, there are no great neighborhoods in Los Angeles.

The next morning I called my various children, friends, and lovers to announce my return, made plans to pick up Marvel that evening, walked to the corner for a *Times*, and read it out on my balcony with a mug of coffee at my side. Los Angeles doesn't have much going for it anymore except its weather; being able to read the paper outside in October is one of the few pleasures we have left.

I went into the small den I'd constructed from a storage room on the second floor of the house and booted up my computer. I'd ascertained from Jo that there was nothing pressing at the office and had decided to take a day for myself before getting back into the swing of things. I sat there reading the scrolling screen. Travel fatigue made it tough, trying to get my head back into reviewing some of my old cases, including a few that I hadn't yet closed, but it beat hell out of wearing a tie, fighting the freeways, punching a time clock, and putting up with crap from a boss. We self-employed people have the best life imaginable—if we can make a living.

By three o'clock I was in high gear. Overdue bills were paid, overdue letters written, and I was feeling almost back to normal. Until something hit my window with a thump.

I work beside a sliding glass door with a peaceful view of the canal, replete with noisy ducks, an occasional rowboat or paddleboat, and every so often an empty Slurpee cup or a used condom floating by. The window overlooking the street is across the room, and when the sound made me glance over there, something wet was running down the glass. I heard a voice, raspy with hatred, scream, "CIA *pig!*"

I ran to the window in time to see a battered brown Dodge van roaring around the corner as if the hounds of Hell were snapping at its tail pipe. On the sidewalk just below my window a can of Budweiser beer was still rolling.

I remembered the writing on my windshield I'd dismissed as a kid's prank, and a strange burning started in my stomach like yesterday's bratwurst sandwich. I didn't realize it then, but it was the icy heat of fear.

At six o'clock I went over to the cinder-block house next door with which mine shared a common front yard. Stewart Channock answered my knock holding a drink, wearing the dress shirt and tie in which he worked all day as a financial consultant, whatever that was. I didn't really know Stewart well; we were more neighbors than friends. We said hello in the parking lot, shared a gardener, and he'd kindly offered to water my plants while I was gone.

"Welcome home," he said. "When'd you get back?"

"Last night, late."

"Come on in. Drink?"

"I need one," I said.

He went into the kitchen and poured me more than a jigger of scotch. I swallowed it down as though I was thirsty.

"Hope I didn't kill your plants—I even talked to them. About football."

"You did a great job, Stewart. I appreciate it. Uh—when was the last time you started my car?"

He frowned, thinking. "Wednesday, I guess. Did the battery die?"

"No, no. Was anything—written on the windshield?"

"Written on the . . . ? No, why?"

I told him what I'd found, and about the beer can incident that afternoon and the brown Dodge van.

He laughed.

"It's not funny," I said.

"Sure it is. Listen, the people walking the streets in this town are Looney Tunes. You start letting them get to you, you might as well go back to Wisconsin to stay."

"Minnesota. But what if this guy thinks I really am with the CIA and wants to kill me?"

"Then he would have done it, and not left his calling card. Come on, this isn't one of your movies."

Right there you could tell Stewart wasn't in show business. Actors call them pictures, directors call them films, and distributors and theater owners call them shows. No one in the business ever uses the word "movie."

"So you think I should ignore it?"

"What's your other option? Go tell the cops someone threw a beer can at you and wrote on your car, but you don't know who he is? What do you think, they're going to stake out the street and wait for him to do it again?"

I nibbled at my drink, feeling more than a little foolish. He was right, of course; I was overreacting. Seven weeks in the North Woods with nothing to do but watch haircuts, eating the Velveeta cheese which was a small town hotel's idea of gourmet food, and living out of a suitcase takes its toll, and I was undoubtedly stretched thin.

"All right, Stewart, I'll forget it," I said, getting up. "And thanks again for the caretaking."

I went back to my own house, picking up the beer can and putting it in the big bag I take to a recycling center every few weeks. At least I'd made two and a half cents on the deal.

Jo and Marsh had invited me for dinner, and it was good to see them again. It was even better seeing Marvel. In the four years he'd been living with me I'd watched him grow from a scared, skinny adolescent who could barely read and write into a handsome, athletic, and witty young man who was beginning his senior year in high school. Considering the adoption had been unplanned and almost out of necessity rather than any desire on my part to share my life with a strange black kid, it had worked out well. He'd become part of who I am, a part I hadn't known existed, and I'd evidently done a damn good job raising him, because he was turning into a real champ.

I spent the evening recounting war stories from the trenches in Duluth, and we didn't get back home until nearly eleven, late for a school night. Marvel went to sleep and I sat up and watched Johnny and then Dave, a habit I'd fallen into on location when there wasn't anything else to do.

The next morning I was refreshed and raring to go, but my feeling of well-being evaporated like a raindrop in Death Valley when I went out to get my car and drive it to my office in Hollywood and saw someone had spray-painted CIA in red letters on the sidewalk, with an arrow pointing to my door.

I've lived in big cities all my life, Chicago before L.A., and I've stead-fastly refused to become one of those urban paranoiacs who triple-lock their doors, scan the street for possible muggers, and sleep with a .44 Magnum under their pillows which will undoubtedly discharge someday and blow off an ear. But this CIA business had me worried.

Trying to keep my mind on my work at the office was a bear. I kept worrying what might be happening at the house while I wasn't there. I decided to go home early.

I'd stopped at the store on my way home and picked up the very basics a gourmet cook like me needs to simply survive a few days— butter, garlic, tomato sauce and tomato paste, several different wedges of cheese that were not Velveeta, and milk. After changing into comfortable sweats and a pair of deck shoes with too many holes in them to wear outside, I went up to my den and sat down at my desk, reading while I ate the linguine with the sauce I'd made from scratch.

Then I heard the raspy shout from the street again. "CIA *pig!*"

This time I got to the window in time to see him. The Pig Man. He was over six feet tall, in his early forties with a droopy mustache, slim and ropy with a slight potbelly, long dirty-blond hair flowing almost to his shoulders from a balding crown, in blue jeans and a turquoise muscle shirt, and just climbing into the Dodge van parked halfway down the street. The set of his shoulders was tense and rigid. As far as I knew, I'd never set eyes on him before.

He sat in the van for a moment. From my vantage point I could only see him from the neck down, his fists clenched on the steering wheel. Finally he banged them on the dashboard before starting the motor and peeling away from the curb, leaving a strip of rubber. It was profoundly disturbing. God knows there are enough people ticked off at me for good reason without having to worry about some deluded stranger.

I dumped the remainder of my lunch into the garbage disposal and poured myself a Laphroaig, neat. I never drink during the day, but I was wound as tight as a three-dollar watch. Anybody bizarre enough to throw a beer can at my window and spray-paint my sidewalk was capable of worse.

Just past three the phone rang. My agent, asking me how it had gone in Minnesota and was I interested in reading for a new series on the Fox network. I was and I wasn't; getting tied down to a six-days-a-week job didn't appeal to me, but the kind of money they pay you for a series did. I was standing in the middle of the room with the phone cradled against my shoulder, pulling yellow leaves off my schefflera plant, when I glanced out the window and saw the brown van come around the corner again and park across the street.

"I'll call you back," I said. I hung up and went to the window, being careful to stay well out of sight. The Pig Man got out, cast a look of loathing toward my house, and went into the building across the street. I waited for about two minutes, then grabbed a pencil and notepad and went downstairs to copy the number on his license plate.

I peered into the front seat of the paneled van, half expecting to see a claymore mine or a flamethrower or a box of hand grenades. All that was in evidence, however, was a crumpled Styrofoam box from Burger King and a few cans of Budweiser, one empty. That was hardly damning evidence; there must be at least a million people in greater Los Angeles who drink Bud.

I came back inside, half expecting a bullet to smash into my back. There were twelve apartments in the building across the street, and I wondered which one he was visiting, whether its window faced mine. I usually leave my drapes open all the time so the plants can get light, but now I pulled them shut. I was as safe in my own home as I was ever going to be, and the security felt woefully inadequate.

Marvel came home and we chatted for a few minutes—it was World Series time and to my horror he was rooting for Oakland. But he had homework to do and repaired to his room, his stereo making the whole house tremble. I tried to read, but I couldn't concentrate. Instead I paced and chain-smoked, every so often sneaking a peek through the closed drapes to see if the Dodge van was still there.

It was.

Somewhere around dinnertime I heard Stewart Channock going into his house. Some human companionship would have been welcome, and I had the urge to walk next door and have a drink with him, but he would have thought it peculiar; we didn't have that close a relationship. We had nothing in common. I don't understand people who move numbers around all day long, and I was sure he was equally mystified by those who chase around after insurance cheats, embezzlers, skips, children kidnapped by divorced parents, and occasionally, people who kill.

I decided I didn't want to be in the house anymore that evening. My paranoia was going to turn me into a candidate for the rubber room if I stayed there much longer. I waited for Marvel to finish his studying and we went out to a Japanese restaurant for sushi and saki. As usual, Marvel talked up a storm, and it took my mind off my troubles.

We got home at ten o'clock, and I noted with relief that the brown van was gone. But in the living room the drapes across the window were blowing. Marvel went over to investigate, and his shoes crunched on long, wicked shards of broken glass that hadn't been there when we left.

"Marvel, stay back!" I said.

He froze, looking at me with eyes that were just this side of frightened. I went past him and pulled the drapes aside.

The window had been shattered, and lying on the carpet amid the debris was a big rock. If I had been sitting by the window with the drapes open, reading, I would have been decapitated. The skin on the back of my neck tingled unpleasantly.

Enough was enough.

The next morning, slightly cranky from a hangover and from the onerous task of cleaning up the glass from my carpet, I was at the front desk of the Culver City division of the Los Angeles Police Department, talking to the desk officer, whose silver name tag said he was L. Tedescu.

I put the rock on the desk in front of him. "My name is Saxon," I said, and told him my address. "This came through my living room window last night."

He looked at it without emotion. "See who did it?"

"I wasn't home at the time."

L. Tedescu's eyebrows—or eyebrow, rather, he only had one that went clear across his forehead—lifted.

"I'm being harassed," I went on, and told him about the man in the brown Dodge van. "From his age and the way he looked, the way he was dressed, I'd guess he was probably a Vietnam veteran with a grudge against the CIA."

"*Are* you with the CIA, Mr. Saxon?"

A real rocket scientist, L. Tedescu. I felt the essence of a headache starting behind my eyes. If I didn't get at least three aspirin down my throat in the next few minutes it was going to be a bitch kitty. "First off, if I were with the CIA I wouldn't tell you. Secondly, I'd take care of it myself."

"Don't even think about taking the law into your own hands, sir," he said pompously. "You'll be the one in trouble."

"If I was going to do that I wouldn't have come here for help. I have the guy's license number." I pushed the number from my notepad across the glass-topped counter. L. Tedescu looked at it as if he could divine the mysteries of the ages from it. Then he handed it back to me. "There's not much we can do about this."

"Why not?"

"He hasn't committed any crime."

"Throwing a rock through a window isn't a crime?"

"You didn't see it. You don't know it's the same man."

"Who else could it be?"

He looked at me, his face a mask of apathy. "You'd know that better than I would, sir."

"Well, what about screaming outside my window? It scares the crap out of me."

"That may be, but it's not a crime."

"Disturbing the peace?"

He shook his head. "We'd have to arrest everyone who raised his voice. Now, if he calls you on the phone and makes threats, that's a crime. But if he does it in person it isn't, and we can't take any official action."

For a bit I was too stunned to reply. The best I could come up with was "That's the dumbest thing I ever heard."

L. Tedescu's eyes turned to slits. "It's the law."

The rock sat incongruously on the desk between us. "He spray-painted the sidewalk. He wrote CIA on the city sidewalk. Defacing public property?"

"Yes it is, and he probably did it. But you didn't see him." He put his hand on the rock and moved it a few inches toward me. "Look, Mr. Saxon—right now, not five hundred yards from where we're standing, someone's probably selling illegal drugs to eight-year-olds. Armed robberies happen at gas stations and convenience marts four or five times a night in this division. People getting behind the wheel of a two-thousand-pound car when they're too drunk or stoned even to walk, driving up on a sidewalk and killing a kid. Rape. Spouse abuse. Child abuse. And I won't even mention the hookers and drug dealers and the knife fights in the bars."

"I understand all that . . ."

"I'm glad you do. Los Angeles just doesn't have nearly enough cops—even if what you know this guy to be doing was illegal, it'd be pretty low on our priority scale." He ran his fingers through his mouse-brown hair. "If he does anything else, if you *catch* him at it, let us know, all right? Otherwise . . ." He turned both hands palms up to show me he was powerless. "I can't even write up a report."

I glared at him for a moment, clenching my teeth to bite back all the angry, frustrated things I wanted to scream. Then I spun on my heel and stalked toward the glass doors. My righteous indignation was like a steel rod up the middle of me.

"Mr. Saxon?"

I stopped and turned back eagerly, hoping he'd change his mind and write up a report, that the police, whose motto in Los Angeles is "To Protect and Serve," would hunt down the Pig Man in the brown van so I could go on with my life and my work and not be spooked by every zephyr that stirred a tree or every stray cat prowling in a Dumpster for its dinner. "Yes, officer?"

He held his hand out to me, and it wasn't until I got all the way back to the desk that I saw what the offering was.

"Did you want your rock?"

It's only a short walk from the police station to the sheriff's office in the Culver City municipal center. Last year's tragic murder of a young actress has made it more difficult to get someone's name and address from their automobile license plate, but nothing's impossible if you have a friend in a high place. At least I hoped she was still a friend.

Female law enforcement officers don't often look like Angie Dickinson or Stepfanie Kramer, but Sergeant Sharyl Capps came pretty close, with a headful of honey-blonde hair, green eyes, and an overbite that could drive a person crazy. We'd met when I was researching my first novel some years ago and had enjoyed a nine-week fling that ended, as most such relationships do, with a gradual distancing that eventually turned to nothing at all. She was almost as tall as I, with several medals and commendations in her service record. I wasn't sure how I would be received, but she smiled when I walked into her office—it wasn't the broadest, most welcoming smile I'd ever seen, but it was a smile nonetheless—and shook my hand in a manner that was a little too business-like, considering.

"It's been a while," she said. The ironic lilt in her voice just made her more appealing.

"I guess it has. I've been busy."

"I know. I've seen some of your movies and TV stuff. I guess you're doing all right. Are you still a P.I. too?"

"Whenever anyone asks me. Sharyl, I've got a problem."

"I know." I suppose I deserved the dig. When I'd been with her I was commitment-phobic, and I guess she was still a little miffed. I winced. Then I told her about my adventures of the last few days. Her face remained passive but the amusement in her eyes annoyed hell out of me. "You're a big tough private eye," she said. "Why don't you take care of it yourself?"

"Take the needle out, Sharyl—this is serious."

"Well, the police told you right. There's not a damn thing they can do." She shrugged. "Nothing I can do, either."

I held out the paper with the license number. "You can run this for me."

She looked at it without touching it. "I'd get my butt in a sling," she said.

I thought about remarking that it would look good even in a sling, but wisely desisted. "I'm not going gunning for him," I said. "Just on television."

"Then what's the point?"

"I'd like to know who my enemy is, at least."

She started to shake her head when I said, "Sharyl, you wouldn't want my murder on your conscience, would you?"

She regarded me narrowly. "Not unless I got to do it myself," she said. She took the paper from me, pointing to a chair opposite her desk. "Park it. I'll be back in a minute."

She left me sitting there with nothing to do. Unlike dentists and lawyers, deputy sheriffs don't have back-dated magazines in their offices to browse through while you wait. I did notice a framed photograph on her desk, a smiling Sharyl and a big beefy muscle-hunk, both on bicycles down by Venice Beach, looking the way Southern Californians in love are supposed to.

In twenty minutes she was back.

"Who's your friend?" I said, pointing at the photo.

"He's my partner. Name's Frank Trone."

"Was that taken one day out on bicycle patrol?"

"None of your business. Look, Saxon, I've already violated procedure here. You want this stuff or not?" She waved some computer printouts at me.

I sighed. Sometimes it seems as though life is one long series of what ifs and might have beens. "Sure," I said.

"The van is registered to one Harlan Panec," she said, handing me one of the printouts. Harlan Panec lived over in North Hollywood, in the San Fernando Valley. Not a high-rent district.

"I never heard of him."

"You sure?"

"Sharyl, if you'd ever met a guy named Harlan Panec, wouldn't you remember?"

"Just for the hell of it, I put him through the computer to see if he had a sheet," she said. "He's a naughty boy. Forty-three years old, dishonorable discharge from the army in '73, misdemeanor possession of marijuana, assault, drunk and disorderly, and several citations for speeding."

I jotted the address down in my notebook.

Sharyl frowned. "Stay away from this guy, Saxon."

I tried to be casual. "Why? He's not exactly a master criminal."

"Because." Her laser gaze reduced me to a small dust pyramid. "You're not nearly as tough as you think you are."

I called a glazier to fix the window, but of course he couldn't come for three days, so I made do with natural air-conditioning and prayed for no rain. The brown van didn't appear the rest of that day, or if it did, the Pig Man didn't indulge his penchant for screaming under windows like Brando in *A Streetcar Named Desire*, but the curiosity that was eating a hole in my gut, the twin of the one caused by fear, got to me by the next morning.

I had to see Harlan Panec, tell him he was mistaken, that he had me mixed up with somebody else, so I could get on with my life without waiting for another rock to come through my window—or worse.

The street address Sharyl Capps had given me was just off Lankershim Boulevard near Vanowen Street, a neighborhood of small industrial buildings and a few houses that were tiny, old, and dilapidated. Not many of the residents spoke English as their first language, and when I pulled my car around the corner at about eleven o'clock they were all out on the street in the sunshine, watching the black-and-white squad cars and the city ambulance, talking in Spanish or Korean or Farsi in the hushed tones reserved for the presence of death.

I pulled over to the curb and watched with them. There must have been twenty uniformed policemen running around on the barren front lawn of the house where Harlan Panec lived. The brown van was parked in the weed-choked driveway, and behind it an ancient Volkswagen Bug. On the sagging porch a woman of about forty, in baggy jeans and a tie-dyed shirt that was a holdover from the Woodstock years, was crying and screaming while a policewoman who didn't look like Angie Dickinson tried to talk to her. There were reddish-brown stains on the hysterical woman's hands and arms. It was hard to tell because emotion distorted her features, but she looked vaguely familiar to me. It took me a few minutes to remember where I'd seen her—going in and out of the apartment building across the street from me.

I got out of the car and stood near the curb as a team of paramedics wheeled a gurney out of the house and lifted it carefully down the steps. I couldn't identify its passenger because he was wrapped in a plastic bag from top to toe, but I knew in my heart it was the Pig Man I'd seen beneath my window.

"What happened?" I said to an Asian woman nearby as they loaded the body into the ambulance. She glanced at me fearfully and moved away. I wandered down the sidewalk and repeated my question to a short, muscular black man in a tank top.

"The woman come over this morning," he said, "an' found him." He rolled his eyes and drew his finger across his throat, making a hideous sound with his mouth. "They got him in the bed."

I shoved my hands into my pockets. That way no one would see them shaking.

When I got home at about one in the afternoon I poured myself a Laphroaig and downed it in two swallows. It was too good—and expensive—to gulp down like that, but sometimes need overcomes nicety. Thus fortified, I crossed the front yard, nearly tripping over a duck, and rapped on Stewart Channock's door. I'd seen his car in its space across the street, so I knew he was home. I'd known he would be anyway.

"Yes?" he said, his voice muffled.

"It's me, Stewart. We have to talk."

"I'm a little busy right now." I heard him move away.

I banged on the door again, harder this time, with more authority.

"Not now," he said through the door.

"CIA pig!" I yelled. There was a pause—a loud one—and then he opened up.

We just looked at each other. Then he sighed and moved aside. "Come on in," he said.

There were two suitcases on the floor near the sofa. "Taking a trip, Stewart?"

"What do you want?"

"You know what I want. Except for a real dumb cop and a real smart lady sheriff, you were the only one who knew about the guy who was hassling me and throwing rocks through my window. Now he's dead."

"That's got nothing to do with me."

"It's everything to do with you," I said. "The guy saw you getting out of my car last week after you'd gone over to start it up for me, right? He recognized you. He must have known you from Vietnam. I happen to know he was in the army in 1973 so it figures. Then he saw you come in here to water the plants, and he thought this was your house."

He shrugged.

"What was it, drugs? You were involved in covert CIA drug-smuggling in Asia and poor old Harlan Panec—that was his name—was in the wrong place at the wrong time and saw you."

"You have a vivid imagination, Saxon."

"A lot of guys who never got over Nam have vivid imaginations," I went on. "They came back home in the early seventies to a country that didn't give a damn, and have been fighting the war in their heads ever since, probably because they realized they'd been over there fighting for a government no better than the sleaziest drug peddler. Panec looked like he was one of them; he had that half-crazy, stretched-too-tight look. When he saw you again after all these years, the poor bastard snapped like a frayed rubber band. But he was too dumb to do anything except throw rocks and yell."

"You're talking crap you don't know anything about."

"Then pay no attention, let me ramble. Maybe you're still with the Agency, maybe not. But whatever you are doing it's probably illegal, so when I told you about the writing on my car, the brown van, the spray painting under my window, you realized you'd been blown. You waited for the van to show up again and you followed it to Panec's place in North Hollywood and cut his throat. Probably not the first guy you ever killed."

"You'll never prove any of this, you know."

"Maybe not."

"But you're going to try?"

"I have to," I said.

He pushed himself away from the door where he'd been leaning casually. "Let's head into the bathroom, shall we?"

I shook my head. "I don't have to go."

"Move it," he said, and there was a gun in his hand. It was a small gun that fit in his palm, the kind women might carry in their purses. At close range it would kill as efficiently as a bazooka. I hesitated, and he said, "Don't be stupid. You know I'll use this if I have to."

"Those are noisy little devils," I said. "People will hear."

He moved toward me. "Do you want to take the chance?"

I didn't. I don't like having guns aimed at me. I should be used to it, but I'm not. On TV, of course, the private investigator would have slapped it out of his hand and overpowered him, but it had already been pointed out to me that I'm not as tough as I think I am.

I walked into the bedroom ahead of him. Another suitcase, half full, was open on the bed. He went over to the dresser, opened a drawer, and felt around inside. Then he pulled out a pair of silvery handcuffs.

"I never knew you were into kinky sex, Stewart."

"Shut up." He motioned with the gun and I went into the bathroom with him right behind me. He switched on the light, and the exhaust fan in the ceiling began humming noisily. There were cute little aqua and black mermaids on the shower curtain.

"Kneel down on the floor by the john. Do it!"

I did it. The porcelain tile was cold on my knees through my jeans. He took my hand and fastened one of the cuffs around my wrist. "Not too tight?" he said. He put the chain around the thick pipe running from the toilet into the wall, then braceleted my other hand and snapped the cuffs shut so I was kneeling over the closed toilet as though at prayer.

"There's no window," he said, "and the fan will muffle the noise, so don't bother yelling. Besides, no one else in the neighborhood will be home until evening."

"And by that time you're in another city with a whole new identity. Stewart, you're a slime."

"There's things you don't understand, so don't be so damned judgmental. If I was such a slime you'd be dead by now."

"You aren't going to shoot me?"

He considered it for more than a moment. Then he shook his head. "Finally you have to say 'enough' to killing." He went to the door. "You okay?"

"I'm real comfy," I said bitterly.

He looked at me for a minute. I suppose he was trying to decide whether he'd made a mistake, whether he should just shoot me in the head and be done with it. But my luck held.

"*Ciao,*" he said, and left me there.

I couldn't hear much through the closed door, but I did hear him leave the house. He was an invisible man, marching through life carrying out his own twisted agenda, and if some other poor fool like Harlan Panec got in his way, he'd take care of it the same way and disappear again, vanishing into the mist like Brigadoon. It takes a special mind-set, I imagine, to live rootless without family or friends, worrying that someone was always in the shadows, watching. Not for nothing were guys like Stewart Channock known as "spooks."

I shifted around on the tile floor, trying to get comfortable, and flexed the fingers of my imprisoned hands. Between the toilet and the cabinet that housed the sink was a wooden magazine rack. From my vantage point I saw two *Newsweek*s, a *Forbes*, yesterday's *Wall Street Journal*, a crossword puzzle magazine, and a couple of paperback books—but I wasn't much in the mood for reading.

I knew what would happen when he got to his car—my making a simple phone call had ensured it—but in the completely closed room I could barely hear the gunshots from the parking lot, and I had no way of knowing who shot whom until Sharyl Capps and her partner/lover from the sheriff's office kicked in the door and told me.

BARBARA D'AMATO

Besides being a playwright, novelist, and crime researcher, Barbara D'Amato has been a stage manager, researcher for criminal attorneys, assistant tiger handler, and assistant surgical orderly (positions not necessarily connected).

Her musical comedies (written with her husband Anthony D'Amato) have played in Chicago and London. Her horror novel, published under the pseudonym Malacai Black, was nominated for an Anthony Award, and her true crime book *The Doctor, the Murder, the Mystery* was featured on the television program "Unsolved Mysteries." But she is best known in the mystery field for her witty and meticulously researched series featuring Chicago reporter Cat Marsala, the latest in which is *Hard Women*.

She also teaches mystery writing to Chicago police officers. So it is no surprise how real and at the same time bizarre the world of Windy City cops is in "If You've Got the Money, Honey, I've Got the Crime."

IF YOU'VE GOT THE MONEY, HONEY, I'VE GOT THE CRIME

Eight or ten of the third watch were standing around in a clump outside the roll call room door. It wasn't considered the thing to do, to file in early and sit meekly in the seats. Instead, the officers hung around outside talking, and they'd go piling in through the door at the very last minute. This always annoyed Sergeant Pat Touhy, which was exactly what it was supposed to do. Touhy folded her arms and glanced with exaggerated patience out the high windows at the amber sodium vapor street lighting that ran along State Street, making the pavement look Venusian and the dark beyond look purple. A few flakes of snow fell, briefly visible as they passed through the light, then vanishing into the dark.

In the hall, Officer Hiram Quail had spent some time talking about a river in Michigan, the Pere Marquette, where he loved to go when he had a few days off, or even just a weekend, and fish for rainbow trout. It made a change, Quail said, from Chicago. And Officer

Stanley Mileski said, "You can embroider that on a sampler!" Then Norm Bennis described the last event of his and Susanna Maria Figueroa's tour last night. Figueroa was a short, energetic white woman of twenty-five. Bennis was a stocky black man, ten years older, who had twelve years on the job, compared to Figueroa's three. He considered himself her mentor. So did she, some of the time.

"The grocer, this little Korean guy," Bennis said, lounging with his left shoulder against the cinderblock wall, "he has a deal with his wife upstairs, she's sittin' up with the baby. They got no store alarm, nothin' like that. Too expensive, or maybe he don't think we'll come, who knows? So if he's gettin' held up, he pushes this button, buzzer sounds upstairs, not in the store, wife calls the cops on her phone."

"Which is not a bad idea," Figueroa said.

"So last night he sees this seriously evil-looking pair come in his store. Chains, black leather with Satan on the back, tattoos, like they're putting a sign up, 'Please arrest me.' They're slouching around lookin' at stuff, see. Grocer pushes his private panic button. Our bad men don't hear it, see, but upstairs the wife calls the police. So Figueroa and me we get the call and we go screamin' over there, like there's an armed robbery in progress, and we go bustin' into the place, the two evildoers are standing there smiling."

"I *hate* that in a crook," Mileski said.

"Absolutely nothin' has happened. One's looking at the videos, is he gonna rent *Grease* or is he gonna rent a skin flick. The other one is deciding between Cheerios and maybe a healthy hot cereal like Wheatena. The shopkeeper has to admit they ain't pulled a firearm yet, and we pat 'em down, they don't have gun one. Meanwhile, one of 'em's saying, 'Well, I know you have to do your duty, officer, but I think maybe my civil rights are being violated here.' This is education at Joliet for you. The other one says do we have probable cause."

"Probable cause!" Figueroa said. "I ask you."

"So by then even the shopkeeper has to admit everything's copacetic, and we stand around with the two non-perps and the Korean, shoot the shit a little, the non-perps do some shoppin', buy a package of cigarettes is all, we look around the store a little and the Korean offers me a Milky Way, but hell, I'm on a diet—"

"Coulda given it to me," Figueroa said.

"And we're about to leave, Figueroa says, 'Hey!' to me. She's pointin' at the non-perps and I gotta admit I don't see anything wrong.

"She says, 'I woulda guessed that guy 5'10" a hundred and forty pounds we came in. Looks one-seventy now.' Damn if she isn't right. Other one's gained a little weight, too.

" 'Hey, boys,' I say, 'gimme just another feel for those guns.'

"Well, they start to run. We flip 'em both, prone 'em out on the floor, and whaddya know. They got shirt pockets, pants pockets, jacket pockets, jockstraps, everything just fulla stuff. They got chocolate bars in the shirt, already gettin' warm, cans of pickled octopus, package of steak strips in the jacket, one of 'em's got videos all around inside his belt. Other one, he's like got a hard-on, I think, but turns out it's a cucumber. And what really gets to me is this: They picked all this crap up while we were talkin' with the Korean and all of us were wanderin' around the store. Is this *bad?* I mean, what kind of idiots do they think we are, we're gonna let them walk out with a couple hundred dollars' worth of groceries in their pants?"

"Sounds like they almost got away with it," Stanley Mileski said.

"Well, yeah. If Figueroa didn't have such a *fashion-conscious* mind, yeah. I guess they woulda."

"You search 'em, Figueroa?" Mileski asked.

Hiram Quail said, "Pat 'em down, did you?"

Mileski said, "Give 'em the giggles; feel 'em up?"

Quail said, "Course, they'd hardly know the difference, male or female, in that uniform."

"Unisex, that's the Chicago Police Department," Mileski said.

"Basically, you look like a really short guy."

"Oh, drop it, Mileski." Figueroa brushed them both off and went into the roll call room. But at the same time, she knew it was true. Except for the difficulty of stuffing female hips and busts into the dark blue pants and shirt, there was nothing particularly edifying about the uniform. And the Chicago Police Department gave women two choices for hairstyles: A. Short. B. Tied up under the cap. Figueroa currently was wearing a very short ponytail.

Norm sidled over and sat next to her. He said, "Don't worry about those guys." She appreciated it, but she was still annoyed.

She was well aware that this was a sensitive area to her. And she couldn't let them see they could push her buttons on it or they'd never stop. Figueroa had grown up in a half-Mexican, half-Italian family—as one friend said, "Just destined to be calm and placid, weren't you?" Traditional roles were important for her older relatives. Nobody but her sister had been supportive at all when Suze decided to be a cop. In fact, they had been horrified. It was unfeminine. Her mother said, "Susanna, you won't look pretty." Both her Mexican and her Italian relatives thought white confirmation dresses with ruffles from top to bottom were the standard against which all female clothing should be judged.

Suze herself, while presenting a tough, decisive front to her uncles, aunts, grandparents, mother and father, nourished a small worm of doubt. Maybe her choices in life *were* unfeminine.

Maybe she was wrong. A divorce the year after she joined the department hadn't helped any, either. Still, she thought she was nice-looking, if not gorgeous, and by God, she was going to do a job that interested her, not just sit around like a cupcake.

Roll call ran its usual course. Sergeant Pat Touhy, herself a tall, strong-looking woman, read some crimes. Also one section of the Illinois consti-tution, which was today's lesson for the troops. Touhy had printed it on the blackboard which stood next to the car assignment sheets and asked several officers to explain phrases out of it. The Chicago Police Depart-ment took cop education medium seriously.

Suze sat through the whole thing with her arms folded, her forehead frowning and her mind grumpy. She wasn't called on, and it was a good thing.

When Touhy gave them the word to hit the bricks and clear, Figueroa and Bennis took off into the night in their old reliable squad car, desig-nated 1-33, meaning first district, car thirty-three.

Figueroa drove. Pretty soon, the seriously macho Mars lights and the seriously macho radio and the seriously macho dash equipment started to make her feel better. Their beat ran along Michigan Avenue past the Chicago Hilton and Towers, the Art Institute and some of the priciest lake frontage in the world. Then they swung back under the El, looking for homeless sleeping and maybe freezing in small, dark, hidden places behind Dumpsters. Snow continued to sift past the streetlights, but melted on the ground.

Not fifteen minutes out of the lot, at 1131 hours, Bennis and Figueroa saw three men talking huddled in a doorway off south State. One of the men was distinctly better dressed than the other two. Figueroa stopped the car half a block farther along—the dome light was turned off, of course, so that it wouldn't go on when they got out of the car—and she and Bennis walked up on the men and surprised them, Bennis going around the block and coming in from behind.

Five minutes later they were calling the dispatcher.

Bennis said, "1-33."

"Thirty-three, go."

"I've got three in custody from a drug arrest and no cage. We need another car to transport the third offender."

Mileski, who was alone in his car tonight, took the third perp. Figueroa and Bennis spent half an hour in the station on the paper and then they were out again.

"Not exactly your difficult bust," Figueroa said.

"Sitting ducks."

"Like taking candy from a baby."

"*However*, quite pleasant for the old personnel file."

The dispatcher said, "1-33."

Suze said, "Thirty-three."

"I have a number-two parker at—"

Norm, who was driving now, swung the wheel. "Watch, it'll be a car in a handicapped zone."

"Ten cents says bus stop."

Meanwhile, the dispatcher said, "1-27."

Mileski said, "Twenty-seven."

"I have a car blocking the alley at 126 North Rush."

"Ten ninety-nine."

By the time Bennis and Figueroa had dealt with their car, Bennis winning the dime because it was indeed a handicapped zone, they heard Mileski call for a tow.

Then the dispatcher said, "1-33."

Suze answered, "Thirty-three."

"We have a disturbance at the Kountry Klub Lounge, 621 north Franklin. That's 621 north on Franklin."

"Ten-four, squad."

"Let us know if you need backup. Seems to be a fight. Bartender called it in."

Norm had always told Suze that the main thing cops did was walk into a situation *in control*. When the civilians were too zonked or too crooked or too angry or too nuts or too injured to cope, cops coped.

Suze walked into the Kountry Klub Lounge in a mood to cope.

After the cold outdoors, Suze felt she had sunk into a pillow of warm beer fumes. The Kountry Klub may have intended to be country, but it had its metaphors a little mixed and had more western than Nashville in its decor. Inside the front door was a saguaro cactus made of green denim with ties of black thread representing needles. It was taller than Norm. There were skulls from longhorn cattle over the bar to Suze's right, an occasional Navajo blanket on the walls, and the dividers at the two edges of the stage, which was at the farthest end of the room, were split-rail fencing. The stage was brightly lit. A drummer was sitting, bored but patient, behind his drums on a raised dais, also bordered with split-rail fencing. Three exotically dressed women sat together on the edge of the dais near the drummer. The apron stage was a large expanse of blond wood twenty feet wide and fifteen deep, raised maybe three feet above the dance-floor/audience-floor level.

Lying in the center of the stage, sparkling in the spotlights, was a glass hypodermic syringe.

Closer to Norm and Suze, in the somewhat darker area intended for the audience, people were milling around and shouting. Looking at them, Figueroa thought, Whoa! There's never been so much denim in such a small space outside of the Levi's factory shipping room. There was denim studded with metal stars and denim coated with rhinestones. Embroidered denim. Slashed denim. Red denim. Even denim shot through with Mylar threads. Suze took stock. Several members of the audience were damaged, one with a bloody nose, another with a deep cut over a cheekbone that was oozing blood, a third with a scalp cut that was *pouring* blood. On the floor, four men were sitting on another guy who was rolling around—trying to roll around, Suze mentally corrected herself—and screaming assorted obscenities. The bartender wore a striped shirt with sleeve garters and a white apron. He went right on serving drinks.

Without consulting each other, Norm and Suze worked as a team, Norm stopping in the doorway and putting out a call on his radio for the paramedics, Suze walking forward and saying, "Now, who can tell me what happened here?"

A woman said, "This man, he was playing and singing, and then—"

"Just jumped down and started swinging at everybody," the man with the bloody cheek said.

"Hey, you yelled at him first, guy," said the man with the cut scalp.

Suze nodded and studied the singer, who was writhing on the floor. He wore Levi's, ones so tight that, even though he was thrashing back and forth and shrieking, he couldn't bring his knees up to his chest. He wore a western fringed leather vest, cut shorter than usual, with dangles of turquoise and silver on the ends of the fringe. Under it nothing. No shirt, just heavy-duty pecs and lats, deltoids, and biceps on the arms, and a sheen that was either oil or perspiration. Suze classified him: hunk type, makes good use of it.

Bennis came up behind her. "You find the manager," he said. "I'll look after little buddy here."

The only person in the place who was dressed like normal folks turned out to be the stage manager, and he was standing next to a light board a couple steps below stage level, off stage left. He responded immediately to Suze's questions. This was a man, she thought, who liked things to proceed on schedule and was unhappy with the present unpleasantness.

"What's the deal here?" she said.

"Your basic fight, I guess," he said.

"Who's been fighting?"

"Mainly Hank. Hank's the act."

"Yeah, I saw the sign on the way in. 'Hank Benton with Faith, Hope and Charity.' "

"That's him. He's a regular with us. He's popular here."

"Not with everybody. The guy over there said somebody in the audience insulted him."

The manager said, "Yeah, well, he was acting funny before that, is why."

"Starting from when?"

"Well, see, he sings eight songs then takes a break. Then he sings another eight. You know. So this one is the finale of this set, 'If You've Got the Money, Honey, I've Got the Time.' His fave, I guess. See, he liked to open this number by me cutting the lights out everyplace." The manager added hastily, "I don't mean the exit lights. We always have them on. But the houselights and stage lights I cut. So he does the first four chords in the dark. Dramatic, he thinks. Then the lights come up and he goes real quick into the song. Which went okay. It wasn't until, uh, maybe close to the end he started making these whooping noises. They weren't in the number, way he usually did it. Then he started doing funny little steps, like making fun o' the song. Which this crowd doesn't like. I mean, we aren't into satire here, you know?"

"Okay," said Figueroa.

"And so somebody said something. Like 'Cut out the stupid shit' or like that. And he yelled back at them. And they yelled back at him. And he dumped the guitar there and jumped into the crowd and started swinging at everybody."

"I see. Why did he do that?"

"Well, jeez," the manager said. He pointed at the syringe. "He took something that didn't agree with him. Right?"

"I guess," she said cautiously. "Has it been moved?"

"It was lying there when the lights came up for the song. Nobody's touched it."

Figueroa was beginning to wonder whether Hank had really injected himself, no matter how it looked. Somehow she could not picture Hank himself bringing that syringe onstage. At the same time, she wasn't quite sure why the picture was so wrong. Figueroa detested the notion of feminine intuition, but she was willing to believe that "cop sense" told her there was an unresolved problem here.

She studied the audience. About half were crowded around Hank and the paramedics, enjoying the unscheduled show. The other half were taking the opportunity to imbibe a little extra alcohol and blunt the rigors of winter in Chicago. Nobody seemed grieved by Hank's collapse.

The manager said, "Can you get him outa here? We got a club to run."

"But nobody to sing."

"The backups can handle half an hour. I got another singer I can call." He smiled sourly. "No lack of out-of-work singers."

Suze pointed at the three women near the drummer. "Those his backup singers?" Well, obviously they were. What else could they be?

"Yeah. Faith, Hope and Charity."

"Uh, is there any unpleasantness, like among the performers?"

"In show business? Unpleasantness? Jealousy? Backbiting? You must be kidding!"

"Like what?"

"Well, Faith just got dumped by Hank the Great. As a girlfriend, I mean. Hope is gonna be fired by Hank because he doesn't think she can sing. This is her last night. Charity wants to go off on her own. And she could, she's good enough, except she's under contract to Hank while the act is here."

"Doesn't Hope have a contract, too?"

"Yeah, but Hank says, 'Sue me,' and she doesn't have the money to sue, plus it'll look bad for her, career-wise. Getting fired. Country singing—even *fake* country singing," he said with a sneer, "is a small world. Hank has the money and the power. The more fuss she makes, the more people hear about it. The drummer hates Hank's guts, too, by the way."

"Why?"

"Stole his girlfriend. Then threw her over for Faith. Who he then dumped, too."

"Sweet fellow, Hank."

"The finest."

"What happens when a performer shoots up onstage and screws up a performance?"

"We just might dump *him*."

"Thanks."

Figueroa walked across the stage to the three women. She glanced briefly at the syringe as she passed it, but left it lying where it was. One mustached kid from the audience was eyeing it. As Suze walked past, she said to him in a stage whisper, "Don't even *think* about touching it." He flinched back. The syringe was four inches long, five counting the needle. Several feet away from it, at the stage apron, lay a silver electric guitar, one of the latest kind, practically all strings and pickups.

As Figueroa approached the women, she could see that the visual motif of this act, costume-wise, was fringe.

"Who is who?" she asked.

"I'm Deloris Michael," one said.

"And in the act?"

"Faith."

Faith was dressed in a bodysuit of see-through white lace. It was made of lace-printed stretch fabric, and covered her from neck to ankle like paint. A fringe about two inches long ran around her at hipbone level. Figueroa doubted whether Faith had any underwear on under the bodysuit and didn't want to stare, but she was suddenly quite sure that Hank had chosen it for exactly that reason. The male audience would spend the whole act trying to tell. She wore high-heeled silvery shoes. Her face was heavily made up in pastel colors—pale pink lipstick, pale blue eyelids, pale skin. Against this, her hair was black, cut moderately short and loosely curled.

"My, my!" Bennis said, approaching Suze, but looking at Faith. Suze stepped back half a pace, offended. To cover her annoyance, she glanced around and saw the paramedics had arrived. They had loosened Hank's Levi's at the waist, which seemed to her to be an excellent idea.

Hope—Lorelei Smith—was gilded. She was sleek, slender, small-breasted and gold all over. Fringed gold bikini top and bottom. Gold high heels. Short glossy gold hair. Gold skin.

"Is that paint?" Figueroa said, pointing at the gold color on Hope's leg.

"Naw. Hank wanted me to get painted, but somebody told me if you paint yourself gold your skin can't breathe and you die. Actually, I oil myself—" She ran a fingertip slowly up from her knee to her hip to demonstrate. Figueroa heard Bennis say "Uhnnn" behind her. "Just a little oil, and then I kinda sift this gold glitter on and it sticks."

Bennis said to Suze, "Look at her. Puts you in mind of Hogarth's Gin Lane and the bizarre excesses at the court of Louis XIII, don't it, Figueroa?"

"Bennis, you're weird."

"I'm weird but I'm cute."

She gave him a look intended to chasten, which made him chuckle.

Charity—Sue Gleason—was yet another type, and Figueroa began to see a kind of sly intelligence operating in the choice of names and costumes. Faith was all in white lace, but Figueroa suspected that nobody would say she looked particularly faithful. Hope was golden. Charity—well, jeez! Figueroa thought—looked like a caricature of what every man would wish somebody would give him as a gift. BIG breasts. Small waist. Lush hips. A corset-style red costume, like something out of an old wild West movie. Two-inch fringe around the top and bottom of the corset, also red. Red lips, red nails, red high heels. Her hair was red too, combed straight with no hint of curl, very lustrous, hanging just below her chin.

Between the three of them, Figueroa thought this was like her own personal nightmare come to life. Here were women who could hardly walk because of the high heels, whose own faces were invisible under the makeup, who you wouldn't know if you met them on the street the next day, but every male in the place was fascinated. Put them outdoors chasing a mugger and they'd be flat on their faces in two steps. Grimly, Figueroa asked Faith, "How long does it take you to put on all that makeup? Not the lace suit, but the eyelashes and the hair and all?"

"Oh, forty-five minutes."

"Forty-five minutes!"

"Yeah. I know it's kinda surprising I can do it that fast. But I've had a lot of experience."

"So what kind of a guy is this Hank?"

"A real turd," said Hope, the gilded one.

"Why?"

"He lies a lot. Promises you things and doesn't follow through."

Faith said, "Yeah. That's his style. Baits you, you know, with how he's gonna help you."

Hope said, "I mean, people warned me. But he seems so sincere when he talks with you. You believe him."

"He sings sincere too," Faith said. "They're both an act."

Figueroa said to Charity, who hadn't spoken, "What about you?"

Charity said, "Hank Benton is slime on a stick."

Figueroa nodded, slightly startled. "What do you three do in the act? Can you tell me?"

"Better," Faith said. They stepped apart, singing "money, honey, money, honey" half a dozen times, swung their upper bodies around, swooped their heads in circles, hair flashing in the lights, fringes swinging, then sang "Ooooooh-ooh-ooh-ooh!" as they came back together.

They put their arms around each other's waists and ended with a "Hmmmmmmmmmmm."

Figueroa said, "Well, thanks. Hang on. I'll be right back."

She walked into the audience area with Bennis at her heels. "Let's wrap this up," he said. "Management's getting antsy."

"Not yet. We don't know what happened."

"Ol' Hank just screwed up is all."

"I don't believe it. Give me a minute."

Hank had stopped thrashing around—whether in the natural course of things by tiring himself out, or because of something the medics had done, Suze didn't know. He was sitting up, but still cursing. The paramedics were checking out the man with the cut scalp and the man with the cut cheek. Figueroa studied Hank. There were no needle tracks so far as she could see on his arms. He had a good deal here at the Kountry Klub. And she deduced from the care he took with his backup singers' costumes that he was very serious about his act. Would he have risked it all to shoot up onstage? But who else could have carried the syringe through a whole set of songs?

There was a reddish rash across the middle of Hank's mostly bare torso. It ran along the area where the turquoise and silver things dangled at the ends of his fringe. She felt the silver pieces. They were bent and faceted to pick up stage lights, but they had sharp corners. Obviously, they poked his skin. Any one of the rash-bumps could be the place something was injected—by Hank or by an enemy of Hank's? There was a largish one on his chest, just under his left elbow, that looked different from the others—bigger, but less red. If he was right-handed, he could have injected himself there. Figueroa pointed to it and Bennis nodded.

"Is he right-handed?" she asked one of the bystanders.

"He plays right-handed."

"So he could have done it himself," Bennis said quietly to her.

"Or someone onstage, in the dark before the last song."

If so, who? Figueroa thought she knew.

"He must've did it himself," Hope said. She patted at some flaws in the gold glitter on her arms.

Figueroa studied Bennis out of the corner of her eye. It was what he believed also, but to Hope she said, "Oh, no he didn't. He couldn't have brought the syringe onstage. He didn't have enough room in that costume to hide two nickels. He wasn't wearing a hat to keep it in. And he couldn't have brought it in his guitar because it's not acoustic. It's electric and it's as flat as a paper plate."

"Underneath?" said Faith, the one in lace.

"Underneath the guitar? Nope. He would've had to hold it against his stomach all evening. That's not the way you people play." She saw Bennis raise his eyebrows in agreement. For him, that was a lot of reaction.

"Any of us could have done it," Charity said. "Bring it in under our hair, maybe."

"Nope. Faith's is too short, Hope's is *much* too short and yours is cut wrong. It's straight. You shake your heads in your act. It just wouldn't work. Now, if you had *big* hair, like Dolly Parton—"

Charity said, "Maybe the drummer did it?"

"Oh, please. Get out from behind all that stuff in the dark and come down off the dais in the dark and find Hank in the dark and inject him and get back up there in the dark, while he plays just four chords? Four seconds, tops! What kind of idiots do you think we—"

Bennis said, "Figueroa," in a cautionary tone. You didn't want any bizarre behavior to get back to the commander.

"Same for your stage manager. Not enough time to get out there, find Hank, inject him, get back and hit the lights. Had to be somebody next to him on the stage."

Faith, Hope and Charity looked at each other.

Figueroa said, "Kind of smart, really, to inject him in the side. He didn't notice, more than to be annoyed, because he was used to those stupid—uh, those silver and turquoise dangles sticking him all the time." And that made it worse, Figueroa thought, that the attacker was smart. That she was smart and didn't have anything better to do with her brains than this.

Faith said, "Well, but you can't tell who."

"Yes, I can. Only one person could have brought the syringe onstage. Nobody else had room."

Charity said, "*Nobody* had room. Lookit these costumes." Her red corset was as tight as the skin on a hot dog.

"Faith is covered by a body stocking, a smooth, transparent body stocking. And Hope's covered mainly by glitter. But you had room. In your cleavage. And I'm ashamed—" Figueroa strangled the impulse to say "I'm ashamed of you." Charity hadn't noticed. She was hopping from foot to foot and yelling. Bennis' eyebrows went up and down with the bouncing breasts.

"Oh, no I didn't!" Charity yelled. "And you can't prove I did."

Figueroa had a moment's qualm. Hank was surely a nasty bit of humankind. Was Figueroa betraying sisterhood? God only knew. God only knew and She was far too pissed these days to tell anybody.

Bennis was a hundred percent with her now. He said to Charity, "C'mere a second." They walked Charity aside.

Bennis and Figueroa went into their one-two punch mode. Figueroa said, "Listen, Charity. Um, Sue. Syringes can be traced."

Bennis said, "She's right. Also drugs—prescription or illegals. Either one."

"Plus fingerprints on the syringe."

"It's gonna go better for you if you tell the paramedics what you used. Help them out."

"I didn't do it."

"See," Bennis said, as if she hadn't spoken, "you are talking here to a coupla street cops with a lotta years in. I mean, drug diagnosis is our thing."

Figueroa said, "Yeah," though she knew Bennis had the years of knowledge, not her.

"I mean," Bennis said, "suppose, just suppose, you gave him some kinda speed, say meth maybe."

Charity's eyes flickered to Hank and back, but she didn't say anything.

Bennis said, "Now, suppose you were judging the dose by what experienced users can take. A thousand, maybe two thousand milligrams at once. And suppose he wasn't a chronic user—which would be the reason you used it, 'cause you knew he would overreact. Well, did you know that 120 milligrams is fatal in non-users?"

Charity's mouth opened a little wider.

Figueroa said, "Yeah. If you overdosed him and he dies and you coulda saved him, you'll be in extremely deep shit."

Bennis said, "And plus, if he dies it's murder. Right now, worst, you got some kinda assault. If he lives."

Figueroa said, "And here you were, trying to shoot him up in the dark. You're trying to skin-pop him, but you couldn't see. Maybe it went in a vein, which might be why it took hold so fast. Maybe it went right to his heart. We're talking possible murder here, no matter how careful you thought you were being." She paused and added, "Your contract calls for you to back up Hank as long as he runs here. You had a chance at a real career—you're the one with talent—and he had you locked in. Unless the Kountry Klub fired him."

"I don't suppose," Bennis said, "you were all three in it together?"

Charity sighed, draping her extremely long eyelashes down over her cheeks. They reached almost to her cheekbones. Suze and Norm said nothing whatever now, just staring at her.

"Oh, shit," Charity said. "No, don't blame them. And yeah, it's meth. Kinda hefty dose." Bennis immediately walked away to talk with the paramedics.

Liking her better, Suze said, "And Hank doesn't skin-pop?"

"No. He doesn't do drugs; he's a juicer; he does booze." A satisfied smile came over Charity's face. "Took him right up, didn't it?"

"It did that."

Twenty minutes later they'd put the incident to bed. Hank Benton was in the Northwestern Emergency Room giving the staff hell. Charity was in the First District station engaging in felony review with the state's attorney. Norm and Suze were gearing up to go back out and look for some more malefactors. Suze Figueroa was feeling a distinct sense of accomplishment. She said, "Let's go, big guy."

"You were mad at me there, weren't you?" Norm said. "When I was kind of ogling Faith."

"For a while."

"I didn't mean it."

"Which part didn't you mean?"

"All of it, matter of fact. I come in here at night, get suited up, see you waiting to hit the mean streets with me, basically." He put his arm around her shoulders. "Soon as I see you, it makes me feel good."

"Without the two-inch nails? Without the three-inch heels? Without the eyelashes?"

"Yeah. Without."

Suze said, "Okay."

What provides more fodder for mystery, deception, and violence than marriage? Husbands and wives often make better adversaries than they do partners.

In "Bad News" Delilah West is hired by a wife to discover why there is suddenly distance between her and her husband, while in "The Lost Coast" it is the husband who hires the P.I., this time Sharon McCone. In each case the P.I.s discover that marriage is anything but perfect.

MAXINE O'CALLAGHAN

Maxine O'Callaghan is a woman of firsts: the first person in her extended family to finish high school, and among the first American women writers to introduce a tough professional woman private eye in Delilah West.

Orange County, California, resident Delilah West made her debut in a short story in 1974, and since has appeared in novels (including *Hit and Run* and *Set-up*). O'Callaghan is also known for her horror/suspense novels (*Something's Calling Me Home* and *Dark Time*).

But "Bad News" is Delilah West's story. Orange County in June is gray and foggy, but Delilah soon finds that getting away to Palm Springs is no vacation.

BAD NEWS

Like cancer specialists and termite inspectors,
P.I.s often are hired to tell people things they
don't want to hear. So I was doing my job,
personally delivering a videotape that confirmed my client's worse suspicions about her
husband. This is not a part of the work that I
enjoy. To make matters worse, Julie Haverson
wanted me to drive over to Palm Springs with
my report, and she was paying too much
money for me to say no.

It was a Friday in mid-June. Forget that
"what is so rare" stuff. Obviously the guy who
wrote the poem never spent much time in L.A.
where June weather means that sullen morning
clouds hang around most days until late afternoon.

From the looks of I-10 everybody in the
L.A. basin had packed up and headed for the
desert. In addition to cars and semis, the road
was bumper to bumper with RVs, Jeeps, mo-
torcycles, and pickups towing trailers loaded
with an assortment of boats, dune buggies, and
dirt bikes. We crept down from Banning past
rank upon rank of huge windmills lining the
sere brown hills along the interstate like something out of Jules Verne. On the radio a disc

jockey announced smugly that it was 117 degrees at three o'clock. Even the sky looked hot. I counted five dust devils whirling through the sand and cactus.

I was cool enough in my metal cocoon. The Astrovan has both front and rear air conditioners. If necessary the powerful unit in back could bring the temperature down low enough to set up a temporary meat locker. Still, call me a pessimist, but in the desert I can't help but feel that I am only a broken radiator hose away from being buzzard bait and bleached bones.

I picked up the car phone and dialed Julie's number to let her know about the delay. I'd tried to reach her earlier, only to catch the answering machine; now, I got it again. It would be my luck to drive all the way out here to find she'd forgotten our appointment and was headed back to the coast.

Our first meeting was a week ago today in Newport Beach. We had sat across from each other on two huge couches in a room built to take in the view of the Back Bay through a good thirty feet of windows. Beyond an expanse of lawn, a high wrought-iron fence, and a margin of tidal marsh, the water was gun-metal gray under low, gloomy clouds.

We got the introductions out of the way, agreeing on Delilah and Julie, although the informality didn't seem to put either of us at ease.

Julie was my age—mid-thirties. Her cream-colored silk shirt cost more than my entire outfit. She wore this tucked into an ancient brown corduroy skirt; there were brown leather flats on her feet, small diamond studs in her ears.

I took a sip of the coffee she had served and put the cup down carefully on the low table between us. Obviously Julie wasn't used to children, dogs, or clumsy P.I.s. The couches were oyster white; everything else was light beige or pale gray except for an oriental rug in rich reds that looked as though it had been spun from silk. The rest of the furniture was antiques, graceful curving shapes and wood that had that unmistakable patina of age and value.

"Neal and I have been married for two years," Julie began. "And we've been happy, much happier than I ever expected to be. I don't flatter myself, Delilah. My father began telling me at an early age that I'd never be much to look at, but I'd still have lots of men chasing me for my money."

She missed being homely by virtue of a good orthodontist and a great hairdresser. She didn't smile often but when she did her teeth were small, white, and even. Coppery highlights glinted in the straight brown bob. With some makeup, a new wardrobe—face it, she'd still be a woman people described as having very nice eyes.

Men have told me I'm beautiful and once or twice I believed it. With her memory of her father's words, I suspected poor Julie never would.

"This is your first marriage?" I asked.

"For both of us."

"So what happened?"

"Nothing much at first." She stared down into her bone china cup. "Neal just gradually became so—so distant."

Which meant, I assumed, the sex had cooled considerably. Then there had been phone calls at odd hours, a charge card slip from an intimate little restaurant down in Laguna that Neal tried to pass off as a business expense.

"You could ask him about it," I said. "There might be a simple explanation." Understand I didn't really believe this; my profession makes me cynical on the subject of fidelity. Still, it seemed a tactful thing to say.

"I've tried to talk to him," Julie said. "But I can never find the right words. Because I'm afraid—what if I'm wrong? He would be so hurt, he might never forgive me."

From the anguish on her face, I knew that whatever he was, whatever he'd done, she loved the guy.

"You'd better think about this," I warned. "Are you sure you really want to know?"

"I have to. He made me believe he really loved me. If that's a lie . . ." She had put down her coffee and picked up her checkbook, her eyes like flint. "Do what you have to do, Delilah. I need to know the truth."

No, there was no way Julie Haverson had changed her mind.

Following Julie's instructions I exited the interstate at Bob Hope Drive and found my way to her street. The town looked torpid and heat-stunned under a brassy sky. Very few people were actually outside the life support bubble of their cars. I saw one old guy on a bicycle, a heart attack waiting to happen.

Julie had come out to the desert because she said the lack of sunlight triggered bouts of depression for her, and she was depressed enough about Neal. She also wanted to provide hubby with enough rope and give me a chance to set up the hanging.

Pretty soon the houses thinned out; up long driveways, these were

white stucco, built low to hug the earth and hide under Mexican fan
palms and tamarisk. The street dipped down into arroyos, places where
you would not want to be caught during one of the wild winter storms
that blow in off the Baja. I drove slowly, trying to read numbers off
mailboxes.

According to my count the next one was Julie's—the house with
squad cars and a coroner's van on the driveway. No mistake, the mailbox
said *Haverson*. Dread crowded my throat as I parked and got out. A
uniformed officer came to meet me and tell me the news.

My client wasn't going to have to hear about her husband's dirty little
secrets after all.

The coroner and the forensics crew were county. Since Julie's house
was located in Desert Edge, not Palm Springs, the cops were local. Chief
Frank Krause was a lanky, knobby man with a flap of belly hanging over
his belt. A tan Stetson covered a head that was bald except for a fringe of
gray hair. The Stetson was off and lying on a patio table. We sat on
cushioned lawn chairs in the shade and sweated. The body had just
been removed from the house, the doors and windows opened to air the
place out.

"You all right?" Krause asked.

I nodded, but to tell the truth it would be a while before I forgot the
sight of Julie Haverson's pale, bloated body. She had been found in a
full bathtub of water, but she was already being bagged when I saw her.

"Who found her?" I asked.

"One of my people. A neighbor called us."

"How long has she been dead?"

"Coroner won't commit himself, but it had to be several days. When's
the last time you talked to her?"

"Last Friday. A week ago today."

She had told me there was no need for interim reports before our
appointment. She said she'd like to hear it from me personally if the
news was good or bad. The only time I'd tried to call was from the car
phone on the way over, and I'd had no reason to suspect anything was
wrong when she didn't answer.

"Do you know the cause of death yet?" I asked.

"Not yet." Krause seemed content to answer my questions, watching
me all the while like a canny old desert tortoise. "Well, you saw her. Not
easy to call, but she was flat on her back in the tub. Doors were locked.
No sign of a break-in. Looked to me like she slipped and drowned.

Then you show up, and I find out she hired herself a private detective. What you were doing for her—you think it had something to do with her death?"

"Could be."

I hesitated. In my profession, cops are not always the enemy, but they are usually not your buddies. So what I was about to do went strictly against the grain. Still, Krause seemed a good man, and if there was any question about the way Julie died, there were things I wanted him to know.

"Chief," I said, "you and I need to watch some television."

Photographs are one thing, but nothing's as effective as video. Ask anybody who saw the tape of L.A.'s Finest beating up a suspect. My camera of choice used to be a fine old Nikon that belonged to my husband Jack. Since I often screwed up the f-stops and the focus, the pictures I produced were usually blurred and marginally acceptable.

My assistant, Danny Thu, has updated my office, introducing me to computers and camcorders. Danny works for me part-time while finishing a double major in business and computer science at UC Irvine. I left the selection in his capable hands and he picked out a video camera that is small and idiot-proof with auto focus, low-light sensitivity, and a high-power zoom lens.

So when Frank Krause and I settled down in his spacious office, where he had not only a television set and a VCR but a couple of comfortable chairs as well, the picture was first-class.

The time and date, registered down in one corner of the frame, shows that I started to tape Neal Haverson's movements on Monday morning at 8:25 A.M. Neal had been out here in Desert Edge over the weekend. I pick him up as the garage door hums open at the house in Newport Beach and his green Porsche backs out. There's just a glimpse of dark hair and wraparound shades until we cut to him unfolding his lean body as he exits the car in the parking lot at Burdick, Fenster and Robb.

According to Danny this firm of stockbrokers is reputable but not big-time. It's also Danny's opinion that serious brokers get to work very early, about the time the market opens in New York. Maybe they keep Neal around for decoration. He has the kind of good looks that are a little too planned for my tastes. The perfect tan, a mouth that crooks easily into a charming smile. No wonder Julie fell for the guy. Me, I'm just the suspicious type.

After the intro there was a minimum of boring footage mixed in with the highlights. A waste of tape to record the man's every action. In-camera editing, Danny calls it. Anyway, there was a complete log, too, of course. I hadn't done the surveillance solo. I explained to Julie I'd need another operative, maybe more if one of us was made. She didn't quibble over the expense. A friend of mine who works out of Long Beach took the first shift; I took the second, and Danny relieved us when necessary. Either we were lucky or Neal was oblivious because he didn't spot any of us.

The very first day Neal leaves the office at 12:10 P.M. and drives over to another building in the commercial complex. A woman stands there waiting, greyhound-thin with full breasts, a long straight fall of tawny hair. She's so perfect you have to wonder how much she owes to plastic surgery. A red miniskirt shows off her legs as she gets into the Porsche. Old Neal was nothing if not predictable.

We cut to the two of them going into that same restaurant in Laguna where Neal indiscreetly charged a meal, Neal's hand resting in casual intimacy on the small of the woman's back.

They adjourn to their respective offices for a few hours of work, then meet for dinner and go on to her place, the activity behind the closed mini-blinds unrecorded but easily imagined. When Krause asked I told him the blonde's name was Suzanne Valco. He expressed no interest in the details of how I knew that, and I was just as glad not to have to explain, the rules about DMV access in California being what they are.

Suzanne was the only woman Neal was seeing, at least that week, but he saw her a lot. And at some of the most expensive bistros and dives Orange County had to offer. While following them around, I ate well, drank a lot of fizzy, non-alcoholic drinks, and listened to too much loud rock music. I might never have a club soda or play the radio again.

The highlight of the surveillance tape came on Thursday, last night, when Neal took his lover home to the house in Newport Beach. Julie's house. I thought about stopping the taping and claiming I had lost Neal, but my client was paying to know the worst. Who was I to censor the material?

After Neal and Suzanne went inside, I sat in my van, having a few dark thoughts about the amount of sleaze I have to witness and wondering what that sleaze was doing to my moral fiber. There's plenty of time to brood on a stakeout. The only alternative is booze, which I've managed to avoid, at least while sitting around in parked cars. So I settled in for a good long spell of introspection, but just then the lights came on in the backyard. I could see the glow on the trees, mostly off to the right side of the house, one palm lit up as though a spotlight was focused on it.

I recalled sitting with Julie, looking out toward the Back Bay, and remembered glimpsing a pool and a spa off on the right side, maybe placed so as not to interrupt the view of the bay or perhaps just situated for privacy.

I hesitated, sighed, then dug out a small flashlight, picked up the video camera, and climbed out of the van. Taping a person's actions is a very sticky situation these days with the possibility of lawsuits always a consideration. The basic rule is you can't stand on private property to point your camera. While I confess to cutting a corner or two, one may as well go along with the legal niceties whenever possible, and I was in luck because along the pool side of the Haversons' backyard ran a convenient strip of public land providing access to the Back Bay.

My flashlight is a very dim hooded light, perfect for cat burglars and other nefarious characters like me. Good thing I'd brought it along because it was damn dark with not a spark of starlight penetrating the overcast and very little spillover from the street lamps. I could hear laughter and the sounds of bubbling water and a pool pump as I picked my way along a graveled path through head-high thorny shrubs to a big old acacia tree. It had been a while since my tomboy youth, but my jeans and Nikes were perfect for climbing. A thick sturdy branch provided an unobstructed view, especially when I used the zoom lens.

The angle was perfect, looking down into the spa, and with the lights in the water and more lights in the shrubbery, you could see everything those two naked, slippery bodies were doing.

Krause sat silently for a moment as that last scene ended, watching the screen dance with electronic snow.

"I didn't think Julie needed to see any more than that," I said.

Krause reached over to turn off the television. "Man's a real piece of work."

"He may be a murderer as well."

Krause gave a noncommittal grunt. "Lots of guys cheat on their wives."

"Lots of guys kill them, too."

"Most don't."

"Most don't have wives as rich as Julie Haverson. Look, maybe he suspected Julie knew about his affair. Maybe he was tired of her anyway and figured it was only a matter of time until she divorced him."

"And maybe his wife died while you were dogging his every footstep, so he has an alibi."

"I didn't do a twenty-four-hour on him," I said. "I tucked him in and my other operative picked him up in the morning. He had all night to come over here."

"Yeah, well, it's three hours round trip plus whatever time it took to do the job. Man looked awful bright-eyed to me every time he went off to work." Krause got up and went over to eject the tape. "Anyway, it's all speculation until the coroner tells us how and when Mrs. Haverson died." He held up the videocassette. "You mind if I keep this for now?"

"Be my guest."

The original was back in my office. I noticed Krause hadn't questioned whether the tape would be admissible if and when Neal was ever charged. I hoped that meant he respected my professionalism but thought it more likely he figured he'd never have to use the tape as evidence.

"Have they scheduled the autopsy?" I asked.

"There wasn't any hurry before. But now—"

He broke off as his intercom buzzed, went to his desk to pick up the phone, listened, said, "Okay, I'll be right there." To me he said, "Haverson's here." Krause tilted his head toward the door, and I saw Julie's husband through the glass, waiting outside.

It was Neal, all right. I'd know him anywhere, with or without clothes. He looked sober and jumpy, a little pale under the tan. A natural reaction to traumatic news, or just a case of guilt and nerves?

"I'm going to push for the postmortem right away," Krause said. "In case we need a statement, you going on back to the coast tonight?"

I wanted to sleep in my own bed and wake up tomorrow to a cool, damp June morning. But I also badly needed a stiff drink, a shower, and, eventually, food. Well, after reviewing the tape and seeing Neal Haverson out there, I thought I could use more than one drink and then I ought not to be driving. I told Krause I'd stay overnight in the area, that I'd call his office when I checked in.

He promised to let me know as soon as he had the autopsy results, put the cassette in his desk drawer, and picked up the phone to tell the officer who acted as receptionist to send Haverson in.

Neal held the door for me on my way out, giving me the once-over as I went past. The flicker of interest in his eyes was pure reflex. He didn't recognize me. He was just doing a quick evaluation and registering approval. And never mind that his wife was in the morgue. My reaction was instantaneous and came strictly from my gut, not my head. I *knew*, all the same.

The son of a bitch had killed his wife.

The Ocotillo Lodge was a nice little motel that didn't bill itself as a luxurious resort. It was clean and moderately priced, with a restaurant next door, the Baja Grill, which specialized in fish tacos. The margaritas were huge, frosty, and potent. I had one as soon as I sat down and another while I ate. Homemade tortillas, fish grilled over mesquite, fresh, chunky salsa.

I managed to put off thinking about Julie's death until I got back to my room and crawled into bed. What I thought was that I ought to be a little careful here. Jumping to intuitive conclusions was the easy part; proving that Neal was a killer was something else again. Furthermore, this wasn't my case. Julie had hired me to get the goods on her husband, and I had certainly done that. Look at it that way, my job was finished. And Frank Krause seemed a competent man. Let him take it from here.

Yeah.

Yeah, but—

What is it with me? Why do I have this little tic of moral obligation that I can't ignore? I hadn't even liked Julie very much. Not that I disliked her. We simply hadn't connected on a personal level. That wasn't unusual. I don't care much for a lot of my clients. But I do care when they wind up dead. And it bothered me that Julie had paid for her husband's alibi. It bothered me a lot.

I punched my pillow, tried to get comfortable in the unfamiliar bed, and listened to the air conditioner buzz.

My father was a cop for twenty years. He used to say that 99% of homicides were totally senseless and usually took place under the influence of drugs or alcohol. Say Julie had been the victim of some random nut case, her death might easily fall into that majority—always assuming she hadn't died accidentally. I didn't think so, but my hunches wouldn't mean spit in a court of law.

Money was at the top of the list for that small percentage of motivated crimes, closely followed by jealousy and lust. Neal rang most of the big bells. But one thing bothered me and was certain to bother twelve ordinary people who might have to decide Neal's guilt. Could he have killed his wife, then gone off to the fun week I'd recorded without showing any stress, anxiety, or guilt?

I remembered a recent news story. Two men kidnapped a young boy on his way home from McDonald's. They tortured and murdered the child—then one of them ate his burgers and fries for lunch.

Not only did I think Neal was capable of murdering his wife and then acting as though nothing had happened, I thought that's exactly what he'd done. Now, the question was: Had he gone on with business as usual, figuring that was the best way to put doubt into the mind of any potential jury? Was the man an amoral monster, incapable of remorse?

The possibility guaranteed some mighty unpleasant dreams.

Morning sunlight lasered in through an opening where the drapes didn't quite meet, a wake-up call impossible to ignore. The inside of my nose burned from the dry air, and pain jabbed at my right temple. Not quite a hangover, but close enough.

I keep an overnight bag in the van, packed with basic necessities. Good thing, since the Ocotillo was short on amenities. I had just gotten out of the shower and was toweling my hair when Frank Krause called.

"Julie Haverson drowned," he said without much preamble. "Doc found a bruise where she hit the back of her head on the faucet, so it was just the way it seemed: She slipped, banged her head hard enough to knock herself out, and slid down in the water."

"And this happened when?"

"Monday or Tuesday, according to Doc. Definitely not Sunday."

"So that's it then?" I sat on the edge of the bed with cold water dripping down my back. "You're calling it an accident?"

"I'm calling it the way it is," he said wearily. "Look, I don't like the guy any more than you do, but the fact is Mrs. Haverson died after her husband left here last Sunday night. And even if there was any suspicion of foul play, we both know for the rest of the week—sixteen, seventeen hours a day—he had a perfect alibi."

He didn't have to remind me who was supplying that alibi.

"If it makes you feel any better," he added, "after the autopsy, I came back here and went over the reports. Went over everything. Hell, I haven't even been to bed yet. Take my word, Mrs. West, there's nothing there. My advice: Stop by for your videotape and then get out of this heat and go on home."

He said he was going home himself, that a man his age had no business staying up all night. If ever I was back in Desert Edge, be sure to come say hello.

And that was that.

Except that after we hung up I kept going over what he'd told me while I dressed and dried my hair. And logic and postmortem findings be damned, I was still convinced Neal had killed Julie.

And now it looked like the bastard was going to get away with it.

What people always say about the desert heat is that oh, yeah, it's hot all right, but it's *dry*. Yes, indeedy. Like somebody stuck you in one of those dehydrating ovens, the kind that turns juicy apricots into fruit leather. Walking from my van into the Desert Edge police station, I felt as if I was wearing heavy wool instead of my short-sleeved cotton shirt and jeans.

Inside, I saw only three officers, and one of them was heading out the back door as I came in. Another sat at a desk in a back corner, smoking and talking on the telephone. The third was the same woman who had served as receptionist the day before, Officer Noonan, according to her ID badge. She was thumbing through a stack of paperwork, looking as though she wished she was elsewhere. The radio on her desk was turned down and registered mostly static. A slow weekend. I wondered if they were all like that out here.

Noonan remembered me. When I asked for the videotape, she looked puzzled for a second, then said, "Oh, yeah, the Chief did say he was leaving it, but then we started talking about the report on Mrs. Haverson, and I guess he forgot. Why don't I have him mail it to you?"

"It's sensitive material," I said. "I'd really like to take it with me. Could you take a look in his office? My name's on the label."

"Well—"

"I certainly would appreciate it."

She nodded and stood up. "Do you know where he put it?"

There was a stack of file folders in her IN tray. The top one was marked Julie Haverson. What the hell—I hadn't made any plans for the weekend anyway.

"Gee," I said, "let me think. Maybe in that big file cabinet—the one over by the TV." The one I knew did not contain the tape.

As soon as she was gone, I positioned myself to block the view of the male cop who was still talking on the phone and flipped open the Haverson file. Pictures of Julie's bloated face made me glad I'd skipped breakfast. I scanned the coroner's report. Description of the bruise, measurement of the faucet. Major factors in estimating time of death: temperature of the house (an energy-conscious 78 degrees), temperature of the bathwater, and the state of putrefaction. No help there.

Three witnesses. Of course, Krause hadn't exactly been beating the bushes. I noted names, speed-read their statements. No time to go over what Neal Haverson had said. I saw Noonan heading for Krause's desk, glancing out at me. I just stood there, trying to look innocent and hoping she wouldn't notice my reading material. She bent down to open Krause's desk drawer, and I quickly closed the file folder.

When she came out of the Chief's office with my cassette, she gave me the once-over. She knew I was up to something, she just didn't know what. I thanked her and got the hell out of there before she figured it out.

"Had it to do over, I'd mind my own business," Henry Volsted said. "People pounding on my door, asking me questions."

Julie's next-door neighbor was a sawed-off little man who looked as though he'd been carrying a grudge of one kind or another for his entire seventy years. He was almost bald, his scalp tanned to a walnut brown. His face was the same shade and so were the scrawny arms and legs bared by madras plaid shorts and a yellow polo shirt. By contrast his wife Eileen was so pale I wondered if she ever went outside the house in daylight.

When Eileen had opened the door I'd managed to talk my way inside by saying I was a friend of Julie's, that I'd arrived for a visit yesterday only to find her dead. And I'd barged on into the living room before Henry arrived. A sofa and two chairs were upholstered in pale green damask, the curved backs outlined with fruitwood. The refrigerated air held a lingering smell of lemon furniture polish. Dozens of small china figurines covered tabletops, the kind of knick-knacks that are too expensive to trust to the hired help to dust. Maybe that's what kept Eileen inside.

"I am sorry to bother you like this," I said. "It was just so awful, driving up and seeing all the police cars, such a shock."

I sank down in a wing-backed side chair as though my knees had given way.

"Are you all right?" Eileen asked.

"I think it's the heat," I said. "Maybe some water . . ."

She nodded and scurried off while Henry jammed his hands in his pockets and glowered down at me.

"I keep thinking if only I'd come sooner—" I broke off to accept a glass from Eileen and sip.

"Oh, I don't know if it would've helped," Eileen said. "She was dead for days, wasn't she, Henry? Best to put it out of your mind and not brood about it."

"I know you're right," I said. "I just thought it might help to talk to people who knew her."

"Then you're in the wrong place," Henry said. "We keep to ourselves, and everybody else does the same. You're such a good friend, how come you're not talking to the husband?"

I explained that I didn't know Neal, that I'd met Julie through some charity work. "He should be grateful to you. Imagine if he'd come home and found Julie like that. What made you suspect something was wrong?"

I knew approximately what had happened from my quick perusal of Krause's file, but I wanted to hear it from them.

"Well, it was the Tremont delivery," Eileen said.

Tremont's, I recalled from the file, was a local grocery store. Julie had called them on Saturday to place an order with instructions for a delivery that day and another one midweek.

"That was late Wednesday," Eileen went on. "I said it was funny, didn't I, Henry?—Julie not answering the door and her car sitting right there in the carport. I said maybe she was in the bathroom." Eileen faltered, looking stricken at her prophetic words. "The delivery boy left the box. I said it was awful, didn't I, Henry?—leaving stuff out in the heat like that. Well, we were gone most of Thursday. I didn't think anything, to tell the truth, until we got home. Then I saw the box was still sitting there. I had a feeling something was wrong—"

She glanced at her husband and got a venomous look in return. I could imagine Henry's response to her worry.

"I had Julie's number written down. For emergencies," Eileen added hastily, least I think she might ever call people just to be neighborly. "All I got was the answering machine. Henry kept saying her husband must've come and they went off somewhere and forgot about the delivery."

"As a matter of fact," I said, "Julie told me Neal might come back out one evening, maybe Monday or Tuesday."

"Well, he didn't," Eileen said positively. "I would have seen him."

Henry snorted. "What got us into this mess," he muttered. "Minding other people's business."

Another day before they finally called the police.

"I guess it didn't really matter that we waited so long, did it, Henry?" Eileen said. "Nobody could help Julie anyway."

* * *

Eileen Volsted might not have seen Neal on Monday or Tuesday night, but that didn't mean he hadn't been here. She had to sleep sometime. Come to that, he could have parked his car elsewhere and walked in. He wasn't invisible. Somebody would have seen him. But with the sun climbing up toward a blistering high noon, I delayed the canvass of the neighborhood and went to Tremont's instead.

I found the delivery boy, Johnny Torres, making up an order in the produce department, glancing nervously at a man who was spraying water on the romaine and bok choy. Torres was young and scared and the more questions I asked the more he lapsed into Spanish. I could understand enough to figure out he'd made both deliveries to the Haversons'. The first time, on Saturday, Julie was there. She signed the receipt and gave him a tip. But Wednesday, no. Nobody there. He saw nothing. *Nada.*

"Por favor," he said. He was very late, his boss would be angry.

I let him go. I hadn't expected much, but it was disappointing all the same. I stood there for a second, dreading going back out into the heat, breathing in the cool, earthy smell of carrots and potatoes.

The man who was spraying the vegetables had worked his way to the opposite end of the long greenery-laden counter. Another man joined him there; they spoke briefly, then ambled down toward me.

They were both in their forties. They wore tan wash-and-wear pants and green knit shirts with a logo: a tree sprouting up in the middle of the Tremont name. The produce man was a little taller and stockier and he had on a light green apron. The other one had a soft full mustache and had a plastic badge that said Manager pinned to his shirt.

"Heard you talking to Torres," the produce man said.

"The cops already questioned him," the manager said, pleasantly enough. "What's the deal?"

"Insurance investigation," was my quick lie.

"Mrs. Haverson's death was an accident, wasn't it?"

"More than likely."

It occurred to me that these two were the curious type who might pick up a wealth of information about their customers, but mostly I was stalling because I wasn't looking forward to going door to door in the hot sun, trying to find out something from the rest of Julie's neighbors.

"Mrs. Haverson had a large policy with us," I confided, "so we like to check things out. Did either of you know the Haversons?"

"Just to talk to on the phone—her, I mean. Never talked to him. How about you, Rick?" the manager said.

"Not that I know of. Of course my memory might improve if I could put my feet up and have a nice cold soda."

"Oh, yeah," the manager said. "Everybody knows a Coke does wonders for the memory." He winked at me. "The stuff this guy will say just to take a break."

By this time I figured that a conversation with these two guys would come up goose eggs, but what the hell, I was also thirsty, so I went along with them back to the staff room, on a first-name basis by the time we arrived. The manager was Ray, Ray Tremont, who said, "I run the place until my dad gets tired of his golf game and shows up."

The crowded staff room held lockers, shelves, a long table, and some kitchen space furnished with a refrigerator and a microwave. The place smelled of popcorn and pizza. Rick took off his apron, sat on a brown plastic chair, and propped his feet on another one while Ray got cans of pop from the fridge. They kept up a running banter as I sipped my icy cola and thought that all I would accomplish here was to provide an audience for their good-natured stand-up routine.

"Do you get a lot of delivery orders?" I asked, casting about for some crumb of information.

"Lots of rich people in Desert Edge," Rick said. "They got better things to do than grocery-shop."

Ray said he took the orders, and that Julie had called hers in herself.

"Do you remember what she said?"

The two exchanged a look like I'd asked the jackpot question.

"She asked for sourdough bread, sliced turkey, lamb chops—" Ray rattled off a dozen more items.

"That was for Saturday," Rick said.

"She wanted extra fruit on Wednesday."

"We carry tree-ripened peaches. They spoil quick."

"Peaches, apricots, raspberries, two cartons of plain yogurt."

Rick grinned in admiration. "Photographic memory."

"A curse," Ray said modestly. "Imagine all the old grocery lists I got stored in my brain."

"What else did Mrs. Haverson say—besides giving her order?"

"Just hello and thank you."

Well, what would she have said? *Gotta run—my husband's filling the tub so he can drown me?*

Rick and Ray looked disappointed when I said I had to get going and thanked them for the drink. "And please tell Johnny Torres I didn't mean to get him in trouble. He isn't, is he?"

"Nah," Ray said. "Dumb to leave stuff in the sun, but what the heck, things happen."

"Screwups," Rick said.

He put his apron back on, and they walked me out, laughing about a major screwup the weekend before.

"A party," Rick said. "All kinds of booze and food—"

"Deluxe catering tray from the deli," Ray recited on cue. "Buffalo wings, blue corn chips, fresh salsa, the works."

"Everything's been set aside ahead of time, of course, except—major botch—"

We were back out in the store by then. Freezer section. Rick pointed to a whole cabinet full of ice cubes in clear plastic and said, "Guess what?"

"Must have been a run on the stuff," Ray said. "All we had left was two bags."

"And ten cases of beer and wine coolers."

"Five cases of Michelob and five Seagrams Mixed Tropicals."

"They put it in tubs or coolers."

"Wanted ten bags."

"We ran all over town. Everybody was short."

"Better believe we laid in plenty this weekend."

"Ice."

They looked at each other and laughed.

I felt a little giddy myself, as if they'd just announced that I'd picked the winner in lotto.

Ice.

I had a very busy afternoon. At five-thirty I was sitting in a little park in downtown Desert Edge, wearing a tank top and a denim skirt, watching the sun slide behind the purple flanks of the Santa Rosa Mountains from a wooden bench that felt as though it belonged in a sauna. A breeze carried a strong scent of drying brush overlaid with the smell of melting asphalt. The temperature was down a few degrees although the sky still glowed bright and hot overhead.

Most people were off having frosty drinks in cool, dim bars. Only a couple of tourists braved the heat, one of them across the park capturing a cactus garden on video. Out on the street, Neal's green Porsche wheeled into a parking space, and he climbed out.

I'd found him easily enough. Not at the house. Bad vibes, I guess. Anyway, he could afford to stay elsewhere. I guessed it would be at one of the most expensive resorts in the area and found where he was registered on the second call. He must have received my messengered surprise.

I stood up and waved. He came over, stopped in front of me. The smooth charm had vanished. With that much fury twisting his face Neal wasn't even good-looking.

"You," he said. "You were in Krause's office yesterday."

"Watching a little TV."

"Shit."

His hands were balled into fists and he was menacingly close even if we were in a public place. I stepped back a pace and slipped my little Beretta mini-automatic from my skirt pocket, making sure he saw it.

He stayed where he was. "I don't care if Julie hired you," he said, suppressing his rage. "What you did was an invasion of my privacy. I called my lawyer, and I can sue your ass."

"One can always sue," I agreed. "Of course, then the tape would be made public."

"All right, let's get to it. What do you want?"

"Just to talk. To tell you I know how you tricked the coroner."

"What?" He stared at me. "You're crazy. I didn't do anything."

"Sure you did. After Julie drowned, you drained out the warm water—"

He stood very still, sweat shining on his face.

"Then," I said. "You put ice in the tub."

He had turned to stone. I began to wish I had Rick from Tremont's around to play second banana and fill in some details.

"I don't think you just piled it in," I said. "You probably worried about frostbite. So you took it slow, ran some cool water and kept putting in the ice. I imagine it took a while and a lot of the stuff."

"That's—that's ridiculous."

"I've got four clerks who remember you, Neal." Danny had a still made from the videotape and brought it over so we could canvass the stores in the area. "Actually, you were pretty damn smart. Oh, I don't mean you're some kind of forensics expert, but you figured keeping the body cold would make it appear that Julie died later, after you were gone. The tricky part must have been knocking her out. What did you do? Grab her by the hair and smash her head back into the faucet?"

"No—"

"Oh, come on. It's my word against yours. The police are closing the file. I just want to know."

"It was an accident," he said thickly.

"Neal—"

"It *was*. I heard her fall—a big splash—and I went in and saw her—" He broke off, remembering.

"And you just stood there and watched her drown. No, wait." I hadn't thought I could feel any more disgust, but I did. "You went out and closed the door and came back when it was over, didn't you?"

Something shifted in his eyes. He shrugged, and the slightest smile hovered on his lips. "Like you said. Your word against mine. Forget the lawsuit. I think I'll keep the videotape of me and Suzanne for a souvenir, and we'll call it square."

"Sure," I said. "You can start a collection."

I gestured to the young Vietnamese fellow who stood way over by the cactus garden, his video camera with its high-powered zoom lens focused on us. Danny gave me a thumbs-up, and I flipped up my shirt collar so Neal could see the remote mike.

"You can't do that," he said.

"Oh, I don't know. I guess a court might find the tape inadmissible, but then again, maybe not. At any rate all the talk shows and those sleazoid news magazines, boy, they'll love it."

He stopped smiling. To tell the truth, for somebody who was about to have his fifteen minutes of fame, the man was downright glum.

MARCIA MULLER

Marcia Muller is the mother of the female P.I. No, strike that. Sharon McCone is the mother of— No, not that, either. Try this: When Marcia Muller introduced Sharon McCone in *Edwin of the Iron Shoes* in 1977, she began a trend that eventually paved the way for the success of Sara Paretsky and Sue Grafton, among others. McCone continues to be the perfect example of the modern female P.I.: smart, tough, very feminine and sexy, to boot. No tricks, no gimmicks, just the Original.

Muller and McCone are past winners of the Shamus Award for Best Short Story, and it's just a matter of time before they take home the prize for Best Novel, as well. It's inevitable.

Stalking has become a crime in the '90s, punishable by a term of imprisonment in some states. McCone is hired by a man whose wife is being stalked and finds out that, as usual, there's more to some cases than meets the eye.

THE LOST COAST

A SHARON MCCONE STORY

California's Lost Coast is at the same time one
of the most desolate and beautiful of shore-
lines. Northerly winds whip the sand into a
dust-devil frenzy; eerie, stationary fogs hang in
the trees and distort the driftwood until it resembles the bones of prehistoric mammals;
bruised clouds hover above the peaks of the
distant King Range, then blow down to sea
level and dump icy torrents. But on a fair day
the sea and sky show infinite shadings of blue,
and the wildflowers are a riot of color. If you
wait quietly, you can spot deer, peregrine falcons, foxes, otters, even black bears and mountain lions.

A contradictory and oddly compelling place,
this seventy-three-mile stretch of coast southwest of Eureka, where—as with most worth-
while things or people—you must take the bad
with the good.

Unfortunately, on my first visit there I was
taking mostly the bad. Strong wind pushed my
MG all over the steep, narrow road, making its
hairpin turns even more perilous. Early October rain cut my visibility to a few yards. After I

crossed the swollen Bear River, the road continued to twist and wind, and I began to understand why the natives had dubbed it The Wildcat.

Somewhere ahead, my client had told me, was the hamlet of Petrolia —site of the first oil well drilled in California, he'd irrelevantly added. The man was a conservative politician, a former lumber-company attorney, and given what I knew of his voting record on the environment, I was certain we disagreed on the desirability of that event, as well as any number of similar issues. But the urgency of the current situation dictated that I keep my opinions to myself, so I'd simply written down the directions he gave me—omitting his travelogue-like asides—and gotten under way.

I drove through Petrolia—a handful of new buildings, since the village had been all but leveled in the disastrous earthquake of 1992—and turned toward the sea on an unpaved road. After two miles I began looking for the orange post that marked the dirt track to the client's cabin.

The whole time I was wishing I was back in San Francisco. This wasn't my kind of case; I didn't like the client, Steve Shoemaker; and even though the fee was good, this was the week I'd scheduled to take off a few personal business days from All Souls Legal Cooperative, where I'm chief investigator. But Jack Stuart, our criminal specialist, had asked me to take on the job as a favor to him. Steve Shoemaker was Jack's old friend from college in Southern California, and he'd asked for a referral to a private detective. Jack owed Steve a favor; I owed Jack several, so there was no way I could gracefully refuse.

But I couldn't shake the feeling that something was wrong with this case. And I couldn't help wishing that I'd come to the Lost Coast in summertime, with a backpack and in the company of my lover—instead of on a rainy fall afternoon, with a .38 Special and soon to be in the company of Shoemaker's disagreeable wife, Andrea.

The rain was sheeting down by the time I spotted the orange post. It had turned the hard-packed earth to mud, and my MG's tires sank deep in the ruts, its undercarriage scraping dangerously. I could barely make out the stand of live oaks and sycamores where the track ended; no way to tell if another vehicle had traveled over it recently.

When I reached the end of the track I saw one of those boxy four-wheel-drive wagons—Bronco? Cherokee?—drawn in under the drooping branches of an oak. Andrea Shoemaker's? I'd neglected to get a description from her husband of what she drove. I got out of the MG, turning the hood of my heavy sweater up against the downpour; the wind promptly blew it off. So much for what the catalog had described as "extra protection on those cold nights." I yanked the hood up again and held it there, went around and took my .38 from the trunk and shoved it into the outside flap of my purse. Then I went over and tried the door of the four-wheel drive. Unlocked. I opened it, slipped into the driver's seat.

Nothing identifying its owner was on the seats or in the side pockets, but in the glove compartment I found a registration in the name of Andrea Shoemaker. I rummaged around, came up with nothing else of interest. Then I got out and walked through the trees, looking for the cabin.

Shoemaker had told me to follow a deer track through the grove. No sign of it in this downpour; no deer, either. Nothing but wind-lashed trees, the oaks pelting me with acorns. I moved slowly through them, swiveling my head from side to side, until I made out a bulky shape tucked beneath the farthest of the sycamores.

As I got closer, I saw the cabin was of plain weathered wood, rudely constructed, with the chimney of a woodstove extending from its composition shingle roof. Small—two or three rooms—and no light showing in its windows. And the door was open, banging against the inside wall . . .

I quickened my pace, taking the gun from my purse. Alongside the door I stopped to listen. Silence. I had a flashlight in my bag; I took it out. Moved to where I could see inside, then turned the flash on and shone it through the door.

All that was visible was rough board walls, an oilcloth-covered table and chairs, an ancient woodstove. I stepped inside, swinging the light around. Unlit oil lamp on the table; flower-cushioned wooden furniture of the sort you always find in vacation cabins; rag rugs; shelves holding an assortment of tattered paperbacks, seashells, and driftwood. I shifted the light again, more slowly.

A chair on the far side of the table was tipped over, and a woman's purse lay on the edge of the woodstove, its contents spilling out. When I got over there I saw a .32 Iver Johnson revolver lying on the floor.

Andrea Shoemaker owned a .32. She'd told me so the day before.

Two doors opened off the room. Quietly I went to one and tried it. A closet, shelves stocked with staples and canned goods and bottled water. I looked around the room again, listening. No sound but the wail of wind and the pelt of rain on the roof. I stepped to the other door.

A bedroom, almost filled wall-to-wall by a king-sized bed covered with a goosedown comforter and piled with colorful pillows. Old bureau pushed in one corner, another unlit oil lamp on the single nightstand. Small travel bag on the bed.

The bag hadn't been opened. I examined its contents. Jeans, a couple of sweaters, underthings, toilet articles. Package of condoms. Uh-huh. She'd come here, as I'd found out, to meet a man. The affairs usually began with a casual pickup; they were never of long duration; and they all seemed to culminate in a romantic weekend in the isolated cabin.

Dangerous game, particularly in these days when AIDS and the prevalence of disturbed individuals of both sexes threatened. But Andrea Shoemaker had kept her latest date with an even larger threat hanging over her: for the past six weeks, a man with a serious grudge against her husband had been stalking her. For all I knew, he and the date were one and the same.

And where was Andrea now?

This case had started on Wednesday, two days ago, when I'd driven up to Eureka, a lumbering and fishing town on Humboldt Bay. After I passed the Humboldt County line I began to see huge logging trucks toiling through the mountain passes, shredded curls of redwood bark trailing in their wakes. Twenty-five miles south of the city itself was the company-owned town of Scotia, mill stacks belching white smoke and filling the air with the scent of freshly cut wood. Yards full of logs waiting to be fed to the mills lined the highway. When I reached Eureka itself, the downtown struck me as curiously quiet; many of the stores were out of business, and the sidewalks were mostly deserted. The recession had hit the lumber industry hard, and the earthquake hadn't helped the area's strapped economy.

I'd arranged to meet Steve Shoemaker at his law offices in Old Town, near the waterfront. It was a picturesque area full of renovated warehouses and interesting shops and restaurants, tricked up for tourists with the inevitable horse-and-carriage rides and T-shirt shops, but still pleasant. Shoemaker's offices were off a cobblestoned courtyard containing a couple of antique shops and a decorator's showroom.

When I gave my card to the secretary, she said Assemblyman Shoemaker was in conference and asked me to wait. The man, I knew, had lost his seat in the state legislature this past election, so the term of address seemed inappropriate. The appointments of the waiting room struck me as a bit much: brass and mahogany and marble and velvet, plenty of it, the furnishings all antiques that tended to the garish. I sat on a red velvet sofa and looked for something to read. *Architectural Digest,*

National Review, Foreign Affairs—that was it, take it or leave it. I left it. My idea of waiting-room reading material is *People;* I love it, but I'm too embarrassed to subscribe.

The minutes ticked by: ten, fifteen, twenty. I contemplated the issue of *Architectural Digest*, then opted instead for staring at a fake Rembrandt on the far wall. Twenty-five, thirty. I was getting irritated now. Shoemaker had asked me to be here by three; I'd arrived on the dot. If this was, as he'd claimed, a matter of such urgency and delicacy that he couldn't go into it on the phone, why was he in conference at the appointed time?

Thirty-five minutes. Thirty-seven. The door to the inner sanctum opened and a woman strode out. A tall woman, with long chestnut hair, wearing a raincoat and black leather boots. Her eyes rested on me in passing—a cool gray, hard with anger. Then she went out, slamming the door behind her.

The secretary—a trim blonde in a tailored suit—started as the door slammed. She glanced at me and tried to cover with a smile, but its edges were strained, and her fingertips pressed hard against the desk. The phone at her elbow buzzed; she snatched up the receiver. Spoke into it, then said to me, "Ms. McCone, Assemblyman Shoemaker will see you now." As she ushered me inside, she again gave me her frayed-edge smile.

Tense situation in this office, I thought. Brought on by what? The matter Steve Shoemaker wanted me to investigate? The client who had just made her angry exit? Or something else entirely . . . ?

Shoemaker's office was even more pretentious than the waiting room: more brass, mahogany, velvet, and marble; more fake Old Masters in heavy gilt frames; more antiques; more of everything. Shoemaker's demeanor was not as nervous as his secretary's, but when he rose to greet me, I noticed a jerkiness in his movements, as if he was holding himself under tight control. I clasped his outstretched hand and smiled, hoping the familiar social rituals would set him more at ease.

Momentarily they did. He thanked me for coming, apologized for making me wait, and inquired after Jack Stuart. After I was seated in one of the clients' chairs, he offered me a drink; I asked for mineral water. As he went to a wet bar tucked behind a tapestry screen, I took the opportunity to study him.

Shoemaker was handsome: dark hair, with the gray so artfully interwoven that it must have been professionally dyed. Chiseled features; nice, well-muscled body, shown off to perfection by an expensive blue suit. When he handed me my drink, his smile revealed white, even teeth that

I—having spent the greater part of the previous month in the company of my dentist—recognized as capped. Yes, a very good-looking man, politician handsome. Jack's old friend or not, his appearance and manner called up my gut-level distrust.

My client went around his desk and reclaimed his chair. He held a drink of his own—something dark amber—and he took a deep swallow before speaking. The alcohol replenished his vitality some; he drank again, set the glass on a pewter coaster, and said, "Ms. McCone, I'm glad you could come up here on such short notice."

"You mentioned on the phone that the case is extremely urgent—and delicate."

He ran his hand over his hair—lightly, so as not to disturb its styling. "Extremely urgent and delicate," he repeated, seeming to savor the phrase.

"Why don't you tell me about it?"

His eyes strayed to the half-full glass on the coaster. Then they moved to the door through which I'd entered. Returned to me. "You saw the woman who just left?"

I nodded.

"My wife, Andrea."

I waited.

"She's very angry with me for hiring you."

"She did act angry. Why?"

Now he reached for the glass and belted down its contents. Leaned back and rattled the ice cubes as he spoke. "It's a long story. Painful to me. I'm not sure where to begin. I just . . . don't know what to make of the things that are happening."

"That's what you've hired me to do. Begin anywhere. We'll fill in the gaps later." I pulled a small tape recorder from my bag and set it on the edge of his desk. "Do you mind?"

Shoemaker eyed it warily, but shook his head. After a moment's hesitation, he said, "Someone is stalking my wife."

"Following her? Threatening her?"

"Not following, not that I know of. He writes notes, threatening to kill her. He leaves . . . things at the house. At her place of business. Dead things. Birds, rats, one time a cat. Andrea loves cats. She . . ." He shook his head, went to the bar for a refill.

"What else? Phone calls?"

"No. One time, a floral arrangement—suitable for a funeral."

"Does he sign the notes?"

"John. Just John."

"Does Mrs. Shoemaker know anyone named John who has a grudge against her?"

"She says no. And I . . . ." He sat down, fresh drink in hand. "I have reason to believe that this John has a grudge against me, is using this harassment of Andrea to get at me personally."

"Why do you think that?"

"The wording of the notes."

"May I see them?"

He looked around, as if he were afraid someone might be listening. "Later. I keep them elsewhere."

Something, then, I thought, that he didn't want his office staff to see. Something shameful, perhaps even criminal.

"Okay," I said, "how long has this been going on?"

"About six weeks."

"Have you contacted the police?"

"Informally. A man I know on the force, Sergeant Bob Wolfe. But after he started looking into it, I had to ask him to drop it."

"Why?"

"I'm in a sensitive political position."

"Excuse me if I'm mistaken, Mr. Shoemaker, but it's my understanding that you're no longer serving in the state legislature."

"That's correct, but I'm about to announce my candidacy in a special election for a senate seat that's recently been vacated."

"I see. So after you asked your contact on the police force to back off, you decided to use a private investigator, and Jack recommended me. Why not use someone local?"

"As I said, my position is sensitive. I don't want word of this getting out in the community. That's why Andrea is so angry with me. She claims I value my political career more than her life."

I waited, wondering how he'd attempt to explain that away.

He didn't even try, merely went on, "In our . . . conversation just prior to this, she threatened to leave me. This coming weekend she plans to go to a cabin on the Lost Coast that she inherited from her father to, as she put it, sort things through. Alone. Do you know that part of the coast?"

"I've read some travel pieces on it."

"Then you're aware how remote it is. The cabin's very isolated. I don't want Andrea going there while this John person is on the loose."

"Does she go there often?"

"Fairly often. I don't; it's too rustic for me—no running water, phone, or electricity. But Andrea likes it. Why do you ask?"

"I'm wondering if John—whoever he is—knows about the cabin. Has she been there since the harassment began?"

"No. Initially she agreed that it wouldn't be a good idea. But now . . ." He shrugged.

"I'll need to speak with Mrs. Shoemaker. Maybe I can reason with her, persuade her not to go until we've identified John. Or maybe she'll allow me to go along as her bodyguard."

"You can speak with her if you like, but she's beyond reasoning with. And there's no way you can stop her or force her to allow you to accompany her. My wife is a strong-willed woman; that interior decorating firm across the courtyard is hers, she built it from the ground up. When Andrea decides to do something, she does it. And asks permission from no one."

"Still, I'd like to try reasoning. This trip to the cabin—that's the urgency you mentioned on the phone. Two days to find the man behind the harassment before she goes out there and perhaps makes a target of herself."

"Yes."

"Then I'd better get started. That funeral arrangement—what florist did it come from?"

Shoemaker shook his head. "It arrived at least five weeks ago, before either of us noticed a pattern to the harassment. Andrea just shrugged it off, threw the wrappings and card away."

"Let's go look at the notes, then. They're my only lead."

Vengeance will be mine. The sudden blow. The quick attack. Vengeance is the price of silence.

Mute testimony paves the way to an early grave. The rest is silence.

A freshly turned grave is silent testimony to an old wrong and its avenger.

There was more in the same vein—slightly biblical-flavored and stilted. But chilling to me, even though the safety-deposit booth at Shoemaker's bank was overly warm. If that was my reaction, what had these notes done to Andrea Shoemaker? No wonder she was thinking of leaving a husband who cared more for the electorate's opinion than his wife's life and safety.

The notes had been typed without error on an electric machine that had left no such obvious clues as chipped or skewed keys. The paper and envelopes were plain and cheap, purchasable at any discount store. They had been handled, I was sure, by nothing more than gloved hands. No signature—just the typed name "John."

But the writer had wanted the Shoemakers—one of them, anyway—to know who he was. Thus the theme that ran through them all: silence and revenge.

I said, "I take it your contact at the E.P.D. had their lab go over these?"

"Yes. There was nothing. That's why he wanted to probe further—something I couldn't permit him to do."

"Because of this revenge-and-silence business. Tell me about it."

Shoemaker looked around furtively. My God, did he think bank employees had nothing better to do with their time than to eavesdrop on our conversation?

"We'll go have a drink," he said. "I know a place that's private."

We went to a restaurant a few blocks away, where Shoemaker had another bourbon and I toyed with a glass of iced tea. After some prodding, he told me his story; it didn't enhance him in my eyes.

Seventeen years ago Shoemaker had been interviewing for a staff attorney's position at a large lumber company. While on a tour of the mills, he witnessed an accident in which a worker named Sam Carding was severely mangled while trying to clear a jam in a bark-stripping machine. Shoemaker, who had worked in the mills summers to pay for his education, knew the accident was due to company negligence, but accepted a handsome job offer in exchange for not testifying for the plaintiff in the ensuing lawsuit. The court ruled against Carding, confined to a wheelchair and in constant pain; a year later, while the case was still under appeal, Carding shot his wife and himself. The couple's three children were given token settlements in exchange for dropping the suit and then were adopted by relatives in a different part of the country.

"It's not a pretty story, Mr. Shoemaker," I said, "and I can see why the wording of the notes might make you suspect there's a connection between it and this harassment. But who do you think John is?"

"Carding's oldest boy. Carding and his family knew I'd witnessed the accident; one of his coworkers saw me watching from the catwalk and told him. Later, when I turned up as a senior counsel . . ." He shrugged.

"But why, after all this time—?"

"Why not? People nurse grudges. John Carding was sixteen at the time of the lawsuit; there were some ugly scenes with him, both at my home and my office at the mill. By now he'd be in his forties. Maybe it's his way of acting out some sort of midlife crisis."

"Well, I'll call my office and have my assistant run a check on all three Carding kids. And I want to speak with Mrs. Shoemaker—preferably in your presence."

He glanced at his watch. "It can't be tonight. She's got a meeting of her professional organization, and I'm dining with my campaign manager."

A potentially psychotic man was threatening Andrea's life, yet they both carried on as usual. Well, who was I to question it? Maybe it was their way of coping.

"Tomorrow, then," I said. "Your home. At the noon hour."

Shoemaker nodded. Then he gave me the address, as well as the names of John Carding's siblings.

I left him on the sidewalk in front of the restaurant: a handsome man whose shoulders now slumped inside his expensive suitcoat, shivering in the brisk wind off Humboldt Bay. As we shook hands, I saw that shame made his gaze unsteady, the set of his mouth less than firm.

I knew that kind of shame. Over the course of my career, I'd committed some dreadful acts that years later woke me in the deep of the night to sudden panic. I'd also *not* committed certain acts—failures that woke me to regret and emptiness. My sins of omission were infinitely worse than those of commission, because I knew that if I'd acted, I could have made a difference. Could even have saved a life.

I wasn't able to reach Rae Kelleher, my assistant at All Souls, that evening, and by the time she got back to me the next morning—Thursday—I was definitely annoyed. Still, I tried to keep a lid on my irritation. Rae is young, attractive, and in love; I couldn't expect her to spend her evenings waiting to be of service to her workaholic boss.

I got her started on a computer check on all three Cardings, then took myself to the Eureka P.D. and spoke with Shoemaker's contact, Sergeant Bob Wolfe. Wolfe—a dark-haired, sharp-featured man whose appearance was a good match for his surname—told me he'd had the notes processed by the lab, which had turned up no useful evidence.

"Then I started to probe, you know? When you got a harassment case like this, you look into the victims' private lives."

"And that was when Shoemaker told you to back off."

"Uh-huh."

"When was this?"

"About five weeks ago."

"I wonder why he waited so long to hire me. Did he, by any chance, ask you for a referral to a local investigator?"

Wolfe frowned. "Not this time."

"Then you'd referred him to someone before?"

"Yeah, guy who used to be on the force—Dave Morrison. Last April."

"Did Shoemaker tell you why he needed an investigator?"

"No, and I didn't ask. These politicians, they're always trying to get something on their rivals. I didn't want any part of it."

"Do you have Morrison's address and phone number handy?"

Wolfe reached into his desk drawer, shuffled things, and flipped a business card across the blotter. "Dave gave me a stack of these when he set up shop," he said. "Always glad to help an old pal."

Morrison was out of town, the message on his answering machine said, but would be back tomorrow afternoon. I left a message of my own, asking him to call me at my motel. Then I headed for the Shoemakers' home, hoping I could talk some common sense into Andrea.

But Andrea wasn't having any common sense.

She strode around the parlor of their big Victorian—built by one of the city's lumber barons, her husband told me when I complimented them on it—arguing and waving her arms and making scathing statements punctuated by a good amount of profanity. And knocking back martinis, even though it was only a little past noon.

Yes, she was going to the cabin. No, neither her husband nor I was welcome there. No, she wouldn't postpone the trip; she was sick and tired of being cooped up like some kind of zoo animal because her husband had made a mistake years before she'd met him. All right, she realized this John person was dangerous. But she'd taken self-defense classes and owned a .32 revolver. Of course she knew how to use it. Practiced frequently, too. Women had to be prepared these days, and she was.

But, she added darkly, glaring at her husband, she'd just as soon not have to shoot John. She'd rather send him straight back to Steve and let them settle this score. May the best man win—and she was placing bets on John.

As far as I was concerned, Steve and Andrea Shoemaker deserved each other.

I tried to explain to her that self-defense classes don't fully prepare you for a paralyzing, heart-pounding encounter with an actual violent stranger. I tried to warn her that the ability to shoot well on a firing range doesn't fully prepare you for pumping a bullet into a human being who is advancing swiftly on you.

I wanted to tell her she was being an idiot.

Before I could, she slammed down her glass and stormed out of the house.

Her husband replenished his own drink and said, "Now do you see what I'm up against?"

I didn't respond to that. Instead I said, "I spoke with Sergeant Wolfe earlier."

"And?"

"He told me he referred you to a local private investigator, Dave Morrison, last April."

"So?"

"Why didn't you hire Morrison for this job?"

"As I told you yesterday, my—"

"Sensitive position, yes."

Shoemaker scowled.

Before he could comment, I asked, "What was the job last April?"

"Nothing to do with this matter."

"Something to do with politics?"

"In a way."

"Mr. Shoemaker, hasn't it occurred to you that a political enemy may be using the Carding case as a smoke screen? That a rival's trying to throw you off balance before this special election?"

"It did, and . . . well, it isn't my opponent's style. My God, we're civilized people. But those notes . . . they're the work of a lunatic."

I wasn't so sure he was right—both about the notes being the work of a lunatic and politicians being civilized people—but I merely said, "Okay, you keep working on Mrs. Shoemaker. At least persuade her to let me go to the Lost Coast with her. I'll be in touch." Then I headed for the public library.

After a few hours of ruining my eyes at the microfilm machine, I knew little more than before. Newspaper accounts of the Carding accident, lawsuit, and murder-suicide didn't differ substantially from what my client had told me. Their coverage of the Shoemakers' activities was only marginally interesting.

Normally I don't do a great deal of background investigation on clients, but as Sergeant Wolfe had said, in a case like this where one or both of them was a target, a thorough look at careers and lifestyles was mandatory. The papers described Steve as a straightforward, effective assemblyman who took a hard, conservative stance on such issues as welfare and the environment. He was strongly pro-business, particularly the lumber industry. He and his "charming and talented wife" didn't share many interests: Steve hunted and golfed; Andrea was a "generous supporter of the arts" and a "lavish party-giver." An odd couple, I thought, and odd people to be friends of Jack Stuart, a liberal who'd chosen to dedicate his career to representing the underdog.

Back at the motel, I put in a call to Jack. Why, I asked him, had he remained close to a man who was so clearly his opposite?

Jack laughed. "You're trying to say politely that you think he's a pompous, conservative ass."

"Well . . ."

"Okay, I admit it: He is. But back in college, he was a mentor to me. I doubt I would have gone into the law if it hadn't been for Steve. And we shared some good times, too: One summer we took a motorcycle trip around the country, like something out of *Easy Rider* without the tragedy. I guess we stay in touch because of a shared past."

I was trying to imagine Steve Shoemaker on a motorcycle; the picture wouldn't materialize. "Was he always so conservative?" I asked.

"No, not until he moved back to Eureka and went to work for that lumber company. Then . . . I don't know. Everything changed. It was as if something had happened that took all the fight out of him."

What had happened, I thought, was trading another man's life for a prestigious job.

Jack and I chatted for a moment longer, and then I asked him to transfer me to Rae. She hadn't turned up anything on the Cardings yet, but was working on it. In the meantime, she added, she'd taken care of what correspondence had come in, dealt with seven phone calls, entered next week's must-do's in the call-up file she'd created for me, and found a remedy for the blight that was affecting my rubber plant.

With a pang, I realized that the office ran just as well—better, perhaps —when I wasn't there. It would keep functioning smoothly without me for weeks, months, maybe years.

Hell, it would probably keep functioning smoothly even if I were dead.

* * *

In the morning I opened the Yellow Pages to Florists and began call-ing each that was listed. While Shoemaker had been vague on the date his wife received the funeral arrangement, surely a customer who wanted one sent to a private home, rather than a mortuary, would stand out in the order-taker's mind. The listing was long, covering a relatively wide area; it wasn't until I reached the R's and my watch showed nearly eleven o'clock that I got lucky.

"I don't remember any order like that in the past six weeks," the clerk at Rainbow Florists said, "but we had one yesterday, was delivered this morning."

I gripped the receiver harder. "Will you pull the order, please?"

"I'm not sure I should—"

"Please. You could help to save a woman's life."

Quick intake of breath, then his voice filled with excitement; he'd become part of a real-life drama. "One minute. I'll check." When he came back on the line, he said, "Thirty-dollar standard condolence ar-rangement, delivered this morning to Mr. Steven Shoemaker—"

"*Mister?* Not Mrs. or Ms.?"

"Mister, definitely. I took the order myself." He read off the Shoe-makers' address.

"Who placed it?"

"A kid. Came in with cash and written instructions."

Standard ploy—hire a kid off the street so nobody can identify you. "Thanks very much."

"Aren't you going to tell me—"

I hung up and dialed Shoemaker's office. His secretary told me he was working at home today. I dialed the home number. Busy. I hung up, and the phone rang immediately. Rae, with information on the Cardings.

She'd traced Sam Carding's daughter and younger son. The daughter lived near Cleveland, Ohio, and Rae had spoken with her on the phone. John, his sister had told her, was a drifter and an addict; she hadn't seen or spoken to him in more than ten years. When Rae reached the younger brother at his office in L.A., he told her the same, adding that he as-sumed John had died years ago.

I thanked Rae and told her to keep on it. Then I called Shoemaker's home number again. Still busy; time to go over there.

* * *

Shoemaker's Lincoln was parked in the drive of the Victorian, a dusty Honda motorcycle beside it. As I rang the doorbell I again tried to picture a younger, free-spirited Steve bumming around the country on a bike with Jack, but the image simply wouldn't come clear. It took Shoemaker a while to answer the door, and when he saw me, his mouth pulled down in displeasure.

"Come in, and be quick about it," he told me. "I'm on an important conference call."

I was quick about it. He rushed down the hallway to what must be a study, and I went into the parlor where we'd talked the day before. Unlike his offices, it was exquisitely decorated, calling up images of the days of the lumber barons. Andrea's work, probably. Had she also done his offices? Perhaps their gaudy decor was her way of getting back at a husband who put his political life ahead of their marriage?

It was at least half an hour before Shoemaker finished with his call. He appeared in the archway leading to the hall, somewhat disheveled, running his fingers through his hair. "Come with me," he said. "I have something to show you."

He led me to a large kitchen at the back of the house. A floral arrangement sat on the granite-topped center island: white lilies with a single red rose. Shoemaker handed me the card: "My sympathy on your wife's passing." It was signed "John."

"Where's Mrs. Shoemaker?" I asked.

"Apparently she went out to the coast last night. I haven't seen her since she walked out on us at the noon hour."

"And you've been home the whole time?"

He nodded. "Mainly on the phone."

"Why didn't you call me when she didn't come home?"

"I didn't realize she hadn't until mid-morning. We have separate bedrooms, and Andrea comes and goes as she pleases. Then this arrangement arrived, and my conference call came through . . ." He shrugged, spreading his hands helplessly.

"All right," I said, "I'm going out there whether she likes it or not. And I think you'd better clear up whatever you're doing here and follow. Maybe your showing up there will convince her you care about her safety, make her listen to reason."

As I spoke, Shoemaker had taken a fifth of Tanqueray gin and a jar of Del Prado Spanish olives from a Lucky sack that sat on the counter. He opened a cupboard, reached for a glass.

"No," I said. "This is no time to have a drink."

He hesitated, then replaced the glass, and began giving me directions to the cabin. His voice was flat, and his curious travelogue-like digressions made me feel as if I were listening to a tape of a *National Geographic* special. Reality, I thought, had finally sunk in, and it had turned him into an automaton.

I had one stop to make before heading out to the coast, but it was right on my way. Morrison Investigations had its office in what looked to be a former motel on Highway 101, near the outskirts of the city. It was a neighborhood of fast-food restaurants and bars, thrift shops and marginal businesses. Besides the detective agency, the motel's cinder-block units housed an insurance brokerage, a secretarial service, two accountants, and a palm reader. Dave Morrison, who was just arriving as I pulled into the parking area, was a bit of a surprise: in his mid-forties, wearing one small gold earring and a short ponytail. I wondered what Steve Shoemaker had made of him.

Morrison showed me into a two-room suite crowded with computer equipment and file cabinets and furniture that looked as if he might have hauled it down the street from the nearby Thrift Emporium. When he noticed me studying him, he grinned easily. "I know, I don't look like a former cop. I worked undercover Narcotics my last few years on the force. Afterwards I realized I was comfortable with the uniform." His gesture took in his lumberjack's shirt, work-worn jeans and boots.

I smiled in return, and he cleared some files off a chair so I could sit.

"So you're working for Steve Shoemaker," he said.

"I understand you did, too."

He nodded. "Last April and again around the beginning of August."

"Did he approach you about another job after that?"

He shook his head.

"And the jobs you did for him were—"

"You know better than to ask that."

"I was going to ask, were they completed to his satisfaction?"

"Yes."

"Do you have any idea why Shoemaker would go to the trouble of bringing me up from San Francisco when he had an investigator here whose work satisfied him?"

Headshake.

"Shoemaker told me the first job you did for him had to do with politics."

The corner of his mouth twitched. "In a matter of speaking." He paused, shrewd eyes assessing me. "How come you're investigating your own client?"

"It's that kind of case. And something feels wrong. Did you get that sense about either of the jobs you took on for him?"

"No." Then he hesitated, frowning. "Well, maybe. Why don't you just come out and ask what you want to? If I can, I'll answer."

"Okay—did either of the jobs have to do with a man named John Carding?"

That surprised him. After a moment he asked a question of his own. "He's still trying to trace Carding?"

"Yes."

Morrison got up and moved toward the window, stopped and drummed his fingers on top of a file cabinet. "Well, I can save you further trouble. John Carding is untraceable. I tried every way I know— and that's every way there is. My guess is that he's dead, years dead."

"And when was it you tried to trace him?"

"Most of August."

Weeks before Andrea Shoemaker had begun to receive the notes from "John." Unless the harassment had started earlier? No, I'd seen all the notes, examined their postmarks. Unless she'd thrown away the first ones, as she had the card that came with the funeral arrangement?

"Shoemaker tell you why he wanted to find Carding?" I asked.

"Uh-uh."

"And your investigation last April had nothing to do with Carding?"

At first I thought Morrison hadn't heard the question. He was looking out the window; then he turned, expression thoughtful, and opened one of the drawers of the filing cabinet beside him. "Let me refresh my memory," he said, taking out a couple of folders. I watched as he flipped through them, frowning.

Finally he said, "I'm not gonna ask about your case. If something feels wrong, it could be because of what I turned up last spring—and that I don't want on my conscience." He closed one file, slipped it back in the cabinet, then glanced at his watch. "Damn! I just remembered I've got to make a call." He crossed to the desk, set the open file on it. "I better do it from the other room. You stay here, find something to read."

I waited until he'd left, then went over and picked up the file. Read it with growing interest and began putting things together. Andrea had been discreet about her extramarital activities, but not so discreet that a competent investigator like Morrison couldn't uncover them.

When Morrison returned, I was ready to leave for the Lost Coast.

"Hope you weren't bored," he said.

"No, I'm easily amused. And, Mr. Morrison, I owe you a dinner."

"You know where to find me. I'll look forward to seeing you again."

And now that I'd reached the cabin, Andrea had disappeared. The victim of violence, all signs indicated. But the victim of whom? John Carding—a man no one had seen or heard from for over ten years? Another man named John, one of her cast-off lovers? Or . . . ?

What mattered now was to find her.

I retraced my steps, turning up the hood of my sweater again as I went outside. Circled the cabin, peering through the lashing rain. I could make out a couple of other small structures back there: outhouse and shed. The outhouse was empty. I crossed to the shed. Its door was propped open with a log, as if she'd been getting fuel for the stove.

Inside, next to a neatly stacked cord of wood, I found her.

She lay facedown on the hard-packed dirt floor, blue-jeaned legs splayed, plaid-jacketed arms flung above her head, chestnut hair cascading over her back. The little room was silent, the total silence that surrounds the dead. Even my own breath was stilled; when it came again, it sounded obscenely loud.

I knelt beside her, forced myself to perform all the checks I've made more times than I could have imagined. No breath, no pulse, no warmth to the skin. And the rigidity . . .

On the average—although there's a wide variance—rigor mortis sets in to the upper body five to six hours after death; the whole body is usually affected within eighteen hours. I backed up and felt the lower portion of her body. Rigid; rigor was complete. I straightened, went to stand in the doorway. She'd probably been dead since midnight. And the cause? I couldn't see any wounds, couldn't further examine her without disturbing the scene. What I should be doing was getting in touch with the sheriff's department.

Back to the cabin. Emotions tore at me: anger, regret, and—yes—guilt that I hadn't prevented this. But I also sensed that I *couldn't* have prevented it. I, or someone like me, had been an integral component from the first.

In the front room I found some kitchen matches and lit the oil lamp. Then I went around the table and looked down at where her revolver lay on the floor. More evidence; don't touch it. The purse and its spilled contents rested near the edge of the stove. I inventoried the items visually: the usual makeup, brush, comb, spray perfume; wallet, keys, roll of postage stamps; daily planner that had flopped open to show pockets for business cards and receipts. And a loose piece of paper . . .

Lucky Food Center, it said at the top. Perhaps she'd stopped to pick up supplies before leaving Eureka; the date and time on this receipt might indicate how long she'd remained in town before storming out on her husband and me.

I picked it up. At the bottom I found yesterday's date and the time of purchase: 9:14 P.M.

"KY SERV DELI . . . CRABS . . . WINE . . . DEL PRAD OLIVE . . . LG RED DEL . . . ROUGE ET NOIR . . . BAKERY . . . TANQ GIN—"

A sound outside. Footsteps slogging through the mud. I stuffed the receipt into my pocket.

Steve Shoemaker came through the open door in a hurry, rain hat pulled low on his forehead, droplets sluicing down his chiseled nose. He stopped when he saw me, looked around. "Where's Andrea?"

I said, "I don't know."

"What do you mean you don't know? Her Bronco's outside. That's her purse on the stove."

"And her weekend bag's on the bed, but she's nowhere to be found."

Shoemaker arranged his face into lines of concern. "There's been a struggle here."

"Appears that way."

"Come on, we'll go look for her. She may be in the outhouse or the shed. She may be hurt—"

"It won't be necessary to look." I had my gun out of my purse now, and I leveled it at him. "I know you killed your wife, Shoemaker."

"What!"

"Her body's where you left it last night. What time did you kill her? How?"

His faked concern shaded into panic. "I didn't—"

"You did."

No reply. His eyes moved from side to side—calculating, looking for a way out.

I added, "You drove her here in the Bronco, with your motorcycle inside. Arranged things to simulate a struggle, put her in the shed, then drove back to town on the bike. You shouldn't have left the bike outside the house where I could see it. It wasn't muddy out here last night, but it sure was dusty."

"Where are these baseless accusations coming from? John Carding—"

"Is untraceable, probably dead, as you know from the check Dave Morrison ran."

"He told you— What about the notes, the flowers, the dead things—"

"Sent by you."

"Why would I do that?"

"To set the scene for getting rid of a chronically unfaithful wife who had potential to become a political embarrassment."

He wasn't cracking, though. "Granted, Andrea had her problems. But why would I rake up the Carding matter?"

"Because it would sound convincing for you to admit what you did all those years ago. God knows it convinced me. And I doubt the police would ever have made the details public. Why destroy a grieving widower and prominent citizen? Particularly when they'd never find Carding or bring him to trial. You've got one problem, though: me. You never should have brought me in to back up your scenario."

He licked his lips, glaring at me. Then he drew himself up, leaned forward aggressively—a posture the attorneys at All Souls jokingly refer to as their "litigator's mode."

"You have no proof of this," he said firmly, jabbing his index finger at me. "No proof whatsoever."

"Deli items, crabs, wine, apples," I recited. "Del Prado Spanish olives, Tanqueray gin."

"What the hell are you talking about?"

"I have Andrea's receipt for the items she bought at Lucky yesterday, before she stopped home to pick up her weekend bag. None of those things is here in the cabin."

"So?"

"I know that at least two of them—the olives and the gin—are at your house in Eureka. I'm willing to bet they all are."

"What if they are? She did some shopping for me yesterday morning—"

"The receipt is dated yesterday *evening*, nine-fourteen P.M. I'll quote you, Shoemaker: 'Apparently she went out to the coast last night. I haven't seen her since she walked out on us at the noon hour.' But you claim you didn't leave home after noon."

That did it; that opened the cracks. He stood for a moment, then half collapsed into one of the chairs and put his head in his hands.

The next summer, after I testified at the trial in which Steve Shoemaker was convicted of the first-degree murder of his wife, I returned to the Lost Coast—with a backpack, without the .38, and in the company of my lover. We walked sand beaches under skies that showed infinite shadings of blue; we made love in fields of wildflowers; we waited quietly for the deer, falcons, and foxes.

I'd already taken the bad from this place; now I could take the good.

A man's home is his castle.

Architectural structures may vary
in size and scale but the importance that men
attach to them can be overwhelming, as Victorian sometimes-actress Bridget Mooney and
Boston P.I. John Francis Cuddy discover.
Whether it's the Brooklyn Bridge—the architectural wonder of its age—or a very modest
house in a very modest neighborhood, to those
who love them they are indeed castles worth
dying for.

JEREMIAH HEALY

In a relatively short period of time Jeremiah Healy has built up an impressive list of credits. His most recent novel, *Shallow Graves* (Pocket Books, 1992), is the seventh in his John Francis Cuddy series. The second book in the series, *The Staked Goat*, won the Shamus Award for Best P.I. Novel, 1986. In the past few years he has proven himself as adept with the short-story form as he is with novels, in anthologies—including the first *Deadly Allies* —as well as in numerous appearances within the pages of *Alfred Hitchcock's* and *Ellery Queen's Mystery Magazines*. He is a former vice-president of PWA, and has just finished a two-year tour of duty as the president of PWA, and as such as an active ambassador of the P.I. form.

A law professor, he combines his knowledge of the law with his abilities to create real-life, credible characters and thoroughly believable story lines. In "Yellow Snow," Cuddy agrees to help an old friend settle a gambling debt, and discovers that even the oldest of friends doesn't always tell the whole truth.

YELLOW SNOW

ONE

Jiggy Doyle sat in my client's chair on a cold February day and let his eyes roam around the office. "Nice setup you've got here, John."

"Thanks."

"I even like the door there. 'John Francis Cuddy, Confidential Investigations.'"

"It kind of came with the office."

"Yeah." Jiggy made the last part of the word a laugh. Jiggy laughed a lot when we were growing up together in South Boston. Now his carrot hair was thinning under a 1986 Red Sox "League Champions" cap, the face fleshy and heavy below the brim. A bulky tweed overcoat I first saw at least a decade ago covered most but not all of the torn sweater under it. His blue jeans were stained and tattered at the cuff, a pair of sneakers nobody would mistake for cross-trainers on his feet. The only concession to currency was the bicyclist's bottle he held in one hand.

I nodded at the bottle. "Still soft for the Gatorade?"

"Never without it. Not since I—well, you know."

I knew. Jiggy had always been a gambler and, until some years ago, a drinker. He drank the way some people talk, which is to say constantly, stopping only to breathe. When his wife Moira finally got him to go into a program, he went over to Gatorade instead of coffee. He said the coffee kept him up but the lime flavor reminded him of a Margarita without the tequila. I didn't think even Moira had been able to control the gambling, though.

"So what's up, Jiggy?"

"I saw you on the tube the other night. About you shooting that guy with the rifle?"

"Mind if we change the subject?"

"Huh? Oh, sure. It's just that I thought to myself, 'Shit, been a long time since I saw old John.' "

I didn't say anything.

Jiggy crossed his right leg over the left, his right sneaker tapping the air rhythmically. His grandmother nicknamed him "Jiggy" for that. To her, it seemed he was dancing a jig with one foot. To me, it seemed he was dancing around something.

"How about you get to it, Jiggy."

He looked down at the bottle, then back up to me. "I need a favor here, John."

"What kind of favor?"

Jiggy blinked, like he hadn't planned on having to explain. "Remember Danny Bennigan?"

I remembered him. Bennigan was cocky and crude, and the closest thing he had to a character trait was his tendency to call everybody he didn't like "fuckbreath." In the schoolyard, Danny organized two other kids into the first gang I ever saw, shaking the smaller ones down for their milk money. When the gang got around to me, I said no. Jiggy sat on one of Danny's boys while I drew Bennigan and the other. The forces of right won out, though I always wondered if Jiggy pitched in because he was my friend or because he had a bet down on me.

"What's Danny into these days?"

"My pocket. I owe him, John."

"How?"

Jiggy gestured with the bottle. "Danny, he's running this game over a drugstore in Dorchester. Second floor, three tables, two poker and one blackjack. Nice place, good action."

"So?"

"So I'm over there the other night—two, three weeks ago—and I hit this streak, see?"

The way he said it, I didn't think it was a winning streak.

"How much, Jiggy?"

The sneaker bobbed to a faster beat. "Thirteen."

"You're into Danny Bennigan for thirteen hundred dollars?"

The foot stopped, then started again. "Yeah."

"Christ, Jiggy, what the hell did you do?"

"I lost, is what I did. Look, I'm over there, see? And I'm at this one table, playing poker, and my luck's not what it might be. So, I notice this guy get up from the other table, and this other guy come in, so I take the chair of the guy that's leaving so the guy coming can have mine."

"To change your luck."

"Right, of course. Change the cards, change the draw, right? Only the stakes at this next table, they're a little steeper than I realize at the time."

"You're betting chips without knowing what they stand for?"

"A sucker mistake, John. Don't you think I know it? But there I am, and before I know it, I'm down altogether thirteen."

I leaned back in my chair, spoke past Jiggy's shoulder. "What did Danny say?"

Jiggy brought his mouth down to the bottle instead of the bottle to his mouth. He squeezed, tilted his head back, and swallowed. "He said he was gonna go after Moira's house."

Moira had inherited the house in Southie from her mother. It was a three-decker on the wrong side of Broadway, but living shelter-cost-free was probably the only way Moira could have made it with a husband like Jiggy making more withdrawals than deposits.

"He doesn't have any grounds for that, Jiggy."

"Grounds?"

"The house is in her name, not yours, right?"

"Grounds. Tell Danny about grounds, huh? He's got this enforcer drives around in a black Trans Am muscle car with some kind of bug painted on the front of it."

"And?"

"And the enforcer's got blonde hair down his collar like a girl plays field hockey."

"I mean, what's Danny going to do about the enforcer?"

"Danny says I'm gonna have a visit from the guy."

"Jiggy. Nobody's going to kill you over thirteen hundred bucks."

The sneaker stopped again. "They start lower and like build to that. I'll make the marker good, but I'm not gonna touch Moira's house to do it, John."

I came forward in the chair. "Okay. Where will the money come from?"

Jiggy's foot hit high gear. "I got a few good tips. They come through, I'm clear."

"And if they don't?"

"That's why I'm here. I was kind of hoping you could go have a talk with the guy."

"The enforcer?"

"Uh-unh. Danny himself. He'll listen to you. He's still afraid of you."

"The schoolyard's a long time ago, Jiggy."

"One thing I learned over the years, John. Life's a schoolyard."

I watched him for a minute, maybe two. I thought about old times and old friends and how you couldn't go back to the one and didn't have that many of the other.

Picking up a pencil, I said, "You got an address for Danny?"

TWO

The address Jiggy gave me was the poker parlor. That afternoon, I wound down Dorchester Avenue, some of the cars at the curb stuck in the snowstorm we'd had the day before. Intersecting the street I wanted, I pulled past the building.

The first floor had a Rexall sign and some used condoms around the edges of a broken window. Otherwise, the "drugstore" was about as lively as a king's grave before the robbers arrive. I checked the other cars on the street. One was a black Trans Am with chrome tail pipes under the bumper and a golden spider painted on the hood.

After a U-turn, I came back, parking my old Honda Prelude in a cleared spot across from the place. Ten minutes later, nothing had appeared at the doorway to the building or in the windows on the second floor. I got out of my car and went up to the entrance. There was a bell that didn't look too far gone, so I pressed it. I didn't hear it ring, so I pressed it again. Still nothing.

I was giving some thought to going through the broken windows of the drugstore when a bolt was thrown on the other side of the door and it opened to the width of a man's face. The guy who stared out at me was about six feet and stringy, left hand on the door and right hand behind him where I couldn't see it. He had brown hair on top in a brush cut and blondish hair fanned out from his neck. The jacket, pants, and shoes matched his car, a little medallion with the spider motif on a gold chain dangling between the lapels. Jiggy must have left out the part about his eyes, though. Hollow and deep and without anything human behind either. A spider's eyes.

"Private club, buddy. Beat it."

"I'd like to see Danny Bennigan."

"Fuck off."

"Tell him it's John Cuddy." I fished a business card from my pocket. Spider ignored the card. "Danny ain't here."

I still couldn't see his other hand. I had a Smith & Wesson Chief's Special over my right hip, but I wasn't keen on waving it around. "Mind if I see for myself?"

A stiffening. "Believe it."

I swung my left hand, edge up, in an arc, clouting his left on the door. I heard a little crack and Spider cursed, the right hand now coming reflexively forward to cradle the injured one. The Ingram MAC-10 in it didn't quite clear the wood, which gave me the chance to step forward and across the threshold. I caught the right wrist in my left hand, jolting the heel of my right up and into his jaw. Spider went slack but not out, and I took the machine pistol away from him. He slumped back onto the stairs that led to the second floor. I hefted the MAC-10, a hideous little engine of death with a rate of fire like the popcorn maker at a movie house. The welcome wagon tried to get up, my right elbow sending him on to Napland.

I closed and bolted the door, stepping over Spider as I climbed the stairs. The six-panel at the top opened without a key, the room behind it furnished for function. Three round tables and seven chairs to a table. A makeshift wet bar with an old porcelain refrigerator. Corduroy drapes over the windows, more for blackout than decoration.

I walked to the tables. Each had a green felt cloth over it, stapled on the underside. There was a dry stain the size of a soccer ball on one of the tables, the stained area lighter than the felt around it.

A short hall ran off the main room with two doors in turn off it. I tried one and found a half-bath that smelled like a plumber's nightmare. I dropped Spider's MAC-10 into the toilet.

The other hall door led to a cramped office with a desk, a telephone, and one chair, standing room only for guests. I rifled the desk. Old magazines, a couple of racing forms, faded gum wrappers. I stopped after I hit the drawer with the used Kleenex.

The desk had a real blotter with leather corners. I tucked my business card under one cowhide triangle and went back out the way I came.

* * *

I looked down at the gravestone, then to the harbor below. Too nasty for pleasure boats, and the working ones were long gone. A few seagulls struggled to take off into the gusty wind at the foot of Beth's hillside.

What brings you here on a day like this, John?

I came back to her stone, shrugging a little at both the question and the cold. "Jiggy Doyle."

Jiggy, Jiggy. Still drinking?

"I don't think so."

And his other vice?

"Still going strong."

Poor Moira. You certainly had your faults as a husband, John, but thanks be that wasn't one of them.

"No, but it could have been."

A pause. *Meaning, you're going to help him with something.*

"Or try, anyway."

Do everybody a favor.

"What?"

Don't die trying.

I drove down the Doyles' street. It was wider than I remembered it. Two teenagers in a driveway tried to tune the carburetor on an old Ford Mustang, the engine sounding rough and raspy as one came down on the accelerator. Next door, a boy jostled what looked to be his sister as they put the stones in the smile of a snowman. Her ski parka was too long for her, his gloves mismatched. A letter carrier nearly slipped and fell as he came off the stoop of Moira Doyle's house.

I waited until the carrier was three doors down before I walked carefully up the stoop and rang the bell. Moira pulled open the front door with an expectant look that turned to disappointment before she remembered to put on a smile for company.

"John Cuddy? It can't be!"

"It is, Moira. How are you?"

She gave me a hug and tugged me inside the house and toward the kitchen in back. There was the smell of hot chocolate from the stove as she pointed to a chair and went to a cabinet over the sink.

I took in the kitchen. Appliances that looked older than the relic in Bennigan's card room. Dingy paint peeling from the ceiling. Both the corners of the linoleum and the corners of the Formica veneer on the table curled upward toward the buzzing fluorescent light, like the petals of a flower toward a dimming sun.

Moira started to pour into a mug before she noticed it was chipped. She dumped the mug into the sink and reached for another in one fluid motion, filling the new one as though each step were a required part of some Japanese tea ritual.

Moira had always been graceful, and more. Half the guys in sixth grade were looking at her before they even understood why. But she had eyes only for Jiggy. Go figure.

They were married as seniors in high school, and it had lasted all the years since, but the milky complexion was a little mottled now and the black hair blowsy. There was also a tightness at the corners of the mouth and in front of the ears, a tension I hadn't seen in her since the days before Jiggy kicked the grape.

Moira set my drink in front of me and tried to settle in with hers, but it didn't work.

"Moira, what's wrong?"

"What's always wrong. Jiggy. You're here, you must know that."

"I was hoping to see him."

"Why?"

"To talk about some things."

"Goddammit, John!" Moira looked away, then bit her lip and looked back. "I'm sorry. I'm—what do they call it, killing the messenger?"

I didn't say anything.

Moira tried some of her chocolate, realized she didn't really want it, and pushed it away, an inch at a time. "I need for somebody to tell me what's going on. If Jiggy won't, I was hoping you would."

"Moira, I can't. When do you expect him back?"

A grunt that would have been a laugh if there were any humor in her. "The twelfth of never."

I stopped. "He's off again?"

"Off? Oh, you mean off the wagon. No. No, he's been faithful to that, John. Once he knew it meant losing me, he's stayed away from the booze. But the gambling, now, that's a different thing entirely."

"Tell me about it."

"What's there to tell you? He gets up, sucks on that Gatorade till he should turn green, then goes to the doggies up in Wonderland or the flats at Rockingham or wherever he can lay down a bet. It's all the man does, but I could take that, John. I have taken it, for twenty-odd—and they have been *odd*—years. But this not . . . knowing, this I can't take."

"Not knowing what?"

Moira thought about something, made up her mind, and left the table. I could hear her rooting around in another room before she returned to the chair.

Moira smoothed out a tightly folded paper on the plastic tablecloth. "Jiggy had this in a hidey-hole, a place he keeps his winnings the few times he has some to hide. I'm pretty sure he doesn't think I know about the place or this."

She turned the paper so I could read it. A binder for a term life policy. Insured: Raymond—God, I'd forgotten that was his given name—Doyle. Beneficiary: Moira Doyle. Face amount: fifty thousand dollars. Date of issue: two days before.

I checked the name of the insurance company on the binder. I knew somebody there. "Jiggy didn't talk to you about this?"

"John, he hasn't talked to me about anything. Not for almost three weeks. Something must have happened, but . . ."

She left it trailing, hoping I'd pick it up. Instead I said, "You hear from him, let me know?"

It took a minute for the hope to leave her eyes. "I used to get mad at him, John. His answer was always 'Don't worry, More, I won't touch the house, not ever the house.' Well, three weeks ago, I started worrying about him, but now that's gone, too. Now I'm just scared. I'm just so scared."

Moira Doyle bit her lip again and turned away from me, standing and hugging herself in front of the sink.

THREE

Back in the office, I called my friend at the insurance company on Jiggy's binder. The policy checked out. Payment on death so long as cause not suicide.

I hung up the phone, but my hand was still on the receiver when it rang. "John Cuddy."

"Kinda anxious there, Cuddy, picking up so fast. You got a guilty conscience, maybe?"

I hadn't heard the voice for a long time, but it hadn't changed that much. A little deeper, a little more oily.

"Danny boy, your butler wake up yet?"

"Yeah. He didn't appreciate the bath you gave his toy."

"He's lucky only the toy went into the hopper."

"Spider, he'd like for you to come calling again."

"His name's really 'Spider'?"

"Come on over and see."

"I think it's your turn to visit me."

"Might leave kind of a mess afterwards."

"Not where I'm thinking."

"Spider, he don't like being this close to cops."

I looked past Danny Bennigan to the blonde bomber, sitting sullenly on a pedestrian ramp and watching the parking lot of the Metropolitan District Commission Police on Storrow Drive. The Mets patrol waterways, parks, and some major roads in and around Boston.

I'd jogged over from the condo I was renting on Beacon Street. Danny and Spider left the Trans Am out of sight. My guess is that Danny had to drive, given the metal splint on Spider's left ring finger.

Bennigan coughed and spit. He was wearing a blue suit and topcoat, both shining a little in the unkind glare of daylight. His chins covered the knot in his tie and flowed over the shirt almost to the points of his collar.

A fat thumb waggled at the MDC station house. "Lifeguards with guns."

I said, "What?"

"The Mets are always at the beaches there. The Boston cops call them 'lifeguards with guns.' "

"Not to their faces."

Bennigan came back to me, shook his head. "This is about that fuck-breath Doyle, right?"

"You tell me, Danny."

"All right, Cuddy. I'll tell you." The air was cold enough that Bennigan's words came out in puffs of gray, like balloons over the heads of characters in a comic strip. "Doyle comes into my place over in Dorchester there and wants to do some business, play a coupla hours. I don't particularly like him, I don't know anybody particularly liked him except you back in school there. But the fuckbreath, he's got maybe three hundred in twenties on him, so I says, 'Okay. You play at the working table, right?' "

"The working table."

"The poker table for the working stiffs. I call that the working table, account of the stakes are limited. Max bump is five bucks, three-bump max per betting round. The other table's blackjack, so you control your own bet there."

"What about the third table?"

"That's the rollers' table. High rollers. I run a simple, clean establishment. Word gets around to the right people, and they refer me clients."

"And you get a cut of the pots."

Bennigan's eyes narrowed. "You telling this or am I?"

"Go ahead."

He took a breath but didn't seem to get any happier. "So, I'm at my place that night, and I turn my back for a couple, three minutes. Before I know it, your fuckbreath friend's at the rollers' table, drinking his green puke from a big plastic cup and playing with this drug baron somebody sent over."

"Local?"

"No. Some fucking South American, he's got this gold cigarette case open on the table next to him, taking a blow once in a while from the snow he's got in there. The baron's also got these bodyguards look like little Indians, you know? I mean, they want to say something to the guy, who looks like maybe he's got some of the blood himself, they walk over to him, cup their hands, like, and whisper in his ear. I had the feeling they was sorry to be in the room, like the poker was taking them away from shrinking heads or something."

"And Jiggy's losing."

"Losing? He's getting creamed. The asshole carries his chips over from the working table and bets them. He knows, he fucking bell-clear knows he ain't supposed to do that with the chips even if he does change tables. Everybody knows that. But he does it and he's losing and the drug baron is getting off on it. Taking the peabrain in the Red Sox hat and the coat like a buffalo blanket. Then Jiggy finally wins a hand, and I'm praying he's gonna have a streak, get even with the board so Spider can throw him the fuck out of the place, when Jiggy, he gets so excited about winning that he spills his drink, the whole fucking cup of it, all over the table."

I tried to picture the light green stain on the felt cloth. "He spills it on the baron's cocaine."

"Right. And his suit. So the baron stands up, and I swear I thought the little Indians were gonna start shooting up the place, and I thank Christ Spider doesn't have his toy out, because I know that would set them off. So I go over to the drug guy and tell him I'm gonna make everything okay. And he says, 'That is correct. You will make up everything.' And I says, 'Wait a minute.' And he says, 'My product, my clothes, my winnings. This man was your guest, and I am your guest. You vouch for him, you make good on his debt.'

"I swear to you, Cuddy, you took one look at this guy and his fucking Indians, you woulda done a striptease for him, he asked you."

I could see where this was going. "What did it come to?"

Bennigan knew what I meant. "Thirteen grand."

Jesus.

Danny looked over at his enforcer. "I tell that fuckbreath Doyle, he comes up with the money by yesterday, or I let the Spider loose on him."

"Jiggy doesn't have that kind of money."

"Moira does."

"He won't touch her house."

"I will."

I shifted toward Bennigan just a little. Both he and Spider noticed and perked up.

I tried to keep my voice steady. "I wouldn't touch the house, Danny."

"You wouldn't. We know you fucking wouldn't, Cuddy. But you're not a businessman out thirteen large. Moira? Moira, she's . . ."

Bennigan stopped. For just a minute, he got a faraway look in his eyes, a look that made him seem younger, and thinner, and—

He snapped out of it. "Moira, nobody's gonna touch her from my end, Cuddy. She's had enough heartache living with the fuckbreath. But Jiggy, now. Jiggy's another story. She can take a mortgage on her house there to pay me, or she can take one out to bury her husband, who's living on borrowed time as it is. Either way, I'm gonna see some compensation for my costs here."

Bennigan moved away, the first few steps surprisingly quick, then slower as he realized I wasn't coming after him. As he drew even with Spider and started up the pedestrian ramp, Bennigan said, "Tell Doyle from me, Cuddy. The fuckbreath pays up by tonight, or he's dead by tomorrow."

Spider said, "Believe it," and followed his boss up the ramp.

FOUR

Two days went by. I didn't hear from Jiggy Doyle or Moira. I didn't want to hear from Danny Bennigan or Spider.

After a long surveillance on another case, I was at home, lying on the couch. I'd been there for maybe an hour when the telephone rang, echoing in the condo.

"Hello?"

"John?"

"Yes."

"It's Moira. Jiggy just called me."

"From where?"

"The Newport Fronton."

"The what?"

"Jai alai. Newport, Rhode Island. He was just calling to let me know he was okay."

"Newport."

"Can you . . . ?"

"I'll be waiting for him after the last—what do they call it?"

"Game or match, I think."

The Red Sox cap was easy to spot, bobbing just high enough above the heads of most of the patrons coming out the main entrance. As the crowd thinned, Jiggy took a pull from the bicycle bottle and looked around, more for transportation than danger. I let him cross against some traffic and move close enough that I wouldn't have to chase him far if he ran.

"Jiggy?"

He jumped a little, then calmed down, taking another snort from the bottle. "Jesus, John, you scared the shit out of me."

"Gives you an idea of what Moira's been going through."

Jiggy inhaled and let it out. "I got a pretty good idea of that already."

I said, "Let's take a ride."

Coming back up Interstate 95, I kept the Prelude in the slow lane, speedometer at fifty-five. For the first ten miles, Jiggy didn't say anything, so I didn't either.

Then, "John?"

"Yeah?"

"You talked with Danny, huh?"

"I did."

"What'd he say?"

"Danny said to tell the little fuckbreath if he doesn't come up with the thirteen large, Spider's going to kill him."

Jiggy closed his eyes.

I said, "Would have been nice to tell me a little more about Spider, Jiggy."

He nodded once.

"And the drug baron at the wrong poker table."

He nodded again.

"And the fact that 'thirteen' had a extra zero after it."

"What difference does it make?"

"The difference is, people do kill you over thirteen thousand."

"No, I mean, what difference does it make, hundreds or thousands, if I don't have it and I won't use the house?"

"Or the life policy?"

The head whipped around to me, the face strobed by the lights of an underpass. "Who told you?"

"Moira. She found the hidey-hole."

Jiggy almost smiled. "I knew she knew about that spot. I figured she wouldn't look there till . . . afterwards."

"After you got yourself killed."

"John, you weren't there. I was having the worst run of cards I ever had. Shit, that I ever even *saw*. Then I realize this guy at the other table—"

"The rollers' table."

"Yeah." A little sheepish. "The rollers' table. Anyway, this South American's got a stack of black chips in front of him like tires at an auto yard. And he doesn't look like he knows shit about poker."

"You see the two guys with him?"

"Danny told you about them, too?"

"He did."

"Well, I wasn't thinking about them. I was just thinking of getting even for a change, maybe even getting a little ahead for once. And I had good hands at that table, John. Good ones."

"It's just that the baron had better ones."

"Right. And then I win that last pot, and it's not a fortune, John, but I jump up a little, I guess, and I wasn't using one of these," he gestured with the bicycle bottle, "so everything kind of spilled over everything."

"Including the nose candy."

"Yeah. The Gatorade made it all turn yellow, like snow some dog pissed on, you know? Anyway, I spent two weeks thinking about how to square things with Danny and I finally come up with something."

"The policy and me."

"You figured it out."

"Tell me anyway."

"I see you on the TV there, I says, 'That's it, John scared Danny off once, he can do it again.' I figure, even if you don't scare him off, you're good with a gun, you'll get that Spider nut off the board. And even if that don't work, the policy will."

"Because I'll make Danny mad enough to kill you."

"Right. Worst case, I'm dead anyway, and this way Moira gets the fifty thousand from the company, which is a hell of a lot bigger bet than I ever brought home for her."

"Moira would really appreciate that."

"Don't go sarcastic on me, huh, John?"

"What you do is, you and Moira take out an equity loan against the house—"

"I won't touch the fucking—"

"—and you figure out a way to pay back the bank, which won't kill you if you can't."

"But will take the house from Moira without paying her any insurance money."

"Worst case, which do you think she'd rather have, you or the house?"

"It ain't what she'd rather have." Jiggy turned to me, an approaching headlight on the lower portion of his face. "It's what's best for her that I care about."

I left it there till we hit Route 128 and swung northeast toward Boston. As I started to talk again, Jiggy said, "I'm sorry I lied to you, John."

"Forget it."

"I won't. But right now I got some thinking to do."

"You want to go home to do it?"

"Yeah." Jiggy closed his eyes again. "Yeah, that'd be nice."

Ten miles later, I turned onto his street. No black Trans Am, but the teenagers were out by their Mustang in peacoats and watch caps, one holding some wires and the other hooking some up. I pulled to a stop outside the Doyle house.

Jiggy said, "Come in for a minute?"

"Maybe it's something you two should talk about together."

"No. I mean, yeah, we will. But if Moira sees you come in with me, she'll know it's all right. That I'm serious about getting this thing done."

He had a point. "Okay, Jiggy. Let's go."

As we got out, I heard a revving engine, the sound like a strong, full-throated roar. I was thinking that the teenagers had done a good job on the carburetor when brakes squealed and Jiggy knocked me down behind a car.

As I looked up, a bullet hit the Gatorade bottle, making a popping sound and sending a spray of liquid onto the snowbank. More slugs stitched their way across the front of Jiggy's coat, tossing up little clouds of gray threads and red mist and bowling him around like an unbalanced top until he went down onto the sidewalk.

I drew the Chief's Special from behind my right hip and came up over the engine block of the car. I could hear a voice from Moira's house as I leveled on the spinning right rear tire of the Trans Am. Just as I squeezed, the car fishtailed, my shot bursting the right front tire instead. The car pivoted on the wheel, slamming into the line of parked cars on my side of the street, sparks flying and multicracked windshield now facing me.

A ball of fire rose from behind Danny Bennigan as he screamed and tried to push the pinned driver's side door of the Trans Am through a parked Plymouth. Spider got out of the passenger's side, having to use his good right hand to work the inside handle. I yelled at him to drop to the ground, but he reached back inside the car and came out with the MAC-10 as Danny tried to climb over the center console.

I yelled once more at Spider. Instead of dropping his weapon, he came at me on full automatic. Instead of running, I dropped him just as the fire got to the gas tank and lifted the Trans Am and what would have been left of Danny Bennigan three feet off the ground.

FIVE

The cops talked to me in the living room, a badge from the fire department joining them because of the Trans Am. In the kitchen, some neighbors took turns making tea and coffee and putting their arms around Moira's shoulders. By the time everybody in a uniform or suit was finished, gray beams of uncertain light were coming through the windows.

I said what I could to Moira, a couple of the neighbors giving me dirty looks as some idea of what had happened became clearer to them. My watch said 6:05 A.M. when I went out through the front door and down the steps to the sidewalk.

I stopped for a minute at the spot where Jiggy had died. There was very little blood on the concrete, his old tweed coat and internal organs absorbing most of it. Where the Gatorade had sprayed, the snow had leached the lime color to a dull yellow. Or maybe the other way around.

I bent down. As I reached my hand out toward it, a voice behind me said, "Hey, don't do that."

Still on my haunches, I turned my head. The snowman kid from yesterday but without his sister.

He pointed the index finger of one mismatched glove. "My mom says you should never eat yellow—"

"She's right," I said, standing and walking back to my car.

P. M. CARLSON

Past president of Sisters in Crime,
P. M. Carlson is best known for her highly acclaimed series featuring statistician, mother,
and quick-thinking amateur detective Maggie
Ryan. There are obvious similarities between
Maggie Ryan and her creator, who has written
a textbook on behavioral statistics, raised two
children, and finds her special interest in the
mystery is the way in which crimes affect sec-
ondary victims.

The similarities between writer and protagonists are less clear with Pat's more recent
detectives. Marty Hopkins is a mother and a
sheriff's deputy in southern Indiana. And the
charmingly amoral nineteenth-century actress
Bridget Mooney lives by rules all her own.

In "The Eighth Wonder of the World; or,
Golden Opinions" Bridget Mooney discovers
the not-so-majestic dealings underlying the
building of one of New York City's most ma-
jestic structures: the Brooklyn Bridge.

THE EIGHTH WONDER OF THE WORLD;
or,
GOLDEN OPINIONS

I scrambled from the stage door, coughing and gasping, heedless of the damage to my beautiful bustled frock. Most miserable hour that e'er time saw! I reckon I'd never been in such a fix. Smoke billowed about me, and sparks rained down. I smelt a dreadful odor and realized that a lock of my unkempt red hair had caught fire. As I knelt to douse it in a puddle of meltwater, I could hear shrieks, thin and terrible against the background roar of the colossal furnace behind me.

The Brooklyn Theatre had caught fire just moments ago, and flames were already lapping at the dark heavens.

The screams behind me tore at my heart, but I stiffened the sinews, summoned up the blood, and crawled gasping along the filthy alley. I heard new cries—the shouts of men on the street ahead, firemen and curiosity seekers who were pouring from nearby saloons and hotels. Legs booted for the December weather pounded by; lanterns bobbed. When I reached the street I tried to stand but my scorched lungs were unable to sustain me and the world swam as I fell against a post.

Clarity returned moments later, and I could again hear the screams and shouts and thudding boots on the cold street. Now I was moving swiftly, being carried along by a pair of strong arms belonging to a sturdy fellow of some twenty years. He wore a cheap rough laborer's coat but his smile was a treasure of kindliness.

"Feeling better, missy?" he asked solicitously.

"Oh, sir, my gratitude is boundless!" I gasped as elegantly as I could. His face registered sudden respect. Perhaps I should remind you that I had recently been tutored in elocutionary skills by the esteemed English actress Mrs. Fanny Kemble, the greatest of her generation.

"Excuse me, madam," he said in confusion, and for a moment I feared that he would bow and drop me. "You won't take it the wrong way, I hope, but for a moment I thought you were a mere actress."

Pleased that he now thought me a lady, I said, "I remain grateful."

My hearty rescuer had borne me a block away from the inferno, and now paused. "Are you better, madam? I can leave you here with your permission, and go back for another poor soul."

Well, I ask you, would any young lady, weakened by smoke and fear, want to be abandoned on the cold street in front of a dry-goods store? The prospect was so dreadful that I was weighing several desperate and perhaps improper means of clinging to my rough-clad hero when I heard a woman's voice call, "Harry! Harry Supple, is that you?"

"Yes, ma'am," said my young man, turning to a carriage that pulled up beside us.

"Harry, it's a dreadful fire! Is it Dieters Hotel?"

The newcomer's voice was educated, and the carriage lanterns gleamed against a shiny painted gig. Well, I reckoned that the well-bred voice and glossy paint signified places far more comfortable than this cold street. I decided to swoon again as Harry Supple answered, "It's the Brooklyn Theatre, ma'am. I was just going back to help the firemen, for I fear there are people dying. But here's this poor lady I rescued with her frock and hair all scorched, and in a faint again, poor thing. A fine lady too."

"Put her in the carriage, Harry," commanded the lady. "She is well-dressed. I'll take her home. Your strong arms are needed here."

Quickly, Harry placed me in the carriage and vanished into the night. The lady tapped the horse with her whip, for she herself was driving, and we moved rapidly away from the dreadful conflagration. I remained limp, with my eyes closed, but I was aware that the lady drove only a few blocks before halting again, calling for servants to help her carry me in.

I was laid on a bed with smooth sheets, and my face and arms were cleansed with moistened cotton cloths amidst soft exclamations about my scorched hair and frock. Then the lady and her maids began to discuss removing the frock, to attend to my needs more easily. Since a pocket that I had sewn into my bustle contained a few items that I preferred not to reveal to the public, I emitted a little moan and fluttered my eyelashes.

"She's coming round," said the educated lady.

It was my cue to open my eyes and say feebly, "Oh . . . what lovely place is this? Am I in heaven, and these the Lord's own angels?" Unfortunately the effect I intended was rather ruined by a spasm of coughing that overtook me.

"Poor dear!" said the educated woman briskly. "You have survived your ordeal, and I believe that when you have taken more good fresh air, you will be able to return to your home."

In the lamplight, I saw that she was a strong woman in her thirties with a pug nose, lively features, and a beautiful smile. I said, "Thank you for your kindness, madam," paused to make sure I had no more coughing to do, and added, "Oh—I remember, the fire! The dreadful fire!"

"Yes. What happened?" The lady's face was as filled with curiosity as the maid's.

"Oh, madam, it was so quick!" I replied. "One of the border curtains high above the stage blew against the flame of a border light, and caught instantly. In a few moments the entire theatre was ablaze!"

"How dreadful!"

"Yes—yes, it was. You are so kind to me, madam, in this hour of misfortune. Permit me to introduce myself. I am Miss Mooney, of a landed Irish family, friends to the Kemble and Sartoris families of England."

Oh, I know, I know, we weren't really landed, unless you count the muddy gutters of St. Louis where Papa spent much of his time. But we were Irish, weren't we? And I certainly knew Kembles and Sartorises. I also knew President Grant—in fact, his daughter Nellie had provided me with the lovely frock I was wearing—but his administration had crumbled in such a flurry of frauds and bribery that I did not wish to mention him until I knew more about this household.

The kind lady said, "I am Mrs. Roebling, and it is a pleasure to make your acquaintance, dear Miss Mooney, though I regret the tragic circumstances of our meeting. Were you attending the spectacle tonight?"

In fact, I had been in the spectacle tonight. But looking around the solid respectability of this room, I hesitated to admit it. Laboring folks like Harry Supple were fascinated by those of us in the limelight, and the higher classes, the noble families of England and the wealthy and politically powerful on both sides of the Atlantic, toasted us. The great actress Mrs. Kemble had married into Southern landed gentry, and her sister Mrs. Sartoris, an opera singer, had wed an English noble. But between Supple and Sartoris lay a large middle class of respectable burghers, the men who ran the shops and built the bridges of the nation, and many of them looked askance at those in my profession until they became rich enough to view us as their playthings.

Bridges! That was it, bridges! On my way to the ferry, I had seen this fine lady often, talking to the workers who were building the great span over the East River. "Mrs. Roebling," I said, "are you by any chance related to the illustrious man who is constructing the splendid bridge to Brooklyn?"

Mrs. Roebling beamed. "Yes. My husband is the Chief Engineer."

I clasped my hands. "What a noble work it is, Mrs. Roebling! When I crossed the East River on the ferry, it was stirring indeed to see those two great towers rising like anthems to the sky!" It was true—the two giant structures rose from the river and upwards, ever upwards, taller than anything for miles around, except for Trinity Church in Wall Street.

Mrs. Roebling leaned back in the bedside chair and smiled sadly. "They were not built without cost, dear Miss Mooney."

"Oh, yes, I have heard of the dreadful caisson disease that has afflicted the Chief Engineer."

"It is dreadful indeed. These last four years my poor husband has suffered so much that he cannot bear to speak to people, nor stir from his room. I write his instructions for him, and carry them to the workmen. And yet, despite the pain and exhaustion, his mind remains clear."

"That is good news, for I had heard that it affects the mind as well."

Mrs. Roebling scowled. "That is not true, Miss Mooney! Who has been telling you such rubbish?"

"A gentleman admirer of mine. But of course you know best, Mrs. Roebling, and I will endeavor to correct his misapprehension when next I see him."

Mrs. Roebling leaned toward me and asked urgently, "Who is your admirer, Miss Mooney? Who is spreading these rumors? Is it Abram Hewitt, the ironmonger?"

She was so intent, looking at me like a hound at a rabbit hole, that I forgot my own difficulties and sat up on the bed. "Mrs. Roebling, please do not distress yourself! I have no desire to sow dissension between the Chief Engineer and the others devoted to the bridge."

"Dissension aplenty has already been sown!" Mrs. Roebling snorted. She looked me over carefully, then sighed. "Ah, well, it cannot be Abram Hewitt. That prim fellow is incapable of behaving in a manner that would lead a lady to describe him as her admirer. Miss Mooney, you would find it difficult to believe the trials we suffer, trying to accomplish what we were chosen to do! The great bridge stands unfinished while the politicians quarrel. This affair with the cable wire—"

Well, that made me prick up my ears, because my admirer was in fact in the wire business. I asked, "What affair with the cable wire?"

"That hypocritical fellow Hewitt is a trustee of the bridge company, as you may know. And he says that those connected with the bridge must not bid on the cable, thus disqualifying my husband's brothers! Yet people believe in his saintliness!"

"You mean Mr. Hewitt has prevented the Roebling wire company from furnishing the wire for the cables?"

"Exactly! Mr. Hewitt said he personally would not bid for the contract. But he's an ironmonger, his company doesn't manufacture wire! Of course he won't bid personally! His cronies will bid instead!" She looked at me earnestly. "It is not merely the unfairness to my brothers-in-law that distresses me. It is the fear that Mr. Hewitt's friends will provide a slipshod product for my—for *our* great bridge!"

Well, naturally Mrs. Roebling would think that Roebling wire would build a better bridge. Still, for such a proper lady, she seemed very knowledgeable. I tried to console her. "That is dreadful, Mrs. Roebling. But surely the opportunity to contribute to this marvel of our age will inspire the company to provide only the best wire! Besides, if Mr. Hewitt values his reputation, he will see to it that his friend's product is excellent."

She said darkly, "Mr. Hewitt is one of Tilden's chief supporters."

"Tilden? They say he has just been elected President of the United States! That is—"

"It is still contested," Mrs. Roebling reminded me. "In any case, just now Mr. Hewitt has great power among seekers of patronage. For all his saintly posing, I prefer the corrupt followers of President Useless S. Grant!"

Well, I was relieved that I had not admitted to my acquaintance with the Grant family. I idly smoothed the skirt of the lovely dress Nellie

Grant had given me, then gasped in shock. I reckon I've never seen a skirt so ratty-looking. The white muslin flounces were caked with mud and soot, and burn marks streaked the splendid mandarin yellow foulard.

Mrs. Roebling saw my dismay and exclaimed, "Oh, my dear Miss Mooney, here I've been chattering on about my problems, while you are the one with troubles!"

"My poor frock! Besmeared as black as Vulcan!"

She picked up a fold of the skirt and inspected it in the lamplight. "The muslin is easily washed," she declared briskly, and turned to the servant. "As for the foulard—Bessie, didn't you boil up the mixture for scorch marks last week? Onion juice, vinegar, white soap, and fuller's earth? And bring the scissors, so we can repair Miss Mooney's coiffure."

I stood to peek into a glass, and for a moment did not realize that the bedraggled Medusa-like creature reflected there was my usually sprightly self. "Oh, my goodness, what will Lloyd think!" I gasped unthinkingly.

When I'd first noticed the border curtain catching fire, I had roused the other actors. Then I'd lit out for the dressing room to exchange my flimsy theatrical costume for my beloved Nellie Grant dress, with its bustle pocket filled with my souvenirs and with a few bracelets I found lying about, left behind by other actresses who were fleeing the blazing theatre. There had not been time to arrange my hair, and the long auburn tresses looked sorry indeed, burnt and damp and snaky with dirty snow. No wonder Harry Supple had not assumed I was a lady.

Slowly I became aware that Mrs. Roebling was regarding me with great suspicion.

"Mrs. Roebling, what is it?" I inquired anxiously, concerned about her sudden change of demeanor.

She asked in a tight voice, "Did you say Lloyd? Is that the name of your admirer, the man who is maligning my husband's ability?"

"Mrs. Roebling, I know that your husband is able! The proof stands proudly in the East River, poised to link these two great cities!"

"It is Lloyd, then," said Mrs. Roebling. "Mr. J. Lloyd Haigh."

I said feebly, "I am sorry, Mrs. Roebling. He appeared to be honorable in all other matters."

And indeed he did appear honorable, my Lloyd. He was a handsome gentleman of some fifty years, with twinkling honest eyes. He was a fine vocalist, a jolly man who was always ready with a compliment that could make a young lady shiver with pleasure. He was also eager to be of assistance in business matters, and had purchased a few old deeds and papers that Aunt Mollie had bequeathed me, giving me over a thousand dollars for them with the explanation that a gentleman of good reputation could use them to obtain loans from a bank, but that a young lady wouldn't wish to trouble herself to learn about interest and repayment and similar tedious matters. Don't you think that was kind of him? Yes indeed. His generosity had enabled me to take a room in an excellent hotel instead of the dirty inn where the other actors stayed. He spoke often of marriage but I put him off.

"Honorable!" Mrs. Roebling exclaimed. She was combing my unsightly hair and gave the comb an angry and painful jerk to emphasize her point. "Those of us who know something of the wire business are aware of certain underhanded practices by Mr. J. Lloyd Haigh's company! But I fear that is of no interest to the bridge trustees."

I waited until the comb was safely through the next red tress before saying, "What you say is shocking, Mrs. Roebling. It is difficult to believe such things of a fine gentleman."

"Oh, yes, he's most persuasive. You aren't the first lady to believe him, and gentlemen are just as gullible. During the bidding, each firm submitted samples of their wire for testing by Colonel Paine with his new device. Mr. Haigh's samples did well. But I suspect Haigh did not manufacture them at his own mill. Instead, he purchased them from a reputable firm, and submitted them as his own."

"Dear me!"

"Of course Mr. Abram Hewitt is trying to assure his success also. Mr. Hewitt cleared out the Tweed Ring from the bridge project, only to arrange for his own friends to profit from it. It makes the Chief Engineer so angry! I believe he would have been up and about years ago except for the nervous exhaustion the politicians inspire in him."

"Poor fellow," I said, reflecting that Mrs. Roebling herself must be able to deal with politicians rather skillfully, or a sick man would not still be in charge of the great bridge. "If a member of the public may offer a suggestion, would it be possible for all the wire to be tested before it is used on the bridge?"

"Yes! Indeed, that may be the answer, testing all the wire!" She thought a moment, smiled, and I breathed a sigh of relief for her kinder mood, for she had finished with the comb and was picking up the scissors. "If Haigh's firm is chosen, we could enforce his honesty, couldn't we?" She snipped carefully. "Still, Miss Mooney, if Mr. Haigh mentions matrimony, be certain to inquire about Miss Jennie Hughes before you accept."

"Accept! Goodness, no, I have no intention of marrying anyone! My Aunt Mollie had a little money from her father, and after she married

Uncle Mike she wanted to buy a"—I had to feign a fit of coughing, because I almost said "a saloon"—"to buy a pleasant riverside property, but they said a married lady couldn't sign for it, her husband had to sign for it."

"That is true." Mrs. Roebling clipped my singed locks into a fringe across my forehead. "A wife cannot enter into a contract, although a single woman can."

"So Uncle Mike signed for the property, and then he mortgaged it, and spent the money. And soon the bank foreclosed and sold Aunt Mollie's property." I didn't tell her that Uncle Mike had lost the money gambling with the sporting men who arrived on the riverboats. The new owner had hired Uncle Mike to work in the saloon, but Aunt Mollie had to take up copying for a trade. From then on she made more private arrangements with bankers, and frequently warned me that for a poor girl marriage was a snare, no different from being a bound servant or a tart, excepting of course in the eyes of the Lord, and the Lord didn't often pay the bills, did He?

Hastily, I added to Mrs. Roebling, "Of course, with a fine husband like the Chief Engineer, marriage is an excellent arrangement."

"Of course," said Mrs. Roebling. "And yet I have heard other stories much like your Aunt Mollie's. Someday we must ask them to change the laws. The difficulty is that we wives have so many duties, we cannot easily spare the time. Meanwhile, you are wise to stay clear of Mr. Haigh. There, Miss Mooney, that is the best we can do with your hair."

"Oh, thank you! It looks quite fashionable," I said, and indeed it appeared much less pitiful and mangy. "You are the kindest lady in the world! And Mr. Harry Supple is one of the kindest men."

"Yes, Harry's a good lad, one of our most trusted riggers. He used to be a sailor, and is good on the wire ropes."

"Do thank him for me, as I was too enfeebled to do so. Now, I have imposed too long on your good graces. My cough is much improved, and my hair is respectable again."

"But your frock, Miss Mooney!"

"I would gladly accept a jar of your mixture to clean scorch marks."

She and Bessie gave me several jars, and an old traveling cape to ward off the winter winds, as my cloak had been abandoned to the blaze. Mrs. Roebling drove me to my fine hotel, saying she would return to the scene of the fire to see if she could help other poor souls.

The next day I rose early, donned the Roebling cape and a feather-trimmed bonnet that dipped low enough in front to hide most of my damaged hair, and hurried to the site of the great fire. The scene was ghastly, and the stench worse. Well over a hundred people had perished, and the firemen were still carrying bodies from the smoldering wreckage. I saw our stage manager, who was delighted that I had survived, but sad to inform me that two of our company had perished, Mr. Murdoch and Mr. Burroughs.

"Oh, no!" The world grew blurry, and I turned and staggered away from the dismal scene. Murdoch and Burroughs were fine boisterous young actors, and we'd had many a jolly hour backstage trading yarns about growing up in St. Louis or Zanesville.

"Bridget, my sweet! Is it you?" cried a gentlemanly baritone.

I turned, and Mr. J. Lloyd Haigh, devilishly handsome in his fine dark cape and checked trousers, ran across to me from the door of the Market National Bank and well nigh hugged my head off. "Oh, Bridget, I was sick with worry!" cried my sweet-scented dandy.

I bowed my head against his elegant woolen cape. "Yes, I would not spend another such a night, though 'twere to buy a world of happy days! But please, Lloyd, I can't bear it here any longer!"

Lloyd pulled out a snowy handkerchief and tried to dry my tears. "Now, now, Bridget, you are safe with me! Let us walk by the river. Tell me, did your Aunt Mollie's business papers burn?"

"No, Lloyd, they are safe."

"Good. Bridget, you are the dearest creature in the world!"

Even through my tears, I could feel the heat of his ardent gaze, and I allowed him to steal a kiss in honor of the great emotion we both felt at my narrow escape. Then he led me away from the scene of the calamity. When we reached the streets near the East River we paused to watch the bridge workers. The great towers, solid and yet airy with their handsome Gothic arches, stood proudly against the gray December sky. Thin ladders stretched the entire height of each tower. Near us stood the stone anchorage building, gray and massive, its top platform spiky with derricks. A few wire ropes had been slung from it to the very top of the two great towers, and thence to the New York side far away. Their scarves blowing in the wind, the laborers were laying slats between these first wire ropes, building themselves a narrow footbridge across the sky. I wondered if handsome Harry Supple was one of the nimble figures I saw scurrying high among the slender wire ropes.

I said, "Lloyd, is it true that your firm might provide the wire for this astonishing bridge?"

"Yes indeed!" He beamed at me. Lloyd had fine teeth and a most engaging smile. "The trustees of the Bridge Company have an excellent opinion of me. That is the most important thing in the world, Bridget, a good opinion. I am fortunate."

Well, I think that riches are more important than good opinion, because generally if a body has money, the good opinion follows along after. As one of Shakespeare's shiftier characters says, "I have bought golden opinions from all sorts of people." But sometimes it's more comfortable not to argue. I said, "It is important indeed. But isn't it true that the Chief Engineer has an interest in a rival firm?"

"Why, what a pert creature you are, my little Bridget, to be so interested in complicated business matters!"

I smiled the way I smiled when I played Juliet, and hoped that my poor hair did not look too bristly in the daylight. "Sir, when a gentleman proposes marriage, of course a young lady is interested in his prospects!"

"Ah, my sweet, of course! Well, my prospects are excellent. Naturally, the Chief Engineer favors his brothers' firm in Trenton. My mill, however, is located here in Brooklyn. Therefore I have the strong support of the editor of the Brooklyn *Eagle*, who is also a trustee of the Bridge Company. I have also another powerful friend among the trustees. Good opinion, Bridget, that is the secret! For when those who hold this good opinion of me gain nationwide power, my prospects will be boundless!"

"You are a supporter of Mr. Tilden, then?"

"A most loyal supporter! And soon my loyalty will be rewarded!" He was glowing with enthusiasm, and I could see that he had reason. If Lloyd helped Tilden's cause, Abram Hewitt and the other Tilden enthusiasts among the trustees would favor giving him the contract, and it would matter little who made the better wire. The Roeblings, I decided, might well lose this skirmish.

"Your loyalty to Tilden is financial also?" I hazarded.

"Naturally. What a lot of questions you ask, you sweet vixen!"

"Then your reward will be financial also!" I clapped my gloved hands and favored him with my sauciest smile.

It was too much for dear Lloyd, who pulled me into the shadowed privacy of the doorway of a saloon that had not yet opened and attempted to steal another kiss. "Yes, my reward will certainly be financial. And more, I hope, when you are my dear wife, and the queen of Brooklyn!"

Sweet-scented though he was, Lloyd was becoming far too ardent for the early morning of a day when I had much to mourn and much to do, seeing as I was out of work again. So, recollecting what Mrs. Roebling had told me, I giggled fetchingly and said, "Mr. Haigh, sir, I have not yet accepted your kind proposal! First I must confer with Miss Jennie Hughes!"

Well, that gave him a turn! His breath sort of hitched, and then he laughed heartily. "That was merely an attempt at blackmail, Bridget, I swear! Scurrilous people told her to say we had wed! I never married Miss Hughes, I never told her I would! She knew I was married already! You mustn't believe silly rumors!"

Hang it, this was worse than I'd expected. I needed to know more. I laughed heartily too. "That is a great relief, Lloyd! I know it's true that many people do scurrilous deeds for the sake of money. Still, a charge of bigamy is serious!"

"It's false!" he exclaimed, clasping both my hands in his and gazing at me most sincerely. "I'm not a bigamist. I divorced my first wife in Connecticut! Bridget, my sweet, these falsehoods pain me all the more, for now I have met you, my truest love! Your bright eyes, your russet hair, the hint of freckles on the loveliest nose in the nation!"

I smiled demurely while I calculated. If he'd divorced his first wife, there must have been a second one, and not Jennie Hughes, for he said he hadn't married her. That made Jennie the third, at least, who claimed to have married him. I silently thanked Aunt Mollie, and Mrs. Roebling, for saving me from becoming a bigamist's fourth wife, surely a fate worse than death, and twice as ignoble.

I wriggled from Lloyd's embrace back to the street and started for the ferry landing. "Come, Lloyd, let us not be precipitous! A young lady must keep her reputation pure. You yourself have taught me the importance of good opinion. I will consider your kind offer."

"Bridget, I will do anything!" he cried sincerely. "I will go down on bended knee!"

Well, I must admit I like to see a handsome gentleman on bended knee, but gentlemen have other virtues too. I squeezed Lloyd's hand gratefully, and by the time the ferry reached New York he had promised me a new velvet traveling dress in exchange for another of Aunt Mollie's old papers. An emerald green dress, I decided, because green looked splended with my hair, what there was of it.

Several days later, after much diligent searching, I had only two offers of work, one from a troupe that proposed to tour to Chicago with two Boucicault melodramas, and another from a Water Street dance hall. Since the duties in Water Street included more than dancing, I chose the touring troupe, and bade my Lloyd a tearful farewell, promising that I'd give him my answer soon.

Oh, I know, I know. Lloyd was a goodly apple rotten at the core, and a proper young lady would have snubbed such a dishonorable fellow; but it's so difficult to find honorable men in these times. And even if you find one he may up and get caisson disease, and lounge about moaning in an upstairs room while you build his bridges for him. My skills did not run to engineering, so it seemed prudent to pursue my chosen profession, while selecting my gentlemen admirers for their generous hearts. And hang it, Lloyd did offer pretty compliments, and elegant green velvet traveling dresses, and useful business assistance whenever I found one of Aunt Mollie's commercial papers! Besides, when Tilden became President, and Abram Hewitt was running Washington, who could guess what splendors lay ahead for my Lloyd, and for his good friends?

But Tilden did not become President. Clever as he was, Abram Hewitt's skills at bribery were no match for those of the party of Lincoln and Grant, and Rutherford B. Hayes overcame popular defeat to triumph in the electoral college by a majority of one. It was many months before I returned to New York and encountered Mr. J. Lloyd Haigh again, and I expected him to bear signs of his disappointment as I sent in a note to his John Street office. But when he emerged he was his old ebullient self, handsome and wreathed in smiles.

"Bridget Mooney!" he cried. "I am delighted! Delighted!"

"I too, Lloyd!"

"You are the most beautiful creature in the world, Bridget!" He looked at me all hot-eyed. "May I beg the pleasure of escorting you to dinner?"

I carefully deployed my parasol in order to keep his enthusiastic attentions at bay and said, "I had hoped to take a constitutional to see the great bridge. They are calling it the eighth wonder of the world!"

"Of course, my sweet!" He offered his arm and we strolled along to observe the work at the New York anchorage. Atop the great stone boxlike structure, workmen with their sleeves rolled up in the June warmth were working with a thick, tautly stretched wire cable that came all the way from Brooklyn, crossing the tops of the towers to this anchorage, looping around an iron horseshoe-shaped holder, and then returning to Brooklyn as it had come. Lloyd explained that it was but one part of the enormous cable that would support the bridge. Working behind the great steel anchor bars, the laborers—one of them was my kindly hero, Harry Supple—attached the cable's horseshoe-shaped holder to a sturdy wire rope that ran over some pulleys back to a great machine. They started the machine. Amidst the ensuing noise and smoke, I saw the machine slowly easing the cable into position so they could attach it to the anchor bars.

Lloyd was observing with interest too. He shouted, "Dangerous operation! If something gave way it would catapult that iron horseshoe across the river, and the cable too! The pull at the hoisting machine is seventy tons!"

I looked at the taut cable stretching all the way to Brooklyn. Seventy tons of tension. "You must be proud to be associated with such an achievement," I shouted.

"Indeed I am!"

"There's such a lot of wire in each cable! It must be very profitable to have such a contract."

"Yes, but—" A cloud flitted across his handsome face.

"But not as profitable as it should be?"

"Hush, little Bridget! It's no concern of yours!"

"The Chief Engineer has set unfair standards?" I hazarded. "Perhaps he is testing the wire?"

"Don't trouble yourself about it, Bridget!"

"I am troubled only for your sake! I worry so, Lloyd!"

I gave him my most anxious look, which put him in a more confiding spirit. "Fear not, I can manage the Chief Engineer, although he is implacable, Bridget! He has Colonel Paine check every wire, right at my mill. And he substitutes Roebling wire whenever he's allowed. Not in the cables, of course, but do you see the wire rope that attaches the cable to the hoisting machine?"

"The one that runs over the pulleys?"

"Yes. That's Roebling wire." He gestured at a woman's figure on the anchorage, and I recognized Mrs. Roebling in earnest conversation with the assistant engineers. "And he has his wife deliver letters to the bridge trustees, trying to undermine the good opinion I enjoy among them!"

The good opinion, and perhaps the profits too. I said, "Your friends among the trustees will stand by you, surely."

"They will! I have my ways!" He beamed at me. "Fear not, Bridget, my profits are secure!"

"I'm certain they are, Lloyd!" I was tired of hollering and turned my attention to the anchorage. With many groans, the great machine had eased its seventy-ton load into place between two anchor bars. Quickly, the workmen drove in a thick steel pin to fasten it securely to the anchor bars. I must admit, I was impressed at the minds that had conceived this bridge, and the methods of building it, wire by wire and stone by stone. I was impressed also by the workmen. Harry Supple's sturdy forearms glistened in the sun. He had driven in the steel pin that locked the straining cable to the anchor bars. It all made me proud to be a part of this glorious age.

It didn't seem so glorious a few days later. I was in Water Street, reassuring myself that the dance hall would still hire me if the theatre companies did not, when a great cannon-sound boomed and crashed through the air. It was a noise to harrow up the soul. People began to shriek. Several ladies nearby, including some reputed harlots, fell to their knees to pray for forgiveness for their sins. With prickling spine, I hastened toward the great noise. There were shouts that there had been an accident at the bridge, and a crowd was forming at the anchorage. Someone was wounded. I ran to fetch a doctor I knew, then asked various gentlemen in the crowd what had occurred. Some said a cable had snapped; some said a bridge tower had fallen; some agreed with the young ladies in Water Street, and believed it was the Second Coming. There were many reports of falling stones, and of a fifty-foot-high splash of water in the East River that had drenched the passengers on the Fulton Ferry.

It was not until the next day that the newspapers pieced together what had happened. While workmen were trying to fasten a new cable to the anchor bars, it had broken away from the machine, shot as though from a catapult toward the Brooklyn shore. It had sheared off a chimney, leaped clean over the great tower, and smashed rowboats before splashing into the middle of the river. Two men working on the anchorage had been wounded, and two killed.

One of the dead was my own dear hero, Harry Supple.

The cause of the accident was the failure, not of the cable wire itself, but of the wire rope that attached it to the hoisting machine. Someone had made sure the reporter knew that the wire that failed had been manufactured by the Roebling company.

The engineers investigated, and issued a report stating their belief that it had accidentally been cut by the sharp iron rim of its own pulley wheel.

Yes, you're right, of course. I knew better too. I vowed by my Aunt Mollie's shade to avenge dear Harry's death. But what could a young lady do? Mr. J. Lloyd Haigh had powerful friends, and no one would choose to believe the observations of a temporarily penniless actress if the esteemed Mr. Haigh denied them. I soon discarded any notion of joining Miss Jennie Hughes and a few of his other wives in publicly attacking his virtue. Many would prefer to believe his protestations of blackmail, and my own spotless reputation might be damaged. Besides, the bridge company trustees doubtless knew the story already, and had granted him the contract despite his nefarious behavior. After all, he had damaged mere ladies, not the gentlemen whose good opinions counted.

My brother, before he was killed by the Rebels, had taught me marksmanship, and the army-issue Colt revolver I carried in my bustle was well-oiled and reliable. Still, I reckoned there were more fitting ways to deal with a low-down skunk who had so thoughtlessly struck down the flower of heroism with a seventy-ton slingshot. Lloyd's proudest achievement was the golden opinion others held of him. That would be my target.

I hocked my emerald green traveling dress—after all, June is too warm for velvet, don't you think?—and accosted a lad, a street urchin of about my height, with the offer to purchase better garments for him if he would allow me to have his. Once he overcame his natural tendency to flee from a lady whose sanity had deserted her, he agreed.

The next day I dressed in the urchin's smelly clothes, tied up my hair to tuck into his soiled cap, and strutted into Mr. J. Lloyd Haigh's mill in South Brooklyn. I spied a foreman who was clearly as Irish as I was. "Me name is Mike O'Rourke, sir," I told him in Papa's best dialect, "just over from the old country, and in need of a job."

"No jobs here, lad," he said kindly. "Try up at the bridge."

"Whisht and haven't I been up there already? Please, sir!"

"This is no work for a boy."

"Sure and I can learn, sir! That gentleman over there—" I indicated the Chief Engineer's assistant, Colonel Paine, who was testing every coil of wire before it was loaded on a flatbed wagon. "He looks at the wire and writes on a paper. That's simple."

My countryman howled with laughter. "Not so simple, lad! We test the wire in many ways. If it's good wire, then we give it a certificate and it may be loaded on. If it's bad wire, it's discarded onto that pile in the yard. Now, would you know good wire from bad? Off with you, now!"

I looked curiously at the flatbed wagon. "What happens to the good wire, sir? Does it go in the bridge?"

"That's right, they drive it straight to the bridge."

"And what happens to the bad wire?"

He glanced at the pile in the yard. "You're a curious puppy, Mike O'Rourke! I suppose they sell it for other purposes."

"What if they send bad wire to the bridge?"

"Well, it won't have a certificate, will it? We caught them one night exchanging bad wire for the good wire they'd stored here overnight.

Now the certified wire goes straight to the bridge, no waiting overnight, so they can't switch it, can they?"

Since I myself, a mere female, could think of several ways to switch it, I decided to investigate further. The certificate was clearly the crucial item; Colonel Paine handed it to the teamster. I bade farewell to the Irish foreman, stuck my hands in my pockets, and sauntered off in the direction of the bridge. Not long after, the flat wagon loaded with wire passed me. I followed and soon saw it turn into the yard of another building where rejected wire was stored. Hiding behind the fence, I watched Mr. J. Lloyd Haigh's men unload the good wire onto a second wagon, replace it with rejected wire, and send the flatbed wagon loaded with the bad wire on toward the bridge, together with the certificate belonging to the good wire that had been left behind.

What would they do with the wagonload of good wire, now that it had no certificate? I slithered an arm through the fence and hooked an apple from the lunch pail of one of Lloyd's men. I had scarce finished it when a teamster climbed into the wagon seat and drove the load of good wire toward the gate. I had to run to keep up with the horses, and was near enough to see them turn into the yard of the building where Colonel Paine tested the wire. Sure enough, soon the same good wire was tested again. I was watching the inspector sign another certificate for it when something jerked me back by the collar.

"You're still about?" cried the Irish foreman, not so kindly as before. "Off with you now, little rascal!" He fetched me a whack with his hand so I skedaddled.

Next day, attired in my serviceable black frock, I intercepted Mrs. Roebling as she started for the bridge. "Forgive me, Mrs. Roebling, but I have important information for you."

She did not pause. "Good day, Miss Mooney. I saw you recently with Mr. J. Lloyd Haigh, against my advice. I fear I have no time for any friend of his." She stalked on stonily.

I hastened along after her. "Hear me out, Mrs. Roebling! I know that your assessment of Mr. Haigh is correct! Please count me a friend of the late heroic Harry Supple, not of a man we both know to be a crook!"

She hesitated, still suspicious, but gracious again. "Miss Mooney, I cannot converse at present, because I have urgent engineering specifications for the laborers on the bridge." She gestured to the packet of papers she carried.

"My message is for them also, and for the Chief Engineer, and for the many members of the public who will tread the bridge in future years.

The wire Mr. Haigh is delivering to the bridge yard has not in fact been approved by Colonel Paine."

She looked shocked. "Oh, you are mistaken, Miss Mooney! Colonel Paine certifies each load of wire, and it is not accepted at the bridge without a certificate!"

"But does Colonel Paine accompany each load from the mill to the bridge? Does he know that it is driven into a building where Mr. Haigh's men exchange the certified wire for wire he has rejected? Does he see the rejected wire continue to the bridge with his certificate, while the good wire is returned to the mill, there to be tested and certified again? Why, some of that wire has probably been tested a dozen times, and has produced a dozen certificates for Mr. Haigh to use on rejected wire!"

"And all the bad wire worked into the bridge cables!" Mrs. Roebling clapped her hand to her mouth in dismay.

"Do you mean it is too late? That the bridge could collapse, and kill hundreds?" In the back of my mind I heard again the horrid thin shrieks from the burning theatre.

"Well," said Mrs. Roebling, "there is a margin of safety, of course, and if we can add good wire to the cables—some two hundred wires each, or even a hundred and fifty—" An enthusiasm glowed in her eyes as she began to calculate, as though solving the engineering problem was her true joy.

I reminded her, "First, you must get the good wire."

"True, Miss Mooney." She looked dejected again. "We have tried so often to convince the trustees that we should change contractors, to no avail! Mr. Abram Hewitt holds Haigh's mortgage, you know, and as he himself lost so much in the Tilden campaign, he has no wish for Haigh to default on his payments."

So that was the source of the "good opinion" Lloyd enjoyed. I said, "Another difficulty is that we are ladies, Mrs. Roebling, and the trustees will not value our observations as highly as those of men."

"That is true, Miss Mooney. We must get a gentleman—I know. The Chief Engineer will send Colonel Paine himself, with some trusted colleagues, to witness the replacement of the certified wire by the bad wire."

"A good plan! Here, I've written the address on this card. Colonel Paine can hide behind the fence there and observe what is done. He and his colleagues can testify to the trustees, and then you and the Chief Engineer can advise them as to the best engineering solution."

"Yes. Surely even Mr. Hewitt will not agree to a swindle that endangers the public! Will you testify against Mr. Haigh as well?"

"Oh, madam, I am eternally grateful to you for so kindly rescuing me, and would assist you if I could, but I obtained this information in a manner that might compromise my reputation. I truly believe that the testimony of a gentleman like Colonel Paine is more likely to bring the desired result."

Mrs. Roebling's pleasant pug-nosed face hid a shrewd knowledge of the world. "I see, Miss Mooney. I would not wish your reputation harmed by Mr. Haigh's falsehoods, for your sake, and because such an event would damage our case. I am grateful for the information, and will not bring your name into the matter."

In fact, I was concerned with more than my reputation. A great advantage of having Mr. Haigh as an eager suitor, rather than a jaded husband, was his generosity. I feared that if he lost the bridge wire contract he would be as poor as I, and so I hastened to ask my shifty admirer to underwrite two new costumes I would need in order to join a touring production of *Two Roses*.

We struck a bargain for the costumes, Lloyd and I. He agreed to pay the dressmaker's bill in exchange for another of Aunt Mollie's old papers and a dozen kisses, and I departed for Buffalo and Syracuse, fully expecting that he would be disgraced before I returned. But no such thing occurred. When I arrived in New York at the end of August, he still held the wire contract for the great bridge.

I arranged to encounter Mrs. Roebling as she left the bridge yard, and asked if our plan had failed.

"Goodness, no!" she exclaimed. "Dear Miss Mooney, you are concerned because as yet there has been no public notice of this affair. You must be patient—the bridge trustees will make it public at an appropriate time. Meanwhile, the soundness of the bridge is assured. The trustees were at last convinced of Mr. Haigh's duplicity, and have agreed that he must replace all the bad wire not yet worked into the cables, and must add one hundred fifty wires per cable to assure its strength, all at his own expense. Further, our inspectors now accompany the loads of certified wire from Mr. Haigh's mill all the way to the bridge yard. Fear not, Miss Mooney, the great bridge is sound!"

"I am glad to hear it, Mrs. Roebling. Are the trustees convinced at last that Mr. Haigh is a scoundrel?"

"Oh, yes!" She laughed merrily. "Do you know, the man had the cheek to tell the trustees that he wasn't anxious about the money it would cost him, he cared only that they should hold a good opinion of him. One of them replied that it was now the unanimous opinion of the trustees that he was a"—her dark eyes sparkled as she looked about to make certain that no one could overhear her before she whispered—"a damned rascal!"

"How shocking!" I exclaimed. "And at a meeting of gentlemen, too! But aren't you disappointed that Mr. Haigh has not been publicly shamed?"

"When dealing with the politicians among the bridge trustees, compromise is often necessary, especially when the news would shame them too," said Mrs. Roebling philosophically. "Someday they will make Mr. Haigh's fraud public. Meanwhile, it is my job to build the eighth wonder of the world!"

I held Mrs. Roebling in the highest esteem, and soon gained further evidence that her assessment of the situation was accurate. When I next saw Lloyd, his splendid voice and hot eyes were as delightful as ever, but he had begun to pinch pennies and I soon found it more agreeable to cultivate other acquaintances. Besides, don't you think a young lady should avoid too close an association with a man who is about to be publicly shamed?

But as the months wore on, I realized that the bridge trustees were not going to put Lloyd's disgrace in the newspapers. No doubt Mrs. Roebling was correct, and they feared that reporters might not follow their lead in assigning all the blame to Haigh, so their own foolish complicity in allowing his fraud would be exposed. They might call him a rascal in a private meeting, but publicly he still basked in the golden opinion of his colleagues.

So, for dear dead Harry's sake, I took the riskier road.

I donned a black wig and a veiled hat and went to the bank. Two banks, in fact, both favored by my clever Lloyd, the Market National Bank and the Grocers' Bank. I claimed that I was a lady from Baltimore who had been swindled by Mr. Haigh, that in exchange for a consideration he had given me a bank draft signed by C. Sidney Norris and Company and it had proved to be a forgery.

I left both banks in a state of excited confusion, particularly the Grocers' Bank, where the manager had blanched when I mentioned C. Sidney Norris and whispered to his assistant, "Didn't we loan Haigh money on a draft from Norris?"

Quickly, I slipped away and changed from my proper wig and veil to a vulgar red dress, rouged my cheeks and painted my lips, and was lounging against the building across the street from Lloyd's office when the police came for him. I hoped to be an invisible part of the passing crowd, but Lloyd's ardent eyes were sharp and he shrieked when he saw me.

"There! There she is! Officer, arrest her! She gave me the forged paper!"

The officer glanced my way and was not impressed. "Not likely, sir. She's a common harlot."

Lloyd jumped up and down pathetically while both officers restrained him. "She did it! She did it!"

I hoisted my skirt an inch and gave them a glimpse of my ankle along with a lewd wink. "And Oi'll do it again if ye want, sir," I said in a lowdown accent, "jist as long as ye pay!"

The officer laughed. "Be off with you, duckie!"

I scampered away.

Oh, come now! Surely you aren't surprised to learn that Aunt Mollie's lovely commercial papers were questionable! In the copying trade my aunt had done many jobs of work for bankers, and became quite skillful at various signatures. From time to time she would bring home an extra copy and slip it into a box which she bequeathed to me, and which I'd kept for purely sentimental reasons, although from time to time brute necessity forced me to sell a bank draft or two to a kindly business advisor such as dear Lloyd. Gentlemen like Lloyd are often eager to assist a young lady who is confused by commercial papers, and will purchase them from her so that she will be spared the unpleasantness of banking transactions. Lloyd had paid me a total of two thousand eight hundred fifty-two dollars for Aunt Mollie's commercial papers. Wasn't that kind of him? And then, because no bank would question a gentleman of such golden reputation, he had borrowed a hundred twenty-five thousand dollars on them from the two banks.

The gentlemen at the banks were not amused to see their assets turn to dust. Mr. J. Lloyd Haigh's arrest upon a charge of forgery was prominently featured in the newspapers, along with his matrimonial escapades and, at last, his bridge wire frauds. Trustee Abram Hewitt, of course, was not mentioned.

Lloyd protested vigorously but as the expenses of making good on the bridge contract had nearly bankrupted him, none of those gentlemen whose golden opinions he had bought in earlier days appeared to defend him.

I know, I know, a proper young lady would never do such a low-down thing to a gentleman admirer. But I've well nigh given up on being proper. Besides, don't you think people should be stopped from marrying so many young ladies and ruining their reputations, and from catapulting handsome heroes to cruel death, and from weakening the cables of the great bridge, which could collapse and kill as many folks as perished in that dreadful Brooklyn Theatre inferno? I know those crimes are not as serious as swindling the gentlemen who run banks, but I'm just a foolish Missouri girl with no sense, who hopes never to hear those agonized shrieks again.

Mr. J. Lloyd Haigh was sent to Sing Sing to repent and break rocks. Mrs. Roebling built her bridge and cared for her invalid. My life for the next two years was singularly eventful, and it was not until the spring of 1883, after a run of good luck in St. Louis, that I returned to New York with my friend Hattie and my ten-month-old niece Juliet James. Wearing one of my new Worth dresses from Paris, I called on Mrs. Roebling. We chatted, and I asked her what she would do now that her bridge was finished.

"No more bridges!" she said vehemently. "I have a son to raise, and after that I may study the law." In fact, some years later, I heard that Mrs. Roebling had earned a diploma from New York University's law program for women. Her essay won a prize. It concerned the unfairness of the law to married women like my Aunt Mollie, who could not own property, while single women could. She thought the gentlemen of the legislature ought to change the law. But they didn't, not for the longest time.

Before we parted, she again expressed her gratitude for my assistance in the matter of the wire fraud, and gave me tickets to the official opening ceremonies for her great bridge.

A wondrous sight it was, and is to this day, Mrs. Roebling's bridge: noble towers pierced by Gothic arches and linked by soaring cables, as graceful and melodious as a song. I reckon I've never seen a finer sight!

Hattie, little Juliet, and I joined a vast crowd to watch President Chester Arthur, Governor Grover Cleveland, the Mayor of New York, the Mayor of Brooklyn, and Mr. Abram Hewitt of the spotless reputation, who all gave addresses to honor the opening of the eighth wonder of the world. Mr. Hewitt specifically declared that Mrs. Roebling represented "all that is admirable in human nature, and all that is wonderful in the constructive world of art." But the most enthusiastic applause came when he stated that all the money raised had been "honestly expended."

The Mayor of Brooklyn praised the beauty and stateliness of the bridge. "Not one shall see it," he declared in ringing tones, "and not feel prouder to be a man!"

Yes indeed.

"Oh, what a tangled web we weave,
When first we practice to deceive!"

Sir Walter Scott, "Marmion"

Scott knew it, but con artists assume they are smarter than the poet. They figure they can keep an eye on all the angles, can outrun all the dangers. But there can be one too many angles to watch, and that's when cons get conned, as one wily pair finds ten miles out of Hot Springs, Arkansas, and another discovers in St. Louis!

SARAH SHANKMAN

Best known for her sexy and saucily witty series featuring reporter Sam Adams, Sarah Shankman has also written a mainstream novel and has been an editor at *Atlanta, New Orleans,* and *Fine Dining* magazines, the last of which provided her favorite kind of research.

What comes through all of Sarah's work is the voice of the South in all its wildly amusing, eye-popping bizarreness. Her latest book, *He Was Her Man,* takes Sam to Hot Springs, Arkansas, where she finds a bevy of con artists, an ex-con who's a card-carrying member of the Graciousness Society, and a former Miss Hot Springs who's misplaced her latest fiancé. This book inspired "What Did You Expect?"

WHAT DID YOU EXPECT?

Olive was saying to her dog Pearl, "Those girls don't know what they're talking about. Do you think they know what they're talking about?" Olive snapped off the TV where Geraldo and the three bottle blondes perched on the edge of their seats like canaries, saying how being a call girl was fun.

Pearl sat back on her haunches and said, "Aooo, aooo," which was what she was supposed to do, and Olive reached behind the counter of the Gas'NGrub for a package of Cheez Doodles, the redbone hound's favorite snack. While she was at it, Olive grabbed herself a Delaware Punch from the cooler. Pearl, impatient, barked twice, but it wasn't going to bother anybody, the two of them being all by their lonesome. Besides, Olive owned the joint, a one-stop gas station and convenience store ten miles out of Hot Springs, Arkansas.

"Hold your horses," she said to Pearl, tearing open the Doodles. "I'll tell you what, dog, when *I* was living the life, no matter what those Geraldo girls say, not a single minute of it was fun. Living in town in Hot Springs, yes, but not the work. Course maybe it's a little different, the way those girls do it, calling on the johns, you have some control, instead of them walking right in off the street, pointing a fat finger in your face like you was supposed to be thrilled to pieces, you'd won some kind of beauty contest. Course, you get down to it, no matter who does the traveling, you close that bedroom door, it's all the same thing." Olive lifted a blue-veined hand and smoothed at the gray curls that had popped loose from the knot atop her head. She was wearing a purple and green muumuu she'd bought in Hawaii ten years ago, nothing under it but rolls of pink flesh and a pair of lilac step-ins. In her pocket was a pair of reading glasses in a red lizard case left behind by her last customer. There was a name and address inside, and she was planning on returning them, but, on the other hand, the glasses worked real fine on the *Enquirer*. She'd just read an article about these eighteen-year-old girl Siamese twins who wanted to marry each other. "That was the fifties," she said to Pearl, "when I was practicing my profession up behind the bank on Bath, right off Central Avenue. Which reminds me, Pearl, we need to figure out what I'm going to wear to Loydell's daughter Jinx's party this evening. My blue? What do you think?"

Pearl gave her a puzzled look like she wasn't sure. Just about then the bell sounded as a four-door silver Mercedes sedan pulled up at the gas pumps. A slender redhead stepped out and reached for the do-it-yourself unleaded supreme.

"Would you look at that? Now that's class." Olive raised up off her stool to get a better look, pulling down her muumuu in the back where it had bunched up. "You see that yellow suit, that's genuine linen. That pretty white blouse is silk and those pumps—that's real alligator, Pearl. Which reminds me of that Japanese tourist at the alligator farm in town was carrying an alligator bag from one of them designers, leaned over too far, big old 'gator snagged her bag like it was his Uncle Elmer he'd always had it in for, chomped it and her wallet, thousand dollars in cash and a whole bunch of credit cards." Pearl barked. "I already told you that one? Well, you look out at that woman there, she'll keep you amused. Ain't she purty? And rich, got to be rich, driving that big car, you see those diamond studs in her ears, see 'em sparkling way over here? That's class *and* money, Pearl. Bet she comes in here and flips out a gold card. Or a platinum." Pearl barked again. "That's right. That's all the metal you see these days, none of them silver dollars I used to collect. We'd drop 'em in the big slots at the Vapors, back in the old days. In town, in Bubbles. Did you know that's what the Yankee gangsters came for the waters used to call Hot Springs, Pearl? Bubbles. Idn't that cute? Watch out, now, here she comes. Wonder what her name is? Rita? Lucy? Something to match that red hair, I bet.''

"Hello there, hello,'' said the woman, breezing in with the same smile you'd swear she used when she had tea with the Queen of England. Olive took a look at the turned-up nose, small white teeth, milky skin, the faintest little laugh lines at the corners of the mouth and eyes—and put her at twenty-eight. Probably be good to fifty. "Beautiful afternoon, isn't it? Oh, my goodness, what a gorgeous dog. Is she a hunter?'' asked the redhead, wrinkling up her nose. She had an overripe accent. Like maybe she was from Charleston, Savannah, thought Olive, one of those. But she had a West Coast kind of body, slim, strong-looking like a young boy's, like she jogged five miles a day or rode a bike.

"Coon dog,'' said Olive. "Redbone hound's the best coon dog money can buy. Pearl here belongs to my grandbaby Bobby.'' At that Pearl flopped right over, belly up, tongue out, drooling like a perfect fool. The redhead leaned over and goosed her for a minute with long thin fingers which were pretty, but looked like they knew a few tricks. On her right hand sparkled an emerald-cut solitaire that had to be at least eight carats, maybe ten. She said, "Dogs are so much better than people, don't you think? I used to keep English spaniels. But I can't now, I travel so much.'' The smile on her beautiful face was a heartbreaker. If it were a record, thought Olive, she'd play it over and over again on rainy afternoons. Then the redhead straightened in one long motion and pulled a bill for the gas from the alligator bag, and handed it to Olive. "Do you mind if I use your ladies' room?'' The pretty lady glanced at her gold-and-stainless steel watch, the kind you see in fancy ads in magazines. "In fifteen minutes I'm due at a meeting in Hot Springs, at the Arlington, and I need to freshen up.''

"Why, not at all. Please help yourself.'' Olive heard herself flossing up her inflection as if she herself were a grand lady with appointments to keep instead of a former hooker/waitress now grocery clerk/gas jockey. Though she did have Jinx's party in town this evening. "You go outside, turn right, around to the side, you can't miss it. But don't you want your change?'' Then Olive looked down at the bill she was holding. A fifty. You hardly ever saw one of those.

The woman's smile tucked in at the corners as she nodded at the bill. "I hope that's not inconvenient.'' She stared back down in her bag, then lifted eyes of emerald—just like the cut of that perfect diamond on her perfect finger. "I'm afraid it's the smallest thing I have.'' Then she did the tiniest little shrug, followed by something you'd say was a bump and grind if she wasn't such a lady and you didn't know that she *really* had to go to the bathroom.

Which set Olive to worrying about the shape the ladies' was in. Oh, she'd emptied the trash like she did every morning, made sure there was plenty of toilet paper and paper towels and pink liquid soap. But she hadn't mopped it. She wished she'd swabbed it down with Lysol and hung some of those little huck towels with the day of the week done in cross-stitch and laid in some of that pink carnation soap her grandbaby Bobby gave her for Christmas four years ago, still in the box, Olive was saving it for something special. But Olive handed over the $32.45 in change and hoped for the best, bathroom-wise. "Thank you so much," said the redhead, stepping outside.

Olive shook her head, turned back to Pearl. "There's them that has, and them that don't. You know that? That's the way God made the world. Course there's them that say there's only so much people stuff in the universe and it keeps getting recycled, so there's always another chance, depending on what you did the time before. Now, I know what *I* want to be next time around."

Pearl sat up and said, "Rowooo, rowooo," like she had a big old coon up a tree and could see the shine of his eyes, *her* idea of Nirvana.

Olive said, "Nope. Don't wanta be like that redhead either, driving that big silver car. I already was a pretty woman, and look how that turned out."

Pearl muttered something deep in her broad chest.

"That's right," said Olive. "*You.* I'm coming back as a coon dog with a momma owns a store full of snacks and nothing better to do than sit around and spoil me all day. Though, I wouldn't mind having that one's figure again, I used to have me one like that—and a pretty pale yellow suit. Wouldn't that look swell at Jinx's party? I think it'd be perfect, early evening do . . ."

Just about then, the lady whose suit she was coveting was striding back to her car, turning and waving with that stiff little motion like you see beauty queens do, when suddenly she screamed. It was the kind of scream that you used to hear from the blonde in monster movies. The kind of scream that let you know the screamer wasn't fooling around. There really was something out there in the dark that was going to scare the bejesus out of you. More likely it'd eat you alive. Olive thought maybe the redhead'd stepped on a snake, so she grabbed her .44 Bulldog from behind the counter, and hit the door yelling "You stay!" at Pearl, making sure she didn't escape.

"Oh, my God!" The lady was still screaming. Then she saw Olive with the revolver and threw her arms up in the air. "Don't shoot, please don't shoot me!"

"Lady, are you crazy?" Olive was looking all around for the snake. Where'd it go?

"I've lost my ring! My diamond ring!"

Her ring? That's what all this hollering was about? Then Olive remembered that emerald-cut sparkler catching the fluorescent lights and she commenced to joining in the screaming. "Where? How? Tell me exactly what you did."

Now the lady was jumping up and down, shaking her wrists. Then stopping to stare at the right hand as if she looked at it long enough, her ring would reappear. "I took it off in the ladies' room to wash my hands, and then, well," she started to wail, "I don't remember!"

"Yes, you do. Just calm down. If you get ahold of yourself, you'll see what you did." Olive knew how that was. How you did things automatically. Driving, even. Like when you were thinking about something real hard, you'd start off in your car in Hot Springs, next thing you knew you'd be in Pine Bluff, forty miles away, not remember a dad-blamed thing.

"I was thinking about Dean, my boyfriend who gave me the ring." The lady broke down into a serious boohoo. Olive wouldn't have figured her for a crybaby, but you never knew.

Olive could hear Pearl yodeling away inside. Pearl was dying to poke her nose in their business, see if it was something she could chase through the brambles, torture across a bog.

"Listen, lady," Olive said.

"Madeline."

"That's a right pretty name, Madeline. Let's just collect ourselves here. I know we'll find that ring."

Madeline was wiping her eyes, making black smudges on her knuckles. That and the runny nose, she looked like a kid.

"Come on, now. You only went from here to the ladies'. We'll retrace your steps, find it for sure."

So that's what Olive and Madeline did. Olive slipped the revolver in the pocket of her muumuu, and together they examined every square inch of the oil-spotted concrete, Olive using her newfound reading glasses. They poked at old chewing gum, at gravel, at weeds growing up through a crack. They inspected every last centimeter of the ladies' itself, including the broken-down old shower, though Madeline swore she hadn't dropped it in there. The more she thought about it, the more she remembered shaking her fingers one last time in the sunshine to make sure they were dry before she put on her ring because she was prone to dermatitis, she had sensitive skin. The ring had simply disappeared into thin air.

Well, it couldn't have done that, said Olive. Things just didn't dematerialize. They weren't snatched up by haints. Olive was a practical woman who'd always lived in the here and now, and by God, that diamond was here, and it was here *now*, and they would find it if they just persevered. So they did the search all over again. Frontward. Backward. Sideways. Widening the area each time, but with no luck. Madeline crying all the while, blubbering like a baby, talking about how much that diamond was worth. A quarter of a million dollars, she said. Insured, of course. But she couldn't report it missing. Not after that robbery that she and Dean had had when she was staying at his beach house last summer, and the thieves broke in and knocked them around and tied them up and took every last piece of jewelry she had. My stars, said Olive. Dean had given her this ring as a sort of consolation prize while they were looking around to replace things with the insurance money. Not that you could ever replace those pieces with sentimental value. Of course not, said Olive, shaking her head, remembering that pink gold locket with the little engraved roses, pictures of her first dog Pokey inside, that a john had ripped right off her neck forty years ago. Thinking about it still made her mad. But because of that robbery, said Madeline, her insurance premiums were already so high, if she reported this . . . Besides, she wanted the ring that Dean had given her, the very one, not some replacement. Then she broke into sobs so heartrending, Olive almost joined her.

After a while Madeline got control of herself, blew her nose in a white linen handkerchief trimmed with both cutwork and lace, rocked back on those alligator heels, and moaned, "On top of that, now I'm late for my meeting. And it's an *important* meeting."

Olive was sure it was. What other kind of meeting would a woman wrapped in linen and silk and alligator and diamonds and gold and stainless steel and a silver Mercedes be going to?

Madeline reached in her bag and pulled out a little notepad and a gold pen. She scribbled her name, Madeline Brooks, and the words Arlington Hotel, Hot Springs. "That's where I'm staying."

Olive nodded. Anybody who knew anything about Hot Springs knew the Arlington. It was one of the grand hotels left from the good old days when Hot Springs was something.

"I hate to leave." Madeline turned her head and closed her eyes and threw her naked right hand over her pretty white silk and yellow linen-covered breast. "But I must. With the hope, of course, that I'll hear from you soon. That you'll call and say that you've found my ring and you're waiting for me to come and claim it and give you your thousand-dollar reward."

Olive gasped. A thousand dollars!

"Cash," said Madeline. "To anyone who finds Dean's token of affection. Oh, Olive, please, please, find my ring." Tears danced in her emerald green eyes.

Olive had never seen anyone with eyes that exact color. "Don't you worry your pretty little head about it. Unless the angels have swooped down and carried it off for the Good Lord to wear on His pinky, you're gonna hear from me soon. I promise you that." With any luck, she'd find it right after Madeline left, bring it into town with her on her way to Jinx's party, stop into the Arlington, call Madeline up on the house phone . . .

"Oh, Olive!" Madeline clasped her to her bosom and gave her a big hug. "I know you'll be my salvation." Reluctantly she stepped into the Mercedes and pulled the door to with that solid kerchunk like a bank vault closing, and waving a sad little Miss America wave, drove off toward Hot Springs.

It's here, I know it's here. Now Olive was down on her hands and knees talking to herself. Wiping the sweat out of her eyes. It could get pretty hot in Arkansas in late April. Hot enough to make an old lady think maybe she was about to get sunstroke if she didn't take a break from searching for that diamond ring, get herself into the shade.

Besides, Pearl was about to have a fit. Howling "Ooohuroo, ooohuroo," in front of the soda cooler as if Olive didn't know how that felt, a woman left lonely, which was the title of her favorite song by Janis Joplin. It was on the album, *Pearl*, she'd named the dog after. Bobby, her grandbaby, hadn't had time to name her before they dragged him off to the slammer.

"Momma understands, sugar." Olive slipped her new glasses back in her pocket, leaned over and gave Pearl a big hug, then reached into the cooler and grabbed herself another Delaware Punch. Whew! There was nothing like an ice-cold pop to make an old lady feel better.

Unless it was a thousand-dollar reward. Olive leaned back on the cooler and took another swig. "How would that be, Pearl? You and me, we'd throw ourselves in that Sunliner." She glanced out at the old black-and-gold retractable hardtop convertible shrouded with a tarp. It was a classic; more than one young hotshot had offered her good money for it, but Olive wouldn't let it go. It belonged to Bobby. He was supposed to be getting out any minute now; she'd been saving the Sunliner for him all this time. Kept it in A-1 condition, too. "Then we'd drive into town and check into the Arlington. No, the Palace. I always favored the Palace, better class of clientele, and I ought to know, having entertained gentlemen from both plenty of times. Get ourselves freshened up, go downstairs, stroll through that pretty lobby, watch ourselves in all those gold mirrors, I bet they make us look slim, take ourselves a table on the veranda, order ourselves a shrimp salad and some real sweet iced tea. Watch the passing scene on Central Avenue. Ask the waiter to call and make us a reservation for a bath and massage in the spa a little later."

Pearl barked.

"You like that? Well, then we'd take us a little nap in our suite, get up and dress for the evening. You remember that frock I used to have of lemon-yellow dotted swiss? It had the most beautiful collar trimmed in lace. I think that's what Madeline's suit reminded me of."

Pearl said, "Ooooruha."

"No, I guess you don't. That was before your time. Anyway, we'd stroll down Central, go look us at some art. There's all these new galleries now across from Bathhouse Row. Back in the old days, before air-conditioning, when we had the legal gambling, you could stand out on the sidewalk in front of those same buildings, the bookies upstairs with windows wide open, hear the results of the races at Santa Anita, Saratoga, Pimlico over the loudspeakers. Pearl, would you *hush up!*"

Then Olive looked out and saw what had the hound so agitated. There was a tramp cutting across the edge of her property, a tall old man in a filthy long-sleeved undershirt and a pair of what looked like green fatigues belted with a rope. He had long gray hair under a straw hat, a scraggly beard, and a sticky-looking handlebar mustache.

Well, God knows there were plenty of folks poorer than her, people who didn't have the luxury of worrying about not meeting next month's rent, worrying about bankruptcy, under the Republicans had already lost what little they had including their homes, lots of which were pretty pitiful anyway. Olive was about to reach back in the cooler, pull out a cold drink to take out to the old man, he looked so hot, when suddenly he stopped at the edge of the pavement, reached down, and picked up something. His mouth fell open like a black cave. He stuck whatever it was in his pocket in a god-awful hurry, and looking behind him like a booger-bear might be after him, took off down the road.

Jesus H. Christ! He'd found the ring!

"Wait! Wait!" Olive ran out after him.

The tramp wheeled with a wild look in his eye. "What do you want?" His voice sounded rusty, like a porch swing that'd been out all winter.

"That's mine, what you've got in your pocket."

"I ain't got nothing in my pocket." He wiped at his nose.

"You do too. You do, and I know what it is. It's a ring! Show me it ain't!"

He stepped back, his eyes slits. "So what if it is? What's it to you?"

"It's mine. It was on my property, and if you don't hand it over, I'm calling the police."

Olive stepped right up close to the bum expecting him to smell like a hog, but he didn't. He was plenty shifty-eyed, though. Real pale-gray eyes that didn't give back any light. Criminal-colored eyes, just like cold cement. She wished that her best friend Loydell was here to get a load of this sucker. Loydell had been the matron for almost forty years for the women prisoners, when there was any, at the Garland County Jail. Loydell knew a real criminal when she saw one. Olive was sure she'd say this fellow was the genuine article, and she wasn't going to spend another single solitary minute feeling sorry for him, especially since he was standing between her and a thousand bucks.

"Are you deaf, old man? I said if you don't give me that ring, I'm calling the cops."

He took the ring out of his pocket—it was the very one Madeline had dropped, big old emerald-cut diamond, bigger than any the tourists had ever picked up at the Crater of Diamonds over near Murfreesboro—and stared at it for a long minute. Then he said, "Can you prove it's yours?"

Well. That made her step back a bit, catch her breath. But she knew whose it was, and she knew who was going to get that thousand-dollar reward for it, and if she didn't, it'd be over her dead body. "I most certainly can," she said.

He waggled a dirty finger in her face. "I don't think so. I think if you could prove it, it wouldn't have taken you so long to say. What *I* think is finders keepers, and I'm the finder."

Olive could see the thousand-dollar reward slipping away. If she called the cops and they came, there was that thing about possession being nine tenths of the law, and this son of a bitch definitely had the ring in his mitt. Which probably meant he'd get the reward. The very idea made her chest hurt.

"Okay. I'll give you fifty dollars for it. For that you can buy yourself a whole lot of Thunderbird."

"Ha! You must think I'm a fool, I'd sell you a diamond like this for fifty bucks. It's worth at least a thousand. Pawnshop'd give me a thousand, for sure. I'll just walk on up the road, Hot Springs's got plenty of pawnshops."

He was bluffing. Olive turned away.

"Okay, okay. Seven fifty. I'll take seven fifty."

"I wasn't born yesterday." She said that over her shoulder, walking back toward the store. Pearl was standing right inside the door, her tail wagging, her nose up against the glass. Every time Olive saw that sweet face, her heart turned over. They were right, what they said about dogs. Nobody'd ever loved her as much as Pearl. She turned back to the tramp. "A hundred's my best offer."

"Five."

At that, she'd still clear another five hundred on the deal. But if she'd just looked harder a little while ago, she could have had the whole enchilada. At five hundred, the suite at the Palace would shrink to a single room. Her long weekend of luxury telescoped to a couple of days. She shook her head. "Two, and that's my best offer."

"Four."

It looked like three hundred was going to be it. Olive tried two twenty-five. Two fifty. But three it was. Three once, three twice, three thrice, she had herself a genuine emerald-cut diamond ring for three hundred dollars on which she could clear seven hundred, she got the reward . . .

But wait a danged minute. Who said she had to call Madeline at the Arlington? If the ring was worth a quarter of a million, she could sell it herself, rake in God knows how much. Now she saw herself back at the Palace registration desk, Pearl loping along beside her, herself saying Thank you kindly, a penthouse suite will be just fine. She was calling room service. She was rustling up some old contacts, getting into one of Jack Graham's high-stakes poker games, winning a few big pots, chucking the Gas'NGrub altogether . . .

"Lady, you gonna give me the cash?" The tramp was waiting with his dirty hand on the counter, palm up.

"Oh, sure. Just a minute." She didn't have but about a hundred in the register, and she didn't want him to see her reach down under for the cash box. Of course, she still had the revolver in her pocket, could feel the weight of it, if he tried anything funny. He smiled. He had nice teeth for a bum. Then he held the ring out in his right hand for Olive to see again, speed her up. Pearl barked, and he leaned over like he was going to pat her. It was then Pearl lunged at him, snapped right in his face.

"Oh, my God! I'm so sorry," said Olive. Pearl, you bad dog, she was about to say, until she saw that Pearl had snatched the scraggly beard and mustache away. Underneath the tramp was smooth and tan and clean and not nearly as old as she'd thought.

"You're not a bum! You're some kind of . . . fake. A phony." And then as she said the words, Olive got it. No indeed, she wasn't born yesterday. In fact, she was so old that she'd forgotten some of what she once knew, what she'd learned living the life. But now she remembered. Bait and switch. A con game, old as the hills. As old as human greed. And she'd been greedy. That's how con games worked, you had to be greedy to get took. She reached for the phone. Now she really was calling the police.

"Put the phone down, lady." His voice wasn't creaky anymore. It wasn't young, either, but it was strong. And mean.

Pearl growled, showing her teeth. She was a big powerful dog.

Shit, Doc Miller said to himself. Goddammit to hell. Mickey'd said they ought not to take this one last mark before they rolled into Hot Springs. But he'd insisted. The lost ring was one they'd pulled a million times, he'd told her, and that was true. It always played like a charm. Mickey working outside, setting up the mark, pretending she'd dropped the ring, waiting up the road while he made the sting, pocketed the cash, left the twenty-five-dollar paste imitation with the pigeon, the blowoff being "Madeline" wouldn't be at the hotel, the mark would keep calling for the reward, then realizing that the pretty lady never was going to be there, probably trying to sell the paste ring for a profit. By then, he and Mickey would be far away. Except, this time they wouldn't. They'd just be up the road, right outside Hot Springs.

It was too dangerous. Mickey'd said that. Awh, come on, he'd said after they'd driven by the little convenience store. You turning chicken on me? It's an old lady—and we'll bag enough to help pay the rent. This one's gonna be expensive, Mick. The big one.

The one he was going out on. Doc's retirement. His last job, not that he'd told Mickey that. He knew she'd be pissed, it'd queer the deal.

But if it went the way they'd planned, oh boy, guys'd talk about it for years. Of course, that wasn't the important part. What was important was getting out of the game—with a pile. And scot-free. He couldn't afford a little sleepover in the county jail right now.

He grabbed Olive's wrist.

"Owh!" she hollered. "Let go, you're hurting me!"

At that, the dog locked onto his calf, her sharp teeth sinking deep. He reached over to a shelf and jerked up a quart bottle of apple juice, knocked the dog in the head with it, hard. The dog's jaw released, and she tumbled to the floor.

"You son of a bitch!" the old woman screamed. His head snapped. The woman had his full attention now. Her face was bright red, her mouth trembling. He watched her hand slide down the front of her big purple and green muumuu, reach into her pocket and find what he was afraid she was going to find. It was a powerful gun, the Bulldog. It'd blow a man's stomach out, splatter his brains all over the wall. He could see what would happen if he didn't reach his hand out, grab her arm, she was holding it way out, too far from her body, asking for it practically, it wouldn't be hard to twist the gun loose, that part was easy, she was an old woman. The part that he'd forgotten (for this scenario had happened before and would probably happen again, obstacles like this having a way of cluttering up the crooked streets of Doc's life) was the sweet shock of release after he'd slipped the safety, squeezed the trigger, and punched three slugs through her gut.

It was one of life's funny coincidences that only moments after Doc had sponged and scrubbed up Olive's crimson mess, the cleaning implements being right there on the shelves of the Gas'NGrub, had packed Olive into the trunk of the Sunliner and driven away, Bobby Adair, her favorite grandson, and the original owner of both Pearl, the redbone hound, and the Sunliner, pulled up into the driveway of that very same one-stop.

Bobby was an innocent-looking boy of twenty-five, clean-featured, with a brown crew cut and clear blue eyes that seemed to look straight through your head, watch the picture show you were running in there. He had a nice tan, a good build, the kind of shoulders you got from working out in prison, the same place he'd picked up the tan. Cons did that, caught themselves some rays out in the yard the last few weeks, so their faces wouldn't shout *Just got out of jail* when they walked down Freedom Street.

Bobby had been looking forward to this moment—seeing Olive and Pearl, not to mention his old Sunliner Ford and his girlfriend Cynthia whose daddy the cop's head he'd knocked which resulted in Bobby's stay at the Tucker correctional facility—for four long years.

But no Olive, no Ford, just Pearl was to be had, shaking her head with its long lovely ears, bawling like a baby, snuffling and scratching to get out of the store.

When Bobby opened the door, Pearl flew like a shot. Then she stood and pointed at where the Ford had been parked and threw back her graceful head. "Ooooooorhuhooooo." She flung one look back at Bobby to see if he knew his role, then took off down the shoulder of Highway 70 toward Hot Springs like they were holding a reservation in her name at the Arlington.

Bobby jumped back behind the wheel of his dark blue spanking-new Mercury Grand Marquis (the one he'd found with the keys in it near Pine Bluff) and followed Pearl in hot pursuit as surely as if she were running through bogs and bushes, about to chop on a big boss coon.

When they got to the city limits, Bobby slumped down, pulling his baseball cap low on his forehead, not wanting to be spotted by a member of the Hot Springs Police Department, the terms of his parole being he could not step foot within fifty miles of the city, his true love Cynthia, or her dad, the cop, who was bad with his hands and his only daughter when he got to drinking, which is why Bobby had brained him with his very own Hot Springs Police Department target-shooting trophy with the little gun on top.

Now an hour or so later, Mickey and Doc were standing in the kitchen of a rambling two-story stone house set back in the woods by the side of a lake five miles west of Hot Springs. They had been going at it for a while, but Mickey hadn't heard anything yet that made sense.

She said, "Explain it to me one more time, please, Doc. I know I'm stupid, don't know what a whole lot of nines are."

"You can cut the sarcasm, okay? I told you, the old lady wasn't going for it." He was rolling up the sleeves of the white shirt he'd changed into, that and some khakis, shucking the tramp duds. "She was giving me a hassle, I decided to blow, and she came after me. I jumped in the car and hit the road. Got here five minutes ahead of you and washed up." He peered into the refrigerator. "There's not a damned thing in here except some ketchup."

"Furnished doesn't mean they stock it with Doritos and all that other junk you eat. You wanted that, you should have sent the landlord a shopping list."

"You can get down off your high horse, okay? What's your damn beef?" He was peering and talking into the knotty pine cabinets now. "Aha!" He pulled out a fresh jar of Miracle Whip and a box of graham crackers. Then he started opening one drawer after another, searching for a knife in the big yellow kitchen.

Mickey couldn't stand drawers being left open. Doors. Tops off jars.

She went behind Doc now, closing things. "I can't believe you're really going to eat that." She wrinkled her nose.

"Look!" Doc wheeled, a cracker thick with salad dressing poking out of his face. "Are you going to ride me all the way through this job? Is that the way it's going to be? 'Cause if it is, I can find another partner like that." He snapped his fingers. "I don't need you, Mick."

"Oh, yeah?" That was a crock. Who'd been in town working the races a couple weeks back, spotted the chance of a big score?

He knew that. "Big deal. Take a finder's fee, you can blow." He crammed another cracker in his mouth. "I'm telling you, I don't need the grief."

"All I'm asking you is, why'd you take the car? It doesn't make any sense. We've run the lost ring a hundred times, *you've* probably done it a thousand, did you ever take a car before this? Did you ever nab something big like that you'd have to dump, something that'd tie you to the mark that easy? Besides, Jesus, Doc, we're not thieves."

His Old St. Nick laugh didn't work with a mouth full of crackers and salad dressing. He followed it with "Nope, we're not. We're hustlers."

Mickey sniffed and started turning side to side, her arms up, elbows bent, still wearing the yellow suit. "Con artists, Doc. *Artistes.*"

"Yeah, we're that alright. Fancy schmanzy crooks. All the partners in the world, I got to hook up with a princess—Jesus, could you stop with the Jane Fonda? I'm talking to you."

"And I'm listening, still waiting for the explanation to why it was— even if for some insane reason, some bolt of inspiration came down and struck you from the blue—you felt compelled to take that car, and I'll admit it's something special. I'd love it myself." Mickey was doing toe touches now in the middle of the green-and-yellow tiled floor, still in her alligator high heels. She was proud of keeping her flexibility considering how much time she spent traveling. "What were you doing back there that took so long, anyway? Usually, you're in, you're out, quick as a bunny on the negotiating. And why was it then you passed me, had to be doing eighty? You didn't toot the horn, I'd have pulled over, you'd have dumped the car, left it on the side of the road. What *was* all that?"

"I wasn't wearing gloves. Needed to wipe it clean. We don't want any screwups, a way the cops can place us here."

Mickey stopped halfway to her toes, bent up so her body was at a perfect ninety-degree angle from the waist. She tilted her face, said in her sweetest voice, "Doc, there'd have been no prints to leave if you hadn't taken the car."

He slammed the Miracle Whip down on the cabinet like a pistol shot.

"Okay! You're right, I'm wrong. I was wrong from the get-go. So what do you want me to do? Kill myself?" He jerked open a drawer, pulled out a cold-forged steel chef's blade, long and wickedly sharp, and held it to his neck. "Okay, Mick. Go on, say the word. I fucked up. One slice, the jugular, it'll be messy for you to clean up, but so what? Yeah? That's it? That's why you're taking your skirt off? Don't want to get blood all over it?"

"No, Doc." She gave him her slow grin. "That's not why I'm taking my skirt off." She paused. "My blouse." It took a minute to undo the little glass buttons. She was wearing one of those lacy flesh-colored bras that could stop a man's heart. "My shoes." Those were quick. "My stockings." Those were slow, slipping the little rubber nib on the garter, letting the silk slide. Pulling them off over her red-tipped toes. You'd never catch a woman wearing panty hose who worked a scam that depended on the weakness of men.

Now Doc, slouched back against the counter, resting his elbows on the yellow Formica, was staring at her.

He took a deep breath. Watching Mickey undress was one of his most favorite things. He was really gonna miss her.

She had one of those faces, Jesus, it was like an angel's. Classy. The cap of red curls above that rounded forehead, smooth and cool, then those wide-spaced eyes of that incredible green, deep and pure with no flecks of gold or brown, just green. Her turned-up nose with the cute little pear-shaped nostrils. Her mouth, God, her mouth was sweet as a plum. And what Mickey could do with that mouth, *say* with that mouth when you got down to the nitty-gritty, he'd never heard a woman say such things. And he'd known some women in his time.

Christ. Why wouldn't he? He was old enough to be her father, almost her grandfather. Maybe that was part of why she turned him on, that old thing about the forbidden, not that he ever would, of course, if he had a daughter, the very thought made him sick, but now there was her back, God, he loved her back, the tender bones of her spine, and though she had definition because she was such a nut about fitness, it was girl definition tapering down to a narrow waist, then flaring. There were those two little dimples, two of his favorite places in the whole wide world.

It hadn't taken long, staring at her back, then watching the way her little ass moved as she walked up the stairs, before she had him in a bedroom.

"Isn't that nice," she murmured, "a king-size bed."

"Clean sheets." He was out of the white shirt and khakis now. "Very considerate."

"Very thoughtful."
"*Very.*"

You know that expression, That dog won't hunt? Bill Clinton used it in a speech up in New York during the Democratic Convention. The Yankees said, What's he mean? As if they wouldn't know, they gave it a minute's thought. Anyway, Pearl was the opposite of that dog. Hunting was what she wouldn't stop. She trudged right on through Hot Springs, right up Central Avenue and Bathhouse Row, the single line of eight old bathhouses that backed up against Hot Springs Mountain. She loped uphill past the Palace and Arlington hotels, past dark green magnolias heavy with creamy blossoms that smelled of musk, sweet dreams, and chivalry long dead. Her pace steady as a metronome, she climbed on out the north side of town, up a two-lane mountain road past a pottery, a flea market, rock shops, billboards for crystal mines where you could hunt for your own, past stone mansions and falling-down shacks and mobile homes, heading on up toward Hot Springs Village where snowbirds perched in condos, and finally turned off at Mountain Valley where the bottled water came from. Pearl went right on humping through mile after mile of Weyerhauser pine forests. Bobby was hunkered down behind the wheel, more worried by the minute. This was looking bad. He was getting the whim-whams on the lonely mountain road broken by only an occasional mailbox. What would Gramma Olive be doing way up here? He shook his head. Nothing good.

Finally Bobby and Pearl came to the edge of Lake Ouachita, as serene a blue lake as you'd ever hope to see. Pearl nosed up a little gravel road and stopped.

She sat down in the middle of the road, her big neat head turning this way and that, her pale eyes mournful. Then she lumbered up and switched back and forth in circles.

Bobby got out, patted her on the head. "Which way, girl? What's the matter? You came all this way and got lost?"

Doc pretended that he was asleep when Mickey slid out of the big bed, silent as a ghost.

He knew where she was going, dressed only in his white shirt.

He'd known that was the point of her little display of gymnastics from the moment she'd given him the slow grin.

One thing he'd never been able to teach Mickey, and God knows she was a fast learner, was this: Never try to con a con man.

She didn't get it. Just because she had an enormous talent for the grift, and maybe throw in the fact that she was beautiful, not to mention one hell of a great lay, she was always thinking she could put one over on him.

Doc'd been working the grift since he was five—his father, a carnie, ran a gaffed wheel, used him as a baby shill—for fifty-four goddamned years. Everything she did, Mickey was clear as glass.

Like he knew she was heading for the Sunliner now, but he also knew it was locked. Both doors and the trunk. He didn't want her to see what was in the trunk.

She'd rolled his pants looking for the keys, just like he knew she would. She hadn't said a word, but he heard the Damn! in her mind. She'd never find the keys, stashed among linens in a hall closet.

He eased out of bed and slid into his soft khakis. Grabbed a slick red windbreaker.

By now she was probably out in the triple carport. There was no locked garage, and he hadn't been thrilled about leaving the Sunliner outside, but he'd figured come dark, there was deep water around here, plenty of lakes, he'd just let the car roll off into one. Windows open, it'd go down fast. With any luck it'd be years before they found it, if ever, and by that time there'd be just a skeleton in the trunk, and he'd be an old man minding his crab traps, strolling on a Sea Island beach, fishing from his johnboat.

Barefooted, he tiptoed down the hall, down the stairs, through the kitchen, past the pantry, the laundry room, a guest bath, and threw open the back door onto the carport.

"Surprise!" he yelled at Mickey. She stood there like a vision in his white shirt against the brilliance, the sun lowering, the sky shot with pink, gold, and vermilion.

He had to give it to her. She didn't even jump. Instead she turned like she'd been waiting for him to come down and try to sneak up on her checking on him. She lobbed him another of her slow grins. This one wasn't about sex, though. It was more sly. This one was about winning.

"Bagged yourself a little trophy, did you, Doc?" Behind her the trunk of the Sunliner stood open. He could see the shape of the old woman. Lumpy inside the blankets and the shower curtain from the gas station ladies' room, she looked like a sack of potatoes.

Mickey's green eyes glowed with bravado. Oh yes, she was clever all right.

Her gaze followed his right hand as it slid to his waist, inched up inside the scarlet windbreaker.

Then smug certainty fled those gorgeous peepers and a question tiptoed in. Followed by a flash of fear.

When she saw the silver of the chef's knife, the very one with which Doc had threatened to slash his own jugular, her eyes widened, then fluttered. Doc reached for her and cut. It wasn't but a minute before he tossed her in the trunk. More baggage.

Pearl stood motionless, muttering to herself low in her chest, gazing out across the still surface of Lake Ouachita. It was growing dark. Wouldn't be able to see a thing soon, thought Bobby. "Are you lost, girl?" he asked again.

The very idea, she seemed to frown at him. Her reverie ended, her ears perked. She shook herself all over. Her pink-brown nose read the air, sniffed the ground, and then she took off with fresh resolve, her tail high, up the winding gravel.

Only a few yards in, it was as if the scent had socked it to her brain; she was galloping uphill, scrabbling up up the steep slope sheering off to the dark navy lake. Pearl accelerated like she had her eye on the prize. Then she kicked it up another gear and she was soaring. It didn't look like her feet even touched the ground, chewing up that gravel road.

Bobby banked hard. It was all he could do to hold the dark blue sedan, even heavy as it was, on the loose gravel curves. This was nuts, he was thinking, the words pounding like he had the bass turned way up. Here he was, not even twelve hours out of stir, wheeling a stolen car like a maniac on a mountain road, wasn't even supposed to be within smelling distance of Hot Springs, Arkansas; get caught, he'd be back in the slammer in a heartbeat. And for what? Had he lost his mind? A dog, not even Pearl, who came from some superlative redbone stock down in north Louisiana, couldn't track a human being in these circumstances, not unless Gramma Pearl had *walked* all this way, which was impossible.

He was going about this all wrong. What he needed to do was catch up to Pearl, jump out and grab her, wrestle her in the car if necessary, head on back to the Gas'NGrub. Wait for Olive.

He punched the gas. Dust rose as the gravel spun and bounced and rattled and drummed off the hubcaps, the Mercury's underpinnings, so loud he didn't even hear his Sunliner heading downhill, down the sharp narrow turn. He couldn't hear Pearl's chop as she took her stand on the outer edge of the curve. "Yo yo yo yo," she sang. "Hunuruhu hoo hoo hoo hoo."

Doc heard her, though. He was cruising down the road, thinking about his plan—he'd look for a place to park, release the hand brake and jump, stand back and watch the Sunliner, the black-and-gold coffin for two, roll and splash and sink. Then he looked up, saw the hound right square in front of him and heard her bawl. She seemed to be shimmering, a ghost dog, against the backdrop of deep blue. The deep blue water he'd been headed for.

Pearl didn't budge. She held her ground and the Sunliner slid and slewed in the gravel and, almost kissing Pearl's cheek, but not quite, flew right over the edge and sank before you could count to three. Doc and Mickey and Pearl's momma all inside.

"Yo yo yo yo." Pearl sang her dirge out into the clear mountain air. "Hoo hoo hoo."

JOHN LUTZ

John Lutz is a former president of PWA, and the creator of not one but two memorable characters. His first P.I. is Alo Nudger, who works out of St. Louis. The second is Carver, who plies his trade in sunny Florida. *Kiss,* one of the Carver novels, won a Shamus Award for Best Novel of the Year. Mr. Lutz has also won the Mystery Writers of America's Edgar Award for Best Short Story, and the Shamus Award for Best Short Story.

His suspense novel *SWF Seeks Same* was made into the highly successful movie *Single White Female,* which he and his wife have seen numerous times. Mrs. Lutz never fails to applaud when her husband's name comes on the screen. Mr. Lutz usually just smiles.

And why not?

In this story, Nudger is hired to find a man's one true love, whom he has only met through a bus window. Those of us who have had experiences like this—catching a glimpse of a stranger and wanting to know about him or her—will follow Nudger eagerly and anxiously throughout this story to its logical end. A happy ending? Is there such a thing, when you're a romantic?

THE ROMANTICS

Jake Adler was a high-tone downtown attorney of the corporate breed. Why he was slumming in Nudger's office promised to be interesting.

Nudger figured the suave, fortyish fashion plate with the graying hair and hawk-handsome features wasn't here to hire him to investigate anything in relation to a lawsuit. And he was sure he didn't owe money to anyone important enough to have retained Adler. This one figured to be personal, something Adler wouldn't want his society friends or clients to know about. Marital infidelity? A ghost from his past? Nudger leaned back in his *eeep*ing swivel chair, into the cool breeze from the laboring window air conditioner, waiting for Adler to unfold.

"When I'm finished talking," Adler said, "it might seem to you I've come here on something of a whim, but it's not that way at all." He was obviously more than a little ill at ease; it didn't go with his well-tailored, commanding physical presence. Signs of humanity on such Leaders of Men showed as glaring flaws.

"I'm nothing if not confidential," Nudger said, trying to relax Adler, trying to imagine the man as the recipient of a whim.

"I know. I checked." Adler glanced around the sparse Maplewood office, sniffed the sugary aroma from the doughnut shop directly below. "And you're honest. Which is why you're here in this burrow with a desk instead of downtown or out in Clayton."

"Your office is downtown," Nudger pointed out, not very tactfully.

"I'm not always honest."

Nudger thought, At least he's honest about it.

Adler crossed his legs, then used thumb and forefinger to sharpen the crease in his expensive pin-striped pants. "But I *will* be honest with you," he said. "That's why I came here. Can you believe that?"

"It's a stretch."

"Well, maybe it doesn't matter. I want you to follow someone, find out about her."

"Who's her?"

Adler cocked his head to the side, smiling faintly. "Ever think about love, Nudger?"

Huh? Another whim? "I've been known to swoon now and then. It usually doesn't work out."

"I don't mean long-term love, where you and a woman share a mutual respect and make an investment in each other's happiness. I had that with my wife until she died last year. And I don't mean temporary lust. I mean *real* love, the kind you remember from your teens, maybe. Or earlier."

Down on Manchester Avenue a horn honked. A bus accelerated with a roar like a lion. The air conditioner drew in some diesel fumes to merge with the pervasive scent of fresh-baked doughnuts. Nudger said, "There are lots of definitions of true love." He couldn't help it; he had the feeling Adler was being candid and had come here to bare his soul. The guy was some lawyer.

"True love is unexpected and instantaneous," Adler said. "It's when you pass a woman on the street, or glimpse her through the window of a passing train, and you know you'll never forget that lightning instant, never forget her face. Something in the eyes, the tilt of the chin, the planes of the face. Has that ever happened to you?"

"It happens to all men," Nudger said, trying to pull Adler back to earth. "If we actually got to meet these women, they might have bad breath. We might not even like them."

"I still remember the girl I sat behind in my high school math class. I was too shy to talk to her, but even now I can recall the nape of her neck, the gentle upsweep of her blond hair, the graceful line of her cheek. That was over twenty years ago, and if I had artistic talent I could sketch her likeness for you with exactness today." An expression of pain and puzzlement crossed Adler's features. "Why is that, Nudger?"

Nudger sighed. "No one knows. It happens, that's all. Something passes between two people, and maybe only one of them realizes it, then they go on their way to their homes or offices and—"

"—And never forget it," Adler interrupted.

"Sometimes. Is that who you want me to find out about, someone you glimpsed through a train window?"

"Bus window," Adler corrected, as if the mode of transportation were important. "Every morning I eat breakfast at the Edgemore Cafe in the Wellington Building downtown. At exactly seven forty-five, a bus slows down and swings wide to take the corner, and I see a woman like the ones we've been talking about."

"She see you?"

"Our eyes have met. And it happens, that arc of emotion. I'm sure she feels it, too. I don't want it to end the way it usually does, with propriety, inaction, and then recollections and regrets thirty years later. All my life I've been a creature of logic, of planning and pragmatism. Not this time. This time I want to find out about her. I want to get to know her."

"You sure about that? I mean, maybe you're still grieving about your wife, not thinking straight."

"That's what a lot of people would say. But why *shouldn't* I learn something about this woman? And prudently, before I approach her? I'm afraid that if she does return my affection, things might get out of control. I want to know about her first, then maybe introduce myself."

"That's a logical and pragmatic plan," Nudger said, "even if it is to satisfy a whim." *Eeep!* He dropped forward in his chair. "Know what? You're a romantic."

"So are you, my friend. I found that out about you."

"But you're a rich and successful romantic. That's contradictory. It doesn't make sense."

"It does if you take into account I'm unscrupulous."

Nudger said, "I can see why you don't want anyone downtown knowing about this. They'd view it as a weakness."

"But you don't."

"No, I guess not."

"I don't want anything in writing," Adler said. "I'll pay you in cash, and I'll want only a verbal report. I need to know about this woman. I need to know what she is to me, why I look forward to seeing her weekday mornings, and why, when I look at her, the moment is so electric."

Nudger's nervous stomach was warning him to be cautious here. "This is crazy," he said. "It'll be a waste of time, won't get you anywhere. She's probably married, might have children. Might have a boyfriend with muscles and meanness. What romantics do is lie to themselves and get in trouble. You defend them in court all the time. Think again about this."

Adler's square jaw set like a building block beneath his handsome smile. He was obviously determined and a man used to having his way, whatever the cost to anyone. "Indulge me, Mr. Nudger."

Nudger considered, then said, "Indulge *me.*"

Adler laid ten crisp hundred-dollar bills on the desk. He knew how to indulge, all right.

Nudger was hired.

He followed the bus until the woman got off at Fourth and Pine, only blocks from Adler's office in the Wayne Building. Nudger recognized her easily from the description Adler had given him: thin, with delicate features and blond upswept hair. He remembered the girl who'd sat in front of Adler in high school; maybe that old chemistry was what was haunting Adler. More likely it was that his wife had died recently. Maybe he was searching for her among the living.

This was no time for amateur psychology, Nudger told himself, as he quickly pulled his old Ford Granada into a No Parking zone and killed the engine. His job was to find out the woman's name, where she worked and lived. And he was a professional and a practical businessman, right?

Right. And one who needed the business.

The woman walked west on Pine. He had to take the chance his car would be towed. The day wasn't starting right. He got out of the car, slammed the door behind him, and jogged across the street to fall in behind the woman.

She had a nice figure, a graceful, hip-switching walk without much motion of the upper body, like an aspiring model practicing crossing the room with a book on her head to improve her posture. Adler wouldn't know that, if he'd only seen her sitting down, through a bus window. Nudger wondered if he should include it in his report. Such a romantic he was after all, as Adler had said. Nudger knew that Claudia, his lady love, would have another word for him.

The blond woman surprised him. He'd been expecting her to enter an office building. Instead she walked north on Fifth Street, then entered the old but elegant Victoria Hotel on Locust.

Nudger went in behind her, closing the distance between them in the crowded lobby.

He got a better look at her then. She was attractive, but not strikingly beautiful. And older than he'd first thought—probably around forty. There was a remote sadness to her features that made her interesting, but she wouldn't launch more than a few ships.

She paused and studied a placard listing the day's activities in the large and luxurious hotel, then walked toward the restaurant.

Nudger found a place at the counter and ordered a cup of coffee, watching in the mirrored wall as the woman sat down at a table with a man with dark hair and a dark mustache. He was about thirty, broad-shouldered inside a tan sport coat that was too tight on him. When he turned to summon a waiter, Nudger saw that he was wearing a ponytail. He was the type that could get away with it and not seem sissified. This was not the kind of guy Adler would be glad to hear about.

The blond woman and ponytail talked until the waiter brought a single order of eggs and toast. Then ponytail stood up, leaned over, and kissed the woman's cheek. She didn't seem to pay too much attention to that, kept chewing toast. Ponytail paid his check at the cashier's counter and walked from the restaurant, not looking back.

The woman ate slowly, daintily, then sat for a long time sipping coffee. She extended her little finger whenever she lifted her cup to her lips. Her cool blue glance slid over the other diners, most of whom had entered the restaurant within the last half-hour.

About nine-fifteen, the restaurant was only half full. Nudger had walked out into the lobby and bought a newspaper from the overpriced gift shop, then returned to the counter and pretended to read while he managed to down his fourth cup of black coffee.

Too much coffee. He had to go to the bathroom, desperately, and wondered if he should chance it. The woman didn't show any inclination to get up and leave.

Had to! The hell with it. His stomach was killing him.

He hurried to the rest room at the far end of the restaurant. Spent only a few minutes there.

When he emerged, the woman was leaning toward an adjacent table and talking to a redheaded man with a plastic name tag pinned to the lapel of his dark business suit. She was grinning with apparent embarrassment, shrugging and holding out her small black purse.

The redheaded guy studied her through his rimless spectacles, then smiled and tossed down the rest of his coffee. An ice-hearted executive type who'd been melted on the spot.

He and the woman talked for a few more minutes, then they both stood up and the man snatched the check from her table. So gallant. A romantic himself. He paid for both breakfasts on the way out of the restaurant.

Out in the lobby, the woman smiled at him and touched his arm lightly, then turned to walk away. The same walk that had fascinated Nudger after she'd climbed down from the bus and set off down the sidewalk.

She stopped when the man said something, then she turned back to face him. Smiled.

He smiled back at her.

Then she shrugged, and they walked from the lobby together.

Nudger told himself she'd misplaced or forgotten her money or credit cards, asked the man to lend her the amount of her breakfast, then charmed him and graciously returned his favor by accompanying him outside. Maybe she was going to give him directions, or show him the sights.

But really he knew that something more than that had occurred between the woman and the redheaded executive type. She'd managed to pick him up smoothly, professionally.

More bad news for Adler.

As he left the Victoria lobby to follow them, Nudger noticed the man with the ponytail seated in a leather armchair near some potted palms and reading *USA Today*.

He got outside just in time to see the redheaded man and the woman climb into a cab and drive away. Three middle-aged women were in line for the next cab the doorman could wave to the curb. Trouble was, no second cab was in sight, much less a third cab for Nudger. Then the light at the corner changed, and the traffic flow on Locust dried up. Terrific.

Nudger watched helplessly as the taxi carrying the blond woman and her pickup turned the opposite corner just before the traffic light changed, and disappeared into glittering and relentless downtown traffic.

He stood frustrated in the increasing morning heat for a while, then decided the only course left to him was to go back in the hotel and start keeping tabs on the man with the ponytail. Maybe he and the woman would get together again before the day ended.

Almost surely they would. Nudger was getting the idea.

*   *   *

Ponytail stood up from his chair and moved around the lobby from time to time, stretching his muscles. He'd apparently lost all interest in his newspaper, which he'd folded and laid on a table for someone else to read. Twice he sauntered outside to smoke a cigarette.

He was back in the leather armchair when the blond woman and the redheaded man came into the hotel. The man had his arm around her waist but removed it just inside the door, and he was no longer wearing his plastic convention ID tag. The woman said something to him, smiling up at him like a flower seeking sun, as they walked to the elevator and he pressed the up button.

Nudger idly wandered over and stood near them, among a knot of people waiting for an elevator. He deliberately didn't so much as glance at them, and he figured they were too interested in each other to look his way.

When the elevator arrived, empty of guests from the upper floors, he pushed in with the other passengers and stood to the side, near the door.

Everyone observed elevator etiquette and didn't speak. The blond woman and the man, and a fat guy with a plastic name tag like the one the redheaded man had removed, got off on the tenth floor.

Nudger followed. The man and woman turned right. Nudger and the guy with a name tag turned left. The chubby conventioneer kept going straight, but Nudger ducked into an alcove with an ice dispenser and soda machines. He peeked around the corner and watched the man and woman enter a room near the end of the long hall.

After checking to find out the room's number, he returned to the lobby.

Ponytail was still seated in the leather armchair. He was staring off into space, absently drumming his fingertips on the chair arms.

Nudger went back into the restaurant, this time ordered a Pepsi, and observed ponytail through the white latticework that divided restaurant and lobby.

"Wasn't you in here earlier drinking coffee?" the waitress asked.

"I'm on a caffeine diet," Nudger told her, realizing he had to use the rest room again, though not so desperately.

The woman stared at him, decided he might be serious, then sashayed down the counter to wait on yet another man wearing a plastic name tag. They were all part of a national luggage wholesalers' convention, according to the placard in the lobby.

The waitress, who had a faint dark mustache and was not a particularly attractive woman, started to walk away, but the guy with the name tag called her back. Gave her a wide, phony smile. Seemed to be flirting with her. Maybe another arc of emotion like Adler described had just occurred and Nudger had missed it. Hadn't even seen a flash.

He didn't miss it when ponytail raised his arm to glance at his watch, then stood up from the leather armchair and swaggered with an air of purpose toward the elevator.

Two elevators were at lobby level. Nudger slowed his pace, then got in the one on the right after ponytail had entered the one on the left.

Then a dozen people began filing slowly into Nudger's elevator. Pressed against the back wall, he heard the adjacent elevator begin its ascent.

Nudger wondered if he'd ever in his life have any luck that wasn't bad.

His elevator made four stops before it reached the tenth floor.

Ponytail had gotten there ahead of him, but Nudger was just in time to see him pause before the same room the blond woman and the man had entered, give a tight little grin, then quickly push inside.

Nudger rode the elevator back down and used a house phone to call Security.

"I don't know what to tell him," Nudger said to Claudia Bettencourt that afternoon in her apartment. She wasn't teaching summer classes this year, and Nudger found himself spending far too much time with her during the day, when he should have been working. Or trying to find work to do, anyway.

Claudia, lean, dark, beautiful, with eyes that held depths Nudger could never fathom, languidly stretched out a tan arm and poured herself a second glass of the wine Nudger had brought with him. It was a spirited Chablis and had a Nevada label. Without looking at Nudger as she poured the bargain vintage, she said, "Tell him the truth."

"The truth will hurt him."

She put down the bottle and toyed with the threads on the glass neck for the cap that lay beside it. It had been a long time since Nudger had brought her wine in a bottle with a cork. He figured, What did it matter? Neither of them was a connoisseur. "I thought you said Adler was a hotshot lawyer," she told him. "Those guys aren't exactly sensitive souls."

"True, but consider why he hired me. I mean, it isn't like a downtown legal shark to ask for that kind of thing. Completely out of character."

"A trick?"

Nudger poured himself another glass of Chablis and took a swallow. He didn't usually drink wine in the afternoon, but this thing with Adler was bothering him. "I thought it might be a trick, but if it is, I don't understand it."

"That's the idea of a trick, Nudger."

He couldn't dispute her on that one. He took another pull of wine, noticing that it tickled his throat. No, more than tickled—burned. Was wine supposed to do that?

"Attorneys are devious," Claudia said. "Consider Henry Mercato."

Nudger did. More often than he would have chosen. Mercato was the divorce lawyer of his former wife Eileen. Was in fact sleeping with Eileen. Which gave Henry a personal interest in helping her to extract as much alimony as possible from Nudger even if it meant dragging him back into court and snatching food from beneath his nose. Not child support, which Nudger would gladly have paid if he and Eileen had been blessed with children, but alimony. No one paid alimony these days. No one other than Nudger. Henry Mercato was that skilled and devious. Eileen, who was at the pinnacle of one of those barely legal home product pyramid sales scams and collected large commissions for doing nothing, needed the money not at all. But she hated Nudger and was motivated. And good at motivating Mercato.

But there was something about Adler. He was like Mercato in some ways. But then he wasn't. There was something else in the man, glowing like a fire beneath a lake. A kind of melancholy that hinted at vulnerability in someone in Adler's profession.

Nudger put down his plastic glass so hard that wine sloshed onto the table. "Damn it, I can't explain why, but even if he *is* a lawyer, I just don't want to hurt the guy."

Claudia smiled. "That's why he hired you, because you had a heart. What he didn't figure on was that you were such a marshmallow."

"Adler called me a romantic."

She studied him over the green neck of the bottle. "Well, I guess you're that, too. You're also a professional who was hired to do a job. Tell your client what you found out, Nudger. In this instance, revealing the truth is the kindest thing you can do for him, though maybe it won't seem that way at the time. Trust me, okay?"

He thought about it. He didn't usually trust people who urged him to do so, but he trusted Claudia. He said, "Okay, he gets the truth."

She smiled at him and he felt something flutter deep in his nervous stomach. Not unpleasantly, though. He reached out a hand and ran his fingertips over her cool wrist.

She said, "You don't have to tell him right away, do you?"

"I'm not meeting him until this evening."

"So there's time to spare for me," she said.

"Always." He meant it. Always.

She got up and walked around the table. The cold breeze from the air conditioner played over her as she passed the window, momentarily molding the thin material of her summer blouse to her lean torso, her teacup-sized breasts, the gentle curve of her waist and hip.

She sat on his lap and he kissed her.

"Adler was right about you," she said.

"That's why he's an ace criminal lawyer," Nudger said, "he has instincts about people."

Claudia didn't answer. She wasn't listening.

She didn't seem to be listening later when he asked her if he could come back tonight after reporting to Adler. He slept over with Claudia often, and tonight in particular he felt like it. Not for more sex. He knew he'd bleed along with Adler when the truth cut deep; he'd need company.

But Claudia was vague about telling him he could return. He suspected why.

He said, "Is it Biff Archway?" Archway was the soccer coach and taught sex education at the girls' high school where Claudia taught English. She'd been involved with him for a while, but supposedly that was over.

"Is what Biff Archway?" she replied, obviously irritated. "Did you see or hear something, Nudger?"

"Is Archway coming over here after I leave?"

"I don't think it's any of your concern."

"I think it is. I don't see how you can say it isn't."

"I told you there was nothing between us other than that we're on the same faculty. We have no choice but to see each other, to get along."

"Well," Nudger said.

"You should trust me. If Biff and I are alone together, you can be sure it's business."

"It's not that I don't trust you," Nudger said. "I don't trust Archway."

"You don't have to." She kissed him lightly on the cheek. "It's me you need to have faith in. I have faith in you."

Guilt, he thought. She knew how to work him.

He glanced at his wristwatch. He had to get moving if he was going to be on time to meet with Adler. He didn't want to leave, but he had no choice.

Claudia said, "Don't worry, Nudger. Really."

His stomach twitched. He couldn't remember a day in his life when he hadn't worried.

"Her name's Doris Vandervort," Nudger told Adler that evening at the counter in Danny's Donuts, downstairs from Nudger's office. He'd jumped right in there with the truth, though he knew it would cause pain.

They were having Dunker Delites and coffee and were the only customers. The shop was usually conducive to confidential conversations. Danny was in the back room boxing up cream horns to sell at a discount by the dozen before they went stale. Staler.

Gazing morosely into his terrible coffee, Adler said, "She didn't look the type." He lifted his half-eaten Dunker Delite, then plunked it down on its plate in disgust.

"She is, though. Security found her undressed in the room, pretending to be her accomplice's wife caught in the act with a lover. She'd managed to unlock the door so they could be interrupted. The mark would figure he'd forgotten or hadn't locked it all the way in his anticipation. The so-called husband graciously accepted money in return for not telling the conventioneer's co-workers and wife back in Tulsa about his indiscretion, and not naming him as correspondent in an alienation-of-affections suit. The woman pretended to help the mark talk the husband into that forgiving and profitable gesture."

"The badger game."

"That's what they call it."

"I thought she was on her way to work every morning when I saw her on the bus. I guess, in a way, she was."

"No," Nudger said, "she was actually coming home from her job as a waitress in an all-night restaurant. A couple of mornings a month, though, she wouldn't go home. She'd go to wherever she and her accomplice were planning to work the con."

"I'm not a criminal lawyer, Nudger. You think there's enough evidence to convict?"

"There would be if the guy she picked up would testify, but he won't. He still doesn't want his wife to find out about his indiscretion, so he'll decide not to bring charges. That's what makes it such a safe con game."

Adler absently prodded his Dunker Delite with a forefinger, as if checking for signs of life. "So she'll walk, after doing something like that."

"Not for a while. She can't make bail, and it'll take the mark a day or so to buckle and drop charges. He'll probably want to make the woman and her accomplice sweat for a few days."

"Still, she'll eventually walk."

"Some of your clients have done far worse and walked," Nudger pointed out. He wasn't sure how Adler was taking this, whether he was angry as well as disappointed. Love could be rough in the real world.

"Well, I wanted to know what she was," Adler said, "and now I do know." He used a paper napkin to wipe sugar from his fingers, then slid off the counter stool and hitched up his belt. It had a buckle that looked like real gold, in the shape of a dollar sign.

"You're not gonna finish your doughnut?"

"Are you kidding?"

"Not so loud. Danny's sensitive."

Adler buttoned his pin-striped suit coat, then extended his hand. "You got the job done, Nudger. Thanks."

"It didn't take long," Nudger said. "You've got a refund coming." He reminded himself to deduct the extra forty-seven dollars he'd needed to get his car back from the city after it had been towed from the No Parking zone.

Adler stared at Nudger appraisingly. "Dumb goes with honest almost without fail. I can't prove I gave you that thousand dollars, so keep it. I would, if I were you."

Nudger didn't argue with such ironclad logic. Did that prove he was more honest than dumb? Or vice versa?

He shook hands with Adler and watched him leave the doughnut shop and stride across Manchester to where his gleaming black Cadillac was parked. The man who'd believed in love and the electric instant. What was the blond woman to him, anyway? A reminder of some childhood imprint even he couldn't recall? Some long-buried Oedipal reflex? A nagging suggestion of something more exciting and satisfying than corporate law?

What was she?

Nudger had his own problems with the female of the species. He asked Danny for a glass of water, then sat at the counter sipping it as slowly as if it weren't free.

Danny walked over and leaned on the counter, took a few listless swipes at it with his gray towel. "You look like you got trouble, Nudge."

Nudger said, "Claudia."

Danny's docile, basset hound eyes rolled their pupils toward the door. "Where?"

"I mean, she's my problem," Nudger said.

"Oh. I thought you meant you seen her coming towards the shop. Crossing the street or something." Danny worked the towel again, moving a few crumbs around, then tucked it back in his belt. "She been going to that shrink again?"

Nudger knew Danny meant Dr. Oliver, Claudia's analyst. The doctor had once told her she should see other men as part of her process of self-actualization. That was when she'd taken up with Biff Archway the first time.

Archway irritated Nudger from the start, and not just because he became something of a romantic rival. The guy was average height but muscular, handsome in a jut-jawed, chesty sort of way. He looked like a former college football star who'd kept in shape and learned how to wear expensive clothes and could afford a spiffy car to impress the ladies. Nudger had checked on him. Archway turned out to be a former college football star who'd kept in shape and spent a large percentage of his schoolteacher pay on clothes and red sports cars. He'd also carried a 3.9 grade point average. He was easy to dislike even when he wasn't hanging around Claudia.

". . . shrink again?" Danny was saying.

"I don't think she's gone back to him," Nudger said.

Danny looked serious. "So is it that Archway bastard?"

"Maybe," Nudger said. "I think he might be going to Claudia's apartment tonight. She wouldn't tell me for sure one way or the other. She says if he is gonna be there, it'll be about the school and it's none of my business."

"*If* he is? She say those exact words, Nudge?"

"More or less." Nudger wondered what significance Danny saw in that.

"I was you," Danny said, "I'd drive on over there and see what was going on."

"Claudia warned me not to do that."

"Her saying so doesn't mean she really don't want you there, Nudge."

Nudger stared at Danny. Occasionally, with childlike clarity of vision, Danny could be very wise about certain matters. Intuitive if not logical. Nudger sensed this was one of those times.

"I don't follow you," he said, thinking he might glean some further insight from Danny. Some faint clue to the true nature of the universe.

Danny placed his blunt-fingered, flour-whitened hands on the counter and leaned toward Nudger. "I figure she might be testing you, Nudge."

"Testing me?"

"Seeing if you love her enough to go to her tonight and tell Archway to scram."

Nudger said, "That's absurd."

"No, no," Danny said, "women think that way sometimes."

"Not Claudia."

"Even Claudia."

"I wouldn't bet on it."

"But you *are* betting on it, Nudge, and the stakes are high." He nodded knowingly and pushed away from the counter, leaving two flour handprints on the stainless steel surface.

Nudger sat silently while Danny went back to his baking. What Danny had said was eating on him, along with his conversation with Adler. In some way it was all connected, and Nudger couldn't figure out how.

He walked around the counter and helped himself to a cup of Danny's sludgelike coffee from the huge, complex urn. It wasn't easy getting the stuff down, but he knew it would keep him awake. Alert. His stomach was kicking violently as he walked toward the door.

"Where you goin', Nudge?" Danny called from the door to the back room.

"Following your advice," Nudger said. "I'm going to see Claudia, whether or not she's alone."

"Good," Danny said, beaming and wiping his ghostly white hands on his apron. It obviously pleased him immensely to see Nudger acting on his suggestion. "It's the thing to do. You can't go wrong."

"I've thought that before and gone wrong."

"It'll work out this time," Danny assured him. "I got a kinda sixth sense about these things. Wanna take her some of yesterday's dough-nuts? That'll get you in tight. I'll pop 'em in the microwave and freshen 'em up if you want."

Nudger said, "I think not."

There was the sleek red convertible, Archway's, parked on Wilmington right in front of Claudia's apartment. Nudger knew it was Archway's car because there was a Stowe High School parking permit dangling from the rearview mirror.

Okay, Nudger told himself, driving around the block and trying to ignore what felt like a sharp-clawed hamster fight in his stomach, so Archway was there. With Claudia. She hadn't said that wasn't going to happen, just said that if it did, it would be strictly business. School business. Her business and none of his. She and Archway would be doing whatever teachers did when they got together professionally. Could be anything. Possibly they were discussing difficult students, discipline problems. Nudger remembered being one of those, but unintentionally, as he recalled. His teachers had been upset. Teachers could be sensitive. Maybe the faculty out at Stowe High School was going on strike.

Or maybe the school had too much money and the faculty was trying to figure out what on earth to do with it all.

The truth was that none of those possibilities seemed at all likely to Nudger. He was thinking of the way Claudia moved when she walked, the way she tossed her long dark hair to get it out of her eyes, the way she smelled.

He slammed on the brakes.

An old, stooped fellow wearing a Cardinals cap, watering his lawn even though it was almost dark out, glared at him as he steered the car into a driveway, then backed it out so it was turned around and headed back to Claudia's apartment and the parking space he'd seen across the street from Archway's sporty red convertible. Staring fiercely from beneath the bill of his red baseball cap, the old guy looked about to throw a wicked fastball at Nudger's head. But he merely lost momentary control of his hose, and its stream of water knocked over one of the two plastic flamingos flanking the steps to the porch.

Nudger knew he should keep on driving, turn the corner, and go home. But he didn't. Couldn't. He parked the Granada and climbed out, plucking his shirt away from where it was plastered to his back with perspiration. He stood still then and stared up at Claudia's apartment.

The lights were off up there.

Well, maybe she and Archway had gone somewhere in Claudia's car.

But there was Claudia's little blue Chevette parked down the block. Nudger recognized it by the dent in the front fender.

His stomach did fast loops.

Don't make an ass of yourself, he thought. Don't jump to conclusions.

But suspicion and jealousy had him like a drug. It was dusk, so it had to be almost dark in the apartment, and the lights were out. Under the circumstances, what would anybody think?

He walked down the block a short distance so he could make sure the dining room light was also out.

Darkness there, too.

So what were the options here? Nudger asked himself. He could go up and knock on Claudia's door, but if she and Archway were up to something, she'd hardly answer.

Or he could sneak upstairs and let himself in with his key, surprise them, and catch them doing . . . whatever they might be doing.

But he really didn't want that. He couldn't bear it if he happened to be right. And Claudia would never forgive him.

Still, he'd know where he stood, however painful the knowledge might be. He thought again of Adler, how the poor guy must have felt learning about Doris Vandervort, his brief but true love. What might passion turn into in a situation like that?

Go home, Nudger told himself. Go home and grow up.

He spun on his heel and was about to walk back to the Granada when he noticed the faint glow from the rear of the brick building. Up on the second floor.

He felt his skin actually crawl. Not very far, but it crawled. The rage in his acidic stomach rose in his throat.

The light had to be burning in Claudia's bedroom! And sometimes she liked leaving the lamp on when—

He swallowed bile and crossed the street, striding angrily toward the building. Then, as he stepped up on the curb, he slowed down.

He'd gained enough control of his anger to be devious.

Opening the street door slowly and carefully so it couldn't possibly be heard upstairs, he slipped into the vestibule. Then he took the stairs to the second floor with equal caution, keeping his feet spread wide and placing them near the wall and the banister so the wooden steps wouldn't creak.

He paused outside Claudia's apartment door. Pressed his ear to the cool enameled surface. Heard nothing.

Standing up straight, he hesitated. Should he do this?

His stomach told him he had no choice.

Slowly he slipped his key into the lock, turned it, then took a deep breath.

He threw open the door and leaped inside.

Only an instant was required for him to take in the scene: Claudia and Archway seated side by side on the sofa in the dim living room, their necks craned so they could stare at Nudger over their shoulders. Even in the dimness the surprise in their eyes was plainly visible. Some sort of machine was set up on a card table, a projector. And there was one of those home movie screens that lowered like a shade over a tripod. On the glowing screen was a young girl wearing only shorts and a flimsy gray tee shirt, running across a grassy field, her youthful bosom jiggling with each coltlike stride, her blond hair flying. What was the deal here? Archway and Claudia watching pornography! Suddenly another young girl appeared on the screen, large but muscular, with a malicious expression on her pug-nosed face. She smashed into the first girl, knocking her to the ground, then dashed out of camera range.

Archway, who'd turned back toward the screen, said, "That's definitely not allowed."

Claudia, still staring at Nudger, gave him the same kind of look the old guy in the Cardinals cap had aimed at him, as if the lawn flamingos were being threatened.

In a voice so calm it scared him, she said, "What's this all about, Nudger?"

"He thought he'd drop by and surprise us," Archway said, sounding amused. The creep had figured it out by the expression on Nudger's face. "You bring a bottle of wine, Nudger? Maybe a bouquet?"

Claudia, standing up now, fully dressed in slacks and a sleeveless blouse, said, "I'm going to substitute for Biff and coach the soccer team for a week while he goes on vacation. He was showing me film so I could understand the game."

Archway had switched on the lamp by the couch and was grinning. Handsome bastard, always at ease, his hair slicked back with some kind of grease you could fry an egg with. He wasn't starting to go bald on top like Nudger. "You think we were watching porno movies, Nudger? What a sick mind."

Nudger realized his mouth was hanging open. His rage had turned to humiliation. His stomach hurt.

"You've made a fool of yourself again," Claudia said.

"Maybe he doesn't believe your explanation," Archway said, trying to make trouble. "Maybe he knows something was going on between us."

" 'Knows'?" Nudger said.

Archway, standing next to Claudia now, slid his arm around her waist and said, "Poor choice of words, I guess."

Anger glowed in Claudia's dark eyes. "*Do* you believe me, Nudger?"

"Of course I do."

"Then get out."

"Wait a minute . . ." Nudger said. He wanted to arrange it so he could leave with a smidgeon of dignity. They should allow him that much.

But Archway saw his opening. He took two steps toward Nudger. "The lady said leave, chum."

"Chum?" Nudger said. "We're not chums."

"Don't be a problem, Nudger, please." Claudia, pleading now.

"He's on his way out," Archway said. "Put this jerk in the past, Claudia."

"He's not a jerk." Now she felt she had to defend him.

Anger and embarrassment pushed reason out of Nudger's mind. He planted his feet wide and crossed his arms. "I'm not leaving," he told Archway. "You are."

"Nudger! . . ." Claudia said.

"I'm not leaving you alone with this creep," he told her.

"I was fine until you arrived," she said. She clenched her fists and slapped them against her thighs. "You *are* a jerk!"

"So long, chum," Archway said, and advanced on Nudger in a crouch. Archway knew karate, or something like it; Nudger had learned that the hard way some time ago.

"You're the one leaving," he said, circling Archway.

Archway spun his body around and tried to kick Nudger in the chest. Did it, too. Nudger said, "Oooomph!" and went sprawling.

He scrambled to his feet immediately. "I said you were leaving," he told Archway, as if he'd been the one who'd landed the blow.

He stepped in and swung hard at Archway's grinning face. Missed clean and felt something slam into his forehead.

Must have been Archway's fist, he figured, from where he sat on the carpet.

Archway was smiling down at him. "Time to say night-night, Nudger."

Nudger struggled to his feet. Said, "Night-night," and swung at Archway again.

Saw a galaxy of stars and discovered he was lying on his back on the carpet. His jaw ached.

"Had enough," Archway asked, "or do you want a nightcap?"

Nudger heard himself groan. He rolled onto his stomach, raised himself to a low crouch, and ran at Archway.

It felt great when his shoulder crashed into Archway's midsection. Both men fell to the floor. Then Archway was on top of Nudger, landing punches to his head and shoulders. Nudger threw him off, tried to stand up and jump on him, but was tripped so that he crashed into the projector. It fell near him and stopped whirring. He thrashed around, tangled in its cord, and stood up just in time to be knocked back down by Archway, who at least wasn't smiling now. Nudger had mussed his hair.

"Both of you knock this stuff off!" Claudia was shouting. She was facing Archway, inches from his face. "Leave him alone, Biff. Go home, please!"

"Me?" Archway looked astounded. "You were telling him to go a minute ago. He's the one who sneaked in here like a terrorist commando. He's the one—"

"The one without sense enough to leave," Claudia interrupted.

"But I don't see why *I* should go."

"Because I asked you to," Claudia said. "Isn't that reason enough?"

"It's not reason enough for Nudger."

"You're not like Nudger. Thank God."

Archway stood for a minute or so with his chest heaving, trying to sort things out while he flexed his muscles. Putting on a show for Claudia, Nudger thought.

Finally he said, "I'll see you at school, Claudia."

"I'll bring the screen and projector," she told him.

Archway snatched up his plaid sport coat from where it was folded on a chair. "If any of that expensive visual equipment's broken, he's gonna pay for it!" he said, pointing at Nudger.

"My pleasure," Nudger said, rubbing it in.

Archway didn't say goodbye to either of them as he stormed out. Nudger heard him bluster down the stairs, then charge through the street door and let it swing wildly behind him until its pneumatic closer calmed it and eased it shut.

Nudger slumped on the sofa. Claudia had her fists on her hips and was staring down at him with anger, and with some other emotion.

She said, "You would have let him kill you before you'd leave us here alone together, wouldn't you, Nudger."

It wasn't posed as a question, but Nudger said, "Yes." And maybe he would have, he realized. It had been headed in that direction.

"Why?" Claudia asked.

"I don't know," Nudger said. It was something he'd have to think about.

"I know why," Claudia said. She sat down next to him and kissed him on the cheek, surprising him.

She kept surprising him.

*   *   *

A year passed before Nudger learned from Gideon Schiller, an attorney in Clayton he sometimes did work for, what had happened with Jake Adler after that night at the doughnut shop.

Adler had paid Doris Vandervort's bail, become her lover, then married her and left the law to own and operate a charter fishing boat down in Key West.

Nudger didn't know how to feel about that. It bothered him and he wasn't sure why. Finally he drove to Key West on vacation and accepted Adler's invitation to go deep-sea fishing.

It was a nice boat, about a thirty-footer. Doris was the crew. She didn't know who Nudger was and neither Nudger nor her husband told her. Nudger watched them together. The two of them seemed happy enough, he decided. In fact, very happy. Whatever romantic whimsy they had forged into reality here in the sun must agree with them.

Adler had put on weight and looked fit in his cutoff shorts and unbuttoned blue work shirt. And there was a new contentment in his once wary and calculating eyes as he familiarized Nudger with the heavy tackle for ocean fishing. Doris smiled a lot and bustled around the bobbing deck, now and then ducking below to ice drinks and work up the lunch that went with the cruise.

Nudger had never been deep-sea fishing, yet somehow an hour from shore he felt pressure on his line and reeled in an odd-looking brown fish about a foot long that flopped around listlessly on the deck. As if it didn't much care one way or the other about being caught.

He stared at it with distaste. "What is it?"

The tanned and content Adler smiled. "I have no idea. There are all kinds of unusual things in the sea. That's what makes it so interesting." He turned slightly so Doris couldn't see him and winked.

Doris popped the tab on a cold can of beer and handed it to Nudger. She grinned down at the fish, then at Nudger. "Gonna keep it? Have it mounted to hang over your fireplace?"

Nudger gave her back the grin. "Sure. Why not? I'll ask the taxidermist to make it look like it's leaping."

He didn't have a fireplace, but he didn't see where that made any difference.

So much of life was in the mind.

What can make you feel more helpless than to be caught in a situation over which you have absolutely no control? While Faye Kellerman's "Holy Water" deals with a kidnap victim, and Max Collins's "Inconvenience Store" a hostage situation, the principle involved is the same. In each story someone is trapped and helpless—or are they?

MAX ALLAN COLLINS

Max Allan Collins has written five novels about Chicago P.I. Nathan Heller. The first, *True Detective*, won the Shamus Award for Best Novel, and the subsequent four books were all Shamus nominees. In 1992 his Heller short story "Dying in the Post War World" was awarded the Shamus for Best Short Story.

In addition to Nathan Heller he is also the creator—along with his partner, cartoonist Terry Beatty—of female P.I. Ms. Tree. While most of Ms. Tree's cases have taken place within the pages of a comic book, she makes an occasional appearance in prose form. "Louise," from *Deadly Allies*, was nominated for an Edgar Award.

He has also written four novels featuring that legendary Untouchable, Eliot Ness. The most recent was *Murder by the Numbers*.

In "Inconvenience Store," Ms. Tree demonstrates that it takes a lot more than being pregnant to take her out of the action.

INCONVENIENCE STORE

A MS. TREE STORY

My pregnancy was pretty much uneventful, with the exception of the hostage situation.

I was in my seventh month and still going in to my office in the Loop—Tree Investigations, Inc.—and had been working more like the CEO I was supposed to be, rather than field agent I preferred to be.

"You know, Michael," Dan Green said, one hand leaning against my desk, "you don't have to be here. You can go home and relax . . . put your feet up . . ."

"Not without help," I said, smiling a little.

Dan, a slender handsome blond in his late twenties, had a hook for his left hand and one of his eyes was glass—souvenirs of a dispute with the crime family responsible for the death of my husband, whose name was also Michael Tree. When Mike died and I took over the agency, I didn't even have to change the lettering on the office door.

"I may be big as a horse," I said, "but I feel great. It's this desk work that's getting me down . . . all this damn peace and quiet."

Dan's slightly scarred face broke into a grin and he shook his head, saying, "You're incorrigible."

"Did you scope out the Bandag account?"

He nodded. "It's a plum. We can subcontract the day-to-day security and still get rich off the deal."

"What does Roger think?"

Roger Freemont was the third partner in Tree Investigations. My late husband's partner on the force, Roger—balding, brawny, bespectacled, pushing fifty—was the company conservative, our voice of reason.

"I think," Roger said, sticking his shiny head in my door, "we should add staff. Hell with subcontracting. Let's make *all* the money."

"Spoken like a true Republican," Dan said.

"When do we have to give Bandag our bid?" I asked.

"Monday."

It was Friday.

"You want to hit the computer over the weekend, Roger," I asked, "and make some money comparisons?"

"Sure," he said, sounding almost eager.

"You *are* a Republican," Dan smirked.

"Do it, then," I said. It was four-thirty. "Me, I'm going home . . . well, first I'm going to *pee* and then I'm going home."

"Thanks for sharing," Roger said.

I bid a pleasant weekend to my secretary Effie and to our receptionist Diane, walking through our modern glass-and-ferns office area on surprisingly springy steps. I may have looked as if I was trying to smuggle a marijuana-stuffed beach ball across the border, but I felt lighter than air.

That evening, in the masculine-looking apartment that had been my husband's, as I sat on the couch watching a rental video of *Basic Instinct*, wondering how anything could be so supremely stupid, chewing on the crust of a Tombstone pizza courtesy of my microwave, I felt an ache in the small of my back (and my back was the only part of me that was small, these days) that might have been a bullet.

"You need exercise, lady," I said to myself (not to Sharon Stone, who was changing her clothes for the umpteenth time on the TV screen), and hauled my butt off the cushions, and stood and held my back with my hands. And groaned.

I glanced toward a window. It was a cool fall evening out there; even with my baggy woolen blue sweater and stretch pants, I'd need a jacket. I ran a brush through the mop of my brunette hair, and had lipstick poised for application when I sneered at myself in the mirror, slung my purse on its strap over my shoulder, and said, "Fuck it."

When my late husband moved into this side-street two-room flat a dozen years ago, Lakeview was a blue-collar neighborhood; now it was Yuppies and gays—safe, as Chicago neighborhoods go. Last year there were only nine murders.

Nonetheless, I was, of course, packing. I'm always reading that "real-life private eyes" don't really carry a weapon. Considering that the mob murdered my husband ten years ago, and that I've lived through perhaps half a dozen attempts on my own life, I'm content to be armed and imaginary.

If you're wondering how I could be pregnant when my husband died a decade ago, I assure you the conception was not immaculate. Suffice to say an old flame flared up, some satisfying if unsafe sex followed, but the relationship didn't last. At an age closer to forty than thirty, however, my biological clock ticking like a time bomb, I decided to keep the child. Ultrasound said a girl was on the way.

The cool breeze whispering through the trees lining the narrow parked-car-choked street was soothing, and Friday night or not, the world seemed deserted. It was just after ten, and too late for people to be leaving, and too early for them to be getting home. I walked quickly, getting the spring back in my step, and the kink out of my low back.

Then I had to pee.

It was closer to walk to the Ashland Mini-Mart than back home. Besides, I could use some of Jon's baklava and maybe a can of sardines. Yeah—that sounded *great* . . .

A corner storefront on Ashland and an east-west side street, the mini-mart was evenly divided between groceries (including fresh fruits and vegetables—typical for Greek proprietors) and liquor. Three of their four coolers were beer and wine.

The well-lighted mart didn't have the modern look of a 7-Eleven; the floor was waxy wooden slats, the ceiling high with rococo trim. You could still squint and imagine the mom-and-pop corner grocery this had been in the 1950s.

"Hey, Ms. Tree," Jon's son Peter said; the dark young skinny handsome kid, in his early twenties, white shirt, black pants, frequently took the all-night shift in this family business. "Pop'll be sorry he missed you. You come for your baklava and sardines fix again?"

"You bet. But can I use your employees-only john? If not, the world's gonna think my water broke."

He grinned and shook his head. "You're a riot, Ms. Tree. Go for it—you know where it is."

I walked back around the counter, saying, "Busy night?"

"So-so. Friday, you always sell plenty of beer and wine coolers. And *lots* of lottery tickets. Payday, and everybody wants that ten-million jack-pot."

"Me too. I never buy lottery tickets, but I figure my odds of winning are about the same."

Then I pushed through the swinging stockroom door and shut myself in the bathroom—the lock was broken, but niceties were not a priority—and enjoyed my twelfth or maybe twentieth urination of the day. Impending motherhood is such a spiritual, uplifting experience.

I was still sitting there when the door opened and I looked up, startled, to see my wide-eyed expression reflected in the shiny badge of a potbellied blue-uniformed policeman. His metallic name tag said HAL-LORAN.

"Sorry, lady," he said, and flashed a pleasant if yellow grin, and shut the door.

A minute or so later, I eased the door open and he was standing right there, staring right in my face—a patrolman in his fifties with the yellow-white hair and red-splotchy complexion of an aging Irish beat cop.

He backed up a step, chuckled gruffly. "Hey, I'm awful sorry. Didn't mean to embarrass you, mother."

"You did give me a start, officer."

He touched his generous belly. "Overanxious. Got me a bad case of the trots."

As he was closing himself inside the john, trots or not, Halloran paused to ask, "When's the little one due?"

"Couple months."

"God bless you both. Shit!" He clutched his belly, shut the door, and, presumably, was as good as his word.

I smiled, shook my head, and coming around the counter asked Peter why he hadn't told the cop the john was in use.

"I was busy with a customer," Peter said, and indeed a guy in a down-filled jacket and plaid hunter's cap was hunkered over the counter, scratching his lottery tickets with the edge of a quarter. "Cops around here don't bother asking—they just go around and help themselves."

"No harm done," I muttered, and headed down one of the four aisles to find my can of sardines.

I was plucking it off the shelf when a harried woman of thirty or so in a tan London Fog raincoat and heels rushed in with a young girl of perhaps seven at her side in a tutu, white leggings, and Reeboks, a light jacket over the girl's shoulders. The mother's heels clicked as she went over to a cooler for some milk. The child, blonde, stood looking at my pregnancy with wide prairie-sky blue eyes in the midst of an angelic countenance.

"You're going to be a mommy," the little girl said.

"That's right, honey. Recital?"

She nodded. "I'm a ballerina."

The mother, with a jug of 2 percent milk in hand, was at the counter, speaking to Peter, crossly, even though Peter was in the process of paying off an instant win to the guy in the plaid hat.

"No butter? No eggs?"

"We're out of both, ma'am. Till Monday."

"That's ridiculous! How am I supposed to make breakfast in the morning? Do you have any breakfast rolls?"

The guy in the plaid cap was giving the five bucks he'd won back to Peter in exchange for five more tickets.

"No, and we're out of bread, too. There's some muffin mix in aisle two."

"How do I make that without eggs? You oughta call this an *in*convenience store!"

I was at the counter now, with my can of sardines; the woman was between me and the plastic-lidded tray of baklava.

"There's a big mini-mart on Southport," I said. "They have everything."

She glanced over her shoulder at me and pursed her lips in contempt; she was blonde but not as pretty as her daughter—not frowning, anyway. "That's out of my way, thank you very much."

I shrugged. "You're welcome."

"Mommy!" the little girl called, from a nearby aisle. "They have Pop-Tarts! Let's have Pop-Tarts for breakfast."

Her mother sighed. "Amy, put those down."

Amy, delighted with her Pop-Tart discovery (Strawberry), twirled in the aisle, a ballerina in Reeboks. "No, Mommy, I love Pop-Tarts! Let's have Pop-Tarts!"

The mother joined the daughter and began scolding her, though the little girl didn't seem to be paying much attention. Nor did she seem to be putting the Pop-Tarts back.

Peter grinned, teeth white in his dark face; he was a handsome devil. "Two baklava tonight, Ms. Tree?"

The guy in the hunter's cap sighed—none of his five lottery tickets had been worth ten million dollars, or five dollars, either. He trudged out wearily.

"Just one," I said, lifting the lid, helping myself to one of the pastries in its paper shell. "Don't want me to get fat now, do you?"

Peter laughed and handed me a small brown paper sack, which I was placing the baklava in when two white boys in ski masks came in, one of them holding a garbage bag open, the other waving a big revolver.

"All your money in the bag, greaseball," the one with the revolver said to Peter.

"Now!" added the other one.

They were skinny, wearing Cubs jackets over heavy metal T-shirts; they had on worn, torn jeans, and Nike pumps that looked like space-man shoes. The one with the gun was taller—or maybe the gun just made him seem taller.

"Take it easy," Peter said, as he opened his register.

"We'll take it easy, all right!" the one holding the bag said, horse-laughing at his own remarkable wit. His voice was thin, whiny.

I thought about the gun inside the purse over my shoulder, but then I thought about the mother and her daughter a few feet away, and I thought about the child in my belly, and I just stood there while Peter piled cash on the counter and the shorter of the pair used his whole arm to push it into the garbage bag.

Then I heard the sound of a flushing toilet and thought, *Oh shit*, but Halloran was pushing the stockroom door open and coming out and the smile on his mottled Irish face had only barely dissolved into a scowl when the three bullets slammed into his blue shirt and sent him back through the swinging door, on his back.

"You fuckin' killed him, man!" the one holding the bag said.

"Shit," the one with the smoking gun said.

The other one dropped the garbage bag to the slatted-wood floor, where money spilled as easily as blood just had, and he pulled a small nickel-plated revolver out of his waistband; he held it in an unsteady fist.

"A cop," he said, brandishing the gun at his taller partner. "You fuckin' killed a fuckin' cop!"

The swinging door waved at us halfheartedly; it was only a three-quarter affair, with space at top, and bottom, with Halloran's dead feet sticking out below.

The two faced each other, guns in hand. For a moment I thought they were going to save society the trouble; then movement behind him caught the corner of the taller one's eye.

"Jesus!" he said, turning, and he fired again, at a blue shape at the door of the mini-mart, and glass made brittle thunder as it shattered and rained to the pavement, and somebody out there yelled, "Judas Priest!"

and Peter ducked down behind his counter, and I did the same on the other side, and the ski-masked pair took cover in an aisle.

Cool evening air and street sounds rushed in from where the glass of the door used to be.

"Who the hell was that?" the smaller one said, as they cowered in the aisle next to where I crouched.

"Must be the dead pig's partner! Shit . . . ."

My fingers unclasped my handbag. To my left, down the next aisle, the mother and her little ballerina cowered together, sitting half-sprawled on the wood floor, the mother looking nearer tears and hysteria than the oddly placid little girl.

From outside a gruff male voice yelled: "Throw out your guns! Walk out slow—hands high!"

"It *is* another cop—what do we do?" the smaller one asked desperately.

"Grab that pregnant bitch!" the taller one said.

The little guy came at me, fast, and I pushed my purse behind the ILLINOIS LOTTERY sign on Peter's counter, back down behind which Peter was looking up with wide-eyed terror.

A gun was in my back and the smaller guy was behind me, as if hiding there; he had room. Still hunkered down in the aisle, his partner yelled out, "We got *people* in here!"

"We got *police* out here!" the gruff voice shouted.

I could see, through the window, between neon beer signs and home-made butcher-paper sale signs, the head of the cop bobbing up behind a car he was using as a barrier; a glint winked off his revolver, as it caught streetlights. Sirens were faint cries that were turning into screams; Halloran's partner would not be alone long.

The little one pulled me by the arm into the aisle with his partner, and down, into a crouching position. I almost fell, but managed to keep my balance.

"Why the fuck did that other cop take so long to come in? If they're partners . . . *Jesus!*" The taller one remained hunkered down, the gun in his hand steadier than that in his pal's.

Peter's voice, as if a ventriloquist's, came from behind the counter: "They always park in the alley but usually come in together. I don't know why he dropped Halloran off first."

"He had the trots," I said.

"What?" the little guy behind me asked, as if surprised I could talk.

"The runs. Diarrhea."

"Ain't that the shits," the hunkered-down leader said, with no irony. Then thought glimmered in his eyes. "Go check the back, Bud."

"I thought you said no *names*, Frank," Bud said contemptuously. "*Duh!*"

Frank pulled off his ski mask; he was hatchet-faced, pockmarked, with dead gray eyes and wheat-color hair that covered his ears.

"They got us pinned in here," Frank said glumly. "We're gonna have a hostage situation soon. They'll know who we are, all right."

"I told *you* we shoulda stole a car," Bud said, shaking his head even as he pulled off his ski mask.

He was round-faced, an odd shape to top such a skinny frame. His head was almost shaved—black five o'clock shadow covering his skull, skinhead style. His acne hadn't turned to pockmarks yet, and his brown eyes were alive, in a stupid sort of way, under heavy eyebrows.

They were kids—just kids, maybe seventeen, eighteen at most. But for street kids, into drugs, as I assumed they were, that was plenty old. Ancient, in some circles.

Frank pointed his gun at Bud, gesturing as if it were a finger. "Check out the back door. If it looks clear, maybe we can make a break for it, 'fore those other cops get dug in."

The loudness of the sirens made that unlikely, but Bud scrambled off to the back room, pushing open the door, stepping around Halloran; then the door swung shut, swaying as Halloran's feet disappeared, Bud pulling him out of the way.

"You left your car running?" I asked Frank. "Out front?"

"Yeah," Frank said, wincing with irritation. Hostages weren't supposed to talk: They were supposed to be quiet and scared.

I said, "You thought it'd still be waiting for you? In Chicago?"

"We left it locked."

"You left your car out front, locked, with the motor running? No wonder you gave up on keeping your identities from the cops."

"Shut up, lady."

"Can I sit?"

"Huh?"

"Can I sit? Pregnant women can't crouch long, you know."

"Sit. Sit! And shut the fuck up!"

I sat, my swollen, stretch-pants-covered legs angling out before me as if I was inviting somebody to make a wish. I could hear whimpering in the adjacent aisle, but I couldn't tell if it was the mother or the little ballerina. My purse, nestled behind the ILLINOIS LOTTERY display, beckoned me; but I couldn't come.

Two explosions echoed from the back room—gunshots—followed by a clanging sound, and Bud saying "Shit!" again and again, at varying volumes, with varying inflections.

Frank sat up, neck straining like a turtle having a look around; the sound of scraping, wood against concrete, sang from the back room.

Cueball Bud came running out, saying, "Cops back there already!"

And, eyes wild in his round face, he crawled on his hands and knees over to join his partner and me in the nearby aisle, the shiny little revolver in one hand, like a child's toy.

"Cops everywhere," he said breathlessly.

"Can they get in?"

"No. Windows are barred back there and the door's steel; I bolted it up, and blocked it with some crates just to make sure. They ain't gettin' in."

"Like you're not getting out," I said.

Round-faced Bud looked at me, astounded. "Who the fuck asked you, fatso?"

I shrugged. "Just thought you better face facts."

Hatchet-faced Frank said, "Such as?"

"Such as you're in the midst of a full-blown hostage crisis." I leaned out in the aisle, nodded toward the street, where the blue revolving lights of several cop cars cut surrealistic paths in the night, and a big Winnebago-style vehicle was rolling in. "Take a look."

Frank and Bud glanced above a row of cornflakes boxes to have a peek. "What the hell's that?" Frank asked.

"That," I said, "is a Mobile Command Unit. Before long they'll be calling you on the phone from there—to start negotiations."

"Negotiations," Bud said stupidly, eyes tight.

I nodded. "So you fellas better decide what you want."

"I just want outa here, Frank!" Bud said.

"It's not that simple," I said.

"What do you know, you fat cow!" Bud shouted, waving his shiny gun at me.

"Play your cards right," I said, "you can trade us for your freedom."

"She's right," Frank said thoughtfully.

"Well, I'm sicka hearin' her voice!" Bud said.

Frank thought about that, too, but his expression turned darker. "You know . . . me, too. Get up and go into the next aisle, mommy—keep that brat and her old lady company."

"You mind if I take a bathroom break first?" I asked.

"You gotta be kidding," Frank said.

"I'm pregnant. I pee a lot. Excuse me for living."

"I can do somethin' about that," Bud said with a sneer.

I smirked, then gestured with two open hands. "What say, boys? To pee or not to pee? That is the question."

They just looked at me stupidly. I'm so frequently too hip for the room.

"Go ahead," Frank said.

"But keep your fat ass away from that back door!" Bud blurted. "If I hear ya movin' those crates, I'll put a bullet in that belly and kill the both of you!"

I hauled myself up. "And here I was thinking of asking you to be the godfather."

In the back room, I could see that the pile of crates and boxes blocking the door were indeed something I couldn't move without getting caught at it—even if I hadn't been pregnant. Kneeling, I checked Halloran; he was dead, all right—on his back, an angled smeary stripe of red on the concrete indicating how he'd been dragged. Three bloody scorched wounds on his chest, poor bastard—I closed his eyes for him. Wished him Godspeed. His holster was empty; apparently Bud had taken Halloran's piece, though I hadn't noticed him having it—probably stuck under his Cubby coat. The officer's nightstick, however, was still there. I plucked it from his belt, took it with me into the bathroom, where I again urinated (I hadn't been lying about the need), even as I stuck the baton up my sweater sleeve, holding its tip in the heel of my hand.

Peter was sitting behind the counter; he gave me a pitiful look, and I whispered from the doorway, "Don't you have a gun back there?"

And he shook his head no, looking ashamed.

He shouldn't have, really: Half the merchants who trade shots with stickup men wind up dead. A fascinating statistic that didn't mean diddly right now.

I came out of the back room, and around the counter; near the LOTTERY sign, where my purse was tucked, I paused. Frank noticed me.

"Get back over in that other aisle," he said, "and keep your big fat trap *shut*."

I shrugged a response and left my purse where it was. Just didn't want to take the chance.

I joined the mother in their aisle; it smelled of chemicals there and I glanced at the shelves and smiled. Then I sat next to the woman, who was huddled with her daughter, who clung to her mutely. The mother's eyes were brimming with tears. She was stroking her daughter's hair.

I sat. Legs stretched out before me.

The woman whispered harshly. "How can you talk to them?"

I shrugged.

"Just leave them alone!" the woman whispered. "Don't say anything to them—you just make them mad!"

Frank's voice called, "Shut up over there!"

As if in response, a grating loud voice, courtesy of a bullhorn, said, *"Send the people out!"*

"Fuck you!" Bud called.

I withdrew the late Halloran's nightstick from my sweater sleeve. The mother looked at me, and it, startled.

"What are you . . ."

I shushed her with a finger to my lips as I placed the baton on a shelf behind me, amid some bathroom supplies.

The bullhorn was barking: *"You boys are going to have a world of trouble if you harm those people. Now, send them out, slowly . . ."*

Frank didn't bother to reply. But to Bud he said, bitterly, "World of trouble. We shot a cop. How the fuck can you get in more trouble than that?"

"You shot a cop," Bud reminded him.

"You're as dirty as me. Felony murder. We'll both go down."

"You gotta deal us outa here, Frank!"

I lifted a bottle of liquid drain cleaner off the shelf. Read the directions; savored the poetry of its warnings . . . "poison" . . . "burns on contact" . . . "harmful to eyes" . . .

The woman touched my arm; squeezed hard. She looked at me with wet, hard eyes and shook her head *no*, furiously.

"Don't you risk my child's life," she whispered.

"I have a child at stake, too," I whispered back.

"I said, *shut up* over there!" Frank almost screamed.

The phone rang and everybody jumped. Me, too. Even Peter—I saw his head bob up.

On his hands and knees, the big revolver in hand, Frank scrambled over behind the counter, as the phone rang and rang, and he plucked the receiver off and was down behind the counter, where Peter was, as he answered.

"How many? I'll you how many. We got a greaseball clerk, a mommy and her little girl, and a pregnant woman. How do you *like* our little party?"

I unscrewed the cap of the liquid drain cleaner; sniffed its harsh bouquet . . .

"What do we *want?* We want a jet! We want a car, and a police escort to O'Hare . . ."

I could guarantee them the police escort.

". . . and then we want the biggest goddamn jet they got! . . . Where?" Frank paused, apparently thinking, then his voice called to Bud: "Where do *you* want to go?"

Bud seemed to think for a while, then his voice called: "Vegas?"

"You moron! Somewhere foreign! Some *other* country!"

"Alaska?"

I would have laughed, except the frozen little ballerina whose head was in her mother's lap was looking at me with eyes that could not widen enough to express her fear.

Frank was saying into the phone, "Never mind where. Just have plenty of fuckin' fuel on board. We'll tell the pilot where to take us . . . and we want money, too! . . . How *much?"*

Frank, despite the lousy luck of his last attempt, called out to Bud for an opinion. "How much dough should we ask for?"

Bud didn't hesitate; he knew just the amount. "Ten million bucks!"

"Get real," Frank snorted. Back on the phone, he said, "A million in cash. Small unmarked bills—nothin' bigger than a fifty."

Shrewd boy, this Frank.

"Okay," he was saying. "Call back when you got an answer for me."

Frank's hand reached up and slammed the receiver on the hook.

I figured drugs were why this skinny pair was after the money—all but forgotten in the garbage bag, bills spilled out on the floor over by the counter, like discarded lottery winnings. But like a lot of addicts, for whom stealing was a job, they had apparently planned ahead, not waiting till they needed a fix, not wanting to go out on a heist in that condition.

Still, sometimes it pays to needle a junkie.

"You boys might be here awhile," I said to Frank as he crawled by. "Lining up that jet's gonna take time. Getting the mayor to approve all that dough—and hauling some banker out of his country club dance to unlock a vault. We could be here for hours."

Bud, from the next aisle, said, "Frank—I'm gonna need a shot before that!"

"Shut up, Bud," Frank said; but he was frozen on his hands and knees, looking at me, thinking over what I said. "You got a point, lady?"

"Frank!" Bud yelled. "We can't wait that long. I'm gonna need a shot! Ask for less money. Get fifty k or something."

"Shut up! Lady—what's your fuckin' point?"

"Let this mother and her daughter go," I said. "It'll buy you some good will, and show the authorities you're reasonable guys. Besides . . . you got me—a pregnant woman—what better hostage could you ask for? Nobody's going to shoot at you guys if you're walking behind a pregnant woman."

Frank's eyes were turning to slits as he smiled. "You could be right about that last part. I don't know about giving up no hostages, though . . ."

"You'll have the cashier," I said, nodding toward the counter, where my purse sat, a million miles away, "and me. One hostage for you, one for your friend. You can take us with you in the car to O'Hare—which you can't do with Mommy and her ballerina here. Let 'em go. You'll be popular."

"Don't listen to her, Frank!" Bud whined. "I don't trust her!"

Frank was studying me, like a lab tech studying a slide. "Who *are* you, lady? Why do you know so much? Why are you so fuckin' chilled out?"

I shrugged. "My late husband was a cop."

That seemed to satisfy him.

"Let the mother and her kid go," I said. "You don't need them. You didn't mean for this to happen, did you, Frank? This is just something that got out of hand . . . let 'em go."

Bud was sticking his head around the aisle to watch this conversation. He was on the floor on his stomach. He looked like a bug with a big head.

He said, "Don't do it, Frank."

Frank was thinking it over. Something had flickered in his eyes— traces of humanity, maybe?—as I'd spoken. Was he looking past me at the woman hugging her child? Was there something human or humane in this lost teenager's white-trash past?

He swallowed and said, "She's right."

"Frank . . ."

"Shut the fuck up, Bud. There's only two of us . . . we can manage better with just her and the guy back of the counter."

"O . . . okay, Frank," Bud said, half sticking out in the aisle on his belly. "But let's shake it . . . I'm gonna need a fuckin' shot before long!"

Bud did seem to be getting the shakes, and it wasn't fear alone. The little hophead, by his own admission, slammed his drugs—injected them —as opposed to smoking or snorting, which meant time was going to catch up with him.

Suddenly Frank yelled; it startled the mother, and the child, and me, too. Peter probably peed his pants.

"Hold your fire!" Frank was calling to the cops outside. "We're sendin' out some hostages!"

Frank crawled back around the counter, so he could get a better vantage point I guess—and it did give him an angle where the cops outside couldn't see him, or get a bead on him—and he said to the mother, "Okay, you and your little girl get up and walk out. Real slow."

The mother allowed herself the briefest smile, and glanced at me with an expression that might have been of thanks, as she helped her child up. She could spare me any gratitude, now or later: I hadn't done this for her.

The little ballerina hung on to her mother's waist as they slowly walked out of the aisle and past the counter where Frank held a gun on them. They walked by the aisle where Bud was taking cover, up to the front of the mini-mart where the mother gingerly opened the metal framework of the shot-out glass door and they were outside.

With a sigh of relief, I watched from my aisle, where I sat leaning back against the shelf of bathroom supplies; I could see the mother and daughter as two cops rushed to help them past the parked cars toward the street filled with squads, moving them toward the Winnebago command center.

"That was the right thing to do," I told Frank.

"Shut up," he said, and he moved out from around the counter.

As he walked past me, I hurled Halloran's nightstick under his feet, and Frank's Nikes hit the baton and he did a crazy, logrolling dance, and as the kid was twisting around, I splashed the liquid drain cleaner in his face and he screamed and I splashed it again and he screamed again.

"Frank!" Bud yelled. "Jesus, Frank!"

He landed hard, on his back, his hands clawing his face and eyes, the big revolver dropping to the slick wood floor and spinning, like a top, till it came to a rest at my feet. I scooped it up, as Frank continued to scream and Bud yelled incoherently.

Before the little hophead could get his wits about him, I came around the other side, up the other end of the aisle, behind him, where he continued to crouch and cower, the nickel-plated revolver in hand, watching his pal wriggle and writhe like an insect under a pin.

Bud's incoherent yelling stopped when I put the nose of Frank's revolver in the back of his stubbly head and told him to stand up.

"You bitch! What did you do to Frank?"

Frank was still screaming.

"Cleaned his drain." I reached my left hand past his left ear; held the hand open, palm up. "Let's have the gun, Bud. Give it to mommy . . ."

He placed the shiny revolver in my palm; swore at me some more.

"March up by the counter. By where your friend Frank is. By the way, we ought to hurry—if he doesn't get some first aid soon, he's going to need a cane and a guide dog."

"You're evil!"

"I guess you'd know. Move it."

He did.

The phone was ringing. The cops were wondering what was going on in here; through the neon beer-ad and butcher-paper sign-cluttered window, vision was only so-so.

"Get that, would you, Peter?" I asked.

Peter's dark face with its wide eyes peered over the edge and the fingers of both hands were pressed against the countertop. He looked like Kilroy Was Here.

"Stand up," I said. "Situation's under control."

I placed Bud's shiny nickel-plated revolver on the counter. Frank was on the floor, on his side, in fetal position, his hands covering his face, and he wasn't screaming now, whimpering instead, saying something about "burning." Bud was standing next to him, looking down like he wished he could help.

Peter, who had answered the phone, covered the receiver and said to me, "They want to know what's going on."

"Tell them to come in and see for themselves," I said, and then I thought about the reporters who'd soon be swarming, and I was rustling around in my purse for my lipstick when Bud pulled Halloran's gun out from under his Cubs jacket.

"I'm going to kill you, you fat bitch," the round-faced little junkie said, his saliva making a mist in the air.

I shot him through the bottom of my handbag and the top of his head.

He flew back, flopping next to Frank, leaving a mist of blood this time, and his body made a squishing sound when he landed on the brain matter he'd spilled. They were both on their backs, but Frank didn't seem to notice the company. He was busy.

The garbage bag of spilled money was nearby—a cheap irony, but it couldn't be helped.

Peter's mouth had dropped open.

I shrugged. "He said he needed a shot."

* * *

One of the first cops on the scene, in the aftermath, was Lieutenant Valer, a thirty-something black good-looking homicide detective I'd known for years.

"How did you manage to be here when all this happened?" he asked. His smile was a wry dimple in one cheek.

"Baby needs baklava," I said, and put two in my little paper sack. Not to mention sardines.

Peter wasn't behind the counter anymore; he'd gone somewhere to have a minor nervous breakdown, I guess. I thought about leaving him some money for the pastries, then decided I'd earned them.

"Excuse me a moment, Rafe? I have to use the john."

Halloran's body had already been moved; lab techs were at work back there.

"You aren't going to touch anything, are you?" one of them said, a snotty redheaded woman in her twenties.

"Well, I might," I said, and closed myself in the john.

When I came out from the back room, Rafe said, "That punk . . . Frank? . . . he's going to be all right. Suffered some burns, but his eyesight won't be permanently affected."

"Swell," I said.

"Those two got rap sheets from here to Wilmette. But they're just kids. Both of 'em under eighteen."

"Pity."

His smile disappeared; his eyes narrowed judgmentally. "You don't care? It doesn't bother you, killing a kid like that?"

"He was pointing a murdered cop's gun at me, Rafe. What would you have done? Burp him?"

He sighed. "You got a point. But you better brace yourself—you're going to take some heat."

I laughed. "It's not politically correct for a hostage to fight back?"

Rafe's wry dimple reappeared in the other cheek. "You're not the average hostage. This won't be the first time you've made the papers."

"It won't be the last, either."

"Yeah?"

"Watch the birth announcements," I said, and took my bag of baklava, and sardines, and walked home.

AUTHOR'S NOTE

I would like to thank the co-creator of MS. TREE, artist Terry Beatty, for the use of our comic-book character in this short story; and Chantal d'Aulnis of DC Comics for granting permission. MS. TREE is a trademark of DC Comics, Inc.

FAYE KELLERMAN

Faye Kellerman, DDS, describes herself as a harried mother who lives in Los Angeles with her husband, novelist Jonathan Kellerman, four children, two dogs, four parakeets, numerous fish, and her newest addition, a homicidal hamster named Charles Manson.

People magazine has proclaimed of her characters: "Peter Decker and Rina Lazarus are, hands down, the most refreshing mystery couple around." And the *Baltimore Sun* has described Faye Kellerman's popular series as "Partly police procedural, partly instruction in Orthodox Jewish practice."

In "Holy Water," Faye Kellerman gives us the lighter side of kidnapping, or in this case rabbi-napping, with a rabbi who—gently—confounds and instructs his captors.

HOLY WATER

Until he felt the gun in his back, Rabbi Feinermann thought it was a joke: somebody's idea of a silly pre-Purim schtick. After all, the men who flanked him wore costume masks. The Marx fellows—Groucho and Karl. Two old Jewish troublemakers, but at least one of them had been funny. The revelers spoke in such trite dialogue it had to be a hoax.

"Don't move, old man, and you won't get hurt."

Although he was fasting, Feinermann was always one to join in the festivities, though this prank was on the early side. So he played along, adjusting his hat, then holding up his hands.

"Don't shoot," Feinermann said. "I'll give you my *humantash*. I'll even give you a shot of schnapps. But first, my two Marxes, we must wait until we've heard the reading of the Megilla—the scroll of Esther. Then we may break our fasts."

Then as he tried to turn around, Groucho held him tightly, kept him facing forward, pressing his arm uncomfortably into his back. At that moment, Feinermann felt the gun. Had he seen it when the two masked men made their initial approach? Maybe. But to Feinermann's naive eyes, the pistol seemed like a toy.

"We're not fooling around here, Rabbi," Karl said.

Feinermann looked around the synagogue's parking lot. It was located in the back alley on a little used dead-end side street. He was alone with these hoodlums, but he had grown up in New York. Hoodlums were nothing new. Although the masks were a little different. In his day, a stocking over the face was sufficient—a ski mask if you wanted to get fancy.

But times change.

The old man had grown up in neighborhoods where ethnic groups competed for turf—the Irish, the Italians, then later on, the Puerto Ricans. Each nationality fighting to prove who was the mightiest. Of course, they all tormented the Jews. Pious old men and women had been no match for angry energy and youthful indignation.

No, hoodlums were nothing new. But the gun in the back was a sad concession to modern times. Had mankind really progressed, the Rabbi mused.

"Come on, Rabbi," Karl said. "Don't make this difficult on us or on yourself. I want you to walk slowly to the gray car straight ahead."

"Which car do you mean, Mr. Marx?" Feinermann asked. "The eighty-four Electra?"

"The ninety Seville," Groucho answered.

"Oooo, a Cadillac," Feinermann said. "A good car for abduction. May I ask what this is all about?"

"Just shut up and get going," Karl said.

"No need for a sharp tongue, Mr. Marx," the Rabbi answered.

Karl said, "Why do you keep calling me Marx?" He pointed to Groucho. *"He's* the Marx guy."

"Your mask is Karl Marx," Feinermann said.

"No it's not," Karl protested. "I'm Albert Einstein."

"I hate to say this, young man, but you're no Einstein."

"Will both of you just *shut* up?" Groucho snarled.

"Then who am I?" Karl plowed on.

"Karl Marx," Feinermann declared. "The founder of Communism . . . which isn't doing too well these days."

"You mean, I'm a *pinko* instead of a genius?" Karl was aghast.

"Just *shut up!*" Groucho yelled. To Feinermann, he said, "You can scream, Rabbi, but no one will hear you. We're all alone."

"Besides," Karl added, "you do want to see your wife again, don't you?"

Feinermann paused. "I'm not so sure. Nevertheless, I will cooperate. You haven't shot me yet. You haven't robbed me. I assume what you want from me is more complex than a wallet or a watch."

Groucho pushed the gun deeper into Feinermann's spine. "Get a move on it, Rabbi."

Feinermann said, "Watch my backbone, Mister Jeffrey T. Spaulding. I had disk surgery not more than a year ago. Why cause an old man needless pain?"

Instantly, the Rabbi felt relief as the pressure eased off his back. "So you're not without compassion."

"Just keep walking, Rabbi," Groucho said.

"Who's Jeffrey T. Spaulding?" Karl asked.

"*Shut* up!" Groucho said. "Just cooperate, Rabbi, and no one will get hurt."

"Mr. Hugo Z. Hackenbush, I have no doubt that *you* will not get hurt," Feinermann said. "It's me I'm concerned about."

"Hugo Hack . . ." Karl scratched his face under his mask. "Who *are* all these dorks?"

"C'mon!" Groucho pushed the Rabbi forward. "Step on it."

As the Marxes sequestered him in the backseat of the Seville, Feinermann tried to figure out why he was being kidnapped. He wasn't a wealthy man, not in possession of any items of great value. His estate —a small, two-bedroom house in the Fairfax district of Los Angeles— would be left to Sarah upon his demise. He and his wife had had their differences, but he couldn't imagine her hiring people to kill him for his paltry insurance policy. Sarah was a *kvetch* and a *yente*, but basically a good, pious woman. And a practical woman as well. The cost of the hit would greatly exceed any monetary gain she'd receive from the policy.

Karl kept him company in the backseat as Groucho gunned the motor. Then they were off. The men were good-sized, capable of doing major physical damage. And they seemed *very* nervous.

Perhaps this was their very first kidnapping, Feinermann thought. It is always difficult to do something for the first time. It was then and there that Feinermann decided to make his abductors feel welcome.

"A nice shirt you have on, Karl Marx," he said. "Is it silk?"

Karl looked at his buttercup chemise. "Yeah. You really like it?"

The old man fingered the fabric. "Very good quality. I grew up in New York, had many a friend in the *shmatah* business. This is an impressive shirt."

"Quiet back there," Groucho said.

The old man pressed his lips together. At least, his discussion with

Karl had produced the desired effects. Feinermann could see the man in the buttercup shirt visibly relax, his shoulders unbunching, his feet burying deep into the Caddy's plush carpeting. The Seville, with its cushy gray leather upholstery and its black-tinted windows, had lots of leg room. It was good that Karl felt at home. He shouldn't be nervous holding a gun.

Groucho, on the other hand, was a different story. His body language was hidden from Feinermann's view. The only thing the Rabbi could make out was a pair of dark eyes peeking through a mask with the bushy eyebrows—a reflection in the rearview mirror. The eyes gave Feinermann no hint as to who was the man behind them.

Feinermann sat stiffly and hunched forward, his elbows resting on his knees. Karl reached into his pocket and pulled out a handkerchief.

"Sorry to have to do this to you, old man."

"Do what?" Feinermann felt his heart skip a beat. "You are going to tie me up?"

"Nah, you're not much of a threat," Karl said. "I'm gonna have to blindfold you. Don't want you to see where we're taking you. Be a good man and hold still."

"I always cooperate with people carrying revolvers."

"Good thinking."

Feinermann closed his eyes as they were covered with a soft cloth, the ends of the kerchief secured tightly around his head. Quality silk—very soft and smooth. His abductors had spared him no expense. It made the old man feel important.

"May I now ask what this is all about?"

"Soon enough," Karl answered. "Don't worry. No one wants to hurt you. They just want a little information from you."

"Information?"

Groucho barked, "Keep your trap shut, for crissakes!"

"Are you talking to me, Mr. Rufus T. Firefly?" Feinermann asked.

"No, not you, Rabbi. I would never talk to a man of the cloth like that." Groucho paused. "Well, maybe I did tell you to shut up. Sorry about that. I was nervous."

"First time as a kidnapper?"

"You can tell, huh?"

"You don't seem like the hardened criminal type."

"I owed someone a favor."

"It must have been a pretty big favor."

"Ain't they all. Just relax, old man. We're gonna be in the car for a while."

"Then maybe I'll take a little rest." Feinermann took off his hat, exposing the black skullcap underneath, and unbuttoned his jacket. "Is this your first kidnapping as well, Karl?"

"Yep." Karl lowered his voice. "I owed *him* a favor."

Feinermann took the *him* to be Groucho and pondered, "Groucho owed someone a favor, you owed Groucho a favor."

"Yeah," Karl said. "It's kinda like a bad chain letter."

A Hebrew proverb came to Feinermann's mind: *From righteous deeds come righteous deeds. From sin comes sin.*

The car ride lasted over an hour. Afterward, the Marx boys brought Feinermann indoors, eased him into a baby-smooth leather chair and propped his feet up on an ottoman. Such service, the Rabbi thought. After the boys had made him comfortable, they removed the blindfold, then left.

The old man found himself in a magnificent library. The room was about the size of the shul's dining hall, but much more fancy. The paneling and bookcases were fashioned from rich, deep mahogany, so smooth and shiny the wood seemed to be plastic. The brass pulls on the cases gleamed—not a scratch dared mar the mirror polish. The furniture consisted of burnt almond leather sofas and chairs, with a couple of tapestry wing-backs thrown in for color. The parquet floor was covered in several places by what looked to be original Persian rugs.

Directly in front of Feinermann's view was a U-shaped desk made out of rosewood with ebony trim. The man behind the desk appeared to be of slight frame, around thirty-five, but bald except for a well-trimmed cocoa-colored fringe outlining his nude crown. Across his eyes sat an updated version of the old-fashioned wire-rimmed, round spectacles. Except these weren't the heavy kind that left a red mark on the bridge of the nose. Mr. Baldy was attired in a black suit, his pocket handkerchief matching the mandarin ascot draped around his neck. He held a crystal highball glass filled with ice, a carbonated beverage and two swizzle sticks.

"May I offer you something to drink, Rabbi?" The bald man stirred his drink. His voice was surprisingly deep. "I'm drinking KingCola—the only beverage considered *worthy* of the Benton's finest imported Bavarian crystal. But we have a full bar—Chivas aged some twenty-five years —if you're so inclined."

"Thank you, sir," said Feinermann, "but I shall be obliged to pass.

Today is a fast day in my religion—the fast of Esther. Eating and drinking are prohibited until tonight's holiday."

The bald man stirred his KingCola. "Interesting. And what holiday is tonight if I may ask?"

"You may ask and I'll tell you. Tonight is Purim—the Festival of Lots —when one righteous woman foiled the plans to annihilate the Jews of Persia."

"And you *fast* on such a day?"

"First came the fasting and praying, then came the celebration. Makes more sense to feast when you're really hungry. Not to mention it's good for weight control." Feinermann adjusted his hat. "Are you this Benton of the famous Benton's crystal?"

The bald man looked up and chuckled. "No, Rabbi, I am not Mr. Benton."

The old man stroked his beard. "I am trying to figure out why his name rings a bell."

The bald man said, "Perhaps you'd recognize the name in a different form. Benton Hall at the university. Or perhaps you've been to the Benton Civic Light Opera Company. Or read about the new Benton Library downtown."

"Ah . . ."

"Mr. Patrick W. Benton is quite the philanthropist."

"So why does a rich philanthropist need a rabbi with a herniated disk?"

"You are not just a rabbi, you are *the* Rabbi."

"I don't understand."

"I realize that. But before we begin, I want you to know that bringing you here was *my* idea, not Mr. Benton's. I work for Mr. Benton, formulating his . . . covert operations."

"Sounds mysterious. Perhaps you're a student of the *Zohar*—our book of mystics?"

"What?"

"Not important. *Nu*, so do you have a name, Mr. Sharp Dresser?"

"Sharp dress . . . you've noticed my *couture?*"

"I like the touch of orange with the black suit." Actually Feinermann thought the man looked like a jack-o'-lantern. But hurling insults was not the old man's style. And now was not the time for insults anyway.

The bald man nodded in approval. "Well, I thought it made rather a bold statement."

The Rabbi said nothing. To him, a bold statement was splitting the Red Sea. "So, Mr. . . ."

"You may call me Philip."

"Philip it is. Exactly what does your Mr. Benton want from me?"

"It is *I* who want something from you, Rabbi Feinermann. I want something not for myself, but for Mr. Benton—for his good deeds. And you, Rabbi Feinermann, are the only one who can help Mr. Benton continue his course of philanthropy. Let me explain."

The old man stroked his beard. "I *knew* this wasn't going to be simple. Kidnappings are never simple affairs."

Again, Philip let go with his pesky chuckle. "Come, come, Rabbi. Surely you don't think we intend for any harm to befall you."

"To tell you the truth, with a gun in my back, I wasn't so sure, Philip. But proceed. Explain away."

"Rabbi Feinermann, you may wonder why a man like me would go to such extreme . . . measures to help out Mr. Benton. It's because I truly believe in his work."

"And what does he do besides erect buildings with his name on them?"

"He *cares*, Rabbi. He has built his empire on *caring*. His multibillion-dollar corporation was one of the first to include the *human* side of business. One of the first to offer complete *major* medical and dental care. And if that was not enough, he included in his medical package—free of charge—optometry, orthodontia, and podiatry services. Do you know how many of his employees have availed themselves of braces, eye-glasses and bunion removal at Mr. Benton's expense?"

"I have no idea."

"Thousands."

"A lot of bunions, Philip."

"Corns are no laughing matter, Rabbi."

"Not at all, Philip."

"It's not just in medical services where Mr. Benton has taken the social lead. His was one of the first major corporations to provide on-site day care, flexible shifts for working mothers and free turkeys on Thanksgiving, Christmas, *and* Easter." Philip paused. "And *kosher* turkeys for our kosher-keeping workers, I might add."

"Sounds like a thoughtful man, your Mr. Benton."

"That he is, Rabbi." Philip tensed his body and shook with gravity. "That's why desperate times call for desperate measures. You being here . . . it was a desperate measure that I took. But one that I hope you will truly understand."

"I'm all ears, Philip."

"Do you know how Mr. Benton made his money, Rabbi?"

"I'm afraid I don't."

"I'm not surprised. He is not a grandstander like your ordinary billionaire."

"I'm not a *maven* on billionaires, Philip. I wouldn't know an ordinary one from an unusual one."

"Well, let me assure you that Mr. Benton is extraordinary."

"I'm assured."

"He made his money right here." Philip held his highball tumbler aloft. "Right in the palm of my hand."

"In Bavarian crystal?"

Philip frowned. "No. In the soft drink industry. *KingCola.* A King as it is affectionately known. 'I'll have a hamburger, French fries and a King.' How many times have you heard that, Rabbi?"

"Not too many. But don't go by me. I don't patronize fast-food places because I keep kosher."

"But even you, as insulated as you are from pop culture, have heard of KingCola."

"Certainly."

"But there's so much *more* to Mr. Benton than KingCola."

Feinermann noticed Philip was shaking again. "We've been over the wonders of Mr. Benton. May I ask what does *any* of this have to do with me?"

"I can sum that up in two words. Cola Gold."

"Cola Gold? Your chief competitor?"

"Our *enemy*, Rabbi!" Philip started foaming at the mouth. "Not just our enemy in the War of the Soft Drinks, oh no, Rabbi. It's deeper than that. Much, much deeper. If it was only money, do you think Mr. Benton would waste his time on them?"

Feinermann thought maybe Mr. Benton *would* bother wasting his time. From his scant knowledge of billionaires, the old man was under the impression that billionaires—and maybe millionaires as well—spent a great deal of time on the subject of money. But he was silent.

Philip went on, "It's the whole CeeGee mentality, Rabbi. CeeGee— that's our code word for Cola Gold."

Feinermann nodded.

"CeeGee's attitude is Machiavellian—only the *product* counts, not the *people* behind the product. Do you know that last year alone CeeGee laid off over two hundred people? And what replaced these people?"

"What, Philip?"

"*Machines!*" Philip spat out. "*Machines* took over jobs that had once put bread on the tables of families. How would *you* feel if a machine took over your job, Rabbi?"

"Not too good."

"Exactly!" Philip pulled an orange handkerchief from his pocket and wiped his face and forehead. "We're not talking about ordinary business competition, Rabbi. We're not just talking about sugar, flavoring and water. We are talking sugar, flavoring, and *holy* water, Rabbi. What KingCola and Cola Gold have going is an all-out *holy* war."

"I see your point, Philip."

"So you will help, won't you, Rabbi?"

Feinermann stroked his beard, then held his finger up in the air. "Yes, I shall help. Call up Cola Gold and ask for the list of those who've been laid off. I could use an extra man to clean up the shul after Friday night kiddush."

Philip bristled. "That's *not* what I had in mind!"

"So if you have an alternative plan, tell me."

Philip pointed a finger at the old man. "It rests entirely in your hands."

Feinermann looked at his hands. All he saw was air.

Philip said, "It has to do with CeeGee's new formula. The one they use to appeal to the youth?"

"Ah yes," the old man said, "I'm aware of it. What is the slogan? 'The new cola for the now generation—' "

"Don't utter those words!" Philip held his ears and began to pant.

Feinermann stood and quickly handed Philip his glass of KingCola. By now the ice had melted and the drink looked watered down. But looked pretty good nonetheless because his mouth was dry from fasting. "Philip, calm down and drink."

Philip slurped up the remains of his soft drink.

"I beg your pardon," the Rabbi said. "I didn't realize it would cause such a reaction. I won't say another word."

Philip took a deep breath and let it out slowly. "It's not your fault, Rabbi. You couldn't have known."

Feinermann said, "I take it by your reaction that the new . . . youthful formula has been successful."

"Youth!" Philip despaired. "What do they know of Mr. Benton's greatness and humanism?"

"Why don't you tell them?"

"As if they'd listen. As if this generation cares about *humanism*. Did you know that soft drinks is a forty-eight-billion-dollar industry? Did you know that colas—both caffeinated and decaffeinated—comprise a forty percent market share? And who do you think drinks cola?"

"Who?"

"Youth!" Philip exclaimed. "Youth, youth, youth! Those rats at CeeGee have not only exploited the workers, they've exploited our youth! Did you know that they've signed DeJon Jonson to a twenty-million-dollar ad contract?"

"He's the fellow with the lamé glove?"

"He's the hottest thing in the recording industry, Rabbi. And CeeGee's got him under *contract.*"

"Twenty million is a lot to pay for a fellow with just one glove. Surely you can find a chap with two gloves for a cheaper price."

Philip glared at him.

"What do you *want* from me, Philip?" Feinermann asked.

"I've tried everything, Rabbi. This is my last desperate attempt to give a victory for *our* side—the side of truth and justice. The key is in your hands because . . ." Philip paused for dramatic effect. "Because *you* are one of the handful of people who knows Cola Gold's secret formula."

The Rabbi's eyes widened. "Me?"

"There's no use in denying it, Rabbi," Philip stated. *"You* are one of the privileged who knows every single ingredient, additive and flavoring, artificial or otherwise, that gives CeeGee's new formula its unique taste."

"Philip—"

"You, Rabbi, have personally checked the formula in an *official* capacity in order to give sanction to the kosher-keeping world that the new formula is as kosher as their original formula. Don't deny it, Rabbi, don't deny it."

"A minute, Philip. Give an old man a minute. Two would even be preferable."

Feinermann needed to collect his thoughts.

He had to think back, because the job had not been part of his regular duties. The assignment had been given to him because Rav Gottlieb, the *mashgiach* for Cola Gold, had come down with a flu named after one of the continents—Asian or African. Feinermann hadn't thought much about it at the time. Gottlieb had been certifying all Cola Gold Inc. beverages as kosher for over twenty years. Still the corporate wheels hadn't wanted to wait for an old man's recuperation. Gottlieb had suggested Rav Morris Feinermann as a substitute.

As Feinermann recalled it, the CeeGee people hadn't been happy to deal with him. Only reluctantly had they parted with the formula, and then they'd sworn him to secrecy. At the time, Feinermann had thought the management overly dramatic.

He stroked his beard—a mistake on his part to underestimate the competition.

Philip couldn't contain himself. "I *want* that formula and you will give it to me. You will give it to me because you, like Mr. Benton, are a humanitarian and have the best interest of people upmost in your mind! If we lose our market share, Rabbi, our sales will go down. If our sales decrease, it will be necessary to lay people off from work. And why? Because a cold, heartless manufacturer prefers to use robots rather than *people.* You're a humanist, Rabbi. You will help."

"But I can't give you the formula, Philip. It would be unethical. And there's also a very practical reason. I don't remember it. All the Latin-sounding chemical names they used for flavoring. Very confusing. Perhaps if you had kidnapped me earlier . . ."

"Had we known about the precipitous rise in their market share, believe me, Rabbi, we wouldn't have waited so long. Still, it's never too late."

Philip pounded the table. "I'll help you, Rabbi. I have lists and lists of chemicals, the finest hypnotists to help you with memory recall. We will work day and night if we have to. I will do anything within my power, sacrifice myself because I believe in Mr. Benton."

"I was never a big student of sacrifices, Philip. The bottom line, my young friend, is I will not divulge anything that was given to me in confidence."

Philip's face turned crimson, his eyes becoming steely and cold. Then his lips turned into a mean smile. "I can see you'll need a bit of *convincing.*" He rang a bell. In walked the Marxes. Red-faced Philip turned to him and with his irritating chuckle said, "Take Rabbi Feinermann to the dungeon!"

The Marxes gasped.

"Not the dungeon," Karl exclaimed. "Not the dungeon, Mr. P. Not for a *rabbi!*"

"To the dungeon!" Philip ordered. "And no food and water for him."

That part was acceptable, Feinermann thought. He was fasting anyway.

*　*　*

The old man told them to walk slowly. His back was sore from the car ride and he was a little light in the head from not having eaten. Then he said, "And just what is this dungeon?"

"Corporate torture, Rabbi," Groucho responded solemnly. "It's better if you don't know."

The Rabbi sighed. "I'll survive. Our people have experienced all sorts of adversity."

"Yeah, you guys have sure had some hard knocks," Karl added.

"If you got any personal role models, Rabbi," Groucho said. "You know, people you admire 'cause they're strong. Maybe now's the time to start thinking about them."

"There is no shortage of Jewish martyrs," Feinermann said. "Take for example, Channah and her ten sons. A bit of a zealot Channah was, but righteous nonetheless. She instructed her ten sons to die rather than give themselves over to the Hellenic ways."

"Did they listen to her?" Karl asked.

"Yes, indeed they did. The youngest was only six, yet he accepted death rather than bow down to the Greek gods and goddesses."

"That's terrible," Groucho said. "A six-year-old kid, what does he know?"

"They were probably more mature in those days," Karl said. "After all, didn't most people kick the bucket around thirty?"

"Still, the kid was only six," Groucho said.

"Surely your corporate torture could not be as terrible as that," Feinermann piped in.

Karl said, "If thinking of this broad helps you along, Rabbi, then more power to you."

"Then I shall think about Channah. And I shall also think about the Ten Martyrs our people read about on Yom Kippur. Our holiest rabbis were tortured to death by the Romans because of their beliefs. One was decapitated, one was burnt, one was flayed and one of the most famous of our sages, Rabbi Akiva, had his flesh raked with hot combs."

"Those Romans were surely uncivilized people!" Groucho exclaimed. "Gladiators, lion pits, and torturing men of the cloth. Even Mr. P. wouldn't do that."

"Comforting," Feinermann said.

"Yeah, Rabbi, that's the spirit!" Karl cheered on.

Feinermann thought: So maybe *this* was his chance to show his faith, like the Ten Martyrs. Always the little Jew against someone of might— the Persians, the Romans, the Spanish of the Inquisition, the Cossacks and, most deadly, the Nazis. Not to mention Tommy Hoolihan, who beat Feinermann up every day for two years as the small boy of ten with the big black *kippah* walked home from *Heder*. Telling his questioning, worried mother that the bruises he'd sustained were from falls. She must have thought he was the clumsiest kid in New York.

Twenty-five hundred years of persecution.

Yet the Jews as a nation refused to die. Could he, like Rabbi Akiva, die with the words *Sh'ma Yisroel* on his lips and mean it?

Feinermann thought about that as the two masked men led him to his destiny.

Perhaps he could die a true martyr, perhaps not. But if he couldn't, he wouldn't worry about it too much. After all, how many Rabbi Akivas were there in a lifetime?

He expected darkness and filth, chains and nooses hanging from the ceiling. And some red-eyed, emaciated rats ready to eat his *kishkas* out. Instead Feinermann was brought into a semicircular projection room. The auditorium consisted of a wide-angled screen and a half-dozen rows of plush chairs, maybe seating for fifty in all.

Not so bad for a dungeon, Feinermann thought.

They placed him in the center row and shackled his feet and hands to the chair. He watched fearfully as Karl took out some masking tape. But all Marx did was tape the old man's eyes open. Not tight enough as to prevent him from clearing his eyes of debris, but firmly enough to prevent him from pressing his lids together.

"Scream when you can't take it anymore." Karl stood up. "Nothing personal, Rabbi, I'd like to help you, but I can't." He moved closer to the old man's ear and whispered, "I'm into Elvis for a lot of bread."

"Elvis?" Feinermann said.

Karl swore and hit his face mask, whispering, "That's Groucho's real name. Don't say nothing or we'll both be in deep water. Let's just get this over with."

As Groucho dimmed the lights, Feinermann waited solemnly, wondering why Elvis didn't hide under an Elvis Presley mask. It would have seemed like a natural disguise.

Soon the old man was sitting in total darkness. All he could hear and feel were the sensations his own body provided—the whooshing of blood coursing through his head, his heartbeat, the quick steps of his nervous breathing.

Then the first outside stimulus. A motor running. The room slowly beginning to brighten as shadowy shapes illuminated the movie screen.

Sound . . . music . . . bad music. Not only was it sappy but old and distorted. It sounded as if it had come from an ancient, irrelevant documentary—the kind they show frequently on PBS.

On screen was a fuzzy, sienna image of a young man digging up potatoes. A voice-over with a reedy mid-Atlantic accent explained that this man was Patrick Benton Senior, the potato farmer. The shack in the background was Benton's house in County Cork. The film went on to explain the hardships of Irish potato farming, including the great famine in the late eighteen hundreds.

A little history lesson never hurt anyone, the Rabbi thought. Still, he wished he could blink in earnest. Next on the screen he saw a boat stuffed with Irish immigrants approaching Ellis Island. He wondered if Tommy Hoolihan's parents were aboard.

Then a cut to a tenement house, not far from where Feinermann grew up. He recognized old buildings that had been razed decades ago. The old clothing, the pushcarts, faces of men and women who still believed in the American dream. Nostalgia gripped his chest. The film switched to an indoor shot—a frame of a woman with a plump face holding a baby in her arms. She looked like Feinermann's mother. In fact, she could have been any one of a thousand immigrant mothers.

Eyes watering, Feinermann knew it wasn't because he couldn't blink. The moisture in his orbs represented something deeper.

The baby had been christened Patrick Junior. Feinermann didn't know Mr. Benton's forename, but he was pretty certain he was looking at the great philanthropist himself. As the film progressed, it was clear to the old man that what he was watching was Patrick Junior's rags-to-riches story. From the son of a potato farmer to the CEO of one of the biggest corporations in the *world*.

Only in America.

The old man watched with rapt attention.

Philip said to Groucho, "How long has he been in there now?"

"Close to six hours, sir."

"Incredible." Philip paced. "Simply incredible. Most ordinary men would have cracked hours ago. Seeing that same story over and over. Are you sure he didn't puke? Puking is usually the first sign that they're coming around."

"No sign of puke anywhere," Karl said. "It's really amazing. That thing is so corny, *I* almost puked. And I only had to sit through it once."

"Maybe it's because he hasn't eaten," Groucho suggested.

Philip thought about that for a moment. "Did he retch at all?"

"Not even a single *gag*," Karl said.

"I just don't understand." Philip pulled out his kerchief and wiped his face. "If psychological torture isn't bringing him around, we'll have to take sterner measures."

Groucho said, "Surely you're not suggestin' *physical* torture?"

"Our market share in the industry is plummeting." Philip wrung his hands. "CeeGee's new formula is wiping us off the map. I've got a five-figure monthly mortgage and a Range Rover owned by the bank. I'm gonna crack that old geezer somehow!"

Over the intercom came Feinermann's voice. "Marxes, can you hear me?"

"Rabbi, it's Philip. We can hear you. What do you want?"

"I think we should talk."

"Are you going to help us, Rabbi?" Philip inquired.

"I will help you, I will help you," Feinermann said.

Philip broke into a wide smile and whispered to his henchmen, "I knew it, I knew it. No one can sit through that much hokey drivel and come out sane." Into the intercom, he said, "I have your word that you will help me, Rabbi?"

"Absolutely, but first I must have your help."

"What do you require from me?"

"I want a few things. First, you must call my wife and tell her I will be delayed. She should go hear the Megilla without me and she shouldn't worry. I'll be home in time to deliver our *shalach manot*—our gift baskets—and our charity to the poor."

"What do I say if she asks questions?"

"Sarah's a practical woman. As long as I can make deliveries tomorrow, she won't care. Next, you must get me a *Megillas Esther*. It's nighttime and I need to read it before I can eat."

Philip said, "I'll find you this . . . Megilla."

"Be sure it's a *Megillas Esther*. There are five *megillos*."

"Rabbi, I assure you you'll get the whole Megilla," Philip said. "Anything else?"

"I'd like to eat after I read. A kosher meal."

"Done."

"Not so fast, Philip. It is *not* enough to have a kosher meal. I must have a *seudah*—a feast. Not a feast in terms of food. I must have a feast in terms of a party, a gathering." The Rabbi thought a moment. "I want to have a feast and I want it to be in your honor, Philip. You have shown me the light."

"Why, Rabbi, I'm so *honored*."

"The Marxes can come, too. That will make it quite a deal. And also, you must invite your Mr. Benton as the guest of honor."

Philip didn't like that idea at all. "I don't know if I can do that, Rabbi."

"You want the help?" Feinermann asked.

Philip thought of his five-figure monthly mortgage. "He'll be there. But you mustn't tell him you were . . ."

"Kidnapped is the word, Philip. But I'm willing to let bygones be bygones. I'm not even angry about it. I think it was the Almighty's way of telling me something."

"You are a remarkable man, Rabbi," Philip said.

"So you will call up our Mr. Benton?"

"Yes," Philip said. "And we will have a feast—to celebrate our new partnership, shall we say?"

"I don't know if partnership is the right word, but if you meet my conditions, I will help you. That's all for now."

Feinermann stopped talking, wondering if his idea would work out. The part about the banquet he'd cribbed straight out of the Megilla. But he didn't feel too guilty about it. If it worked once, maybe it would work again.

Left alone in the library, Feinermann read the Megilla aloud, intoning each word with precision, stomping his foot loudly whenever he came to the name of the evil Haman. According to Jewish law, Haman was so wicked that one's ears were not even supposed to hear his name. And also according to Jewish law, one was required to hear every word of the Megilla, including the name of Haman. A difficult dilemma, Feinermann thought.

When he was done, he closed the Hebrew text, imbued with sense of purpose. He buzzed Philip and the bald man came in, a grin slapped upon his face.

"We have prepared a most sumptuous kosher meal for you, Rabbi Feinermann. I've phoned Mr. Benton and he can't wait to meet the man who will bring KingCola back to its rightful number-one position."

The bald man rubbed his hands together.

"Now don't worry if it takes a little time to recall the formula in its entirety. We have an excellent staff who'll be at your beck and call . . . Tell me the truth, Rabbi. Did they indeed use trichlorobenzodroate? I'm not a taste expert, but I swear I detect a little trichlor in their new formula."

"I don't remember, Philip. And even if I did, I couldn't tell you."

"B-b-b . . . but you swore," Philip stammered.

"I swore I wouldn't tell Mr. Benton that you abducted me—a big concession on my part. *And* I swore to help you. I will help you. But I will not give you Cola Gold's formula!"

A buzz came over the intercom. The secretary said, "Mr. Benton's limo has just pulled up, Mr. P."

The bald man began to sweat. Out came the kerchief. Feinermann noticed it was a new one—white linen, starched and ironed. Philip said, "So help me God, if I hadn't asked Mr. Benton to come personally, I'd tear you limb from limb."

"Not a smart idea, Philip. And against religious law as well."

"Banquet in my honor! This was just a ruse, wasn't it!"

"It worked for Queen Esther—"

"Shut up!"

"Are you going to let me help you or are you going to sit there like a lump and sweat like a pig?"

Philip glared at him. For the first time, he realized he was working against a formidable opponent. "Just what do I tell Mr. Benton?"

Feinermann held up his hand. "You let me handle your Mr. Benton." He stood. "First, we will eat."

The meal started with cabbage soup. The main course was boiled chicken with vegetables, kasha and farfel stuffing and a salad of chopped onions, tomatoes, and cucumbers. Dessert consisted of apple strudel, tea and coffee.

Feinermann wiped his mouth with satisfaction while studying the faces of the men who had abducted him—introduced to Benton as chauffeurs. Elvis and Donnie were in their thirties; both had bad skin and little ponytails. Without the masks and the guns, they were not impressive as thugs. But Philip had gotten them for free. You buy cheap, you get cheap. The old man noticed the food was not to their liking. He expected that. But Benton had cleaned his plate.

Everything was going according to plan.

The Rabbi asked for a moment to say grace after meals. While he gave benedictions to the Almighty, he sneaked sidelong glances at the great industrialist/philanthropist.

Patrick Benton had been a tall man in his youth. From the film, Feinermann remembered a strapping man of thirty whose frame easily topped those around him. But now with the hunched shoulders and the curved spine, Benton didn't seem so tall. His eyes were watery blue, his skin as translucent as tracing paper. What was left of his hair was white. The Rabbi noted with pride most of his own hair was still brown.

Finishing up the last of his prayers, Feinermann sat with his hands folded and smiled at Benton. KingCola's CEO smiled back.

"I don't know when I've eaten such tasty . . . nostalgic food. All these exclusive restaurants I go to, where everyone knows my name and kisses my keister." He waved his hand in the air. "Food that doesn't look like food and the portions aren't big enough to feed a flea. Damn fine grub, Feinermann." He turned to his assistant. "Philip, make a note of where the chow came from. This is the kind of cooking I like."

The bald man quickly pulled out a notepad and began to scribble.

"So," Benton harrumphed. "I understand you have a way to help out KingCola. Philip was sketchy with the details. Give me your ideas, Rabbi."

"Mr. Benton, first I want to say what an honor it is to meet you, even though this was not my idea."

Philip turned pale.

"Not your idea?" Benton questioned.

"Not at all," the Rabbi said. "I'll be honest. I didn't know you from any of the other philanthropists with names on buildings until Philip here convinced me to come and meet you. Even so, I wasn't so crazy about the prospect. His idea of help and my idea of help weren't exactly the same thing."

Benton looked intrigued. "How so?"

"You see, Mr. Benton, I worked with Cola Gold in a very tangential way. Even so, it was necessary for me to learn the formula of their new line of cola—"

"*Good God*, Rabbi! *You* know the formula? That would be worth *millions* to me!"

"I take it you'd pass a few million to me in the process. But that's not the point. I can't give you the formula. That would be unethical."

Benton sat back in his seat. "Yes, of course." He ran his hand through thin strands of white hair. "However, there's nothing . . . unethical . . . about you making . . . suggestions for additives in our competing brand of new-generation cola."

"The problem is, Mr. Benton, I don't know anything about new generations, period. I am from an old generation."

Benton turned to Philip. "So this is why you interrupted me at the clubhouse?"

"Hold on, Mr. Benton," Feinermann said. "Don't be so rude to Philip. The man is not my best friend, but he does have your interest at heart. I don't have any suggestions for your new-generation drinks. But I have a lot of suggestions for your old-generation drinks."

"What old-generation drinks?" Benton asked.

"That's the problem," the Rabbi said. "There *are* none. Mr. Benton, I watched your life story, many, many times. Not my doing, but be that as it may, I feel I know you quite well. We have a lot in common. We both had immigrant parents, grew up dirt-poor in New York, the first generation of Americans in our family. We were the dreams and hopes of our parents who sacrificed everything so we could have it a little better, *nu?* We lived through the Depression, fought in World War II, gritted our teeth as our hippie children lived through the sixties. And now, in the waning years of our lives, we sit with a sense of pride in our lives and maybe bask a little in our grandchildren. Am I not correct?"

Benton stared at Feinermann. "Exactly! I see you as a man with vision! Philip, *hire* this man on as a consultant. Start him at—"

"Wait, wait," Feinermann interjected. "Thank you for the offer, but I already have a job. And I'm not so visionary. I know how you feel because we're from the same generation. I saw your mother, Mr. Benton. She looked like my mother. She probably knocked herself out chopping meat by hand and scrubbing floors with a sponge."

"Her hands were as rough as sandpaper, poor woman."

"And I bet she always had a pitcher of iced tea in the icebox when you came home from school. Maybe some shpritz from a bottle with the cee-oh-two pellets?"

Benton smiled. "You've got that one down."

"No cans of cola in her refrigerator."

"Just where is all this leading?" Philip asked.

"Shut up!" Benton replied. "We're reminiscing."

Again, Feinermann wiped his mouth. "I'll tell you where this is leading, Philip. Pay attention because it has to do with business."

The bald man wiped his forehead. "I'm listening."

Feinermann said, "You have a multibillion-dollar business that provides beverages to America. And *all* of your products are aimed at the young or the ones who wish they were young. Not that I have anything against the new generation, but I can't relate to them. And I don't drink the same things they drink. I want my glass of tea with a lemon. I want my old-fashioned shpritz without essences of this flavor or that flavor. What ever happened to tonic water and ginger ale, for goodness' sake?''

"We have ginger ale," Philip protested. "King Ginger."

"Ach!" The Rabbi gave him a disgusted look. "Relegated to the back of the cooler. The young people think it's a drink for stomach maladies."

"You have to realize that New Age drinks comprise a measly three hundred and twenty-seven million dollars of market sales," Philip said. "Ginger ale's a drink with no appeal."

"It appeals to me," Feinermann insisted.

"The Rabbi's got a point," Benton said. "The New Age drinks do appeal to the older set. And let's not forget the growth rate, Philip— fifteen percent as compared to two percent in the industry as a whole."

"There you go," Feinermann stated. "When are you companies going to wake up and realize there is a whole generation out there waiting for you to appeal to them?" He turned to Benton. "You gobbled up dinner tonight because it reminded you of your mother's cooking."

Benton bit his lip. "I see what you're saying. But Rabbi, you have to realize that carbonated beverages is still a youth-oriented market."

"Because you *choose* to woo the youth. What about me?"

"The elderly market is tricky," Benton said.

"Even if you convert them to your product, they're just going to keel over anyway," Philip said.

Benton glared at his assistant. "I beg your pardon."

"No . . . I mean . . . not you, Mr. Benton—"

"Calm down, Philip," Feinermann said with little patience. "Yes, we're all going to die. Even your Mr. Benton here. But I see your point. So don't market the old-fashioned drinks. Make them *family* drinks. Seltzer, tonic water, ginger ale—promote them as new lighter, less sugary drinks with a history of *America*. Show teenagers and grampas drinking them at the family barbecues. What could be better?"

Philip said, "I've got the hook, sir—a New Age drink with a touch of nostalgia."

"I like it, Philip," Benton said.

"And what about iced teas?" Feinermann said.

Philip said, "Only a four-hundred-million-dollar share of the market."

Feinermann said, "But combine it with your three-hundred-and-twenty-seven-million-dollar New Age share, Philip. That's almost a billion dollars."

"Man's got a point, Philip."

"Tensel's has a lock on tea, sir," Philip said. "Besides, I heard Heavenly Brew is coming out with a new line. Lots of teas for such a little market share."

"Ah, Heavenly Brew. That's not *tea*. Not tea the way Mr. Benton and I remember it."

Benton nodded. "True. We had tea that ratted the guts. How about a new full-flavored tea drink, Philip? It just might work, sir, especially if we get a decaf version."

"Very good, Mr. Benton."

Feinermann said, "We're a lost generation, Mr. Benton, just waiting for someone to sing our tunes. Stop regurgitating old cola recipes and expand your horizons."

Benton exclaimed, "Glad you brought all this to my attention, Rabbi. Philip, make a note to bring all this crap to the board's attention this Thursday. And, Rabbi, you will join us at the meeting, won't you?"

"Thursday I have a funeral to preside over. I'm afraid I must pass. Besides, I've stated my piece. Perhaps now your Philip will leave me in peace?"

"Absolutely! Philip, stop pestering the Rabbi."

Philip nodded like a Kewpie doll.

Feinermann stood. "If you don't mind, I'd like to take my leave."

"Certainly, Rabbi," Benton responded. "And anytime you need anything, just ask."

"Thank you, Mr. Benton." The old man shook hands with the philanthropist and bade him goodbye. As he was accompanied back to the car, walking in the cool March air, he reflected on how much he missed his childhood. Not the part about being beaten up by Tommy Hoolihan . . . and he didn't miss the cholera and polio, either. But he did miss his youth—a generation that grew up without TV. And a good glass of ginger ale . . . corporations do forget about the elderly—a reflection of society, he supposed.

Ah well, at least he'd sleep in his own bed tonight.

When they arrived at the Cadillac, Feinermann said to Philip, "You don't have to come back with me. The Marxes know the way."

"The Marxes?" Philip said.

"Private joke, Mr. P.," Donnie/Karl said.

Philip shook hands with the Rabbi. "I'm sorry if I inconvenienced you."

"No problem," Feinermann said. "I'll integrate the experience into next week's sermon." He opened the door to the backseat. "By the way, Marxes, what did you do with the face masks?"

"They're in the trunk," Elvis/Groucho said. "Why?"

"Unless you're planning another abduction, give them to me," Feinermann said. "I'll use them in the Purim festivities! Why let them go to waste?"

Amos Walker and Lydia Chin
have little in common beyond the fact that
they are both private investigators. Walker is a
P.I. in the true Chandler mode, hard-boiled
and cynical, while Chin is a Chinese American
female, small in stature but large on brains. In
this instance, however, both find themselves
working for wealthy clients who think their
money can buy anything, even justice.

S. J. ROZAN

S. J. Rozan's short stories have appeared in *PI Magazine*, *The 4th Womansleuth*, and *Alfred Hitchcock's Mystery Magazine*.

A New York City native, Rozan is an architect and has worked as both a self-defense instructor and a photographer. Rozan applauds the diversity of New York City and meshes elements from these wide-ranging experiences to create the unique team of tough and sexy detectives, New York City native Lydia Chin and fortyish army brat Bill Smith.

In "Film at Eleven" Lydia Chin and Bill Smith discover that seeing is not necessarily believing in this tense, fast-moving tale of betrayal and B-movies.

FILM AT ELEVEN

I had followed the case long before I became a part of it because the dead woman was Chinese. Not Chinatown Chinese, like me: Patricia Lin had been uptown Chinese, a doctor's daughter raised on ballet lessons and music classes, summer camps and private schools. When she'd enrolled at the College of Communication Arts, where she'd met the man alleged to have murdered her, Patricia Lin had been slumming.

I hadn't known Patricia Lin. I wasn't tied to her by blood or marriage, home province or village, but she was Chinese, so I followed the case.

It seemed over, of course, before I ever got involved. There was the finding of the body, the arrest, the trial. There was Mitch Ellman, with his gloating, victorious grin, his short blond hair lifting in the wind outside the courthouse as reporters crowded near him. When we'd seen his arrest on the eleven o'clock news his hair had been shoulder-length, tied in a ponytail. I wondered if he would grow it again, now that he'd been found not guilty of murder.

There was the jury forewoman, short-tempered, correcting a reporter: the jury's task had not been to find on the defendant's guilt, but on the question of whether the prosecutor had *proved* the defendant's guilt, which he had not done. She sped away in a taxi as the camera returned to Mitch Ellman being hugged and pounded on the back by his family and friends. His lawyer, Jay Berlow, known to those of us in the crime-related occupations as a high-priced oil slick, beamed beneficently in the background.

I was disgusted that night when I turned off the news, and my mother had to listen to me spout for a while. She sat silently hemming a pair of my pants until I stopped for breath. Then she said, "How do you know he's guilty? Maybe he's innocent. This is America."

My mother says "This is America" the way I imagine Dorothy explaining the Technicolor miracles whirling around her by saying "This is Oz."

"He's guilty, Ma," I said. "Did you see his face? Hear his voice? His body language?"

"Body language?" She looked at me blankly. There really is no Chinese word for it, and the phrase I had dredged up to use has a more formal, ritual meaning.

"Never mind," I said.

"Never mind" always annoys her.

"Arrogant girl." She pursed her lips. "You think because you waste your time with criminals and policemen you know everything. Always so sure. One day you'll be surprised—"

"Not by you, Ma. Everything that happens you turn into a complaint about my profession. The only surprise is how you'll do it."

"Oh, smart mouth," she said. "But wait. One day—whoosh! The world will show you where you belong." She nodded sagely to herself.

I went to bed.

The case didn't become mine until three months later. It was April by then, a time of soft nights and warm, breezy days. A phone call came from John Kimball, a lawyer I didn't know, but that wasn't unusual: a lot of my work is for lawyers, and lawyers talk to each other. Kimball said he'd gotten my name from a colleague, and would tell me about the case when we met at his office.

So we met at his office. It was on the forty-fourth floor of a blue-glass building on Park Avenue just north of Grand Central. The lobby was polished green stone and the directory was one of those computer touch-screens. I was early so I stood and played with it, moving the little orange person down the blue hallway. It told me where to find John Kimball, with a map and everything, and it told me where the ladies' room closest to his office was, just in case.

When it was time, I went up. The firm's name, O'Herlihy Davis Kimball, was spelled out in big stainless steel letters on the taupe wall opposite the elevators. I wondered if lawyers didn't use commas or ands because they didn't want to pay for the extra stainless steel.

To the right was a glass wall with glass doors where a woman with big glasses sat behind a taupe counter. To the left was a taupe door with a tiny sign: ODK DELIVERIES. I suppressed the urge to go that way, strolled briskly to and through the glass doors.

By the time I was seated in John Kimball's office I had seen more shades of taupe than I'd ever thought possible. I was glad I'd dressed conservatively, brown suit and white cashmere sweater, low brown heels and briefcase; it would be very easy to stick out like a sore thumb around here, and as a small, young Asian woman I usually stick out like a whole sore hand anyway. Especially in the kinds of places I sometimes go.

Right now, though, I wasn't the only small young Asian woman in the place.

"Miss Chin, this is Janet Woo," John Kimball said, reseating himself behind his broad, glass-topped desk, his back to a window I could see Chinatown from. "Janet, this is Lydia Chin, the private investigator I was telling you about." Janet Woo half-rose from her chair, smiled shyly. We shook hands, Janet Woo and I, while John Kimball went on explaining to me why I was here. Janet Woo's hand was soft, dry, and limp. Kimball's had been fleshy and firm.

"Janet has a story I want you to hear, Miss Chin," he said. "I'm hoping you'll be able to help us."

"I hope so too," I said politely, and I did hope so, because O'Herlihy Davis Kimball did not seem like a client that would need to pay my bill in barter instead of cash.

Janet Woo gave me a serious look, her head held low; she gave John Kimball the same look, and it seemed to me she held her head even lower.

"Go on, Janet," Kimball ordered, leaning back in his chair. He was a big man in a pale blue shirt, navy suit, blue-striped tie. His hair was beginning to thin and his chin was pointy. He wore a gold wedding band on his left hand.

Janet Woo wore no jewelry at all, and her only makeup was lipstick of the shade you wear less to attract than to keep people from noticing you because you don't wear makeup. Her blouse was high-necked, her skirt a noncommittal, below-the-knee length, and her long, straight black hair was pulled back from her face with two silvery clips. I had time to catalog all this because she sat staring at her hands, saying nothing.

After a full minute's silence, Kimball asked, a little coldly, I thought, "Do you want me to start?"

Janet Woo nodded.

"Miss Chin"—he turned his intense blue eyes to me—"do you remember the Patricia Lin case?"

"Yes, of course," I said, surprised.

"Can you summarize it?"

I could and did, although it felt a little like a high school pop quiz. "Patricia Lin's body was found in Central Park. She had been strangled somewhere else and dumped there. She had died during or soon after having sex. The man she'd been dating, Mitch Ellman, was arrested, tried, and acquitted."

Janet Woo did not look at me while I spoke, and she blushed faintly. John Kimball's eyes, on the other hand, never left me.

"How do you characterize the verdict?" he asked.

I thought. "I don't have access to all the facts."

"Nevertheless."

I looked at Janet Woo, and then back into Kimball's eyes. They matched his shirt perfectly, I noticed.

"I thought the verdict was wrong."

Kimball nodded, and Janet Woo seemed to soften a little.

"Why," Kimball asked, "do you think he was acquitted?"

"Because the evidence was all circumstantial. And because he had a very expensive, very slimy attorney." In a lawyer's office, I'd learned, you don't say "lawyer."

"Janet . . ." Kimball said; when she didn't respond he went on. "Janet has some evidence pertinent to that case."

Janet Woo looked up hurriedly. "I don't know if it's evidence," she said. "I only think so." Her voice was high and hushed, breathy. Oh well, I thought, at least it's a voice.

"I don't understand," I said. "Mitch Ellman's been acquitted. What good is evidence now? They couldn't try him again even if he confessed."

"Not for murder," Kimball said. "But if it were solid evidence the Department of Justice might be willing to undertake a civil rights prosecution."

"Civil rights?"

"It's a violation of someone's civil rights to kill them."

I almost laughed. I controlled myself and said, "I'm glad to hear that."

"Yes." Kimball frowned. Nothing funny about the law. "Well. I'm a friend of Janet's family, and recently Janet came to me. She didn't know where else to go. She feels she cannot tell her family what she has told me. In fact it would be a disaster if her parents found out. Isn't that right, Janet?"

She nodded. John Kimball waited a few moments, then said, "Janet knew Mitch Ellman too. Didn't you, Janet?"

I wondered if the whole rest of our meeting was going to be a silent-response Q & A, but suddenly Janet Woo spoke up.

"I dated him."

I waited, motionless, afraid any movement or sound would stop her again.

"I studied acting at CCA two years ago," her soft voice went on. "I dated Mitch Ellman. Not for long."

"Why not for long?" I finally asked, when it was clear she was stalled.

"He was . . . exciting." She started slowly, then warmed to it. "Wild and . . . powerful. He attracted me." She gave me an earnest look, as though trying to make sure I believed such an odd thing could happen, a shy woman attracted to a powerful man. "For a while we dated," she said, "without . . . physical intimacy." She blushed furiously; even the part in her hair grew crimson. "But he became more insistent. And I also . . ." She swallowed. "We began to have sex."

This last line was delivered in a whisper so low I had to lean forward to hear it.

"Go on, Janet," Kimball said.

Janet Woo jumped in her chair. Maybe she'd forgotten he was there. She looked at him, then at me. I tried to smile encouragingly.

"But . . ." She straightened her skirt and continued. "At first it was exciting. Then it got frightening. I stopped seeing him."

"What about it," I kept my voice soft, "was frightening?"

"He likes to"—she looked at Kimball's desktop, but not at him, then down at the taupe carpet—"to tie you up. If a man likes to do that, that can be exciting"—she brought her eyes to mine again—"but only if you trust him. I found I couldn't trust Mitch. Sometimes he hurt me. He always scared me. He . . . I didn't know what he would do. I was afraid. So I stopped seeing him."

Janet Woo was staring into her lap now, twisting her hands. I looked at John Kimball, raised my eyebrows inquiringly. As hard as this might be for Janet Woo, I didn't see that it added significantly to any case against Mitch Ellman.

John Kimball seemed to sense what I was thinking. "Tell Miss Chin," he said to Janet, in a voice with an edge of demand in it, "what you told me about Patricia Lin."

She raised her head and blinked. She said softly, "I think there is a tape."

"A tape?" I repeated, not sure what she meant.

"A video," she nodded.

I didn't know what expression was on my face, but she looked down again, spoke to her hands. "He liked to tape us. Not every time, just some. The camera was hidden; at first I didn't know. Then he told me. I even saw one. The important thing," she said with a rush, "the important thing is, the times he taped were the times he scared me most. He changed then. Well, not changed: he got more like himself, got . . . wilder. Those were the times he hurt me. If he . . ." She swallowed again, preparing for the words she was about to say. "If Mitch killed Patricia Lin while he was having sex with her, it must have been one of those times. It must have been while he was taping it."

"Oh," I said. I let my eyes wander to the window, where pretty, innocent clouds floated across Manhattan. "Oh."

"Do you see, Miss Chin, why I called you?" John Kimball's edgy voice almost made me jump, the way Janet Woo had done.

"I think so," I said.

"If we had that tape," Kimball said, "we could take it to the FBI."

"But we don't know if there really is one."

"No."

"And if there is, why on earth would Mitch Ellman give it up?"

"Mitch Ellman," John Kimball said carefully, "obviously finds Asian women . . . attractive."

I looked at him coldly. "I suppose," I said, "that I might get him to go to bed with me. I don't think that necessarily means he'd give me a videotape that could send him to jail for the rest of his life." And I'm a private eye, not a concubine, you stuffed-shirt lawyer, I thought.

"He wouldn't have to give it to you." John Kimball ignored my attitude, which gave me time to get myself back under control. "If you could swear you'd seen it, the FBI could get a search warrant. Once they found the tape, they could use it."

"If it exists," I said.

"If it exists."

I looked at him steadily for a few moments, then looked at Janet Woo. She instantly dropped her gaze to the floor.

"What do you want me to do?" I asked.

"Get the tape," Kimball said. "Or at least see it."

"Do you care how?"

Kimball frowned again. "Yes. Nothing that will discredit this office, or expose Janet to any publicity." Janet's eyes widened. "I think I should be informed of what you're planning, and how each step is progressing," Kimball said.

"That may make it harder."

"It's necessary."

I thought, letting the carpeted silence settle in the room.

"I can see a way to do this," I finally said. "It may work. I'll need to bring my partner in."

Kimball seemed taken aback. "I didn't know you had a partner. I was told you were a sole proprietor."

"I am. So is he. But we work together well, and we work together a lot. If it makes you feel better, think of him as someone I'm hiring to work on the case. It'll cost you the same either way."

"There's an issue of privacy here, Miss Chin."

Janet, whose issue it apparently was, nodded, her face very serious.

"Mr. Kimball, there's an issue of privacy in every case I take. The only way I can think to pull this off—and it's a long shot—will involve two people and some money. And some risk. Bill and I know how to watch each other's backs. Do you want us to try?"

"What are you thinking about?" Kimball asked.

I shook my head. "I want to try it out on Bill first. If he thinks it might fly, I'll outline it for you before we start."

"And you'll keep me apprised throughout the course of the investigation? I really will require that, Miss Chin."

"I understand that, Mr. Kimball."

"And your partner? He's a sole proprietor also, you say? No staff to share this with, no chance of accidental slips?"

"He's been an investigator for twenty years. I think he's learned to keep his mouth shut." Something they don't teach lawyers, I thought. Along with manners.

"All right," John Kimball said. "Talk to him and get back to me."

"Fine." I smiled. "Now, so that we all know what we're talking about, shall we discuss fee?"

The air was cool and breezy but the sun was warm when I came out onto Park. I found a pay phone on the corner and called Bill.

He was at his office, and picking up the phone.

"Smith," he said.

"Chin," said I.

"So what?"

"I'm wearing heels."

"I'll be right over."

"I'll buy you lunch."

"That's your best offer?"

"Wear a tie."

It would have been a shame to waste the outfit, so we met at the Mesa Grill, a southwestern place in the Flatiron district where the clientele and the prices are usually too upscale for me, but the food is good.

I took the bus down Fifth; there was a limit to my splurging. The restaurant was bright and airy, ceiling fans spinning, stainless steel handrails and bar. Stainless steel was becoming a theme of the day.

Bill was waiting when I got there, at a balcony table. We could watch the comings and goings from there. There was, as far as I knew, no need for that in our present circumstances, but it was the table I'd have chosen if I'd gotten there first, too.

He stood when he saw me, but he didn't pull out my chair. Bill's twelve years older than I am, and sometimes there's tension between the things he does because they're ingrained, and the things I can put up with. But mostly we've worked it out.

"Hi," I said. He leaned to kiss me. He had on a gray sport jacket and a black knit tie. "You should wear a tie more often."

"You should take me to lunch more often. What's the occasion?"

"We have a wealthy client."

"What you mean we, white man?"

"No, you're the white man. I'm the Chinese woman."

"Did I get that wrong again? Damn."

The waiter came, bringing blue corn chips and salsa loud with cilantro. We ordered, and he left. Bill asked, "Who's our mysterious benefactor, and how do you know I'll take the case?"

"For the same reason he knew I'd take it. You won't be able to resist." I told him who, and what.

When I was through, he was quiet, sipping a Mexican beer. "Mitch Ellman," he mused.

"You see?" I said. "You can't resist the chance to nail the little worm, can you?"

"He was acquitted," Bill said.

"Oh, come on! You don't believe there's any chance he didn't kill her, do you?"

He put his beer down on the sand-colored tablecloth. "No," he said. "I don't."

The waiter came with lunch. Mine was mesquite-grilled salmon with a yogurt-dill glaze, though as Bill pointed out none of that was native to the Southwest except the mesquite. He had a chick-pea and tomatillo tortilla.

"You're only eating that because you can pronounce it," I accused.

"Possibly true," he agreed. "I'll examine my motives in the small, dark hours. Do you have a plan for Mitch Ellman?"

"I do." I tasted my fish. It was smoky and smooth. I ate a baby carrot and told Bill my plan.

He nodded a few times while I was talking, asked a few questions. When I finished, we ate in silence for a while, and I knew he was going over it in his head, looking for trouble spots we would have to deal with.

"It could work," he said, as I reached my fork into his plate for a bite of tortilla. "You should wear a wire." He thought. "Unless you're afraid he'll find it?"

"He'll never get that close, if that's what you're really asking."

"Of course it is."

"Relax."

"Okay."

So we decided to do it. Bill had a few more suggestions, and we played around with the plan through the warm apple tart, which we shared.

There were risks, of course, and we discussed what they were and how to minimize them. Then we went on. That's one of the great things about Bill: he never suggests, as everyone else who claims to care about me does constantly, that I should avoid something just because it's dangerous.

Over his coffee and my peppermint tea Bill said, "Tell me about the client."

I'd already told him who the client was, but I knew he didn't mean that.

"Him?" I asked. "Or her?"

"Which one did you dislike more?"

"I didn't really dislike her," I began.

"No," Bill said. "But she gave you hives."

"Well, she's such a cliché. The terminally shy Chinese girl, afraid of bringing disgrace to her family but dynamite in bed. I have a cultural issue with that."

"I wouldn't touch it. What about him?"

"You're the one who should have a cultural issue with him. Pompous rich white guy, patronizing and totally unsympathetic."

"What's the issue?"

I gave him a narrow-eyed stare. "If I didn't know you to be, deep in your heart, the perfect model of a caring, empathic, antimacho postfeminist male—"

"Yo, my sister, you wanna step outside?"

"You and who else?"

"Every other antimacho postfeminist male in here."

We looked around at the cutting-edge crowd of photographers and architects finishing their lunch.

"Well," Bill said, "maybe not. Let's get back to John Kimball."

"Pompous rich—"

"I heard that part. So why is he bothering?"

"With this case? I get the feeling he thinks he's stuck. And resents it, by the way. He's a friend of the family."

"Why didn't he just send her home? 'Thank you, Janet, but there's nothing that can be done about that case anymore. I suggest you go home and forget it.'"

"You underestimate the terminally shy Chinese. It took her months to work up to this, and I'm sure the only way she did it was by convincing herself it was more important than saving face. So following up on it becomes the Correct Thing to Do. She'd lose face in her own mind if she let it drop now."

"And you think he knows that?"

"She may have told him she'd go to the police or something if he didn't help her. We can be very insistent."

That, of course, was all wrong, but it seemed right to us at the time.

When we left the restaurant Bill went back to his office and I went across Fourteenth Street to Paterson Silks. The next few moves were mine; I'd call Bill when everything was set.

And, of course, I'd call John Kimball, to keep him apprised.

At Paterson I bought a few yards of wine-colored raw silk. I bought thread, lightweight silk for a lining, and a pattern, and took them home to my mother.

"This is what people wear now?" she sniffed, examining the pattern.

"Fancy Hong Kong ladies," I said. "Businesswomen. That's a very high-class suit."

She gave me a long, appraising look. "If you let your hair grow," she said, "if you did something about your nails, and put some color on your face . . ."

"I'll fake it, Ma. Can you make the suit?"

She gave me a look full equally of disapproval and disappointment. "Ling Wan-ju," she said, "did you ever bring me a pattern I couldn't make?"

It took her four days to make the suit, and it was very high-class indeed. I could never have afforded it at a tony boutique uptown, but my mother spent thirty years as a seamstress in a sweatshop in Chinatown, and the truth is that everything that's sold at those tony boutiques is made in the sweatshops of Chinatown.

By the time the suit was ready the operation was ready, too.

I had called the CCA Film Program, spoken to the director, Harry Lang. I explained who I was and what I wanted. He believed every word of it. Three days later, in my new suit, a pale pink blouse, and a little too much gold jewelry, I was sitting in a fluorescent-lit classroom, being introduced to a special meeting of directing students by Harry Lang.

"This is Ms. Lydia Chin, of Black Tiger Films in Hong Kong," he told the eighteen or twenty students who had gathered to meet me. CCA, on West Forty-fifth Street, is one of those specialty institutes you find on every other block in New York. A CCA degree, students hoped, would get you a foot in the door in TV or film; or, in the case of the acting students, in to see agents and casting directors you would otherwise not get close to. CCA did, in fact, have its share of well-known alumni; but it wasn't UCLA.

"And this," Harry Lang went on, "is her American associate, William Smith."

"Hardball Productions," Bill said, giving them a California smile. He was California all the way, tan jacket, linen shirt, ironed jeans, cowboy boots. He even wore tiny round sunglasses, and a thin silver chain around his neck with a tiny silver rattlesnake hanging from it.

"I don't know how many of you are familiar with Black Tiger," Lang was saying. "They're a fairly new studio. About four years old, am I right, Ms. Chin?"

"Not even," I said with a smile and a British accent, because Hong Kong English is British English. "Closer to three and one half."

"Yes," said Lang. "Well, for such a short time, you have an impressive record." He was holding in his hand our impressive record, which I'd made up and had printed yesterday, along with the letterhead it was printed on. Copies had been distributed to the students as they arrived.

"Thank you," I said. "You have to understand that in Hong Kong there is a time pressure which perhaps is not felt in Hollywood." I smiled knowingly at Bill. He smiled knowingly back.

"The Hong Kong film industry has experienced explosive growth in the last decade," I told the students. "To stay competitive a studio must produce quantity as well as quality. It is not unusual for a director, under contract to a studio, to make four films a year."

I looked out over my audience, saw all their little eyes light up.

Mitch Ellman's little eyes, in the second row from the back, were as bright as anyone's.

He was, I noticed, wearing the ponytail again.

"However," I went on crisply, "you have all probably heard of Hong Kong's difficulty in holding on to talented professionals in these troubled times. Fear of 1997 is rampant, and many people have, unfortunately, chosen to leave the island.

"There has developed quite a competitive situation in regards, especially, to directing talent. Many studios, faced with rising demand and a shrinking talent pool, have, I regret to say, resorted to the use of . . . mediocre talent."

Bill grinned. Mediocre, his face said, was a kind word.

"But Black Tiger refuses to do that," I said. "I don't know how many of you are familiar with our films." I looked around the room. All the glowing little eyes were trying hard to look familiar. "If you know us, you will know that there is a . . . philosophy, a series of threads that runs through our work."

I could almost hear the mental keyboards clicking as résumés were rewritten to highlight philosophical threads running through people's work.

"This is a hard world, ladies and gentlemen," I told them, sweeping the room with a long, slow glance. I let my eyes rest, for a moment, on Mitch Ellman's.

A smile touched the corners of his mouth and his gaze merged with mine with a presumptuous intimacy.

It made me want to get up and sock him.

Bill, seeing our eyes meet, frowned slightly, uncrossed his legs, crossed them the other way. I shot him a swift look, began again.

"Black Tiger is unafraid of the darkest recesses of this world. We believe it is the mission of the media—even the so-called entertainment media—to lift the curtain from the hidden pain in the human soul." I went on like that for a while. They ate it up.

"However," I said, building to my finale, "it takes a particular sort of artistic vision to do what we do. An unflinching vision, a courageous vision. Without that, works of our sort can become mere exploitation films, violence and sex, blood and fear without meaning. Vision in Hong Kong," I swept the room again, "is becoming scarce. I have come to America in search of vision."

Bill and I searched for vision in the halls of CCA for two days, and a dreary search it was. In a stale screening room with a sticky carpet we saw at least one work by each directing student, including four who had not made it to the meeting. We asked for a second film from five of those students, and viewed them with the student present. We discussed, commented, asked the student to explicate. We heard some thoughtful, intelligent presentations, and we heard a lot of nonsense.

And we heard, of course, from Mitch Ellman.

We heard from him last, because we set it up that way. Two others of the final five were also good-looking blond men, and I displayed a great deal of interest in their work. I made eye contact when we talked, touched their manly arms with my manicured fingertips. Bill smoked and grew progressively more sarcastic and nasty in his questions and commentary. At one point, in the middle of a film, he got up and stalked out. Just before Mitch Ellman's turn we had a fight.

"I don't know how you people do it in Hong Kong," Bill's snarling voice was loud, "but the casting couch is passé, here."

"Don't be ridiculous," I answered airily. "That was very interesting work. A fresh approach—"

"Approach? You practically ran him over. And there was nothing fresh about it. You have a very stale technique."

"It worked on you."

"My mistake."

"I can't believe you're jealous of men twenty years younger than yourself."

"I can't believe you're making cow eyes at men ten years younger than *your*self."

That was an exaggeration, but anything for art.

"I think we'd better have the next one in." My voice was icy. "Don't you agree?"

He gave me a silent stare. Then he stood abruptly, stuck his head out the already open door, and called, "Ellman!"

Mitch Ellman, cassette in hand, came in struggling to keep his face straight.

"Hello, Mitch." I gave him a warm smile, ignored Bill as he sat heavily in the row in front of me. "What do we have?"

"Hello, Ms. Chin." Ellman grinned, his eyes catching mine as though there were already secrets between us. "Hi, Mr. Smith." You couldn't miss, in the way he addressed Bill, the derisive generosity of the young toward the over-the-hill.

Bill didn't miss it. He turned, gave Ellman a long, cold stare, turned back to the screen.

"This is called 'Within Wheels,'" Ellman said, putting his tape into the VCR. He sat beside me, smiled at me as the lights went down.

As it had when our eyes first met, my skin crawled now, so near Mitch Ellman. The way he leaned a little too close; the way his teeth seemed pointed when he smiled; the way his eyes held mine too long every time they met: I wanted to get up and move, to put actual, physical distance between us.

I didn't. I sat there, smiled back, and he rolled the film.

His second film was like his first, dark and pretentious, filled with rats and trash cans and lonely beer bottles rolling in the gutter and steam rising from street grates in the rainy New York night. I asked him whispered questions all through the thing, forcing myself to lean close, to touch his hand. Bill kept his eyes fixed on the screen; you could see the anger expanding and surrounding him like the blue halo of cigarette smoke he was producing.

"Mitch"—I smiled again when the lights came up—"I like this very much. Let me see . . . do I have your résumé?"

"Oh. Yeah, sure," Mitch Ellman said eagerly. "I gave it to you yesterday." He produced another copy while I fanned through the papers in front of me. I read it over, nodded, passed it to Bill. Bill barely glanced at it, dropped it onto the chair next to him.

I shifted my eyes to the back of Bill's head, then to Mitch again. "I think," I said, "that I shall have to call you, Mitch."

"Great," he said, seizing onto my eyes. "When?"

"Soon," I told him, indicating Bill. "Thank you for coming."

"Sure," Mitch Ellman grinned. "Sure."

Bill grumped and glowered as we left CCA, kept it up the whole time we were hailing a cab. It was rush hour on the West Side; it took a while. He stood in the street with his arm in the air, wearing more California clothes—a rumpled linen jacket over a white T-shirt—while I stayed demurely on the sidewalk in a blue silk dress my mother made me last year.

"How're you doing?" I asked when we were safely and privately in the cab.

He leaned back against the seat. "I could do without the cowboy boots," he grinned.

"They make you look sexy."

"They do?"

"No, wait, I meant bowlegged."

"I thought bowlegged men were supposed to be sexy. It's because their—"

"I don't want to hear why. I can guess."

"You want to investigate?" He lifted his sunglasses and leered.

"No." I leaned back against the seat of the cab, too. "I also don't ever want to see another movie."

"That'll make you a cheap date."

"And speaking of cheap," I said, "that's a pretty chintzy place, CCA. Where's the glamour? Where's the glitz? Where's the excitement of life in the fast lane?"

"Where," said Bill, "is Janet Woo's transcript?"

That sat me up again.

"What are you talking about?"

"This afternoon," Bill said, "while you were making eyes at muscled young blonds, I was making eyes at muscled young blondes. Two charming work-study students in the registrar's office. Janet Woo never went to CCA."

I stared at him for a moment, then leaned back again. "Oh," I said. "Ho. What do you suppose that means?"

We discussed what we supposed it meant for the rest of the ride. At the end of the ride we sat in a diner on Canal Street and discussed it some more. We discussed what we supposed some other things meant, too; and then we thought of things we hadn't even wondered about, and discussed them as well.

We took turns filling in the details, convincing each other. It didn't take all that long, that part. When we were convinced, we discussed what we were going to do about it.

When we'd settled on a plan I had another cup of tea and he had a cup of coffee, to celebrate.

"What if we're wrong?" I said.

"It's the same as with the tape," Bill said. "This is bait only the guilty will rise to."

Bill's a fisherman; he was probably seeing trout in a sun-dappled stream when he said that.

Me, I was seeing *Jaws*.

It was time to call John Kimball and give him an update.

"Things are going well, Mr. Kimball." I was in my office, which is a room I sublet from a travel agent on Canal. This way people coming to see me can pretend they're looking for a cheap flight to Taiwan. It saves a lot of face.

"Have you found out yet whether the tape we discussed actually exists?" Kimball got right down to business.

"No." I sketched out the rest of the scenario for him. "If it works out, I'll call you tomorrow night with the final details."

"Fine," Kimball said, and hung up.

One friendly guy.

I let Mitch Ellman stew until the next afternoon, then called him at CCA. Last year, before his arrest, Mitch had been a work-study student himself, answering the switchboard three afternoons a week. Wouldn't that have been convenient, I thought, as I sat on Hold while someone raced around looking for him. I was sending very strong ESP signals to the receptionist to just come back so I could leave a message when Mitch Ellman's eager voice blossomed in my ear.

"Can you meet me for a drink tonight?" I asked, after he was through telling me how glad he was I'd called. "We're staying at the Paramount."

"Great," he said. "Great. Will you be," his voice lowered, "alone?"

"Yes." I lowered my voice, too. "Bill has plans. I don't expect him back until . . . late."

"I'll be there," Mitch Ellman promised me.

The bar at the Paramount Hotel is a dark place of sharp edges and things that reflect. Wearing a black velvet cocktail dress and a rhinestone choker I sat in a black leather booth softer than my best pair of gloves. I sipped a club soda with both lime and lemon in a black glass and watched for Mitch Ellman. The quiet music in the air was jazz piano and bass. Bill would have known who the musicians were.

When Mitch came through the dark glass doors I didn't stand or wave to him, but when he spotted me I lifted my drink and smiled.

He made a beeline across the room. He was wearing a loose double-breasted suit and a wide silk tie, right in the heart of fashion. His ponytail was tied back with a black leather thong.

"Hi, Ms. Chin," he said, a little breathlessly, when he reached the table.

"Hello, Mitch." I smiled my quietest smile. "Please sit down. And please call me Lydia." I signaled a waiter.

Mitch slid onto the opposite banquette. "Lydia." He leaned toward me. "You look great."

"Thank you, Mitch." I wondered, now that my arms were bare, if he could actually see my skin crawl.

The waiter came. Mitch ordered a martini. He looked around the bar, at the chic patrons, the hard edges and soft lights. "Is this where you always stay when you come to New York?"

"When I can," I told him. "Bill likes the Plaza. But I prefer things that are . . . new."

"Bill and you," Mitch said, bringing his eyes back to me, "you work together a lot?"

"Hardball Productions is our American distributor." I sipped my drink, smiled at him again. "But I work with many people, Mitch."

His martini arrived, in a wide black glass. He lifted it. I lifted mine. "To the future," he said, and our eyes locked. I pulled mine away.

After we drank to the future, I put my glass down. "Unfortunately, Mitch, I don't have very good news for you."

His face clouded. "What do you mean?"

"I don't think I can offer you anything, Mitch."

"What? But I thought you liked my work. When you saw 'Within Wheels'—"

"I do like it, Mitch. You have a fresh, raw approach, a sharp, dark vision. I believe you would be an asset to Black Tiger. That's why I called you." I drank again. "Right up to this evening I believed I could persuade Bill to my point of view. But he doesn't like your work as much as I do, and I can't seem to change his mind."

"Yeah, my work," Mitch sneered. "I'll bet that's what he doesn't like."

I smiled over my drink, didn't answer.

"Look," Mitch said, "do you have to listen to him? He's just your distributor. Why can't you do what you want?"

"Hardball is investing a large amount of capital in the development of Black Tiger; very valuable to us in the current economic climate. I'm afraid I can't go against Bill's judgment. Especially when I have only . . . feelings . . . to go on."

He leaned a little closer. "Feelings?"

"I think," I said, drawing his eyes into mine, "I *sense*, that there's something in you, Mitch. Something wild and raw and untamable. Something animal. Exciting. Beyond the rules, beyond the boundaries. Something I would like very much to—to meet." I traced the back of his hand with my fingertip, watched his pupils widen. "It's that," I whispered, "that's what I wanted . . . for Black Tiger."

Then I slipped my hand away, picked up my drink. "But Bill doesn't agree. He doesn't have my certainty, my sense of your potential. He's only seen the films we've seen, and based on them, he doesn't think you have it, Mitch."

"Doesn't think I have it?" Mitch's voice was husky.

"He thinks you're young. He thinks—no, forget it."

"Tell me what he thinks."

I shook my head.

"Tell me!"

I let my own eyes widen; then I told him. "He thinks it's fake, Mitch. The wildness, the power I see in your work, that I sense in you: he thinks it's phony. He doesn't think you have . . ." I searched for the word.

A different voice said, "Balls."

My head and Mitch's snapped up at the same time. Bill loomed over our table, dressed completely in black. He still had the sunglasses on.

"I don't think," Bill fixed his black-glass stare on Mitch, "that he has any balls."

"Hey—" Mitch began to rise; I put a hand on his arm.

"What are you doing here?" My words, to Bill, were as cold as I could make them. "I thought you and Paul—"

"I'll bet you did. Paul's twelve-stepping; we ran out of things to do. What's *he* doing here? Going over his résumé?"

"Please sit down. You're making a scene."

"You usually like that. Maybe you should know that about her, Ellman. She likes public scenes. And Chinese food."

"Hey—" Mitch began again.

"Come on," Bill said, grasping my arm. "Bedtime."

I pulled sharply away. "I'm not finished."

"Yes, you are."

"No, she's not." Mitch was finally on his feet. "The lady says she's not finished, bud."

Bill looked at him in surprise, then laughed. "Lydia," he said, his eyes still on Mitch, "did I ever tell you about the dogfight I saw in Tijuana? Doberman and a cocker spaniel. Doberman just about chewed the spaniel's balls off. Not that it was much of a mouthful—"

"Stop it!" I ordered. "You're being ridiculous. You're drunk. Go upstairs. I'll be up soon."

"Now," he said.

"No," I said, my eyes burning through his dark lenses, finding his eyes. "Soon."

He stood for a moment, shoulders tight, hands curled into fists.

Then his hands opened, his shoulders dropped. He laughed.

"Okay," he said. "Why not? I'll see you later, sweetheart. Enjoy your drink." He turned his head suddenly, barked at Mitch. Mitch flinched. "Night, Spot," Bill said. He was laughing as he turned and left.

"Hey—!" Mitch started after him.

"Sit down," I said sharply.

He stopped. After a few seconds of staring at the black glass doors still swinging from Bill's exit, Mitch sat.

His face glowed red. I signaled the waiter, who, like half the bar, had been watching us anyway. I pointed to Mitch's drink.

"That bastard," Mitch growled, after the waiter had brought his second martini. "That motherfucking bastard!"

"Yes," I said, sipping my drink. "With money."

"Fuck his money!"

"I never do that."

Mitch stopped, confused.

"For money," I said. "I'll do many things for money, but that isn't one of them."

Mitch frowned, the confusion growing. "You mean—you and he—" He looked over his shoulder to the door, turned back. "I thought—"

I laughed. "Oh, Mitch, just forget it. You're so young. Perhaps Bill's right. I may be wrong; this whole thing may be a mistake. Let's just finish our drinks and say good night, what do you say?"

"No!" he burst out. "You're not wrong. I *do* have it! I have what you need, you and Black Tiger both!"

Another laugh; I tried to make it tinkle. "Why, Mitch, how sweet. Still, it won't do any good. Bill's a bastard but he's a businessman. If he can't see anything that's worth risking his money on—"

"What if he could?"

"Well, if he could, it wouldn't matter to him that he doesn't like you."

Mitch's face, which had been fading back to its normal pallor, reddened again. "But, Mitch—"

"There is something."

"Excuse me?"

"There is something." Mitch had slurped up half his new martini. His eyes were shining now. "There's a film I didn't show you."

"Mitch, I don't understand. If you have a better film, why didn't you bring it?"

"It's not better. It has—technical difficulties." He grinned. "But it shows what you want to see. It shows I have more balls than that drunk cokehead motherfucker ever dreamed of!" He pounded the table with the flat of his hand.

I raised my eyebrows, in awe at his manliness. "I would have liked to have seen that, Mitch."

"I can still show it to you. I can show you tomorrow. You can—"

"I'm afraid I have meetings all day tomorrow. And we're leaving the following morning for Los Angeles. Early," I added.

"It's short. It just takes—"

"I have meetings all day, Mitch."

He gulped some martini in agitation. Then suddenly he brightened. "Tomorrow night. Whenever you say. I can bring it here."

I considered. "Well," I said slowly, drawing it out, "well, I suppose that's possible. Bill's planning a late night, but I had no intention of accompanying him."

"Can I then? Can I bring it up?"

I looked at him thoughtfully. "You say it's—different? Unusual?"

He nodded rapidly, eyes huge.

"I suppose, if I liked it," I said, "I could persuade Bill to view it when he returned. He doesn't like to go directly to sleep, in any case."

"Well, then? Well? Can I bring it?"

I thought I'd better agree before he crawled over the table and into my lap.

"Yes, Mitch. Bring your film tomorrow night. I'll look forward to it."

I called Bill as soon as I got home.

"Let me speak to the Doberman," I said.

"Is this that Siamese cat with the rhinestone collar?"

"That dogfight thing wasn't fair. I almost cracked up."

"Just keeping you on your patent leather toes. Did it work?"

"Uh-huh." I told him the plan.

"All right," he said. "I'll meet you there around nine."

"How about seven?"

"Okay, but why?"

"Because I'll never get a suite at the Paramount again. If John Kimball's cash advance is covering this, I think he should buy us a room service meal."

"Heartless hussy."

"We could have told him we needed the suite tonight too, for authenticity. Think of all the money we're saving him."

"It's a warm, cozy thought. I think I'll go to sleep curled around it. Unless you want to come over—?"

I hung up.

Then I called John Kimball, to apprise him.

"He fell for it, Mr. Kimball. He's coming to the hotel tomorrow night."

"Good, fine. How is it exactly arranged?"

I'd been expecting that question. "Mitch will show up at ten-thirty, with his tape. That will give us time to view it, remove it from the VCR, and for me to make the switch. Bill will come charging in at about eleven-thirty, drunk and looking for a fight."

"How will he get in?"

"I'll leave the door unlocked."

"Then what?"

"Bill and I have a roaring fight. Yelling, screaming, things thrown and broken. I hustle Mitch out with the dummy tape, telling him I'll call him in the morning."

"And?"

"And we pack up and bring the real tape to you."

"It sounds as though you've thought of everything, Miss Chin."

I thought it sounded that way, too.

The next morning I'd intended to sleep late, but I was too keyed up for that. After breakfast I did some errands for my mother, then grabbed my rollerblades and did an hour in Battery Park City, back and forth on the Esplanade. At eleven I went up to the dojo and took a Tae Kwon Do class. Finally, just after two, dressed in a loose green jacket over a short black skirt, carrying a suitcase that was nearly empty, I went uptown and checked into my suite at the Paramount.

I told the desk clerk my husband would be in about seven. She smiled and said that was fine. I spent the afternoon just playing tourist on the Upper East Side. At six I went back to the hotel to take a nap. I was still asleep when Bill came in.

"Lydia?" I heard his voice from the outer room. "It's me."

"I'm in here," I called.

"Are you decent?"

"No."

"I'll be right there."

"Don't you move."

I washed my face, brushed my hair, slipped my skirt back on. When I came out to the other room he was fixing himself a drink from the bar near the windows.

"Hi," he said. "You have a crease down your cheek. Want a drink?"

"The usual," I said breezily. I crossed the thick carpet, felt the pile squash under my stockinged feet. I flopped onto a huge ice-blue sofa, stretched myself out.

Bill brought me a club soda with lime. He sat at the other end of the sofa. There was room for two more people between us.

"I can't believe we're finally alone in a hotel room and all you want to do is have dinner," he said.

"At least I invited you. I could have asked Mitch."

"I doubt if he'd have been the gentleman I'm planning to be."

"Thank you for letting me in on your plans. How about some music?"

We had music from the stereo, and dinner from room service, and bizarre, out-of-scale reproductions of famous paintings to look at on the walls. It's a cutting-edge place, the Paramount. We had fun, eating steak and grilled capon and berries with crème fraîche. We talked about the city and we talked about the music, and then we talked about the plan.

We went over it again, coordinating with each other, making sure we hadn't overlooked anything so big we hadn't noticed it. We gave each other what-if situations and decided how to handle them. Then we had coffee and tea. Then it was time to get ready.

I went into the bedroom, laid out my things from the suitcase. I showered in the huge marble bathroom, dried myself on towels that seemed an inch thick. I blew my hair dry and dressed.

Bill was still in the outer room; he'd had less to do. I clipped on the tiny remote microphone. "Is it working? Can you hear me?"

"It's not clear," Bill called.

I moved it. "Is this better?"

"Maybe I should come in and show you how to do it." I could hear the grin in his voice.

"I've worn one before."

"Not like this. It's brand new, I just bought it. I think I should come adjust it for you—"

"If you come in here I'll shoot you."

Talking about my gun reminded me, so I checked it. Everything seemed perfect. I clipped it to the waistband of my silk pajamas and covered it and the mike and everything else I was wearing with my yellow silk kimono.

"Jesus," Bill said as I came into the outer room. "That's just how I always imagined you'd look in a kimono."

"You've imagined about that?"

"Incessantly."

"That's an invasion of privacy. I think it's illegal."

Bill had opened the windows; he's a big fan of open windows. The mild April air whispered in, moving the hem of my robe. Bill watched that happen, and he smiled.

Then he said, "I think I'd better disappear. In case he's early. In case he doesn't knock." He asked, "Nervous?"

"A little," I admitted.

"It'll be fine," he said. "It'll go perfectly."

"I bet you say that to all the girls."

"Uh-huh. And I'm always right."

He showed me where the recorder was hidden. He kissed me on the cheek. Then I was alone in the room, waiting.

Mitch was a little late. At the time it annoyed me; later I saw it as a blessing. I let myself think nervous thoughts: he'd changed his mind, he wouldn't come. He'd come, but too late. And the worst: he'd come, but he'd bring a different tape from the one we wanted, some murky, incomprehensible garbage I'd have to watch.

I drank some more club soda, paced around the room. I felt silk brush my calves as I moved, felt my heart beat, felt the reassuring solidness of my gun under my left arm. I sat in front of the big-screen TV flipping channels. I was in the middle of some murky, incomprehensible garbage when a knock came on the door. It made me jump.

I turned off the TV, opened the door. "Mitch, you're late." I stepped aside to let him in, unlatched the door before it closed.

"I'm sorry, Ms. Chin—Lydia," he breathed. "Bad traffic. I jumped out of the cab and ran the last ten blocks."

"Did you really?" I smiled. "Such devotion. Would you like a drink?"

I waved him in the direction of the bar. He gaped, and seemed frozen with indecision; then he poured himself a large tumbler of Glenlivet.

Bill had said the Glenlivet was the most expensive thing there.

"God, Lydia," Mitch said appreciatively, raising his glass to me, "you are gorgeous."

"Thank you." I smiled graciously. "Did you bring your film?"

"Yes." He grabbed up an envelope he'd put down on the bar. "It's here. You'll love it, especially you. I'll bet you've never seen anything like it."

"I've seen a lot, Mitch."

"Not like this."

He slipped the tape into the VCR, took the remote in hand, sat down beside me on the ice-blue couch.

He was right. I'd never seen anything like it. But he was wrong. I hated it.

There were no titles or opening credits. Just the coarse-grained static of blank videotape; then, suddenly, picture. We were looking down on a large rumpled brass bed. For a short time, silence and stillness. I lifted my eyebrows at Mitch, but he wasn't watching me. His eyes were on the screen, his lips slightly parted. It struck me that he'd watched this tape before.

I heard laughter. Two naked figures danced into the frame, touching and teasing each other. One was Mitch Ellman. The other I recognized only from the graduation photos and family portraits we'd seen on the eleven o'clock news.

It's a shock seeing someone alive for the first time after you know they're dead. I was just getting used to that when, on the screen, Patricia Lin shoved Mitch Ellman away. Laughing, she bounced onto the bed. He laughed too. Then he bent over her. His blond hair covered her face as he pinned her wrists over her head with one hand, kissed her hard. She lifted her lips to his, responding.

Grinning, he snatched up a cord dangling from the brass headboard, tied it around her right wrist. She turned her head to see; he quickly did the other. She arched, laughed again.

He moved slowly down her body, caressing, kissing her. He tied her ankles to the bed, her legs spread wide; she laughed. He moved back up, touching, stroking. They kissed. He moved, made her strain to follow him. He touched her and she moaned, twisted in her bonds.

He mounted her. It was short and violent, animal sounds and the sounds of skin. Spent, he pulled away and stood up.

She raised her head, her face puzzled. She whispered, "Mitch?"

He grinned. "Wait," he said. He walked out of camera range. Patricia Lin lay still on the bed.

I wondered if she was afraid.

Then Mitch Ellman came back into the frame.

He wasn't alone.

Another man, also nude, was with him. I couldn't see him clearly. "Patty, this is a friend of mine," I could hear Mitch say. "He wanted to meet you."

Patricia Lin, bound to the bed, turned her face to the stranger. She looked at him; then a wide, wild smile split her face. "Well," she said huskily, arching toward him, "come meet me."

As the stranger leaned over Patricia Lin I saw his face.

It was John Kimball.

I shot Mitch a glance. He was enrapt, his eyes shining.

In the film, Kimball mounted Patricia Lin.

In the hotel suite, the door flew open.

"Turn it off!" a voice yelled.

It was John Kimball.

Mitch's mouth fell open.

"Turn it off!" A silenced automatic stared from Kimball's right hand.

I grabbed the remote from Mitch, turned the film off. Mitch didn't move.

"Take it out," Kimball said, "and give it to me."

I started toward the VCR.

"Not you." Kimball waved me back to the sofa. "You, Mitch."

Mitch jolted himself from the sofa, stumbled to the VCR. He handed the ejected tape to Kimball.

Kimball put it in his pocket. "Sit down."

Mitch sat next to me again. Kimball looked quickly from Mitch to me and around the room.

"Now what?" I asked, dropping the British accent. Mitch's mouth opened again.

"Now we sit and wait for your partner," Kimball said. As though that sounded like a good idea, he dropped himself onto an ice-blue armchair, positioned to keep the gun on us and an eye on the suite door.

"Then?" Mitch choked.

"Then he kills us," I said, before Kimball could answer.

Mitch's eyes widened. Kimball shrugged.

"You got greedy, Mitch," he said.

"Mitch was blackmailing you," I said to Kimball. "Over the tape. That was why you wanted it. You were planning to kill him, but you couldn't risk it before you had the tape."

"Hey," Mitch blurted. "Hey. There's another. There's a copy in my safe deposit box."

"This is the copy from your safe deposit box. I saw you pick it up this morning," Kimball said. "There's no other. Why would you risk that? You're a greedy bastard but you're not that stupid."

"Hey—"

"Shut up, Mitch. I'm tired of hearing you. You're a whiner. You whined the night we met in that goddamn yuppie bar and you've been whining ever since. It'll be a pleasure having you out of my life."

Voices and laughter came from the corridor. Kimball lifted the gun warningly. The voices died away.

"Now you," Kimball said to me, "I do regret having to do this to you. You're smart and cute. We could have worked well together."

I could feel my face redden angrily and my shoulders square.

"You know," Kimball said to Mitch, "all of a sudden I don't trust her. I think you'd better tie her up." He waved the gun at me. "Use your belt, Mitch. Who knows? Maybe she'll like it."

I stood, turned my back as the gun directed me to do. Mitch loosened his own belt, pulled my wrists behind me, started wrapping the belt around them.

"Don't do that," Bill's voice said.

It came, not from the suite door, but from the bedroom doorway.

Kimball whipped around, stumbling and firing a shot which caught Bill in the chest, threw him against the wall. I shook off the belt, yanked my gun from its clip, fired at Kimball. I hit him in the wrist. His gun flew across the room as he yelped and grabbed his arm.

"Don't move!" I ordered him. "I'd love to kill you."

Bill stood slowly.

"Are you okay?" I asked, my heart racing.

"Uh-huh. I just wish they'd make a vest that could stop the kick along with the bullet."

"What the—?" Kimball groaned.

"What the hell—?" Mitch croaked.

"What the hell took you so long?" I snapped at Bill.

"You had everything under control." He rubbed his side through his Kevlar vest. "I thought we should get as much as we could on tape. Nice shot, by the way."

"I was aiming at his guts."

"Oh. Lousy shot, by the way."

"I don't believe this," Kimball said, leaning over his wrist.

"Well, it was good, Mr. Kimball," I said, "but not that good. Bill got suspicious because CCA had no record of Janet Woo. I didn't like her anyway. Hopelessly shy, terrified of disgracing her family: so Chinese."

Bill brought Kimball a towel from the bathroom to wrap around his wrist.

"But a woman like that studying acting?" I went on. "That was a mistake, Mr. Kimball. Of course, that was the true part. She was an actress, wasn't she, just hired for the role?"

Mitch finally found his voice. "You mean," he choked, "there's no Black Tiger? No Hong Kong?"

"Not in your future, Mitch. I'd wondered how a work-study student at a second-rate school could have afforded such a high-priced lawyer. After I'd met you I wondered about your fancy clothes. And you're back in school this year, and not even on work-study—after the cost of a trial like that.

"And you, Mr. Kimball. You didn't like it that I had a partner, but you didn't mind it so much once you found out that he worked alone, too. And you wanted to know everything we were planning. I thought that was strange. Most attorneys like to know as little as possible.

"So Bill and I worked out a hypothesis. And we tested it. And you're right on time, Mr. Kimball. Halfway between when Mitch came and when you expected Bill to show up."

"What if you'd been wrong?" Mitch asked wonderingly.

"If we'd been wrong, Mr. Kimball wouldn't have come. We'd have taken the tape and there'd have been a civil rights prosecution and everything would have been lovely."

"Civil rights?" Mitch was still behind.

"That's just the beginning," I said. "There's also extortion for you. And kidnapping and attempted murder for you," I turned to Kimball, "just based on tonight. Plus whatever's on the rest of the tape, which thank God I didn't have to see."

"He killed her," Kimball said through teeth clenched in hate or pain, or maybe both. "I didn't even know it was happening."

"You were there," I said. "Now she's dead."

While I'd been chatting with Kimball and Mitch, Bill had called hotel security. They'd called the police. All of them stormed in at once now, and there was a lot of general confusion and people growling orders.

They took all the guns and they took everyone's name and statement and finally they took Kimball and Mitch and the tape away.

They needed to take us away too, down to the precinct where they could ask more questions and take more statements and yell at us; but Bill persuaded them to wait outside on the ice-blue side chairs in the corridor while I changed.

I showered again, because watching that film had made me feel as though someone had spit on me in the street. When I was through I packed up my lingerie and my own Kevlar vest. I put my jacket and skirt back on and went out to the other room.

There was music from the stereo. Bill was on the sofa with a drink and a cigarette. I went and sat next to him. He put his arm around me and I leaned on his shoulder.

"What's the music?" I asked.

"Brahms. Piano Quintet."

I looked through the torn place on his shirt to the bruise under it. "Does it hurt?"

"No," he lied. He sipped at his drink. "It was hard watching that film, I'll bet."

"He called her Patty," I said. "He tied her up. She liked it."

I didn't know I was cold until I felt Bill's arm pulling me closer, all solid and warm.

We sat like that for a while, until Bill's drink was finished and his cigarette was gone and we had no more excuse to sit quietly by ourselves. Then we got up, took our things, and left our suite at the Paramount. We joined the cop in the corridor, who was finishing a cigarette of his own. The three of us rode silently down in the elevator, crossed the marble lobby past the black-glass doors. A uniformed doorman held the street door for us.

Outside, the sidewalk was crowded with reporters. On the street were a couple of TV remote broadcast vans. I looked at my watch; the ones who'd been quick enough could have gotten the arrest of Mitch Ellman and John Kimball on the eleven o'clock news. There were bright lights and microphones for us, too, but we pushed past them. As we climbed in the police car and pulled into traffic I imagined the entire Paramount Hotel, with its polished lobby, dark, sharp-edged bar, and ice-blue suite, fading to black.

LOREN D. ESTLEMAN

Loren Estleman and his Detroit-based P.I., Amos Walker, have combined for three Shamus Awards, two for Best Short Story and one for Best Novel, *Sugartown* (1984). His most recent Shamus nomination came for his story "Safe House," which appeared in *Deadly Allies*. He is also the author of the acclaimed Detroit Trilogy, *Whiskey River*, *Motown*, and *King of the Corner*.

In "Slipstream" Walker parlays being at the scene of an accident into a job working for the most hated woman in America.

SLIPSTREAM

The blue flashers made me slow down. The red flashers made me pull over and stop to see if I could help scrape someone off the pavement. When the state troopers and the county sheriffs both come out, it means there's been more than just a merger of fenders.

The light bar on the EMS van was stuttering in a desultory kind of way, splashing colors off the dewy asphalt and into the faces of the usual human detritus that gets pulled into the slipstream of accidents, fires, and drive-by shootings: guys in quilted vests and baseball caps, cigarette-puffing women in head scarves and denim, teenage boys reeking of Stroh's, and big cops in leather jackets writing birthdates and license numbers into spiral notebooks with doodles on the covers. The air smelled of scorched metal, gasoline, and carbon tetrachloride. A plume of dank smoke hung over a charred blob of something that might have been a Ford Escort or a Cadillac Seville or the tail section of the *Hindenburg*, kneeling on bare wheels with its front end accordioned against the trailer of a flatbed truck parked across Square Lake Road, somewhere in No Man's Land between Southfield and Iroquois Heights, seven miles north of Detroit.

"See anything you like, mister? Oh, Christ."

This cheery greeting, altered when I turned to face him, came from a man mountain in a Chesterfield with velvet collar and a tweed cap, who answered to Killinger. He wore amber shades astraddle his Irish pug and an impressive set of handlebars that must have set him back an hour each morning in the bathroom. He topped off at six and a half feet, high normal among the Michigan State Police, and dressed out at around two hundred fifty.

"Evening, Lee," I said. "This is a piece out of your pen, isn't it? I heard you were commanding the Northville post."

"Your hearing's just fine. I'm meeting friends for dinner at the Machus Red Fox. Or I was." He checked his watch, a steel aviator type. "They probably think I've pulled a Jimmy Hoffa by now. Anyway I caught the squeal and that makes me the ranking officer on the scene. What about you?"

"Just rank. I thought I had a client up in the Heights. If she'd said over the telephone her missing Ambrose was a pit bull I'd have saved a trip. Is that a K?" Two EMS attendants in navy were busy zipping up a vinyl bag on a stretcher on the gravel apron.

Killinger nodded. "Charbroiled in the can. The M.E., who's been and gone, thinks male, between twenty and twenty-five, but he says he's been wrong before. Sheriff's men put out the fire. No skid marks. Poor son of a bitch came over the hill and met God."

"What was the truck doing blocking the road?"

"We'll know that when we find the driver. He might've jackknifed and been trying to straighten out when the car came. Probably he was drunk. Ninety-nine times out of a hundred that's the case when somebody rabbits."

"No witnesses?"

"Just rubberneckers. Video arcades must be closed."

"What'd you get on the plate?"

He might have smiled under the mustaches. In any case it wouldn't have meant anything. "Rita Donato."

"Seriously?"

"No, I always joke around whenever I help pull a Crispy Critter out from under a steering wheel in my supper suit."

"Then that'd make this—?" I nodded at the bag being slid into the back of the van.

"At a guess, Albert. The son. Heir to the department store chain, currently in receivership while the widow of its late humanitarian founder stamps books in the library in Milan on a three-to-seven for income tax evasion." Then he did smile. "Didn't I call him a poor son of a bitch?"

Walter Donato, dead five years, had been named for his adoptive parents and reared in Dearborn, where he inherited his foster father's five-and-dime at age thirty and within sixteen years ran it into the largest chain of cut-rate department stores in the Middle West. After spending several millions of his personal fortune probing fruitlessly into the mystery of his birth, he had diverted his energies toward the establishment of a foster-care foundation that became a model of its type and put his face simultaneously on the covers of *Time* and *Newsweek*. When bronchial pneumonia took him at sixty-two, the President of the United States authorized an annual grant in his name to be awarded to deserving projects in the area of child placement. The local archbishop had been overheard to remark—and was censured by Rome for so doing—that he'd consider nominating Donato for canonization if he were anything but a Baptist.

The take on his widow was different. A former professional dancer, Rita had met Donato shortly after the death of his first wife, married him within six months, and buried him before their second anniversary. The terms of his will placed her in sole charge of the store chain until the majority of his son Albert, a role she took far more seriously than those of helpmate and stepmother. She remodeled the stores from top to bottom, threw out all the no-brand merchandise, and replaced it with clothing lines named for TV miniseries actresses whom she hired to do commercial endorsements. In no time at all she had stores on both coasts and became a sought-after speaker at gatherings of women who wore shoulder pads and hyphenated their surnames. When the Democrats finally got into the White House there was even talk of a cabinet post.

Just about then someone in the IRS found out she hadn't paid taxes in three years, each of which showed more profit than the chain had seen during Walter's lifetime. After the usual protracted trial, appeal, and counter-appeals, reparations forced the Donato organization into Chapter 11 and Rita into the federal penitentiary at Milan, Michigan, pronounced M*eye*-lin, where at the time of the accident that took the life of her stepson Albert she had served eighteen months. In the meantime some things had come out about her general comportment that removed her name from *Cosmopolitan*'s list of the twenty most admired women.

Albert Donato's death and its circumstances led all the local news reports and received heavy national play for the better part of a week. The Oakland County Sheriff's Department traced the truck driver, one Owen Subject, to his house in the suburbs and arrested him for leaving the scene of the accident with a charge of manslaughter to follow; too much time had elapsed for a blood-alcohol test to be considered conclusive, and so no drunk-driving accusation was made. An independent trucker, Subject told the cops he'd been on his way home from delivering a diesel tractor to a farm implements dealership in Iroquois Heights when he swerved to miss a deer and wound up stalled across Square Lake Road. Albert Donato's Chrysler LeBaron had slammed into him and burst into flames, panicking him into running. Subject's bassethound features and free-standing black hair became a staple on the front pages of both Detroit papers for days. Then another one of the mayor's relatives got caught dealing dope and the story went inside.

That was when a party named Sporthaven with caps on his teeth and a brown leather portfolio under one arm looked me up in my little toy office on West Grand River and asked me to drop in on Mrs. Donato in Milan.

"*Hell* no, I never said it. They made that one up at Channel 2 and all the networks took it and ran with it. That's what convicted me. Otherwise I could have bought my way out."

We were sitting in the visitor's room—a not really uncomfortable place with orange scoop chairs and laminated tables that looked more like the cafeteria in an auto plant than a room in the House of Doors—Rita Donato, Lawyer Sporthaven, and the detective in the story. She had on a cotton blouse open at the neck, twill slacks, and loafers, no stripes or work denims. Things are a little more relaxed in the federal lockup, and if you can afford them you'd be surprised how much you'd be willing to pay for the simple comforts. They didn't include hair dye, and hers had gone back to its natural gray, but it was done in a style becoming to her lean angular face, parted to the left of center and curling in at the base of her neck. She was fifty and looked it, but a patrician fifty, and the large round lenses of her glasses masked the bags under her eyes.

The question, asked by me and answered by her, was whether she had really been overheard to say that only losers pay taxes.

"Pity," I said. "Nobody ever says what everybody says they say." I lit a Winston and waited for the conversation to come to a point, any point. So far all she'd done was sit across the table from me with her legs crossed, bouncing one foot and holding up one end of an interview for "Prime Time Live." I had the impression she was starved for company.

"A man named Killinger gave me your name," she said then, without transition. "I gathered he's something with the state police."

"Commander. He issued me my license the first time."

"He was decent enough to come here in person and tell me about Albert before I heard it on the news. He mentioned your name and what you do. He didn't say why. Maybe he knew the local authorities were going to sweep Albert's death under the rug."

"Are they?"

"Sporthaven tells me they're about to drop all charges against Owen Subject."

I looked at the lawyer's young-old face: nipped, tucked, stitched, peeled, creamed, and smoothed by many hands until it had all the character of a rounded stone in a riverbed.

"I got it from a legal secretary at County," he said. "Albert should have had his car under control. The trucker took adequate steps to avoid hitting an obstruction in the road."

"What about his leaving the scene?"

"There was nothing anyone could do. The car was instantly engulfed. Even had he stayed and risked his life to pull Albert out of the car, a corpse would have been all he saved."

"That part's true enough," I said. "I saw the car."

"They're blowing it off." Mrs. Donato had both feet on the floor now. "If Albert were anyone but my stepson they wouldn't have dared. Read the polls. I'm the most hated woman in America."

"What do you want me to do?"

"Investigate Subject. Killinger said he thought there was alcohol involved. If he's got a record I want it brought out into the open. If it leads to something else I want that to come out too. I'm no wicked stepmother, Walker. I was very fond of Albert. I won't have his life wiped off the books just because the woman his father married made a mistake in arithmetic."

Sporthaven reached inside his portfolio. "Under the conditions of her personal bankruptcy, Mrs. Donato cannot own anything for five years. However, my firm has authorized me to issue you a letter of credit for up to five thousand dollars." He handed me a crisp sheet of expensive bond containing three paragraphs printed in boldface with justified margins. "Should you be successful, whatever is left is yours. Your standard fee is guaranteed, of course."

"Of course." I folded it as carefully as if it were the Declaration of

Independence and interred it in my inside pocket. "What if nothing turns up?"

"Come now." The woman sat back and recrossed her legs. "In your profession and mine, where would we be if we went around looking for the good in everyone?"

I spent an hour in the periodicals section of the Detroit Public Library downtown reading up on the accident. I knew most of the details, but I needed one in particular. When I had it I went back to the office and rummaged through my desk looking for business cards. I still have every card that was ever handed me. Twenty minutes of that and I had a match. I propped it against the base of the desk lamp, looked up Owen Subject in the metropolitan directory, and dialed the number. His wife answered, a break. She said Owen wasn't home; another break. I read the name and title off the business card and arranged an interview at the house for seven that evening. She said Owen would be in by then.

The house was in Redford, one of a tract of brick ranch styles that had been poured in an ice cube tray and dumped out in the pattern in which they were formed. A small woman with red hair and gray roots snatched the door open under my knuckles.

"Owen? Oh." She clutched her quilted housecoat together at her throat.

"Anson Wold, Mrs. Subject. We spoke earlier. I'm with Midwest Casualty. It *is* Mrs. Subject?" I handed her the card.

"Yes. I'm afraid Owen isn't home yet. I expected him before this." She stood aside.

The living room was full of glazed furniture and factory art. Stacks of supermarket tabloids occupied most of the chairs. The same alien seemed to have cropped up on the front pages of most of them. I found space on the couch.

"I just need a couple of details before I can finish processing Mr. Subject's claim. I understand the truck is his property."

"Yes. Um, I didn't know he'd filed a claim. He's been so busy with this court thing. They arrested him, you know." She perched on the edge of a straight-back chair.

"Released on his own recognizance, I believe."

"Right. Even at the arraignment the judge knew they had no case."

"I imagine your finances are pretty tight with his truck in impoundment."

"Well, there's not much coming in. But the mortgage is paid off and so is the truck, and we have enough in savings to take care of incidentals."

I made some scratches in my prop notebook. "He must be a hustler. Making a go of a small business in this economy is a twenty-six-hour-a-day job."

"That's what I said when he left the trucking company and made a down payment on the rig. I told him if he lost the house I'd leave him. It was tough at first, but then he got a loan and right after that work started coming in. We're better off now than when he was punching the clock, and his time's his own." That made her think to look at her watch. "I can't imagine what's keeping him. He was just going to see the lawyer."

"Where did he get the loan?"

"Loan? Oh. Do you need to know that?"

"It's for Records."

The magic phrase brought her to her feet. "I forget the name of the company. I think there's a card." She went to a desk holding up a telephone shaped like a duck and pawed through drawers. "He got the name from a friend in the union. He almost gave up. He'd tried all the places that advertised in the yellow pages and on television. Here it is! Ever hear of them?"

I looked at the card she brought over. "Oh yeah," I said. "I've heard of Gryphon Collateral."

I spotted the blue Chevy two turns after I left Redford.

It was a closed tail and he was good, but traffic was light at that hour and the routes I take around the city are my own and make no sense to anybody but me.

I had three good chances to shake him. I didn't use them. Thanks to Mrs. Subject I had a fair idea who was sending his kid through medical school, and it was handy to have someone close by I could ask questions of in case I hit a wall.

When I turned into the driveway in Highland Park the guy kept driving, reading the numbers on both sides of the street as if he were looking for one in particular. I heard him cut his motor down the block while I was waiting for someone to answer the front door.

"Chevies. What's the world coming to?" Barry Stackpole trained a pair of graphite binoculars through the window of his home office. "Something important went out with bulletproof Cadillacs."

"Ten'll get you twenty when you run the plate it'll kick out Gryphon Collateral," I said.

The room, converted from a small bedroom on the second floor, was full of books and videotapes that had boiled out of the shelves onto the desk and chairs and all but a narrow twisted walkway on the carpet. Some of the books bore his byline. All of the tapes belonged to the program he had hosted on local cable until someone decided that reruns of "Three's Company" would skew better in his time slot. The program, titled "Know Your Neighbor," had highlighted a different Detroit area crime figure each week. Barry had been a Mob watcher only a little longer than he'd been getting around with one artificial leg, two missing fingers, and a steel plate in his skull, souvenirs of the first time someone had suggested canceling him.

He put down the nocs and limped over to the desk to pour scotch into two glasses from a bottle of Glen-Something. "I want to thank you for bringing him here, Amos. I still have three limbs I don't know what to do with." He handed me a glass. "Cold steel."

"Hot lead." I lifted mine and tossed it back. "I brought him here on purpose. When he reports the address and they look it up, maybe they'll panic and do something dumb."

"Here's hoping they do it to you." He drank and leaned a hip against the desk. "Gryphon, you said?"

"I hear they got two floors of a high-rise in Southfield, no more dealing loans over a card table behind Tino's Billiards on Livernois."

"Michigan," he corrected. "Livernois was Jake the Shake. Gryphon's lost a lot of color. They figured out they don't make anything when they have to break bones. That's when they added Collateral to the company name. Small business is their specialty. If you can't pay they grab a piece or take it out in trade."

"That explains why Owen Subject isn't hurting for money."

"Milton Thorpe."

"Is that a name or another toast?"

"Milton likes to block roads," he said. "He used to use cars, but someone got around him once by going up the bank. A truck is better. He used a truck the day he capped Guillermo Zuma."

"Zuma I heard of. Someone named Milton Thorpe doesn't sound like he attends the same cockfights."

"Zuma always had a WASP front for him. This one had ambition. Loan sharks generally have plenty of indy truckers in inventory. And Milton Thorpe juices most of the sharks in town."

"I don't remember Zuma getting killed in a crash. I heard it was bullets."

"You can't count on a crash. He got it from the car following behind.

He couldn't go forward on account of the truck blocking the road and he couldn't back up because the car was on his bumper. They squoze him in between, put it in Park, got out, and shot him and his driver in the barrel. Cops down in Ecorse snagged the trucker out of the river three days later."

"Owen didn't show tonight," I said. "His wife was worried."

"He'll turn up in three days. That's how long it takes the gas to bring them to the surface."

"Lucky for Albert Donato he was driving so fast. It saved him from getting shot."

"It would explain why Subject powdered and left the truck behind. Nobody told him there might be flames. The car with the guns would have done the same once Albert was toast." Absently he scratched the wrong leg. "That store receivership wouldn't have lasted long. What was a kid with his bucks doing playing around with someone like Milton Thorpe?"

"Maybe he wasn't. Maybe it was a message for his stepmother."

"Are you suggesting your client might not have come across with the whole story?"

"I'm shocked too." I drained my glass and set it on Barry's face on the back of one of his books. "Thanks for the whiskey and information. I'll be taking my tail and leaving."

"Don't forget you owe me a bottle."

"I can't afford your brand."

"Hell, neither can I. That's why I give out information." He stopped smiling. "Stay alive, buddy. Don't leave me alone with the politically correct."

"Don't worry. I'm fire-retardant."

I left the driver of the Chevy looking for a space near my building and went up to place some calls. First I tried Rita Donato at Milan, but after a long wait some prison brass came on and said she'd used up her allotment of calls for that period and would I care to leave a message? I hung up and got Lee Killinger at the Northville state police post.

"I'm out the door, Walker. Unless you're calling for an address to send money you borrowed from me, which no keyholer will do ever, I got no time for you."

"Sorry to hear it, Lee. So will a lady dispatcher I know at the Brighton post. Wasn't her kid born just about the time you transferred over on your last promotion?"

"You can only draw that one so many times before it misfires," he said after a pause. "What is it this time?"

"I'm wondering if Rita Donato ever had any dealings with a drug lord by the name of Milton Thorpe."

"That's federal."

"I hear the computer in Lansing has coffee all the time with the one in Washington."

"Anyway, all that would have come out during her trial. When they really want you they dig deep."

It was a point, one sharp enough to deflate. I asked him to feed it through anyway. He said he'd get back to me in twenty-four hours and banged off. I was getting to be as unpopular as my client.

Next I called Owen Subject's wife to ask if her husband had showed up. I knew what the answer would be when she speared the telephone halfway through the first ring. It was three minutes after ten. He'd been missing eight hours. I said something comforting. It made me unpopular with myself.

The next morning I was shaving with the bathroom door open when the TV morning-show hostess, a blonde on Percodans, reported that the body of a middle-aged male had been found snagged in brush on the American side of the Detroit River south of Flatrock. I wiped off the lather and made a call.

"Wayne County Morgue. Fitzgerald."

"Walker, Fitz. How was Bingo Saturday night?"

"I'm still answering the phone here, ain't I? What's the rumpus so bright and early?"

"I may have an ID on that floater they gaffed downriver."

"Too late. His wife identified him an hour ago."

"How'd she take it?"

"Better than the son. He was leaning on the old lady when they left."

"Son?"

"Clean-cut kid. You wouldn't think he came from such rotten loins."

"Fitz, I have an idea we're not both talking about Owen Subject."

"Never heard of the gentleman. Customer's name is LoPolo."

I groped for the pack in my shirt pocket and realized I was wearing my robe. "LoPolo comma Francisco in parentheses Pancho Polo?"

"Yeah, all of those. Plenty of places he could've landed between Bogotá and here, but he chose the Renaissance City. Two in the melon. Nine millimeter."

"Didn't he used to work for Guillermo Zuma?"

"Uh-huh. Some folks thought he'd step into the old man's pointy patent leathers. He didn't and I hear it made him surly."

I found a half-smoked Winston in the ashtray and set fire to it. The smoke cleared the bees out of my skull. "Have you got an address for LoPolo?"

"His wife left it. Second." He came back on after twenty. "Nice little cottage on Square Lake. Probably thirty-two rooms. Number's—"

"Not necessary. Thanks." I broke the connection and tried Killinger in Northville. The turn-out sergeant I spoke to said he wouldn't be in until eight. I finished grooming, dressed, and drove to the office. The blue Chevy followed.

"I said twenty-four hours," Killinger growled when I got him. "It's been ten."

"Forget it. I'm betting five thousand dollars Rita Donato didn't know Milton Thorpe from Robert Young." I told him about Francisco LoPolo and where he'd lived.

He blew air. "Snaps right in there, doesn't it? What about the trucker?"

"He'll pop up in a couple of days. By then he'll be the forgotten man. How'd you like a plush office in Lansing?"

"Depends on the deposit."

I told him.

When the messenger came, shortly before noon, I tipped him, opened the manila envelope, studied what was inside, and transferred it to a No. 10 I'd already addressed and stamped. I slipped it into my inside breast pocket. Before I went out I checked the load in the Smith & Wesson .38 I'd had longer than my wife and clipped it to my belt.

The man behind the wheel of the blue Chevy shielded his eyes with his left hand when I came out of the building and lost himself in a map of what looked like Nebraska. He jumped when I tapped on his window with the muzzle of the revolver. I made a twirling motion with my free hand. He cranked down the glass.

I got out the envelope and held it in front of his face. It was addressed to the Detroit office of the Drug Enforcement Administration. His lips moved as he read. His hair was moussed forward rather than slicked back and he had on turquoise-colored contacts, but the rest of him had plainly come from someplace where the written language included tildes and accent marks.

"Yeah?" he said. "So?"

"Oh, the repartee." I pocketed the item. "You probably saw the messenger deliver it in a different envelope. It was sent by Owen Subject's wife. She found it among his papers. You know, 'To be opened in the event of my etcetera.' It's going to a safe deposit box I keep up in Iroquois Heights." I pointed at the blue cellular telephone standing to attention at his elbow. "Tell Milton he knows where to reach me when he's ready to deal."

"Milton who? I don't know you, mister."

Grinning, I holstered the .38 and walked. Only the faces change. The patter stays the same.

My car was parked in the deserted service station across the street. Once behind the wheel I shook the silver-dollar-size object out of the envelope and clipped it to the sun visor. The messenger had come from Lee Killinger, not Mrs. Subject.

I don't keep a safe deposit box in Iroquois Heights. Mostly what I keep there is away. But the road that leads there is one of the few empty stretches in the metropolitan area and crosses Square Lake Road, where Albert Donato got cooked to death and near where Francisco LoPolo had lived in dope-financed splendor until somebody shot him in the head and tipped him into the river. I made a face at the doohickey on the visor. For a man who didn't own a computer or even a digital watch I was counting an awful lot on modern technology not letting me down.

I picked up the truck at Thirteen Mile Road. A big yellow tanker labeled CAUTION TOXIC CHEMICALS, it wheeled into my lane from the right without stopping for the light, forcing me to use the brake to slow down. The Chevy, which had been hanging back a block and a half since I left downtown, closed in then. This would require timing.

Although it was cool September, my window was open to allow maximum oxygen into the car and my brain. Now I poked my cigarette butt into the slipstream and rolled up the window. I wanted as little resistance as possible when the time came to maneuver.

It came sooner than expected. The traffic had thinned out to just us three, but we were a mile south of the Square Lake crossing and the straight stretch that afforded an unobstructed view in both directions. The tanker accelerated with a black jet of diesel smoke from its stack and went into a hard turn. Its rear tires skated sideways, laying down molten rubber. The truck filled my windshield.

My instincts screamed brake. I didn't listen. I wrenched the wheel left and leaned with the inertia. My tires yelped. Thanking God and Goodyear for steel-belted radials, I stood on the brake then, and while my insides were still straining toward the firewall I straightened the wheel and banged the lever into Reverse. The tires spoke again. My rear wheels struck the curb with a vibration I felt in my teeth. I spun the wheel and hit the accelerator. The blue Chevy slid into view square in the middle of the windshield. I saw the driver's narrow dark face, his eyes and mouth forming a triangular rack of O's, one hand diving inside his coat.

I hit him hard.

The Mercury was fifteen years older than his little outsourced GM and outweighed it by fifteen hundred pounds. His front end crumpled like foil, throwing belts, bursting hoses, and spraying steam. After killing the ignition I unbuckled myself and piled out behind the .38.

I didn't need it. He hadn't worn a seat belt and was sprawled over the console, out cold and bleeding from the piece of scalp that was caught in the jagged star on his windshield. I found his pulse, unburdened him of the 9-millimeter Beretta he carried in a shoulder rig under his coat, and used it to cover the driver of the tanker. That was unnecessary too. He was sitting hunched over the wheel of the stalled truck with that poled-ox look that says the round is over.

That's how things looked when the state police radio car arrived carrying Commander Killinger, its roof-mounted halo homing in on the little electronic gizmo attached to my visor.

The matron held the door for my client more in the manner of a maidservant than a turnkey, which meant all her bills were being paid. Prisonwear today was a pink cashmere sweater and pleated skirt split as if for riding. Mrs. Donato nodded to Sporthaven and sat down opposite me with the table in between.

"You've been busy," she said, when I'd delivered my report. "Do you think this Hidalgo will testify against Milton Thorpe?"

Feliz Hidalgo was the name on the green card the state police found on the driver of the blue Chevy. I moved a shoulder. "If the cops match that Beretta I took off him to the slugs they dug out of LoPolo's brain, he might trade his boss for a sentence less than life. If he's the pro I think he is, they won't. The tanker driver is another story. I hear he's talking already. That ties Thorpe to the attempt on me."

"I don't want that. I want him to answer for Albert."

"That's up to Hidalgo. Or Subject, if he surfaces. The judge put out a warrant on him when he didn't show at his preliminary this morning. No body yet, so it's possible he just ran."

"So Albert wasn't the target after all. They wanted LoPolo that night."

"It makes sense," I said. "LoPolo lived on Square Lake and always took the same route home from his headquarters in Detroit. He drove a gray Cadillac, Albert drove a gray Chrysler. They look alike to the owner of a Chevy. Your stepson just got sucked up in the slipstream. Later, when they found out their mistake, they took LoPolo out more quietly."

"Poor Albert. I really was fond of him."

"You'll get over it. In time," I added sympathetically. She was as easy to feel sorry for as a battlewagon.

Sporthaven shifted his briefcase. "You've earned the five thousand, Walker. Send us the bill when you buy a new car to replace the one you wrecked."

"Thanks, I'll get it fixed. I've seen what the new ones are worth." I rose. Rita Donato's eyes followed me up.

"I won't forget you when I'm paroled. That may not sound like much now, but I won't be your average ex-convict any more than I was your average rich widow."

"Just don't put your first hundred million into electronics," I said.

Despite the fact that TV and the movies would like to make you think clients of P.I.s and lawyers are all well-to-do, there are times when they are rather simple people—of simple means and even, in some cases, simple minds.

Fairly new talents, Jan Grape and Cathy Pickens have given their protagonists such simple qualities, but each quickly learns that having simple clients does not always lead to simple cases.

JAN GRAPE

Jan Grape has been invaluable to PWA since she joined. For the past couple of years she has been the editor of the PWA newsletter, *Reflections in a Private Eye,* and she is the first person to ever refer to it as RIPE.

Of late, she has become very much in demand as a short-story writer, appearing in the anthologies *Deadly Allies, Cat Crimes III, Invitation to Murder,* and many others. Somehow, she also manages to find the time to run—with her husband—their bookstore in Austin, Texas, Mysteries and More, and to host a mystery convention there in May of 1993. She is also working on her first novel.

Happily, she found the time to pen—or compute?—one of her Jenny and C.J. stories for this collection. Her story in the origin *Deadly Allies*—featuring these characters as well—was singled out by many reviewers as one of the best stories in the book. We're anxious to hear what the reviewers think of this one.

SCARLETT FEVER

ONE

It was one of those crisp, autumn-tinged November mornings that central Texans rarely get. The heat often begins in April—simmers —builds to a boil in August and barely slackens until December. With the heat people snarl, cursing the weather or each other. Some folks go limp with exhaustion or shoot someone to relieve the pressure cooker. But when the jet stream pushes cool Canadian air down across the plains and deep into the heart of Texas, people actually smile at each other and say inane things like "Isn't this weather great?" and "Reckon we might have some winter after all."

The old Balcones Fault line runs through the center of Austin, dividing the city east and west. The eastern side slopes to gently rolling hills. The western side is rougher terrain, full of limestone cliffs and hills and canyons. My office, on the fourth floor of the LaGrange Building, is in northwest Austin and the building sits on a small hill. My apartment is only a few blocks from the LaGrange.

It was 7:58 A.M. when I arrived. My partner,

Cinnamon Jemima Gunn, or C.J., as she is known to most folks, is always in the office by 8 A.M. We had just completed a big insurance fraud investigation and were behind on our paperwork and I had promised to come in early. Okay, so eight is not exactly early to those who get up with the chickens, but it was early for me. I don't do single digits of the day well.

The telephone rang as I walked in. C.J. answered. "G&G Investigations," she said, then listened briefly. "Yes, Mr. Porter, Ms. Gordon just walked in. Will you hold a moment?" Her professional tone clashed with the surprised roll of her eyes when she noted the early hour.

C.J. punched a button, held the receiver out, and with a wry expression said, " 'Bulldog' Porter wants *you*, Jenny."

Bulldog King Porter, one of the best criminal defense attorneys money can buy, had sent work our way before. It began with us doing a bang-up job on the Loudermilk case, making Bulldog happy and a nice piece of change for us. His nickname came from being tenacious in court.

"You talk to him."

"I don't have time. He gets off on 'those old rum-running days in Galveston,' and ties a person up for hours."

Bulldog's stories can be endless, depending on his mood. I hurried into the inner office, not wanting to leave him dangling. "Mr. Porter, how are you?"

His voice held a chuckle. "I thought we'd gotten past that Mr. Porter and Mrs. Gordon stuff by now, Jenny."

"Well, we have, Bulldog, but . . ."

"Young lady, you don't have to be polite to an old curmudgeon. Can't say I deserve politeness even from a pretty lady like you."

I could picture him, the widow's peak and the thick steel gray hair, his piercing blue eyes startling in his seventy-eight-year-old face. I swiveled my chair around and looked out the window. A northerly wind swirled leaves around like a giant cake mixer whipping batter. Thick white clouds with black-streaked bottoms looked as if they would develop into thunder-boomers soon. "I'm sure you didn't call just to pass out compliments, Bulldog."

"Quite right. Complimenting you is a pleasant chore, but I will get to the point. There's a young man I'd like you to see."

"Fine. One of your clients?"

"Not exactly. He's the son of an old and dear friend. The boy's about your age. His is an unusual story I think you should hear. He's looking for a young woman who's disappeared. Someone special, but he . . .

well, perhaps he should tell you himself. He does, however, need a good investigator and you lovely damsels at G&G fit the bill." Bulldog held a whispered conversation on his end and when he came back asked, "Are either you or C.J. available today? Perhaps right after lunch?"

"Yes, I believe so," I said, knowing full well we had all day free. "How does one o'clock sound?"

"One is fine. Wilson Billeau is my young friend's name. Thank you, Jenny, this means a lot. Wilson's like the son I never had. His father, Jud Billeau, and I were deputy D.A.s back in the fifties and sixties and we . . ."

Damn Sam. I choked back a sigh. He could go on for another half-hour, but for once I got lucky. Bulldog's secretary, Martha May, interrupted him, saying he had a long distance call on another line. "I'll finish this story one day, Jenny. You'll enjoy it. And listen, I appreciate this."

"Don't mention it, Bulldog."

Hanging up, I walked out to our kitchen/storage room, grabbed a mug of coffee, and went to fill C.J. in on the conversation with Bulldog.

"Who does Porter think we are, the frigging Bureau of the Missing?" C.J.'s haughty tone made it all sound distasteful. She slammed drawers, shoved things around on her desk, and said, "A missing person, huh? Sounds boring, too."

Hoo boy, she's in one of her moods, I thought. But despite her gripes, I knew she'd never want us to refuse a paying customer.

My partner was a Pittsburgh police officer for eight years before moving back to her native Texas. She stands six feet tall, is built a lot like Racquel Welch, and reminds me of Nichelle Nichols, the actress who played in *Star Trek*, except C.J.'s skin tone is darker. Her tongue can be as sharp as a surgeon's scalpel.

Good paying customers are her favorite kind. C.J.'s not money-hungry, but her favorites are the ones with cash. We operate on a slim margin and, because of her excellent business head, manage to stay afloat.

"And who's going to pay for this?"

"I assume Mr. Billeau is paying. Bulldog didn't exactly say. Who cares? As long as we get paid."

"You got that right. I've been going over the bank statement this morning."

"We're not overdrawn?"

"No, but damn these companies who run sixty days behind. Afraid we could be in deep doo-doo before then."

Bank statements are Greek to me and I round everything off to the nearest dollar. C.J. knows her balance to the exact penny. I'd once of-

fered to keep our office books, but she said not until our sun goes super-
nova. She does the books, but it makes her cranky.

"Well, if the client's due at one you can grab his check out of his hand
and hot-foot it to the bank before it closes."

"Aww, shit. Somebody has to worry about money around here."

"I know, and you do it so well I don't like to deprive you."

"You just remember to get a retainer. We don't do freebies." The
computer keyboard began clicking again. "Why don't you get back to
your desk and finish your reports?"

"Yessum, Miz Gunn, whatebber you say, Miz Gunn."

"Smart ass. You ain't the right color to talk the talk."

"Discrimination again. Boy, the things I have to put up with around
here." A Post-it notepad hit the doorjamb as I went through it.

I was tempted to say, Yah-ha ya missed me, but instead, I stuck my
head around the corner of the door. "Are you going to join me when our
client arrives?"

"Afraid not, Jen. I've got too much to do. These invoices need to go in
tonight's mail."

"You just don't want to listen to a tale of lost love."

"You got that right. I heard enough of those when I was a cop." C.J.
came to the door to stand in front of me. "Besides, you're so much better
at that than I. You get all full of empathy and the client loves that shit."

"Okay, I'll wing alone, but if you think you can cut out early . . ."

"You just call me when the action begins." Her laugh was evil.
"That's what I crave, Girlfriend. The excitement."

"You are *so* bad." I went back to my expense reports, glad she'd
lightened up a bit.

Mr. Billeau walked in right on time. He probably wasn't thirty yet, but
he had one of those faces that would look boyish for the next thirty
years. His thick auburn hair was cut short, not quite a crew cut. He had a
narrow waist and broad shoulders that looked like he wore football pads.
His plaid western shirt was clean and his stone-washed Levi's and
scuffed cowboy boots—the working-type, not the fancy dress ones—
completed the picture. A burnt-orange-and-white gimme cap with a
U.T. Longhorn logo was tucked under his left arm.

"Mr. Billeau?" I held out my hand. He looked as if he wasn't sure
what to do and then took it. His hand was limp, but I gave him a firm
shake and almost laughed at his surprise. Some men get uncomfortable
when shaking hands with a woman. "I'm Jenny Gordon. And this is my
partner, C.J. Gunn."

C.J. gave him a brief nod and went back to her monitor. Damn her, I thought, she could be a little more cordial, but she winked as I led the way to the inner office.

"We can talk more comfortably in here." Once inside I indicated an upholstered customer chair for him and turned to walk behind my desk. I stopped. He had followed only to the doorway.

"Mrs. Gordon, I'm not sure about this. . . ."

I put on my most disarming smile. "Fine, but you've made an effort to come here. Let's discuss it. If you decide there's nothing I can do to help, you can be on your way. It won't hurt my feelings."

He stared at his feet. When he finally looked up, I could see he'd decided to give me a try. "Mrs. Gordon, if you can help, I'll be obliged."

He sat down and began staring at his feet again. He looked like a kid in high school taking a history test and looking for answers he'd written on his shoe tops.

Maybe he found something because he suddenly began talking. "I'm a country boy, Mrs. Gordon." He raised his head. "Probably a little dumb, too."

I smiled reassuringly after telling him to call me Jenny.

" 'Bout all I'm good at is farming. My grandpa left me a little place out near Dripping Springs. Nothing much, but it's mine. I raise a few chickens—milk a few cows. I work hard all week and come Saturday night, I like to go into town maybe have a few beers."

"Sounds normal to me."

He began twisting the gimme cap in his large hands. "There's this one place I like to go to—the Lucky Star Bar and Grill. You heard of it?"

I admitted I hadn't.

"They have these girls that dance."

"With the customers?"

"No, ma'am. I mean dance on stage. They take off their clothes, too." He blushed. "For several weeks . . . one girl. She was so lovely and I, uh, I sorta fell for her."

I nodded, not wanting to interrupt.

"Every man who came in—fell for her. I mean, this girl—pretty as a speckled pup—dancing in this joint. She made you feel special. Everybody stopped whatever they were doing just to watch Scarlett dance."

"Scarlett?"

"Yes, ma'am. Her name is Scarlett Fever."

I almost made a joke, but he was so doggone serious. "What happened?"

"It's driving me crazy. Ten days ago her name was gone from that big sign out front. I went in and asked the bartender. He said Scarlett was

gone. I asked where. He said maybe Los Angeles or Las Vegas. He
didn't know. He thought she'd moved on to a bigger city where she
could make bigger money.

"Miss Jenny. I've gone to Dallas, Los Angeles, Las Vegas, Houston,
even Nashville. I can't find a trace. And, ma'am, I've got to find her. She
and I . . . Oh, we never went out or nothing, but I knew from the way
she looked at me—we were meant to be."

Could anyone be so incredibly naive? He was such a country bump-
kin. "Wilson, this world is full of big cities. Bigger and better places than
Austin, Texas. She could be in any city."

"Yes, ma'am, I know it's hopeless. I might be dumb, but I'm not
stupid." He blushed again. "It was crazy to come here. Take up your
time." He studied his feet again. "But the crazy part. I'm afraid something bad has happened. I'll never believe she left without saying good-
bye. And I don't know where else to turn. Mr. Porter said if anyone
could find Scarlett, you could."

"His vote of confidence is nice, even if it is somewhat skewed."

Forlorn couldn't even begin to cover his hangdog expression as he
realized what I was implying. That I probably wouldn't be able to find
her either.

C.J. had nailed it when she said clients love it when they feel you
care. The police don't have time to give them personal attention. That's
why they come to a private eye in the first place, but that's also why it
hurts when you can't help.

Girls like Scarlett change locations about as often as the weather
changes in central Texas, and they never leave a forwarding address. I
knew what the odds were. An impossible mission, right?

No one was more surprised than I when the next words came out of
my mouth. "Wilson, it's not hopeless."

Did I really say that? "There are a couple of things I can do that might
produce a lead."

"Like what?"

Yeah, like what, smart ass. Me and my big mouth. "First, I'd check
where she worked. Maybe someone there knows something."

"Jim, the bartender, didn't know anything."

"Maybe she had a girlfriend and confided in her. What about the
other dancers and the waitresses and the musicians?"

"I've already asked. Nobody knows nothing."

"Maybe they were leary about why you wanted to know. People
working around singers and dancers, especially pretty ones, learn they
have to be careful about giving out information. You can never tell who

might be a sicko or a pervert. They might talk to me." A faint hope shone in his eyes. And strangely enough, I started having a little hope myself.

There were a few other places I could check—the owner of the club— the person who wrote the checks. Maybe a talent agency or a dancers' union. Surely a young woman moving on to greener pastures didn't do it entirely on her own. Someone, somewhere, knew Scarlett and knew where she had gone.

"Wilson, why don't you give me a couple of days, let me see what I can turn up. That way you'll at least have the satisfaction of knowing you gave it your best shot."

"I'll be happy to pay whatever it costs. I've got money saved. A lot of money."

I almost said we could talk money later, but C.J. would have killed me. "Okay. A three-hundred-dollar retainer to begin. That's two days. We can settle expenses afterward." I pulled a standard contract out of the top drawer of my desk.

He took out his billfold and handed me six fifty-dollar bills. "I feel better already. Just knowing someone will be doing something. I haven't been able to eat or sleep."

Wilson Billeau walked out feeling hopeful and I wondered if I had lost my cotton-picking mind.

TWO

C.J. and I went into our missing persons routine. She began a paper chase via computer and since legwork is my specialty, I drove out to the Lucky Star Bar and Grill.

Beginning in front of the State Capitol Building and driving south on South Congress Avenue, you pass through the downtown area, cross Town Lake, and continue along where eventually the area becomes a strip of nightclubs, bars, motels, and prowling grounds for pimps and prostitutes. It's a scuzzy area only a few short miles from the state's political power.

The club was on South Congress, a mile or so west of Interstate 35. It had a western motif, a big white Lone Star on the roof, and country music twanged inside; also, as suspected, no one thought it was unusual that Scarlett had left. Dancers work here and there—leaving when the mood strikes.

Oh, she had mentioned moving on, but who knew which bright lights had lured her. One day she just ups and doesn't show.

Jim, the bartender, looked like a Mexican *bandido*, but was talkative except he didn't have a clue about Scarlett. I thanked him for his time and asked if he had a photograph of the girl. He found a black and white eight by ten publicity shot that the club had put in the lobby for promotion.

At the front door I had to pause to allow a young woman carrying a guitar case to come in, and Jim called out to me. "Hey, Detective Lady, this here's one of Scarlett's friends. I'll bet Delia Rose can tell you what you want to know."

The young woman was short, around twenty, a few pounds overweight, but chunky, not fat. Her straight blond hair was pulled back into a ponytail. Her blue eyes, more knowing than they should be at her age, told of all the hard knocks she'd received in her short life.

The bartender introduced us and Delia Rose and I slid into an empty booth. I told her I was a private investigator.

"And you've been hired to find Scarlett?"

I nodded.

"I'm sorry," she said. "Scarlett talked about going to Vegas, but I don't know if that's where she went. She didn't even tell me good-bye. I'm a little hurt, too, because I thought we were friends."

"Maybe she left with a boyfriend," I said. "Was there a special guy? Someone you remember coming in to see her?"

She began shaking her head before I was through talking.

"Look," I said. "She was a beautiful girl. Surely there was someone . . ."

"Not really. She flirted with everyone, but I don't think there was a boyfriend."

"Or a girlfriend?"

Delia Rose blushed. "She didn't have any designs that way either and believe me I would have known."

"Who of the regulars did she pay attention to?"

She thought a moment. "Only one guy—a farm boy. Sweet kid. He had a funny name."

"Wilson Billeau?"

"Yeah, that was it. Wilson Billeau. He had the fever for Scarlett Fever." She realized her joke and we laughed.

"He's my client."

"Scarlett was nice to his face, but she made fun of him behind his back." Delia Rose looked wistful. "Man, I wish someone would get that kind of hots for me."

I stood. "Well, I appreciate your help. If you think of anything, will you call?" I gave her my card.

Delia Rose arched an eyebrow and smiled. "When you find her, tell her I said to drop dead, okay?" She smiled wistfully again and that's when I knew she also had the fever for Scarlett.

"Will do," I said.

Before I was halfway to the door, Delia called me back.

"I just thought of something. The day before Scarlett left, an older man came in. She was dancing and suddenly got a sick look. When she came off-stage he grabbed her arm and said, 'We have to talk.' Scarlett pulled away and told him to leave her alone. His face got all red and Scarlett had this funny look. Not scared exactly, but sorta like resigned.

"The old guy doubled up his fist and I thought sure he was going to hit her. Jim saw the guy was acting up and came over. Told him we didn't want any trouble and asked him to leave."

"Did you ask her about this guy afterward?"

"Yeah, but she said she didn't want to talk about him and for me to forget it. So I did. I guess I forgot all about it until just now."

"What did he look like?"

"Let's see, I can't remember much. Maybe late fifties. Dark hair, turning gray. Jim might remember. He got a better look."

She called Jim over, but he couldn't add much more. He said the guy was plain vanilla. "Some old fart. Dressed in a business suit that went out of style twenty years ago."

"I remember thinking at the time he reminded me of a movie star," said Delia Rose. "One of those older guys, but I can't remember who."

They couldn't think of anything else and this time I really did leave.

I tacked Scarlett's picture to the wall next to my desk hoping to be inspired. A striking dark-haired woman, twenty-two or thereabouts. Her eyes were dark, too, but with only a black and white photo, I couldn't be sure of exact colors. A smile extended to her come-hither eyes, yet there was an innocence, too. Try as I might, I couldn't see much to make her star-quality. Dark-haired beauties aren't exactly a novelty. Obviously, you had to have seen her dance moves.

Strippers don't belong to a union, but C.J. traced the photographer who'd taken the publicity picture. I talked to him and to the talent agency that had booked Scarlett into the Lucky Star. Sure they knew her, but she hadn't confided any plans to them.

C.J.'s nimble computer fingers found no records of credit cards or bank accounts. Scarlett Fever didn't have a car registration or a driver's license, either, but C.J. discovered Scarlett had a room, for the past six months, at the Stagecoach Motel, a half-mile south of the Lucky Star. She was registered as Scarlett Fever O'Hara.

A trip to the motel seemed logical. It was sleazy-looking, more like a place for rent-by-the-hour trysts than a home for a young girl. The manager was also a sleaze-bag, but he took my twenty-dollar bill greedily and gave me the key. The room was pathetic; an old iron bedstead held a sagging mattress; a vanity-type dresser from the fifties stood against one wall. Worn carpet and torn drapes over yellowed window shades completed the decor. I found a rust-speckled can of Lady Schick shave cream and one lipstick tube, fire engine red, used down to the metal. Nothing else to show a young woman had lived in that depressing room for six months—no clothes, no receipts, no pictures. Scarlett appeared and disappeared—end of story.

As I left I asked the manager how Scarlett got around as she didn't have a car.

"How should I know? Walked maybe?"

My twenty must not have extended to his answering questions.

It was discouraging, although I hadn't expected much to begin with. Yet one tiny cell in the back of my brain kept taunting in a singsong voice, "Nah-na, nah-na, nah-na—you've forgotten something."

C.J. and I checked and double-checked every scrap of information we had. It was wasted time.

At the end of two days I called Wilson Billeau. He didn't seem surprised. The slight hope he'd nursed must have dwindled soon after he'd left our office.

"Thanks for trying, ma'am. I know you did your best."

"Wilson, I believe things happen for a reason. Scarlett came into your life. Maybe to remind you that you ought to do something besides muck around with cows and chickens. I'll bet if you tried, you'd find a young lady who'd like to live on a farm in Dripping Springs."

"I guess. I promised myself I'd put this all behind me if you couldn't find her, but I can't give up yet." His voice didn't sound as if his heart was in it, but he was determined.

I wished him luck and broke the connection.

C.J. said Wilson's money helped to ease our cash flow, but the whole episode left me feeling sad for a couple of days. Soon though, we both put the missing Scarlett Fever out of our minds.

THREE

Three weeks later, I unfolded the morning newspaper, the *Austin American Statesman* and there she was—Scarlett Fever O'Hara. The grainy picture was the same publicity photo I had and she was identified only as Scarlett. The headline for this rainy December day read SCARLETT IS DEAD. The story said a hooker's nude body had been found in one of Austin's better downtown hotel rooms. The woman had been beaten severely and then stabbed to death.

Unholy murder served up with notes of Christmas cheer.

A man registered to that room as Marshall Tolliver from Houston was now in police custody.

C.J. called me at home. "Did you see her?"

We discussed the murder for a few minutes and I said I'd better contact Wilson Billeau. "I hope he's already seen the paper because I'd hate to be the one to tell him."

There was no answer when I called Wilson, so I tried Bulldog Porter. The attorney said one of his informants had called him soon after the girl's body was found and he'd notified Wilson of the girl's death. He said Wilson had gone to the funeral home to make arrangements for her and would drop by Bulldog's office later. Bulldog said he would give Wilson our condolences.

My next call was to Lieutenant Larry Hays. Larry works in the homicide unit of the Austin Police Department. He and I have been good friends for years. I'd first met him when he and my late husband, Tommy Gordon, entered the police academy together. They were partners until Tommy left APD to become a private detective.

After Tommy's death Larry took a brotherly role with me. One I was grateful for, except when he got too protective. Especially where it related to the detective agency. Larry is sensitive, witty, and stubborn as only a Swede can be. He is also one hell of a good cop.

When he returned my call, I asked, "What's the story on the dead hooker?"

"The one known as Scarlett? What do you know about it?"

"Nothing about the murder, but . . ."

"Just a minute." Larry put me on hold, briefly. When he came back, he said in his official voice, "Meet me at Casa Mañana!"

His gruff, insistent order hit me the way that tone usually does and I almost told him to go take a flying leap from the Congress Avenue bridge, but in a conciliatory tone he added, "Please, Jenny. I could use your help here."

I said I'd be there by one-thirty.

Casa Mañana is a Tex-Mex restaurant near APD headquarters and the officers frequently go there for lunch. It's a converted old stucco house, yellow with green trim and the feel of a cantina. Inside were plain wooden tables covered with oilcloth and the tables at each booth had Mexican tile tops. The food is excellent, the price is reasonable, and the service is top-notch.

Larry is attractive, long-legged, and wears a size thirteen shoe. He's five years older than me and I was unmerciful when he turned forty recently. He was seated in the corner booth when I arrived. Two iced teas, hot salsa, and tortilla chips were already on the table. I slid into the booth and he said, "Where you been keeping yourself?"

"C.J.'s been cracking the whip. We've hardly had time to go to the bathroom."

"That explains your pained expression."

"If I have a pained expression, it's because you haven't called or come by to see us."

"Hah! I used to complain when we had one homicide a month. Little did I know those were the good old days."

"Makes you wonder what's happening to our normally laid-back capital city."

"Fast growth, drugs, and hard times."

We were interrupted by Paco Hidalgo, the owner, as he placed chicken enchiladas—with all the trimmings—on the table and refilled my glass. The chips and salsa I'd been nibbling called for constant mouth-cooling, but I get anemic if I don't get my quota of Mexican food.

"I hope you don't mind, I ordered your usual. Thought we could save time." Larry began eating without waiting for my reply. "Tell me what you know about Scarlett."

I filled him in on Wilson Billeau and the saga of Scarlett, and on everything C.J. and I had done. "Everyone I talked to was convinced she'd left for more bucks and glory elsewhere." It was difficult trying to talk and eat too, but I managed. "What's the story on this guy you've arrested?"

"Tolliver tells a straightforward tale with only one twist. Says he was in town for a sales conference and he picked her up yesterday afternoon at the hotel bar." Larry was shoveling his food and didn't let the talk slow him down. "They spent a short time talking and indulged in a little slap-and-tickle. Tolliver figured she was a hooker, working the convention, but he didn't mind."

"Does he have a record?"

"Nope. He's squeaky clean."

"Then what's the twist?"

"Somebody slipped him a Mickey Finn," he said. "We had a few last year. Hookers setting up and rolling out-of-towners. First one I've seen this year, though."

"But why did he kill her?"

"The captain thinks Tolliver woke up earlier than expected. Caught the woman with her hand in his billfold and flew into a rage." Larry finished his food and Paco unobtrusively removed the plate.

"You don't agree?"

"I don't know. Maybe I've got a burr up my tail. I think his story about waking up at one o'clock this morning and finding her dead in his bathroom is the truth."

I shuddered. Finding a woman in the bathroom stabbed to death gave me the willies.

"It won't be easy to prove his innocence. He claims he never saw the knife before, but it was there in the shower, his prints on it. Two points in his favor is that he didn't run. He called us and waited until we showed. His hands were also unmarked."

"Why wouldn't he hide the knife?"

"Exactly. Or wipe his prints. Tolliver says he picked it up without thinking." Larry lit up one of his favored cigarillos. "He wasn't too coherent during questioning, he acted much like a person would if they'd been given a Mickey."

"Do you have a better ID for the girl than Scarlett Fever O'Hara?"

Larry nearly choked on his iced tea. "Are you shitting me? Scarlett Fever O'Hara?"

"She danced at the Lucky Star Bar and Grill as Scarlett Fever. But she was registered at the Stagecoach Motel under Scarlett Fever O'Hara."

"The Stagecoach Motel, huh? We don't have that yet. Where is it?"

"On South Congress just before you get to 71."

"I'd better make a trip out there. They took her prints at the morgue and are running a search with AFIS [Automated Fingerprint Identification System]. If she's been arrested, we'll get a positive ID and her real name."

"She'd moved out, the place was empty. It's probably been rented to someone else by now." When I saw his face, I knew I'd said too much. "How could I know it was going to be a murder investigation? That was three weeks ago."

Larry tried, but couldn't hold his serious face. He smiled. "You bribed the clerk?"

"Let's say I donated to his favorite charity."

"I'll still need to talk to him—the sooner the better." He punched his cigarillo out in the ashtray, stood up and grabbed his wallet. "Thanks for the info, Jen."

"Thanks for lunch. You *are* buying?" I walked with him to the cash register.

"Sure. You saved me some legwork. That's worth lunch."

"Christmas will be here soon," I said, as we walked into the bright sunshine.

"And someone's daughter won't be home. God, I hate this time of year." He walked with me to my car. "That photo didn't do her justice," he said, as he bent to give me a brotherly good-bye kiss.

I headed for the interstate wanting to get back to work before I started thinking about Wilson Billeau and his beautiful dead Scarlett and got depressed.

FOUR

Damn Sam. I was northbound, four miles from my exit, when it hit me, that niggling little thing I'd overlooked earlier. Dancers work out all the time, they have to to stay in shape. Why not strippers? Especially one hoping to latch on to a star. Neither C.J. nor I had thought about checking for a dance studio or health spa. I found a clear space in traffic, wrenched my car across the lanes, squealed off at the exit, crossed under the underpass, and headed down the southbound entrance ramp.

Once I was going in the right direction, I picked up the cellular phone and dialed. "C.J.? What dance studios or panting palaces are near the Lucky Star or the Stagecoach Motel?"

"What do you think I am? The frigging information op . . ." She caught on fast. "Scarlett, huh?"

"You got that right. Why didn't we . . . ?"

"It was slim-to-none. She wasn't into ballet."

"Yeah, but." I couldn't explain the feeling, some inner instinct. "It's a long shot."

"I've gone out on a lot less before, Girlfriend." She gave me names and addresses of two dance places and three health clubs in the area. "Let me know what you find out."

The dance studios were a bust, ditto the first health club. The next sweat box on the list didn't sound promising because of its name, but nothing ventured and all that.

The Texas Gym and Health Spa was three miles south of the Lucky Star. For boxer and weight-lifter types only, I thought. A dirty beige concrete block building, it looked like it went out of business in 1969. A sign in the front window said OPEN. I walked in and the stale odor of sweat almost made me walk back out again. The reception area was small, a motel-style counter and doors on each side leading to open hallways. LADY'S GYM right and MEN'S GYM left. So it *was* co-ed. A door behind the counter led to what probably was an office.

A man of indeterminate age came out from the men's side. He had on sweatpants and a form-fitting T-shirt which didn't do a thing for the extra fifty pounds he carried in his belly. His arms and shoulders were huge, but his face drew your attention. A deep red scar began at his nose and curled down across his chin. His small eyes were buried in folds of fat. How could *he* convince anyone they needed to shape-up?

"Are you the manager?"

"The manager ain't here now. I'm his helper." He spoke slowly, like he had to think about what I said and then think about what he was going to say before he said it.

"When do you expect him?"

"Tonight. He's got a funeral this afternoon."

That one threw me. "What?"

The man guffawed. "That's right, Brother Adkins owns this gym and he's a preacher, too." He scratched his chin along the edge of the scar. "Brother Adkins says the body is a Holy Temple and we should treat it as such."

A strange combination, if you ask me, but perhaps it did make a sort of weird sense. "Guess I never thought of it that way."

"Can I show you around?"

"No, I really needed to talk to . . ."

"I'm Buddy. He leaves me in charge when he's gone. I'm sure I can tell you . . ."

Taking the photo out of my purse, I said, "I'm Jenny Gordon, a private detective. I'm trying to find this young woman." I held the picture out. He took it and studied it as if memorizing some state secret.

Eventually he looked up. "She sure looks like Miss Henrietta, but it can't be. This girl is older and too painted up."

"Miss Henrietta?"

"She's Brother Adkins's daughter." He looked at the picture again. "I'm sure it's not her."

"Where would I find Miss Henrietta?"

"She's gone. Brother Adkins said something about her going up to Dallas a few days ago. I don't think she's come back yet."

This was maybe even a longer shot now, but I'd already started down this path and hated to give up. "And you're sure this isn't Henrietta Adkins?"

Buddy looked again. "No, it's not Miss Henrietta, but it looks like her older sister."

"Does Miss Adkins have an older sister?"

"I don't think so. Brother Adkins never told it to me. Henrietta never said nothing about a sister either." Buddy stared at me, his gaze almost as intent as the one he'd given the photo. "Did you say you was a cop?"

"No. I didn't say that, Buddy. I'm a private detective. Looking for this missing girl."

"Oh yeah. You said that when you come in."

"I'd like to talk to the reverend. Maybe he saw this girl. Someone said she used to work out here."

"I didn't never see her." He looked at his watch. "He'll have go to the cemetery for the grave side."

"Will he come back here after the cemetery?"

"Maybe. In an hour . . . I guess."

"Thanks, I'll come back in an hour." I stopped at the door and asked, "Is Miss Henrietta a dancer—like a ballet dancer?"

"No way. Dancing is forbidden by the Word. It's a sin and ab-bomi-nee-tion for a woman to call attention to herself." He stumbled over the four-syllable word.

"I understand. Well, thanks and don't work out too hard, you don't want to strain a muscle." Buddy gave me a puzzled look as I left. It taxed his brain too much to figure that one.

A hamburger emporium was a block down and across from the gym. I went inside, ordered a large iced tea, and found a pay phone.

"C.J.?" I told her about Brother Adkins and his daughter. "Can you check family records to see if there's another child, an older girl?"

"Like a black sheep daughter?"

"Maybe. Something's there, but I don't know what or how it connects."

"No problemo." Our other phone line rang. "Check you later, Girlfriend. Bye."

I sat in a booth facing the gym and sipped on my drink. I took out a pocket notebook and tried to make sense out of what I knew and what I didn't. Mostly, I doodled.

All the tea I'd had for lunch added to these extra ounces soon sent me scurrying to the Ladies'. I hated to leave my looking post, but when you gotta go . . .

A maroon station wagon, a sign on the side reading Texas Gym and Health Spa, had pulled up while I was answering nature's call, and I saw a slender man in a dark leisure suit walking up to the gym's entrance. That must be Preacher Adkins, I thought, hustled out and drove across the street.

The reception area was empty. I crossed behind the counter and stuck my head into the office. The man I assumed to be Adkins was bent over the open drawer of a file cabinet.

I knocked on the doorjamb.

He whirled around. "Who are y—you?" The gray eyes in his narrow oval face showed surprise. He was about six feet tall, his muscular arms and legs were well defined under the suit. A product of his own sound-body dictum, probably. He had graying hair, thin, disapproving lips, and a deep cleft in his chin. It was the Kirk Douglas dimple that fit Delia Rose's description of an older movie star.

"Sorry. I didn't mean to startle you, Brother Adkins. I'm Jenny Gordon. I'm trying to locate a missing girl who supposedly worked out here. I'm hoping you might know her." I noticed the faint indentation in Scarlett's chin on the photo I handed to him. Hard to deny family genes, I thought.

He took the photograph and glanced at it briefly. "I don't know her. She may have been in here, but I don't think so."

"Are you sure? I was told this girl resembles your daughter."

"You've been talking to Buddy," he said, handing the picture back. "You can't pay too much attention to him. His brain is addled from taking too many jabs to the head. Every photograph he sees of a girl looks like Henrietta to him. He has a big crush on her."

"Then this girl *doesn't* look like your daughter?"

"No." He evaded my eyes and his voice grew indignant. "My daughter is younger, more beautiful and innocent. She has blue eyes and blond hair. Henrietta would never paint herself up like a harlot either."

"Is Henrietta your only daughter?"

"My *only* child. My wife died in childbirth."

The part about his wife was true maybe, but I didn't believe for a minute he only had one child. "I'm sorry."

"It was a long time ago. I'm sure the Lord had a greater need for her than we did."

"This young woman is lying stone-cold in the Travis County morgue.

Unloved and unwanted," I said, hoping for some reaction. "Somebody's family will miss her this Christmas."

His voice took on the timbre of the hell-fire and brimstone evangelist. "I read about this harlot in the newspaper. She was a sinner, a whore. She doesn't deserve a Christian burial."

"That's one way of looking at it," I said. "Whatever happened to Christian forgiveness?"

"The Lord Almighty is the only One who can forgive sins. He will finally turn away from you if you keep rejecting Him, just like some parents have to turn away from their children."

He'd justified it all in his mind and I didn't have any argument for that. "Thanks for your time," I said, anxious to get away from this holier-than-thou Bible-thumper. No wonder Scarlett wanted to be anonymous. Henrietta probably felt the same way. "I'd like to call Henrietta . . ."

He pointed a finger at me and shouted, "Get out of here, you Jezebel! And you stay away from Henrietta. She has nothing to do with harlots and whores."

I'd never been accused of being a Jezebel before. It was time to go before he started throwing stones at me.

FIVE

Information poured from the office printer like hail coming from a Texas tornado cloud, amazing my technological aptitude of a horntoad with its speed. C.J. got all the information we needed without ever leaving her desk.

Two legal document copies blew away all my theories. Texas birth certificates require a response to: Other Children Born to This Mother? and more specifically: How many other children are now living? Henrietta Jo Adkins was the only child born to Mary Madeline Fever Adkins. A death certificate for the wife of Stephen Adkins showed Madeline died on January 29, 1970, the day Henrietta was born, from heart failure. "Fever" wasn't just part of Scarlett's clever stage name. It was also her mother's maiden name. I'd been so sure there was an older daughter that Henrietta Adkins and Scarlett Fever O'Hara had to be one and the same.

"Any other proof?" I asked C.J.

"Uh-huh. Scarlett was arrested for solicitation twice under the name of Henrietta Jo Adkins. The Austin Police Department AFIS computer matched their fingerprints."

Preacher Adkins's attitude still infuriated me. "That sanctimonious bastard doesn't even intend to bury his own flesh and blood. Doesn't he care that Wilson is claiming the body?"

"No, because the heartless S.O.B. disowned her completely, but I hope he feels some fear right about now."

"Is the ID positive," I asked C.J.

"Uh-huh. Lieutenant Hays confirmed it, too."

I'd been so sure there was an older daughter. And Preacher Adkins infuriated me. "That sanctimonious bastard doesn't plan to do anything about burying his own flesh and blood. And he doesn't know or care that Wilson is claiming the body."

"He's one heartless S.O.B. But I'll bet he's a scared S.O.B. right about now."

"Because his daughter was identified as a hooker?"

"You got it," said C.J. "His little church flock will probably tar and feather him. His reputation is ruined and—"

"Maybe he killed her to keep his reputation intact."

"Good thinking, Jenny."

"We seem to have a plethora of male suspects," I said.

"Marshall Tolliver, the man found in the room with the very dead Scarlett, and Preacher Adkins. Who else?"

"Buddy, the pug-ugly down at the gym. Except I can't see him being smart enough to carry out the complications of Mickey Finns. And . . . Wilson Billeau."

"Surely you don't think our good old country boy killed the girl he claims to love? Besides, he's our client."

"He's technically not ours anymore. It's happened before, even to us." I knew she didn't want to be reminded about when her cousin Veronica and Veronica's baby had been killed, so I continued.

"If we rule out Buddy," I said, "we still have three viable suspects. You do know it's not exactly our business to get into an active homicide case."

"Larry Hays would never forgive us."

"Understatement of the year. Yet you and I know what a heavy caseload he has. He won't devote much time trying to solve a hooker's murder."

"What have you got in mind?"

"Not a darn thing, but if we put our heads together, we should be able to come up with someone who might have wanted Scarlett dead."

"Exactly, and who was around to do it."

We brainstormed for an hour and couldn't figure out how to bypass Larry without causing trouble. "Maybe we should lay low and see what happens."

"I'd much rather stir things up and see what happens," said C.J. with an evil grin.

"What do we do about Mr. Tolliver?" I asked.

"After what Larry told you earlier, we can probably rule him out. If we talk to the hotel employees we might corroborate his story."

"Larry's team has already done that, I would imagine."

"Okay, let's head out to Dripping Springs to see what Wilson Billeau has to say and come back by the Lucky Star. We can stop in there for a cold beer. Talk to some folks."

C.J. drove us to Wilson's house with the top down on her Mustang. It was a great evening for a drive, but I didn't feel much like talking. I kept thinking how Wilson was really a sweet kid and how it would upset me if he was involved. C.J. knew how I felt, or maybe she even felt the same way, because she kept quiet too.

Bulldog Porter's Lincoln Towncar was in the driveway and he greeted us at the door, a finger to his lips. "Wilson is lying down. He could use some feminine company. I'm not too good at this."

We walked into the living room and sat down. "The police called my office a short time ago," said Bulldog. "They knew I represented the man who claimed Scarlett's body and made the funeral arrangements. They said she'd been identified as Henrietta Adkins, but I can only say the name Wilson always used."

Wilson had heard us come in and he joined us. "Do you know if the police have arrested the man who killed her yet?" he asked without preamble. "Bulldog said they cleared that man from Houston and he was released from jail." His face showed the ravages of grief and his eyes were red-rimmed. He was suffering. If it was an act, it was the Oscar-winning performance of the year.

C.J. and I looked at each other. An unspoken message passed between us. *This* young man can't be the killer.

"We haven't talked to the police in the past few hours," I said. "I think our friend in homicide will call when APD makes an arrest."

Wilson said Scarlett's father still wanted no part of claiming her, so the funeral would be as he'd planned, tomorrow at 2 P.M. He said he hoped we'd come. We said we'd be there and he went back to the bedroom.

I could tell Bulldog was grieving along with Wilson. He obviously had unusually strong feelings about his friend's son.

Bulldog said, "I've told Wilson the police will do their best, but they'll soon give up unless the killer drops in their lap. They don't have the time to devote to a long investigation. Wilson would like you to take the case when the police give up."

We finally agreed to do what we legally could.

Bulldog was nodding off as we left, but Wilson came out to walk to the car with us. "Jenny, would you and C.J. promise me one thing?" For the first time since we arrived, his voice had some emotion. "No matter how long it takes or how much it costs, I want you to keep on looking. I want whoever killed her to rot in jail."

"We'll do our best," I said. "But as far as the jail term, Wilson, you know today's justice system—the killer may only serve a short time or get off completely. It's up to a judge and jury."

C.J. and I headed back to Austin.

"I can't help feeling sorry for him," I said. "For someone who'd never dated that girl, much less had a relationship with her, he's in bad shape. Did you see those big sad eyes?"

"She represented a fantasy to him, a dream," said C.J. "A dream that died. That's what had been worrying me. I was afraid he might have been too obsessed. That when he'd found out she was a hooker he didn't want anyone else to touch her."

"I know. Deep down I was afraid of the same thing. Are you convinced he's innocent?"

"Yes. And if Larry has cleared Marshall Tolliver—that poor sucker from Houston—there's only one suspect left."

"Scarlett's unforgiving father," I said.

"And if Larry's as smart as I think he is, he's already checking Adkins from top to bottom. Let's go to the Hyatt for some fajitas," she said. "We can eat and talk about our options."

"I can't do it. I had a humongous lunch. We could go over to my house and I'll fix a salad and grill a steak or a chicken breast for you."

C.J. is a big gal and eats like a construction worker. Luckily she never gains an ounce, but she also lifts weights, swims, and does martial arts training.

When we reached my apartment C.J. parked and opened her car door. "I hope you have a cold beer—I could use one, maybe even two."

We went inside. I went to the kitchen and got out a couple of Light Coors. "I'll make up the bed in the guest room for you and we won't worry about you driving home tonight."

"That works for me," C.J. said and popped the top on her can.

I popped mine, too, and checked for my telephone messages. One was a hang-up and the other was Bulldog Porter. "Jenny? Are you there? Wilson has talked himself into doing something drastic. He's on his way now to talk to Scarlett's father. He thinks Adkins had something to do with killing her. I dozed off, but he left me a note. Wait, I've got Adkins's home address here."

Papers rustled noisily, then Bulldog gave out the preacher's address. "That's just off William Cannon and West Gate. We've got to stop him. I'm heading over there now." A moment later Bulldog said, "It's 9:05."

"Holy shit! That was over forty minutes ago," said C.J. "Let's go."

The barely sipped beer went down the drain and we left. The address where Preacher Adkins lived was five or six miles farther south and two or three miles west of the Lucky Star Bar and Grill. It was a yuppified suburban area a good thirty to forty minutes from my apartment even at this time of night and using the freeway.

"MiGod, C.J. Did you see this coming?"

"No way. But in hindsight, I should have. Wilson is a man in pain and he wants a killer brought to justice."

"And I just *had* to remind him justice was blind and deaf."

"He didn't need you to figure that out, Girlfriend."

"I know, but damn. Damn, damn."

As we raced down Interstate 35 I called Larry's house and office. No answer at either place. I dialed his pager and punched in our number. He still had not responded when we exited on William Cannon Drive and turned into a subdivision. The houses along here were a little older than others in the upscale section down the block. When we neared the address, I spotted Larry's car parked behind two patrol units, their red and blue lights stabbing the darkness.

A Special Missions Team was there, tall men dressed in black, with helmets and equipment hanging from everywhere. The SMT officers carried heavy firepower and looked like alien warriors from *Star Wars*.

Two uniformed patrolmen kept back a small knot of thrill-seekers and as we parked I saw the SMT squad move out, surrounding the house.

Bulldog's Lincoln Towncar was angled up to the edge of the lawn two houses away. We parked on the opposite side of the street. When he saw us he opened his car door and waved us over. "Can you find out what's going on?" he asked. "No one will tell me anything."

"They haven't let you talk to Wilson?" I said. "Don't they know you might be able to talk some sense into him? Come on, we'll try to find someone in charge."

The three of us walked slowly toward the house, edging our way through people politely so the uniformed officers wouldn't think we were troublemakers. As we reached one of the patrolmen, a shot was fired inside the house.

A second shot followed, moments later. Both shots sounded like they were from the same handgun and not one of the rifles the SMT officers used.

"I don't think Wilson has a gun," said Bulldog.

The SMT squad swarmed in. Someone yelled "He's down!"

I knew it would be a while before we would know anything. Two ambulances squealed up, one behind the other, and the silence when they turned off the sirens was exquisite. The EMS attendants ran inside the house.

"That's a good sign, isn't it?" asked Bulldog. "Someone needs medical attention."

"It could mean anything, Bulldog," I told him. "Don't get your hopes too high."

When the Medical Examiner's station wagon pulled up a few minutes later, I had to catch Bulldog when he slumped. I eased the old man to a sitting position on the ground. C.J., with tightened lips, said she was going to find Larry Hays and get some answers.

Time passed and I couldn't get Bulldog to return to his car. We sat in the dewy grass and I kept my arm around his shaking bony shoulders. Neither of us talked.

When C.J. returned to where we sat, one of the EMS attendants followed and I could tell from her face the news was grim. "They're both . . ." She shook her head. "Looks like they fought. The preacher had a gun. After he shot Wilson, he killed himself."

Bulldog started having chest pains. "He was my son," Bulldog said. "His legal father was my best friend, but no one except his mother and I ever knew."

The EMS guys began checking the old man.

C.J. took me aside. "The police found news clippings of Adkins being convicted of child abuse. He'd beaten up on Scarlett for years. Larry Hays had already found out that Adkins had served time for that conviction in another state and had been released from prison six months ago. There was also a letter of resignation to his church in which he admitted killing his daughter. Claimed she was a seed of Satan and had to be destroyed."

The medics reported that Bulldog didn't have a heart attack, it was emotional stress. They put him on a stretcher, saying a checkup at the hospital was routine procedure. I said I'd ride with him in the ambulance. C.J. said she'd meet me there.

The EMS wagon was ready to roll, but I couldn't get in yet. "Naive little shit." The tears I'd held back slipped out. "What could we have done differently, C.J.? What more . . ."

"Nothing," she said, putting an arm around me. "Not a damn thing."

"Why? C.J. Why?"

"The Scarlet Fever got hold of Wilson and never let go."

The author thanks Kenny Rogers for writing and recording the song "Scarlett Fever," which inspired this story.

CATHY PICKENS

The editors of *Deadly Allies II* are delighted
to introduce South Carolina attorney Cathy
Pickens, whose first story debuts here. "Uncommon Law" features Avery Andrews, recently returned-home lawyer.

A descendant of a family that has been in
South Carolina for three hundred years, Cathy
Pickens has been a church organist, a Scottish
clog dance instructor, and now teaches law and
ethics at Queens College in Charlotte, North
Carolina. While her lawyer's eye was on civil
litigation, her mystery writer's gaze was taking
in the scene: "Avery's bizarre clients are
Southern eccentrics. Visit any small-town
courthouse on criminal docket day and you'll
meet more folks than could ever populate a
book—and plenty so strange that no reader of
fiction would believe them."

The South is known for its hospitality, but
in "Uncommon Law" Avery Andrews finds
one more guest than she bargained for.

UNCOMMON LAW

My new AVERY ANDREWS, ATTORNEY-AT-LAW sign
rattled as I struggled with the lock on the front
door. The phone inside started ringing.

Damn. Had I remembered to turn on the
answering machine last night? I convinced the
lock to turn on the sixth phone ring. On ring
seven, I dashed across the front room and
grabbed the receiver.

"Miz Andrews? That you? Pee Vee Probert.
How you doin'?"

"Fine, Pee Vee. How about yourself?" Pee
Vee is a regular client, one who has taught me a
lot about redneck weekend-binge drinkers and
county-jail habitués.

"Reckon you could come down and spring
me?"

"Already?" My voice registered my surprise.
Pee Vee knows the unwritten protocol better
than I do—calls from the detention center generally don't start until late Friday night, and it
was now early Friday morning.

"Got started a little early," he acknowl-
edged. "A few beers with the guys after the
second shift and wouldn't you know it? Out of
a whole county full of guys, they arrested me."

The unfairness of life. "Not driving." It was

a wish rather than a question. Pee Vee knew how much time he'd do if he picked up a DUI/3d offense.

"No, ma'am. I know better'n'at. Wadn't riding, neither. Never left the parking lot."

I could picture him, thumb hitched in the belt loop riding low on his skinny hips, proud of not being dumb enough to get arrested driving—or riding—drunk. Of course, nobody's dumb enough to get arrested for riding drunk, since there's no law against it. But Pee Vee, in his limited way, knew that if anybody could manage it, he could.

"And?" I said, prodding him to explain. Some clients are a bit reluctant to explain—not from any remorse, but from misplaced pride, as if telling what they'd done was immodest, beyond the bounds of simple propriety.

"You know Peanut Potts? Bad to hold his licker and striped snake mean when he's drunk. He'uz razzing Hub—you know Hub? You did that malicious damage to property thing for him?" He rolled the statutory offense off a practiced tongue. Pee Vee knew a thing or two about malicious damage himself.

"Um-hum." I remembered Hub. A behemoth. He'd come to court wearing a T-shirt strained full of holes by his beer belly. His brain, however, did not strain the confines of his skull. Hub was a gentle sort, but my first meeting with him resulted from him busting windshields with his head because somebody's said he couldn't do it. He could. And had been fairly pleased, if a bit bruised.

"We'uz at Eli's, and Peanut starts in on Hub 'bout Hub's old lady dumping him. Then Peanut starts telling Hub that I'uz the reason she left. That she wanted a quick little pricker 'stead of—"

"And you were arrested for?" I did not want to hear a recitation of Hub's and Peanut's drunken but, I'm sure, literate comparison of sexual merit.

"Assaulting and battering Peanut up side the head."

"You hit Peanut?"

"Yep." Again, that sense of self-satisfaction from a job well done seeped through his speech.

"Was he . . . hurt?" I asked carefully, not wanting to hurt Pee Vee's feelings. But he's only five feet tall, one of the few adults I know shorter than I am. How much damage could he have done?

"He's down to the hospital. They wouldn't let me call to find out this mornin'. I thought you could. And let me know?"

"Sure," I said. "But finish explaining about the fight."

"Well, one thing led to another. You know how that is."

Actually, I didn't know how it was since I've never stood around in a parking lot talking trash until the discussants parted ways for the hospital and the county lockup.

"And Peanut starts pounding on Hub pretty bad. You know Hub, he's a nice guy and don't really got any idear how big he is, so he's getting the shit stomped outta him. 'Scuse me. I shouldn't'a said that."

"That's Okay." Chivalry isn't dead. "How big is this Peanut fellow?"

"Big as a dray horse. Got fists like salt-cured hams. Done time for killing a man. Got dishonorable discharged for it. 'Coz it was in a fight. Not a war."

"How did Peanut end up in the hospital?"

"I laid him out with a tire iron." He pronounced it "tar arn," but the clinical accuracy of his choice for equalizing his size disadvantage couldn't be questioned.

"You beat him with a tire iron." I tried to keep the hysterical edge out of my voice, to sound matter-of-fact.

"Oh no. I didn't beat him. Just took one haul on it and he was out. To get him off Hub, you know. Then I took Hub home so's his wife could doctor him up."

"I'm not sure I'll be able to get bond set today. They may want you to cool off over the weekend."

"Hmm." He sounded dejected for the first time in our conversation. "That'd sure be a shame. Missin' a weekend and all."

The source of Pee Vee's dismay was that beer, pool tables, and tire irons aren't allowed in the county lockup. Life, liberty, and the pursuit of happiness.

"I'll see what I can do."

I called the clerk's office. Jean Bartlett answered. Jean knows the normal course of the flotsam and jetsam of Camden County's criminal court system better than most women her age know how long a rinse and set at Angie's Vanity Box take. She said she'd let me know.

The red light on the answering machine blinked at me as I replaced the receiver after doing what I could for Pee Vee. I'd remembered to leave it on after all.

I punched the button and turned to Adamia, my life-sized human skeleton and only officemate. She sat with her back to me, peering out the front window, her right thighbone demurely crossed over her left. "Nice start to the day, huh?"

As the phone message started, I dumped a pencil stub from the A&W

root beer mug by the phone and scrabbled among the clutter for a scrap of paper.

"Avery, this is Laurel Cross. You probably don't remember, but we were in high school together. I'm in town. And I need a lawyer. Couldn't believe it when I saw your name in the book. Thought you were in a big firm in Columbia. It's about a divorce. Well, actually, I guess, about a marriage. Talk to you later." Laurel rushed her message, ending with the bright, brittle *bye* of someone not used to talking to machines.

The second message was also rushed. "Hi again. Forgot to leave my number. I'm at the motel. Room 115. If I don't hear from you, I'll try back later. Bye."

As I flipped through the Dacus, South Carolina, phone book for the Dacus Motel's number, the front door creaked open. Melvin, my neighbor, stood there. Even with a four-foot-long iron stake and a coil of green wire in one hand and a flashlight and hammer clutched under his other arm, he looked every inch an accountant.

"The computers," he said.

I nodded. Melvin and I have known each other long enough for me to understand completely. He'd really said, "We need to ground the electrical outlets to our computers, and I'm not going in that basement by myself."

Melvin Bertram and I share a sprawling pink Victorian circled by wide porches, the former Baldwin and Bates Funeral Parlor. My parents had been mildly surprised when I'd left a partnership at the Calhoun firm in Columbia and come home to set up a solo practice in Dacus. Whether they were more surprised by my coming home to a small town or by my combination office/home in the old mortuary, I wasn't quite sure.

My upstairs living quarters are not as elegant as my downstairs office since funeral visitation had been confined to the large ground-floor parlors and chapel, now my offices, and, in the other half of the building, the office of Melvin Bertram, CPA. After a rocky start, Melvin and I had established a good working relationship. He'd set up my bookkeeping system, although my cash flow demands nothing more sophisticated than the shoebox method: everything in a shoebox until the end of the year. In return, I supply the rare bit of legal advice. Melvin is the only one who knows that I spend most of my working day feeling like a wet-behind-the-ears legal fraud.

Neither Melvin nor I venture downstairs to our mutual basement if we can help it. I'd never been past the first room into any of the warren of storage rooms we supposedly own. But it was either go downstairs or hire an electrician. Melvin is a do-it-yourselfer, everything from cooking to changing his ancient Plymouth's oil. And alone, I couldn't afford an electrician.

Melvin turned without waiting for acquiescence. I tossed the phone book onto the paper pile on the desk and trailed obediently after Melvin through the main hallway and down the basement stairs.

The fluorescent lighting flickered, then hummed, glaring off the scratched stainless steel and glass-fronted cabinets of the embalming room. A gray metal table sat in the middle of the room, spotlit by a hanging lamp. The air was a wet cold and the sweet biology-lab formaldehyde smell masked odors I didn't want to think about. I half-expected eerie music and maniacal laughter to swell from some hidden alcove.

"We ought to sell this stuff," Melvin said, always the accountant.

"Where do we need to run the wires?" I said, wanting to get out of the basement quickly rather than look around for investment opportunities.

We crossed the tomb-quiet embalming room to a small door half hidden by a small cabinet. Melvin fiddled with the lock. Like everything else in the house, it was old and stubborn. "From the old blueprints, the unfinished basement starts behind this room. We can run ground wires from both our outlets down through the common wall. Shouldn't take long." Characteristically, Melvin had everything planned.

Uncharacteristically, however, Melvin froze. He'd snapped on his flashlight and was groping for the light switch when he stopped. Over his shoulder, in the beam of the flashlight, I hoped I wasn't seeing what I saw.

Suspended in the beam of Melvin's flashlight, like a levitation act, was a body—somebody.

My fight-or-flight response is usually in good working order. But I couldn't move. Melvin found the switch, and the bright glare overhead pinned us like possums in a headlight. Neither of us said anything.

The body lay on a wooden table against the far wall, still as a dead man. He wore a severe black wool suit, the scratchy, awkward-to-wear kind, and a white shirt and dark tie. His greased gray hair lay like plastic mannequin hair; his skin was the bloodless gray-pink of the dead and carefully made up. As the final cruelty, his lips had been set in a slight grin so his dentures showed. Judging from the deep wrinkles lining his face, this small grin was not an expression he'd worn in life. It made it more painful to see in death.

"Who is he?" I whispered. We stood like mourners at a funeral, not too close but mesmerized, looking for some sign that this had once been alive. My hands were clasped in tight fists against the damp cold.

"I have no idea."

"We'd better call—" Who? A funeral home seemed the natural place for a dead body. But this was no longer a funeral home. And this guy certainly hadn't been included in the contract when we bought the place.

We left silently. Exactly like mourners and as much at a loss as if he'd been a loved one we would miss. Our loss, though, was what we'd do with him, not what we'd do without him.

"Call L.J.," Melvin said when we had fled upstairs to the sun-filled front hallway.

I was so intent on getting to the phone in my office that I almost missed the woman sitting in my lone client chair. Clients in my office are something of a rarity, so I should have noticed immediately. I smiled hello, said—as professionally as I could—that I'd be with her in a moment, and breezed into my office. Melvin, with his flashlight, wire coil, iron stake, and hammer, followed.

The phone on my desk startled me by ringing as I reached to pick it up. "Avery Andrews's office," I singsonged automatically.

"No wonder this gahdam number sounded so familiar."

I hesitated. "L.J.? I was just calling—"

"You got a dead body for a client," she boomed. Sheriff L.J. Peters isn't easy to interrupt.

"The dead ones are yours, L.J. I—" My brain wasn't firing on all synapses. I was supposed to be the one announcing a dead body.

"This one's over at the motel and she's got your phone number in her purse—"

"Whoa," I said. "Back up—"

"—Laurel Cross. You used to hang around with her in high school." L.J. could make eating lunch with someone sound like grounds for a federal RICO racketeering action.

"Laurel? She called this morn—"

"Get over here now."

"But—" The phone clicked, then hummed a dial tone. I stared at Melvin.

"That was L.J. Laurel Cross—a friend from high school—is over at the motel. Dead." I realized how stunned I was when I heard my own voice.

"Oh, Lord." Melvin shed his electrician's tools noisily onto my desk. "L.J.'ll be worse than her usual self-important self now that she's got a case to solve. Two, actually," he added, always a stickler for details.

I walked into the front office to find where I'd left my briefcase. "She doesn't know about the body in the basement," I called over my shoulder. "Maybe we should just leave it there so we won't have to tell her," I said half-seriously.

The woman I'd forgotten was still sitting in my client chair. She raised her eyebrows ever so slightly.

"Um," I fumbled. "I'm sorry. Did you have an appointment?" I knew full well I hadn't scheduled any clients that morning. I remember the few clients I have.

"Certainly," she said. "I'm Edna Lynch."

Edna Lynch. "The investigator?" If this had been a Three Stooges skit, I would've slapped my forehead with my palm. "I do apologize. It's just . . . well, we've had an unusual morning. And . . . somehow, I was expecting someone . . . different."

That was an understatement. I know it's corny, but when I called Lynch Investigations, I'd expected Paul Drake to show up, or Magnum P.I., or even Columbo. But here was Aunt Jemima. She was taller than my own near-munchkin proportions, and she had the thin arms and legs and padded body that middle-aged moms get. Her hair was permed into unbelievable sausage curls but she'd had sense enough to keep her own steel-gray color. She wore polyester pull-on pants with a matching sweater set and thick-soled shoes. She looked like any retired cotton mill grandmother who puts fatback in her green beans for Sunday dinner. She didn't look like a private investigator.

"You said you might need an investigator. I'm licensed. I've got references. And I'll be glad to show you what I can do." Her watery brown eyes bored into mine. Her face was surprisingly bony for such a grand-motherly body, her skin smooth and milk chocolate. Her eyes sat in deep, sunken sockets. She knew exactly what I was thinking, and she was calling my bluff.

I stalled. "We've got a problem," I started, groping for my business voice. I fought against sounding like a whining child trying to explain some inexplicably stupid act.

"A body in the basement," she said. "And forgive my eavesdropping, but Sheriff Peters just called about another body at the motel."

I nodded. I had no idea where to start this conversation. I didn't have a pending case for her to work on; I'd only wanted to start interviewing investigators. But if I put her off . . . I'd handled things badly, but I had too much on my mind this morning to settle in over a cup of tea and talk divorce investigations. I fumbled for a tactful way out of my political incorrectness.

Melvin hovered nearby like my embodied conscience, making matters worse. "A private investigator. Fascinating," he murmured. He had that ready-to-settle-in-for-a-chat look. His ingenuousness seemed to disarm Edna somewhat.

She turned back to me. "You sound like you've got some unexpected things to deal with this morning. Why don't I—"

"The body, Avery," Melvin interrupted. "L.J.'s got her hands full right now. Why don't we ask Ms. Lynch to find out who our downstairs tenant is? That'll make deciding where he should go next a bit simpler, don't you think?"

Edna Lynch tried not to look interested.

"Why not?" I said, wondering how "we" would pay the grandmother private eye. "Will it take long, do you think?"

"I can't get involved in a murder investigation unless the police are notified," she said, shaking her head.

"No, no. Not murder. He's just—there," I said. "He's embalmed and everything. I assume, I mean he must be left over, from when this was a mortuary. We found him this morning and we want to get rid of him."

"He's downstairs?" Edna slung a lumpy suitcase-sized black vinyl bag over her shoulder. "I'll need to get a picture of him first. I'll get back to you this afternoon with something."

I gave a small nod, speechless. She marched off with Melvin toward the basement stairs while I rummaged around under the front desk for my briefcase. Maybe I should go upstairs to bed and try again tomorrow. This day was too strange already.

I carefully nosed my 1969 Mustang between two county police cars in front of the Dacus Motel. The overhang on the long cement block building half-shaded a line of doors painted different discount paint colors. Flimsy webbed lawn chairs alternated with the doors down the long porch. Places like the Dacus Motel are pre-interstate-highway anachronisms, left alongside back roads, infested with weeds and broken windows. The Dacus Motel had, in a manner of speaking, survived, but it hadn't thrived. It was Dacus's only motel, too old to succeed but not too close to the road to cater to the rent-by-the-hour crowd.

Room 115 wasn't hard to spot. The door stood open, with yellow crime scene tape stretched from the door down the iron porch supports and back to the window. The porch was crowded with uniformed police officers, smoking, spitting, and watching me get out of my car. A major crime doesn't come along everyday.

"It's damn near time you got here." L.J.'s voice sounded from the darkened doorway. A camera flash backlit the sheriff as she hove into view. One of the uniformed county cops held the yellow tape while I scooted under it. L.J.'s mother had named her Lucinda Jane, hoping a dainty name would somehow save her from looking like her daddy. It hadn't worked. From size-eleven black safety shoes to close-cut black hair, her six-foot, two-hundred-and-something-pound frame was awesome. Especially if, like me, you could remember that same voice echoing in the grammar school restroom. Every time L.J. sounds perturbed, I gulp, swallowing the memory of being body-slammed against the restroom wall in the fourth grade. I gulped now. I knew L.J. didn't intend to slam me against the wall, but childhood fears grow up hard.

The smell of musty bed linen, spent gunpowder, and urine coated the dingy room. On the gray-green linoleum floor, between the front door and the bed, lay Laurel Cross. A small, crusty round hole bore in the side of her head, just above her ear. All I could think was that the floor looked too cold and dirty to let her lie there.

"Why'd she call you?" L.J. asked around the wad of gum in her mouth.

A foolish part of me likes to bait L.J. "What makes you think she called?"

"Two things, wise ass. One is that the manager placed the call for her through the switchboard. And the other is that you told me so yourself."

I nodded, mentally retreating from verbal battle. I'd come unarmed. "I don't know exactly why she called. The message on my machine said something about a divorce. That's all."

The guy puffing fingerprint powder around the room pushed past me to dust the bedside table.

"Any idea why she was in town?" Standing, L.J. plopped one black military-issue brogan on the seat of the only chair in the room.

"Nope. That's all she said. I might still have the tape, if no one has called and recorded over it."

"You remember her, don't you?" L.J. asked, nodding toward the body. "She was one of the popular kids."

The challenge in L.J.'s voice was clear. No high school kid ever sees herself as one of the popular ones, but L.J. had never been close to being popular, in her eyes or anyone else's. She still wasn't. She was elected, but that's not the same thing.

The corpse on the floor had that nobody's home look. The thin, white-blond hair was shoulder-length now rather than the waist-length I remembered. And her waxen face had a few more lines. Laurel had been the closest thing Dacus'd had to a flower child. Marching in the war moratorium at the college was tame stuff by most standards, but then trendy things reach Dacus three years after they've trended out everywhere else. She'd been scandal enough for Dacus, with the rumors of drugs and even a New York abortion.

I'd always liked Laurel. In person she was never as outrageous as the stories about her. Sitting beside her in art class was as close to the wild side as I ever got. We molded clay into pots and mashed them flat, and she reported on the weekend concerts at The Farm, the outdoor cow pasture concert hall I'd never frequented. I'd always seen her as gentle and artistic, a truly free spirit. Whatever she was, I'd found it appealing. She was what I was not.

I went out to stand on the motel porch. Watching the yellow crime scene tape dance in the breeze from a passing truck, I found myself grieving for Laurel and for who we used to be.

L.J. ambled out and stuck a manila envelope in my direction. "What'd'ya make of this?"

The envelope held a sheet of notebook paper, a news clipping, and a photograph. The sheet of lined paper had been folded and refolded so many times it was almost in pieces. The looping, childish scrawl read:

> *In your eyes I see the me I long to be*
> *Two parts of a whole formed in the dusty pink sunrise of dawn.*
> *To you I pledge the me you have created*
> *As we become one*
> *As a shooting star with the night sky.*
> *As we love one another, making a bond and not a bond of love,*
> *I will cherish you forever.*

It read like the painful anguish that masquerades as poetry for the teenaged lovelorn.

The newspaper article was neatly clipped and recent: LAKESIDE DREAM HOUSE DESIGNED BY OWNERS. I remembered seeing the article—an interview with Mark Guildman, a high school classmate of mine—in the Saturday *Home* section a few months earlier. Smiling in the newsprint photo, a couple sat on the deck of a sprawling house. The lake glinted in the background. Mark hadn't changed much since high school. Mr. Most Likely to Succeed had made a bundle developing and selling his grandfather's land, and he'd married a woman from Charleston. They looked like Barbie and Ken dolls.

The third item was a color photograph of another couple sitting in a grassy field. They were in each other's arms, reclining slightly on the grass and smiling. The trunk and lower branches of a tree sheltered them. It took a second for me to recognize Mark Guildman. His hair was 1970s shaggy and his sideburns were two caterpillars crawling down either side of his face. Laurel Cross, though, was easy to recognize. Except for being dead, she hadn't changed much.

The photo brought a wash of forgotten memories. I turned to L.J. "The summer we graduated, remember? Laurel and Mark were dating then. Surprised everybody. But then Mark went to The Citadel to school and Laurel, well, just left." Had it been as long as it seemed?

"You think she saw this stuff in the paper about his house and decided to renew old acquaintances?"

I shrugged and handed the envelope back to L.J. Renewing old acquaintances didn't sound like Laurel. She might run into you somewhere and exclaim, "I *knew* I was going to see you soon. I had this vision" or whatever, but coming back to Dacus for the heck of it wasn't her style. Getting away from too-small Dacus had been too important to her fifteen years ago. She wouldn't just wander back now. Not without a reason.

"What'd'ya make of it?" L.J. asked again.

I shrugged. "I don't know. You're the sheriff. What do you think?"

"I think she came to see Mark Guildman and you. She only made two phone calls: one to you, which you say you got, and one to Guildman, which he says he never got. Since you two are the only ones she tried to contact—"

"—by phone," I interjected.

"—stands to reason you're the only ones who knew she was here. What'd she want to see you about?"

"I told you. She said something about a divorce."

"If you're holding out on me, Counselor . . ." L.J. let the threat trail off.

I'm constantly reminded that law enforcement was an unnatural career choice for L.J.

I had turned my car toward town when I remembered that I'd neglected to report our basement tenant. How a dead body in a basement could slip my mind . . . I'd call her. No sense giving L.J. news in person that I could give her over the phone.

As I pulled in front of the stately pink Victorian creature I call home and office, Edna Lynch's serviceable Chevrolet pulled up to the curb behind me.

She bustled out and onto the sidewalk, tugging her knit top over her hips. "Glad I caught you," she said matter-of-factly. "I found out who he is—was." I had a clear impression that Edna was back with a vengeance. She wanted to shove it in my face. But she didn't. She just gave me the facts. Smugly.

"Edwin Masey. There's a signed death certificate on file, so there should be no problem about failing to report an unexplained death," she said.

"What's still unexplained is what he's doing in the basement." I wrestled with the lock and pushed open the door for her.

"He died about two years ago, right before Mr. Bates retired from the burying business," she said. "Seems he and Bates got into it over some money."

Inside the front room, Edna settled into the client chair and I took the desk chair. She continued. "Seems Masey ran a lot of scams. Masey borrowed money from Bates, used his burial plot as collateral. Trouble was, he'd given a lot of people his burial plot as collateral, and Bates was at the end of a long line. Then Masey showed up needing that burial plot for its intended use. Bates was furious." She allowed herself a small smile. "What goes around, comes around. Apparently Bates decided to get even and just didn't bury him. The moral is, don't mess with your mortician. He might not have a forgiving heart."

"How in heaven's name did you find all this out so quickly?"

"Contacts," she said simply. "Know Zebulun Canty? That fella always sits on the courthouse steps, wears that red stocking cap even in July?"

I nodded. An assortment of Dacus's answer to village idiots decorate the courthouse steps on all but the coldest days. They're such fixtures nobody pays them much attention, unless one of them looks like he needs a hot meal the last few days before the Social Security checks come in.

"He was the Baldwin and Bates's gravedigger. He knew all about how Masey rooked Bates. Didn't take long, after he gave me Masey's name, to check the death certificates."

"I'm impressed." I leaned back in my armless chair. "Is there, um, any way to say thanks to Zebulun Canty? Or have you taken care of it?"

I've heard of withering glances, but this woman had mastered a glare that put Mammy Yokum's triple whammy to shame. "Zebulun Canty don't need no thank-you's. Don't be fooled by how folks look. The man can afford to hire an accountant," she said in a tone that let me know she knew I couldn't.

I hesitated before broaching another uncomfortable topic. "And how much do I owe you?"

"I'll send you a bill," she said, standing. "I charge thirty dollars an hour, and it only took an hour."

"That's fantastic." I could probably find thirty dollars. "I'll be calling you on those other cases. As I said, none of them are to the point where I need an investigator. But I'm sure glad to know who to call. Thank you." And I meant it.

The hard lines around her eyes softened a bit, but she didn't smile. Instead, she gave a curt nod as she gathered her elephantine vinyl bag, pulled her sweater top down over her fanny, and left. Paul Drake, she wasn't. But then, Paul's constant flirting got irritating after awhile. As soon as I convinced Ms. Lynch that I wasn't ordinarily a narrow-minded bigot, maybe we'd get along just fine.

As I phoned Melvin with the news of the deceased Mr. Masey, I remembered to pop the minicassette out of my answering machine. No one else had called. Laurel's message should be intact, but I didn't want to replay it. Melvin agreed to make whatever arrangements one makes for an unwanted embalmed body. I didn't ask if we could just board up the basement and forget it was there.

A nap was what I had in mind as I climbed the narrow servant's stairs to my apartment, but I stopped first at the bookcase just inside the door and pulled off the *Dacus High Chronicle*, my senior yearbook. I seldom open it. The dust of remembering always leaves me fuzzy around the edges.

Mark Guildman, in the traditional senior picture, looked young and self-absorbed. His shaggy brown hair wasn't as long as it had been in the photograph with Laurel, but then he'd had a whole year between photographs to grow those sideburns and become a senior. Mark also appeared in half a dozen club photos. He'd been president of the Future Business Leaders. I didn't spot him in any of the basketball team's game pictures, but he was there in the team photo. Looking back, it had been a predictable route from here to his Charleston wife, new home, and money.

Laurel appeared in only two pictures: a single shot of her in the class section, her thin face and light coloring faint against the black drape all the senior girls wore, and another in the Drama Club photo.

I wished I had a copy of that much-folded sheet of notebook paper L.J. had shown me. Something about that poetry . . .

On a shelf that needed dusting, I found the tiny volume of Kahlil Gibran's *The Prophet* tucked between *Kenilworth* and Zora Neale Hurston. The shelves with the mysteries on them get dusted more often than these.

There it was: "Love one another but make not a bond of love." The opening of that chapter of *The Prophet* explained everything: "And what of Marriage, master?"

I threw the book on the chair, grabbed my car keys, and clattered down the back stairs.

The courthouse library was small but it had what I needed. I'd run across the old opinions while researching a point of law for a divorce case a few months earlier, so it didn't take long to unearth them. I made a few photocopies, then went across the street to the Law Enforcement Center to find L.J. Just my luck, she was in.

I handed her the photocopies. "The phone cassette is at my office. You might need it."

L.J. tilted her chair back—it leaned more easily than mine—and thudded both her feet onto the desk in one quick move. "So?" she said, wiggling a toothpick to the corner of her mouth with a practiced tongue.

"You'd better question Mr. and Mrs. Mark Guildman. It's likely one or both just found out that his marriage is bigamous."

L.J. raised her heavy eyebrows, but she wasn't about to commit herself with speech.

I motioned toward the photocopies on her desk. "Those are 1945 and 1946 Attorney General's opinions and a 1960 case, *Johnson v. Johnson*. They say that, in South Carolina, you don't have to have a marriage license to have a marriage. Neither do you have to live together as man and wife. To create a common law marriage, all you have to do is agree to become man and wife. There's no case on point," I continued, "but I suspect that all one would have to do is exchange vows, say, in the middle of a field under a spreading oak tree."

L.J.'s feet hit the floor. Her chair didn't even creak. "You saying that the victim and Guildman were married?"

"I'm saying there's a possibility they might have been."

"Gahdam lawyers. Do you know the simple words 'yes' and 'no'?"

"It doesn't matter whether they were really married or not. I'm saying there's enough evidence to *believe* they were married. It could've caused problems, what with Mark's land development plans and big bank loans and his new wife and her money, if there was a hint of scandal. Apparently Laurel took things seriously enough to save that picture and what might have been their marriage vows."

"Must be a witness. Somebody took that picture."

"Maybe not. Cameras can be set to take pictures automatically. And you don't need witnesses to a common law marriage."

For a few quiet minutes, L.J. shuffled through the photocopies I'd handed her. "Guess I'll be calling on Mr. and Mrs. Mark Guildman at their lovely new lakefront mansion."

L.J. didn't even say good-bye.

Back at the office, I was shouldering open my front door when the phone started ringing. I dashed behind the desk to answer it.

"Gawd a'mighty. Miz Andrews. You gotta help me!"

It took a second to recognize the high-pitched wail on the phone. Pee Vee Probert. "What's the matter? Whoa! Calm down!"

He was sputtering and yelling and cursing. I could imagine him dancing from one foot to another like an enraged leprechaun stomping out a fire.

"He's trying to get me out. Gawd he'p me."

"Pee Vee. Slowly. Explain yourself."

Pee Vee snorted, exasperated. "Peanut. They're going to let me out!"

This morning, Pee Vee had been disappointed at the thought of wasting a sober weekend locked up. Now he sounded like a candidate for a rage-induced seizure at the thought of getting out.

I chose the most likely tack. "Who is letting you out?"

"These bullet-headed mother-f-ing cops!" he shouted. Considering that the phone hangs right beside the intake desk, surrounded by cops, Pee Vee was really winning friends down at the detention center.

I tried another tack: "What about Peanut?"

"He's f-ing bailing me!"

Ah, pay dirt. "The man you assaulted and battered with a tire iron is posting your bail?"

"I didn' battery him. And—" More confused harangue from which I gathered that no bail had yet been set, that Peanut was trying to get the magistrate to set it, and that the cops had allowed Pee Vee this special phone call because they thought it was an f-ing joke and they were laughing their heads off and pissing their pants.

"Hold on, Pee Vee. I'll call the magistrate and get this straightened out. And I'll come over and make sure we get it worked out." I choked, struggling not to laugh.

I hoped Melvin would be free for supper tonight. I didn't want to think about how easy things were to start and how hard they were to end or about dirty gray-green linoleum. I wanted to spend time with someone who wouldn't be dredging up the circular past. But then, you don't walk away and leave your past. You take it with you, and it comes around again to meet you. Things were easier to start than to finish, and they always come back around.

I decided I would drive out to The Farm, where the giant oak still shades what has changed over the years from cow pasture to rock concert site to cow pasture. I'd say a prayer for Laurel—and for Edwin Masey. But first, I'd make sure Pee Vee stayed in jail where he would be safe. Prayers probably wouldn't help him as much as the loan of a tire iron.

"Love makes the world go 'round."
And when it ends, the earth may not cease
spinning. But for the discarded lovers the rup-
ture can be just as jolting. And the obsessive
passion they bring to revenge may be more
consuming than the original love.

In Ben Schutz's "What Goes Around," a
rejected lover tries to trick a P.I. in the process of his vengeance. And rock star Don Shannon's former lover in Marilyn Wallace's
"Desdemona's Handkerchief" finds the fall-
out of revenge can be as dangerous as the
revenge itself.

MARILYN WALLACE

One of the most versatile of writers, Marilyn Wallace began with an award-winning police procedural series in which she probed the moral dilemmas of police work and delved into the effect of the crimes on the women who were most intimately affected by them. From these sensitive portraits it was a natural progression to move on to the rich and harrowing world of suspense novels (*A Single Stone, So Shall Ye Reap,* and *The Seduction*).

But Marilyn Wallace is best known for her work in revitalizing the mystery anthology, having created and edited the *Sisters in Crime* anthology series. There she built a community of contributors and a community of readers. In "Desdemona's Handkerchief," Wallace has created a darker community that makes demands that go beyond the bounds of friendship.

DESDEMONA'S HANDKERCHIEF

I will be hang'd, if some eternal villain
Some busy and insinuating rogue,
Some cogging cozening slave, to get some office
Have not devis'd this slander.

Othello

Dreams suck.

I learned that the hard way from Don Shannon, lead guitarist for Glory. He discarded women the way some guys throw away guitar picks, whenever he was bored or tired of the feel of one. He had a gift for painting beautiful happily-ever-after pictures and then using them to wipe his own snotty nose. At least that was how I saw it, and as one of the founding members of a sorority of the tossed-aside, I had plenty of company.

Don Shannon could blow riffs on the theme of love with his eyes, his hands, and his wonderful, warm mouth, but he was always just playing, one of those master technicians whose dazzling runs made you think, in the beginning, that his fingers were greased with God's own special, soulful magic. When you hung around for a while, you realized it was nothing more transcendant than dexterity.

Knowing Don made me tougher, more careful, a little more wary, and by the time it was pretty much over between us, all I could see whenever I looked at him was a lizard: dangerous, heavy-lidded, ready to flick his sticky tongue at anything in range. People, he once said, believe the lie they most want to hear and by the time they figure out the truth, it's too late.

That Don Shannon didn't live to a wise and serene old age was no surprise to anyone who read the entertainment section of the *San Francisco Chronicle*, or for that matter, any major newspaper in the past decade. Men under twenty-five and women over thirty-five adored him. Everyone wrote in parts for themselves to play in one of his incarnations: playmate to rock's drug-crazed *enfant terrible;* lust-object of a swaggering sex idol; beneficiary of his final transformation into a yogurt-swilling, tofu-powered megavitamin-optimized Clean Machine. A media junkie to begin with, when Don discovered health he became a walking endorsement for the healing power of antioxidants and positive thinking, and got himself gigs as the face and voice of Rockers for Rainforests, the Parasanctus Foundation, and Nature's Whey, a miracle product you could either drink or bathe in to promote that youthful glow.

And glow he did. When I met him, Don was forty-nine; most people thought his face was a dewy endorsement of the miracles of surgical enhancement, but he insisted he'd found his personal fountain of youth in daily injections of vitamin B_{12}, claiming it was the source of his energy, bounce, radiance. He could even, he said once as he winked at a nubile MTV interviewer, pop a quick pick-me-up on the road, to get him through the night.

But his metamorphosis barely affected anything beneath that taut, thin skin. Whenever a chorus started to sound too familiar, he played the existential freedom riff for all it was worth, and then took off in search of the next set.

People still talk about where they were when they first found out about Don's death, the way my parents and their friends talk about finding out about Kennedy's being shot. I had just driven back from a carousel restoration job in the wilds of Sonoma County and was sitting at Café Puccini on Columbus sipping a latte. I glanced at the guy at the next table to check him out just as he picked up his newspaper—and was nearly blasted out of my chair by the headlines. SHANNON DEAD! they screamed. FANS IN SHOCK.

I slapped my hand on the table and said "All *right!*—I actually said it out loud, kind of like a testifier at a revival meeting—but this was San Francisco and the guy didn't even sneak a peek over the top of his paper. I licked at my foamy milk as though nothing had happened. Before I drained the coffee, I admitted a bit of generalized philosophical regret for a life ended. I meditated on the "apparently natural cause of death" cited in the article. As far as I was concerned, a big hate by a jealous band member or a betrayed woman were righteously natural responses to Don's behavior.

I met Don Shannon on June 23, 1991. San Francisco was in the middle of its annual week-long hot spell, the temperature pushing ninety and the cooling fog hiding out somewhere west of Honolulu. Being a dual Shakespeare and film history major had left me basically unemployable, and after eight lean months I had finally found work that didn't make me rail about hypocrisy and exploitation and the contemporary capitulation of quality to the almighty gods of commerce. Restoring antique carousel animals was actually fun, and Ginny Fratelli had been teaching me lots of little tricks with paint and wood putty. I was practically high all the time just from the excitement of learning.

Ginny had sent me over to the NightFlame, a small club on Folsom undergoing its fourth renovation in ten years. Someone had found two horses in a closet and thought it would be a kick to get them cleaned up and put them in the front room, kind of like Gilley's-by-the-Bay.

Hot and dirt-streaked from poking around in the storage room, I came upstairs to take a break and was chugging an Anchor Steam when Don Shannon sat down beside me, looked at me in the mirror, and said, "Just my luck. A woman with clear eyes and the fire of holy life burning behind them."

Whatever that meant.

I didn't really care because he kept staring at my reflection, his eyes drawing me down, down, into the center of a whirlpool. It was spooky, and very tender. And he *was* Don Shannon, lead guitarist for Glory. I tried semi-hard to convince myself that I didn't care, but within forty-eight hours, I was his woman. That's what he said, anyway. The soundtrack swelled with violins: he petted me, pulled pretty bracelets out of his leather jacket, saved a seat for me up front in the van when the band did a two-week tour of Southern California.

Carousel horses pranced on out of my consciousness, but I didn't think it mattered since Ginny was cool and loose. "New clients, new ideas—something good's going to come out of my association with

Don," I told her as I boarded a plane. He was taking me with him to New York and I was thrilled, a Big Apple virgin eager to have that particular cherry popped. Somewhere in Brooklyn, Don mentioned that he'd left his credit card at the hotel. I paid for dinner. Then, the band's manager walked out in a snit because he thought the hotel Don had chosen was too expensive. And then Don asked me if he could borrow four thousand dollars.

"Just till after the concert on Long Island. We sold out the place. Going to be big money. Record contract is practically a done deal anyway. I'll have it back to you, what, five days, a week at the most." He said it without whining or pleading. Just the facts, ma'am, and I felt dumb to wonder why he didn't have at least that much stashed somewhere. Big star and all that.

The old windbag from Hamlet was right on about being neither borrower nor lender. But where's Polonius when you need him? I hardly have to say it; of *course* I didn't ever see a penny of that money again.

Which made me feel like a colossal jerk . . . until I met the others. It's strange comfort to know you're not the only one to make the same stupid mistake; Cathy Beaman clued me in on that one. Glory was doing a show at the NightFlame. I was working on the wooden horse. Cathy was doing their books.

She was an accountant, trying to cut loose her card-store and drycleaner clients and break into the restaurant and nightclub scene. I was on the way out; she was next in line. For Don Shannon, that is. Even so, and after only one meeting, I thought she was hip, a kick to be around, and I liked her. He was looking for something from his women, old Donnie was. Cathy is fair and I'm dark, and she's three inches taller than I am, but we're both hiding a fierce starstruck wonkiness. Plus, I'm forever embarrassing people by holding eye contact longer than they expect, strangers, friends, and lovers alike, and Cathy does the same thing.

Talk about your instant sisterhood.

You automatically have a lot in common with another woman who's about to be used and abused by the man currently giving you grief. I knew instinctively when I saw the way Don looked at Cathy that it was time to cut my many losses, so I left my best Calvins in his apartment and pleaded with Ginny until she let me paint horses again.

I was only a little surprised when Cathy called me three months later and asked if I'd meet her for a drink. When I showed up, I was introduced to Marikko (seven thousand dollars), Linetta (a mere two thousand), and the biggest fish of all, Debra, whose bank account was down twenty-two thousand dollars, doled out in three installments to Mr. Macho Shannon.

Cathy (four thousand, like me) had called us together for a purpose. "We need to help out Don Shannon, ladies, put his unethical, cheating, lying buns into reorganization. Chapter eleven for the emotionally bankrupt, you take my meaning."

We realized we had a shared agenda: to vent a little about Don's self-serving pathological inability to learn that it wasn't nice to hurt people. To imagine exquisite ways we could do him grievous bodily harm. And to see if we could get our money back. We concocted then rejected about a hundred different schemes and finally decided to check with a lawyer Linetta knew. When the evening was over, we drifted out of touch and nothing ever came of the plan.

A couple of days later, I ran into Carlo, Glory's thin-lipped, twitchy drummer, and we went out for sushi. After the fourth little pitcher of sake, Carlo confessed that he couldn't understand. Why did Don, who was such a shit, get all the wonderful women and then treat them like dirt? He'd happily tap my cymbals (his words) or for that matter, Cathy's or Linetta's or Debra's, or any one of Don's cast-offs.

I thought it was weird for him to say that. I had this spooky feeling that Carlo had been skulking in the shadows, spying on us, and I felt like a bit player in a Friday-afternoon episode of Don Shannon's personal soap opera.

A week after the funeral, Lieutenant Tony Fillipo, a stubby man with a cigar poking out of the corner of his mouth, announced on the six o'clock news that Don had died from Provocaine poisoning. "Based on the coroner's findings," Fillipo declared, gesturing with Sidney Greenstreet fingers as though he were wearing a diamond pinky ring, "Don Shannon's death is now officially classified as a homicide. Provocaine is a dental anesthetic, and when it's taken in the quantities found in the victim's body, blood vessels collapse, convulsions follow, and cardiac arrest results."

Not a pretty picture to contemplate, even for someone still smarting from the bumps and bruises of rejection. I'd have bet a gilded ostrich and two painted stallions that someone had replaced the B_{12} in one of Don's ampules with Provocaine. Permanent exile on an island with Lawrence Welk would have been a more just and fitting fate for Don Shannon—even *he* had the right to wake up one morning and see the light.

Clearly someone else didn't have as much faith in the perfectibility of the individual as I did.

By the next morning, the *Chronicle* article said that Valium (Don once told me it promoted harmony and kept him from transmitting his worries to others) had enhanced the effects of the Provocaine and sent Don's big old heart muscle into a big old wrenching spasm. I thought idly about congratulating whoever did it, and I took a little quiet pleasure knowing that the sisterhood of Shannon throwaways had reached capacity.

Five days after the Provocaine story broke, as I was rounding the corner onto Sanchez on my way home, I nearly collided with a stocky man. He'd combed his wavy brown hair into a high pompadour and wore a bite-your-nose meanness around his mouth that made me wish he was in a different county. Startled, I must have frowned as I tried to pass around him, but he blocked my way.

"Something wrong? Help you, miss?"

The edge to his voice told me he meant the kind of help that muggers offer little old men in cardigans as they leave the bank. And then it came to me: This was Don's Colombo, his television cop. Tony something. And despite his question, he wasn't working on his politeness merit badge.

"Miss Shea?" he said, proving my point, since not a single Boy Scout had any reason to know my name. The cigar shifted wetly in his mouth as he spoke, and I tried not to laugh.

"Have we met?" I put on my best Audrey Hepburn face and tried to look interested.

He flashed his ID. "I need to ask you a few questions about Don Shannon. Maybe we could go sit down somewhere so we can talk. Why don't we go to your place, you can take off your shoes, you know."

"Slip into something comfortable? Just ask your questions, Lieutenant."

"Don't get smart with me, sister. Broad like you, giving Shannon all that money . . ." The ridge between his eyes deepened into a frown. "Look, lady, either we find someplace to talk or you can come down to my office. Your choice."

This was a man with a low tolerance for humor. I batted my eyes and let my hands flutter in the air. Vivien Leigh would have been proud. "Really, my apartment's a mess. I didn't have any time to clean this whole week. Oh, gosh, could we maybe have coffee on the corner?"

He seemed satisfied that I was done smart-mouthing, so he followed me back to Noe. We found seats at the counter in the Greek bakery. I didn't mind answering his questions, really, because all I had to do was tell the truth. I gave him straight answers and even tried not to push his buttons, but Tony Fillipo was stuck in some Jimmy Stewart mentality where good girls don't go around sleeping with rock musicians and paying for the privilege. At least those were the signals I picked up from him. He spent most of the interview treating me like a bug he'd found in his baklava. When he left, frustrated and empty-handed, he was muttering under his breath.

That made me very happy.

I read every issue of the *Chronicle*, amazed at how many different ways they could write about nothing for an entire week. I came across outraged letters from loyal Shannon fans in the *East Bay Express*, the *San Francisco Weekly*, and the *Bay Guardian*. Some suggested that the CIA or Newt Gingrich or Saddam Hussein or Jerry Falwell or even Tipper had been the power behind a conspiracy that had gotten Jimi, Janis, and now poor Don. Front-page interviews with Boots, the bass player, or Carlo, or Lieutenant Fillipo all proved as empty as Don's checking account.

Then, the media started to shine the bright lights on how the police were handling the case.

Why were there no suspects?

What happened to the much-touted leads?

When were they going to present a theory to explain Don Shannon's death?

First Lieutenant Fillipo, then Chief Grogan, finally even Mayor Sinclair took the heat, and then the press started back in on Fillipo. After one gruesome interview in which Fillipo looked like he was about to punch the plastic-haired guy with the microphone, I almost felt a twinge of sympathy. Fillipo was twisting in the wind of public scrutiny, and all his little professional warts had suddenly gone neon.

So I was more than a little surprised to see Cathy Beaman's face on page one of the *Chronicle*, Tony Fillipo's sausage-fingers pushing down on the top of her head as she got into a squad car. As I read the report, my hopes sank and my head clanged. It was truly damning, especially the part about the empty box and three cartridges of Provocaine found under Cathy's bathroom sink. Cathy Beaman was being charged with Don's murder.

Nobody who knew *him* doubted that her reasons might be well grounded, but all of us who knew *her* doubted that she'd be careless enough to leave a box and three unused ampules of the drug lying around. Cathy is an accountant, a meticulous person. She'd never forget to figure equipment depreciation in someone's tax returns, and she wouldn't neglect to clean up after herself, either.

According to the newspaper, her lawyer was a white-haired Mel Belli look-alike, full of bombast and social contacts. Of course she couldn't put up the twenty-five-thousand-dollar bail: she'd loaned all her money to Don Shannon, and he'd had the bad manners to get killed before she could figure out how to extract payment.

When Cathy called me, I had the feeling she needed a friend.

Lieutenant Fillipo, looking at his shoes, nearly bowled me over as I hurried down the corridor in the Hall of Justice. I was a few steps away when he grunted, "You lost, Miss Shea?"

"Not at all. I'm right here." I shifted my canvas sack and tried to look as though I knew what I was doing, but he came up and stepped in front of me. "I'm visiting someone."

"Who?" he demanded, close enough for me to nearly choke on the old-socks smell of stale cigar smoke on his shiny jacket.

"Cathy Beaman." I said it like a declaration of war.

An oily grin slid across his face. "Popular customer. Every reporter this side of the Rockies been trying to get tight with her. You wanna see our star, you gotta follow procedure." He pointed with his head toward a door marked VISITORS; he was still smirking when he turned and walked toward the elevators.

I couldn't shake the feeling I'd just stepped in something squishy and unpleasant as I headed for the visitor's entrance. The woman at the desk said she'd have to check with Cathy, and ordered me to put my package on the counter. For an hour I waited, filling out forms while the guard tore apart the sandwiches and confiscated the cabernet I'd brought along. The place felt creepy, and I pictured poor Cathy sinking into a depression. In black-and-white, of course, with maybe Susan Hayward as her cell mate.

Finally, a dumpy, scowling matron ushered Cathy into the windowless room. Her long gold hair was pulled back into a shiny ponytail; a thick layer of mascara and some glistening mauve lip gloss spoke volumes for her mental health. But her face was sullen and her eyes cold.

"Height of fashion, right?" She snapped the collar of the baggy orange jumpsuit like Joan Crawford primping for a close-up. "The accommodations are *très elegante*, my dear. And if you like nightmares, the food's a dream."

I hauled the canvas bag from between my feet and pushed it across the table toward her. "They took away the file I was trying to smuggle in. Actually," I said, pleased to see the little upturn at the corners of her mouth, "I brought a bottle of BV cabernet. Guard swears I'll get it back on my way out. We'll do it later."

While I babbled, she fished out the bottle of mineral water and the sandwich, then neatly rearranged the turkey, smoked gouda, and tomato, and slid the smeary chunks of avocado back into place. By the time I finished pointing out that the shampoo I'd brought needed really thorough rinsing, she'd devoured the first half of the sandwich.

She swigged the Calistoga, wiped her mouth, and looked at me. "Someone set me up. Someone got their hands on some Provocaine and planted that box of cartridges in my bathroom."

"You have any ideas?" The names and faces of Don's women charged through my mind, a legion group, so diverse you'd have thought Don Shannon invented affirmative action. So why did this unknown someone choose Cathy?

If you were looking for someone to set up, she got points for having an apartment on the ground floor, and for working regular hours. I wondered if that was enough to make her a prime candidate.

Between slugs of Calistoga, she wiped her mouth on the cloth napkin I'd brought from home. "I don't have an alibi, you know. Home alone, doing my nails, that's what I told them, even showed them my pretty toes but that didn't help." She bit into a chocolate truffle and closed her eyes to keep the pleasure private. "They said I was obsessed with him, and that I was angry that he'd dumped me. Okay, so I was angry. So were you. And Linetta. All the others, too. Angry? Damn right."

"If angry was all it took, we're all guilty," I assured her. "You need anything else? Skin cream, makeup, books, I don't know, whatever." Suddenly, the bond of shared hatred for Don Shannon just didn't compensate for the smell of urine and disinfectant and the lighting that made me feel half-blind, the oppressive grayness of the place. "Listen," I said, trying not to be too obvious, "I have an appointment. But, really, if you need anything . . ."

"I need *help*, Frannie, and my lawyer can't concentrate on anything but my boobs when we're in the same room. He hasn't gotten the message yet: *Someone's setting me up*. Maybe it's Carlo. When Don would take me out drinking after gigs, Carlo would get this look like he'd happily drop me from the south tower of the Golden Gate Bridge and turn me into a statistic. Maybe it was some jealous woman, *any* jealous woman. I don't know how those drugs got in my apartment. All I know is that I had nothing to do with that box of Provocaine, and I need *help*."

A flurry, like a series of complicated chord changes, jammed into my brain.

My own life was tangled enough already.

Maybe she's desperate from being in this awful place.

It might be me sitting in that chair.

The last one started my heart banging in my chest, hard and thumping as though I'd done some heavy-duty drug.

"Okay, listen to me, Cathy. Maybe Carlo or someone else did have something to do with it. You say you were set up, and I believe you. But proving it is going to be a different story."

Her laugh was harsh. "Lawyer's going to be useless. He's got brains in his . . . well, maybe even not there."

"So wear a jacket, armor, whatever, so that he's not distracted by your chest. Has he told you that if you can prove you were set up, then you'll walk? So you don't have to have an alibi. That's not going to matter. All we have to do is find out who put that stuff in your apartment and you're out of here." I rushed through my words in a burst of adrenaline-charged optimism but Cathy caught me up short.

"How do I know I can trust you? You could be the one who planted that box." Her eyes narrowed and she leaned back in her chair. "You haven't told me where you were that night."

"Honey buns," I said wearily, having told the story to Tony Fillipo at least three times, "I was checking out a carousel in Santa Cruz."

She looked down at the floor, and her eyebrows flickered with a question. "Okay, but you have to swear on your boyfriend's dick that you're telling the truth."

My current social life made that oath about as meaningful as a Charles Laughton book of beauty hints. "Sure, fine. You, too. This will only work if you're totally straight with me, right?"

"I had nothing to do with that box of Provocaine the cops found in my bathroom. Believe it—or don't. That's the truth." She brushed her ponytail free of the collar of her jumpsuit as the matron signaled that we were out of time.

Cathy was led away, and I practically ran to the exit and into the sunshine, gulping the cool air as though I'd been about to drown. I was excited about helping to get Cathy off—Scout's honor, it felt good to do something that would make the world a better, more just place.

I dove into the work like Rosalind Russell covering a fast-breaking story, and started making phone calls.

"I know you're busy," I commiserated when Debra Wilson complained about having to meet a printing job deadline. "Just come to the

Café Puccini tonight for an hour. Listen, it's a pretty strong bond, to be one of Don's women. No one else knows what it's like. In the end, it's all we've got. Each other. It might have been you in Cathy's place."

She finally mumbled something that sounded like an agreement.

I was still buzzing with excitement when we all gathered at a small marble table right under a speaker blaring *Tosca*, and brainstormed how to help Cathy. Four former Shannon victims, we pored over newspaper clippings and expressed regret that we weren't the ones to have written his requiem, to carry a musical metaphor perhaps a little too far.

"If only I'd followed through after we got together the first time," Linetta said quietly into her house red. "It was an opportunity to feel whole and empowered and we missed it."

This is northern California, you understand, and Linetta was speaking the *lingua franca*. She's a therapist and I don't think she can help it. It's probably part of the licensing procedure in the state to pass a fluency test in New-Age-Speak. But she managed to put her own spin on it when she added, "On the other hand, my inner child is fucking thrilled to know that Don Shannon finally got to eat his own dirt."

My outer adult agreed enthusiastically.

"You have a baby?" Marikko asked, tilting her head so that her raven-dark hair slid in a silken swish away from her face. Delicate and serene in her leather skirt and motorcycle jacket, she got dreamy-eyed when the language became more complicated than direct nouns and verbs. "You really think Cathy killed that little turd?" she added.

Linetta nodded vigorously, her wild, glistening curls bouncing vehemently. "Bitch. Beat me to it."

We had to spend two more hours talking about karmic debt and appropriate responses and enabling behavior and silent rage before we could figure out how we could help Cathy, who Debra, finally, poetically, pointed out in practically the same words I'd used earlier, was a symbol for all of us and any of us.

"The whole case," I said in my best Paul Muni voice, "stands or falls on the drugs. Without that box, without the cartridges of Provocaine, Cathy's in the same position as the rest of us. We've all got motives, and so does she, and so do I don't know how many others all over the country."

"Maybe," Debra said dryly, "they'll make a movie of Don's life called *A League of His Own*. Enough of us out there for ten, twenty baseball teams."

I ignored her. "We need a contact in SFPD. Someone who can tell us if they've checked that box for fingerprints." Tony Fillipo hardly qualified but he was the only cop I knew.

Linetta sipped her drink thoughtfully. "Maybe I can get to someone. An old business, um, acquaintance. It'll take a while, I may have to, you know, do some favors."

Debra ran her finger along the edge of the table. "What about Boots and Carlo? If they were tired of putting up with Don's tantrums and not getting paid on time and . . ." Her voice trailed off and ended in a deep sigh. "This is above and beyond, you know, but I'll bet on Madonna's twin peaks that I can get Carlo to tell me anything I want to know. Now don't you all go turning green with envy. This is my good deed for the year." She drained her beer, then shook her head. "The decade."

This was starting to sound promising, a synergy of estrogenic intelligence making us, collectively, ever so much more effective than if we'd tried doing this on our own. Excited, I said, "There must be some way to trace the drug. Where it came from, who bought it, when, how."

"My dentist is very, like, friendly," Marikko said quietly. "I bet if I ask at the right time, he'll tell me the manufacturer, maybe even give me an address." She blushed from her own boldness.

I could hardly believe that her synapses were firing fast enough to grasp my next thought: Any one of us might have a friendly dentist . . . Any one of us probably could have laid hands on Provocaine without much trouble.

"Okay. Marikko, you find out who the manufacturer is," I said, switching gears so I wouldn't get swept into paranoia, "and then I'll see what I can get on how Provocaine is distributed. Linetta's going to talk to her cop friend, and Debra'll get chummy with Carlo."

We toasted woman-power and drifted off into the fog, to continue our split-screen efforts to help Cathy Beaman.

I was washing my hair and only half-heard the knock on my door. Finally, when I turned the water off, Marikko's tiny voice called, "Frannie, hurry up. I have to leave. He's downstairs."

As I wrapped a towel around my dripping head and let her in, I wondered if it was nature or nurture that made Marikko incapable of dealing with hard information, such as who *he* was and why I should care if *he's* downstairs. She was done up in purple spandex, her face whitened so that she looked like a character in a Noh play.

"Here." She thrust a piece of paper into my hand and wrinkled her nose. "Why would anyone want to be in New Hampshire?" She shrugged her tiny shoulders and turned to the stairs, waving as she disappeared down the twisting flight.

I was going to have to pay long distance charges to do my Sam Spade. DynaDont was in Manchester, New Hampshire, and it was prime time on the phone lines.

I dried my hair, spritzed it, tousled it with the blower again, and finally decided that I'd better get the call over with.

I dialed the number. After eight rings, a weary voice answered. "Yes?"

I pictured Margaret Rutherford, dumpy and gray-haired, pushing a mop with her chapped hands.

"Is this DynaDont? I need to talk to someone who knows about Provocaine."

A slight throat clearing, and then a definitely Barbara Stanwyck voice demanded, "What is it that you want to know?"

Not the cleaning woman, I realized, and I started again winging it on an improvisation on the theme of Robert Mitchum. "I'm working for Horace Rumfeldt. The famous San Francisco lawyer? A box of Provocaine is evidence in one of his big cases, and I need to know how it's distributed."

Her silence stretched on and on, so I jumped in again. "This isn't some kind of secret, right, so why don't you tell me and make it easier."

She sighed. "We do our own distributing directly to dental offices. Each lot of cartridges is tracked from the minute it's packed into boxes until it reaches the dentist. We have strict procedures. What the dentist does after that is his business."

My mind was spinning with questions. "How many clients do you have in the San Francisco area?"

This time her laugh was quick and hearty. "How about more than three hundred? And who they are I'm not telling you. For all I know, you're just trying to steal my client list so you can peddle your own wares to my customers. Listen, that's all I have to say to you."

"Someone's life is at stake here." I stifled my own laugh; cheap, rip-off grade-B scenes just seem to play themselves. But I'd hooked her.

She answered in kind. "Okay, you've one more minute. One. One more minute."

"How do you keep track of what goes where?"

I winced. Really professional, that question.

But she gave me the whole spiel. "Every batch of Provocaine has a lot number and an expiration date printed on each of the fifty ampules and then again on the box. A lot is a thousand boxes of fifty. We slap a sticker on the box and put its twin on the shipping slip and we always know where any particular box is until it gets to the dentist."

"Where would I find this lot number?"

She made a sharp *tsk*ing noise, then went on. "It's on the end flap of the box. It will say something like Z2234, right near the expiration date. The drug loses its potency after two years, so the first thing you'll see is the date, oh five slash ninety-three or something like that. Then a letter followed by four numbers. Date and number are on each cartridge, too, in case some pea brain takes them out of the box."

"And you keep track of lot numbers and who got what, right?"

"Yes, for our records. Controls and all that. I'm sorry, but I'm hanging up now."

And she did, but she'd given me a lot to think about.

Maybe Team Beaman could find out which local dentists received Provocaine from the same batch the cops found in Cathy's bathroom. And we might then discover a link between that dentist and someone who had reason to permanently anesthetize Don Shannon. If Linetta's SFPD connection made a quick trip to the evidence room, we'd be in business.

Linetta answered on the first ring. "Frannie. I was just trying to call you. I spoke to my friend. He said the box was clean. No prints."

That was *not* what I wanted to hear. "Okay, call him back and tell him we need the lot number and the date on the—"

"End flap, I know, he told me already." Linetta dictated a jumble of numbers and letters. "He's smart about stuff like that. He couldn't get over that there weren't any prints. Oh, damn!" she yelled. "I gotta get outa here! Talk to you later. Oh, wait. He said the box had a funny smell."

My scalp prickled. "What kind of smell?"

"He wasn't sure. Maybe like burning rope, he said, or an old gym locker, something nasty like that."

Or fat little cigars, I thought as I hung up. Suppose Lieutenant Tony Fillipo, frustrated, losing face after becoming a fixture on the nightly news, knew a friendly dentist . . . Imagine that this dentist's office was easy to break into, if you knew what you were doing . . . Consider Fillipo's scorn for someone who would sleep with Don Shannon *and* give him money, his low tolerance for uppity remarks from women, Cathy's incurable case of bad-mouth.

But mine was not to wonder why, or even who. *When* was the operative word here. The expiration date on the box in the SFPD evidence room was 1195, twenty months from now. If we were lucky we'd get the right answer to my question about when it was manufactured, and more importantly, when it was shipped.

Hang on, Cathy, I thought as I dialed the DynaDont number again. We're coming to spring you. You'll be out of there in no time.

Cathy Beaman lived a brisk, downhill walk from my Noe Valley apartment. I stopped on the way to pick up a sourdough baguette, a ball of fresh mozzarella, a ripe tomato, four Godiva chocolate truffles, and a bottle of BV Private Reserve cabernet. By five, I was knocking on her door. "Cathy?" I called softly.

"Go away," a tired voice called after the fourth knock. "She's not here."

Of course. She'd been the paparazzi's darling all day, and here I was dropping by to celebrate her release. "It's me, Frannie. I brought provisions. We did good, didn't we?"

The door opened a crack and her nose poked out; I caught a glimpse of one very tired, dark-rimmed eye. "You alone?"

"Just me and some great Italian fast food." I rustled the bag. "I'll take my chocolate truffles and go away if this isn't a good time . . ."

The door creaked open and Cathy shook her head. "If I don't talk to a real human being instead of those jerk reporters, I'll lose what's left of my mind. God, it's good to see you."

She stepped aside and I walked into the dark hallway, holding my breath against the still-rank smell of an apartment that had been closed up for three weeks while the garbage ripened. Mothers warn you to wear clean underwear in case you're in an accident and have to be rushed unconscious to a hospital. As though the first thing the ER doc will do is check your panties and then decide whether you're worth saving; nobody warns you about making sure you've taken out the garbage in case you get sidetracked to jail.

"Sorry about the smell. You believe this? *I'm* the celebrity. It's totally trippy. People follow you around. Offer you money. Promise to make you a star. Everyone wants a piece of you, a front-page piece, a big-screen piece. Stardom." Her voice was sharp, high, like a guitar string that's been twanged too often and can't hold its note anymore. "As someone must have said in one of your old flicks, I'm blowing this burg as soon as I can pack."

I hate it when people call movies "flicks." I got busy putting the food out on her chipped plates, feeling more than a little sorry for poor Cathy. At least I still had the fake Fiestaware I bought before Don Shannon. I glanced around her Italian-modern apartment, my eyes drifting toward the very unaccountantlike jumble on the refrigerator. Instead of a calendar with notices of doctors' appointments and *Sylvia* cartoons, the door was plastered with curling, yellowing Don memorabilia—a picture of both of them standing on a bed in a hotel room; clippings of pre-concert interviews with the great man and reviews of his shows and albums, notes he left her to pick up the dry cleaning or to apologize for going out with the guys when the two of them had other plans.

"That was pretty amazing, you finding out that the lot number was for a batch manufactured two weeks *after* Don was killed. I still can't believe anyone could be that dim. Whoever dropped that box of Provocaine in my apartment should have bothered to find out about lot numbers and expiration dates."

I let her pat my back for me. I *was* proud that we'd proven that the drugs had been planted. According to DynaDont's records, the lot found under her bathroom sink was shipped exactly eighteen days after Don's body was found. The drugs in Cathy's apartment, her lawyer had argued, couldn't have killed him.

She was released. The press had a field day. Spencer Tracy would have been proud.

"I owe you, Frannie. Thanks." Finally, I thought I saw a glimmer of warmth from Cathy, but she snapped back to her old suspicious self in a blink. "Why were you so nice to me?" she asked bluntly.

"I plead temporary insanity." My back was to her as I piled slices of tomato on a plate. "Listen, I told you—it could have been any one of twenty, fifty women. I believed you and I wanted to lend my support."

She didn't say anything smart to that, and I turned to read her face. It was stone, unsmiling, Edward G. Robinson. Finally, she said, "The tomato's going to slide off the plate. I never bought tomatoes when I was with Don. He hated them."

I righted the plate before the slices took a final juicy trip toward the floor, set the food on the table, and we sat down.

"What's next for you?" Maybe she'd turn human if we were talking about the future instead of the past. But she was stuck on Don, her voice sharp with venom and blame.

"He did so much damage. It wasn't right. His balance sheet was *way* off."

It was sad that she'd let him get under her skin so permanently, like a bad tattoo she'd have to look at every day. I felt a kind of pride that I'd let go of him much more easily, cleaned my own house, so to speak, so that the stink of Don Shannon was long gone.

"So," she said as she speared a tomato slice with her fork, "Iago planted Desdemona's handkerchief on Cassio to make Othello think she was playing around."

I stared at her with sudden understanding. "Just like someone, Fillipo I'd guess, managed to get that box of Provocaine into your bathroom."

She sipped her cabernet and smiled, and I heard an echo of her voice in the visiting room, telling me that someone had set her up, saying only that she hadn't left that box in her bathroom, never denying anything else.

I set my wineglass on the table and met her gaze. "But poor Desdemona was true to Othello, wasn't she? She was framed for something she *didn't* do."

Cathy held a gleaming chocolate between thumb and forefinger, examining it as though it were a jewel before she bit it in half and chewed dreamily. "Don was really nice that day, so, I guess I'd have to say, so dignified. What's that funeral line? It's from *MacBeth*, I think."

" 'Nothing in his life became him like the leaving it,' " I whispered.

"That's it." She popped the rest of the truffle into her mouth. "I knew you'd understand."

Close-up on Peter Lorre, the gleam of puzzlement in those bulging eyes—tricked again. Fade to black. Roll credits. My money was on Cathy Beaman for Best Actress in a Distorting Role.

BENJAMIN SCHUTZ

Benjamin Schutz won a Shamus Award
for Best P.I. Novel with the third in his Leo
Haggerty series, *A Tax in Blood* (Tor, 1987). His
most recent Haggerty novel, *A Fistful of Empty*,
was nominated a couple of years ago in the
same category. His Haggerty short story,
"Mary, Mary, Shut the Door," which appeared
in *Deadly Allies*, swept the MWA Edgar and
PWA Shamus Awards for Best Short Story of
1992.

In "What Goes Around," Haggerty comes to
the aid of a colleague who, on her first case, has
run into something that requires the one thing
a new P.I. lacks—experience.

WHAT GOES AROUND

In the darkness things always go away from you.
Memory holds you down while regret and sorrow
kick hell out of you.

        James Sallis, The Long-Legged Fly

Trickle down was so much bullshit. If you let the rich get richer then some of that money just had to trickle down through their tightly clenched fists. The only thing that "trickled down" as the economy came to a halt was misery. A monsoon of misery. Lost jobs, lost homes, lost dreams, lost hopes. All of which was good for business. My business, private investigation.

I was going through our weekly collections, counting up the slow pays, deciding which ones we were going to put on hold, who we were going to introduce to our lawyers.

"Call for you, Leo, line one," my secretary, Kelly, announced over the intercom.

I picked up the phone. "This is Leo Haggerty, what can I do for you?"

"Mr. Haggerty, my name is Gina Logan, we met once before . . ."

"Where was that?"

"The Virginia Investigators License Course last year. You taught the section on professional ethics and liability."

"That's right."

"Well, I was the one who talked to you after the class."

"The adoptee, right?"

"Yes, that's right. I'm surprised you remembered me."

"You asked some very good questions. Did you ever find your mother?"

"Uh, yes I did."

I thought about asking her how it had gone, but didn't. A triumph she would have already declared; a fiasco was none of my business.

"Well, how can I help?"

"I'd like to buy a little of your time, if I could. I need a consultation. I think I've made a big mistake that might cost me my license."

"Okay. How much of a rush is there? I'm just about ready to leave the office. Can it wait until tomorrow?"

"I don't think so. Is there any way we can meet this evening?"

"Tell you what. I'm going over to Artie's for dinner. Can you meet me there in say thirty minutes?"

"Sure, whatever you say."

"Okay. The manager's name is John, tell him you're meeting me. If you get there first, ask for the last booth on the upper level and ask him to keep the one next to it empty."

"Sure thing. Listen, thank you very much. I'll look for you there."

Artie's was my favorite restaurant. Its fine food and bustling crowds were welcome antidotes to my life alone. A year's worth of meals there had earned me some consideration.

I finished my work with the billing logs, reviewed tomorrow's schedule with Kelly, and left to meet Gina Logan.

On the way over, I tried to remember what she had looked like. Nothing came to me. I'd check her ID anyway. I parked at Artie's, entered, and waved to John. The end booth was empty. I pointed to it and he nodded that it was fine.

I slid in and John came over. We shook hands and I asked him if he could keep the next booth empty.

"Sure. You working?"

"Yeah. I'll try to keep it brief."

"No problem. Just let us know when we can open it up."

"Thanks, John."

I ordered the calamari and waited for Gina Logan. Fifteen minutes later I looked up from my plate to see a woman standing there.

"Mr. Haggerty, I'm Gina Logan." She put out her hand. I stood partway up, shook it, and motioned for her to join me.

She set her bag aside, took off her raincoat and said, "Thanks for seeing me on such short notice. I really appreciate it."

"No problem. Why don't you tell me what your situation is. Don't give me any particulars, keep it real general," I said and forked some squid into my mouth.

"Okay. I'm a free-lance investigator. I've been trying to supplement that with direct referrals, maybe start my own shop some day. Anyway, about ten days ago I got one, my first one, in fact. So I met with the client. He tells me he thinks his wife is having an affair. He wants me to follow her to see if it's true. He's going out of town for the weekend, a business trip. It's the perfect opportunity for her if it's true. So I got the details on the wife, a retainer for two days of my time, and I tailed her."

"When did you start?"

"The next day. He was going from my office to the airport. This was Thursday evening. I started with her around eleven-thirty."

"In case she was having a nooner."

"Right."

"So what happened?"

"Well, she wasn't going out on her lunch break, but . . ."

A waiter appeared to fill her water glass and ask if she wanted a menu.

"No, thank you. A cup of coffee would be nice though."

"Anything else for you, Mr. Haggerty?"

Yeah, a refresher course on manners. "No, I'm fine for now." I set my fork down.

When the waiter left, I looked up from my plate. "Sorry, that was rude of me. I guess I've been eating alone too long."

"No need to apologize, I'm fine. I never eat this early anyway."

"Well, if you change your mind . . ."

"Thanks, but coffee will be fine."

"So, you were saying . . ."

"Where was I . . . oh, right, she didn't leave her office for lunch but at five she came out of the front of the building, stood on the sidewalk for a couple of minutes, and was met by a man."

"Not her husband."

"Not even close. They walked down the street to a restaurant with a bar, went in, had a few drinks, stayed for dinner, then went back to his car. He drove her to her car and followed her home. Where he spent the night, departing around ten-thirty the next morning."

"You've got opportunity and inclination. Job well done. You confirmed that the guy wasn't her cousin or brother, right?"

"Yes. I did stay awake through your lecture, you know." She smiled.

"Apparently. I hope it wasn't too difficult to do."

"Not at all. Your stories were a great relief. At least, to me they were. To know what kind of mistakes you'd made over the course of your career, and what you'd learned from them. That was why I called you. I figured that if anyone would understand how I'd gotten myself into this jam, you would. I even have a quote from your lecture on my desk. I start off each day looking at it."

"What did I say? I'll be honest, I didn't prepare that talk. I was winging it."

"You said, 'It's not the mistakes you make, but what you make of them that's important. Nothing will make you a better detective, faster, than a good mistake, if you let it.' "

I thought about all the qualifiers I'd trim that brave talk with now but kept them to myself.

"So far, you've done everything right. Where's the mistake?"

"You asked if I checked the guy out, right? I did. I ran his plates through DMV and got his name, address, and so on. Monday I called him, posing as a cosmetics salesperson, and found out that he had no female family in the area who could use our free samples. Anyway, Monday evening my client calls me and I have to give him the bad news. I've done this before, so I go into my newscaster imitation, and give him the facts, no nonsense, straight out, boom-boom. I tell him I have pictures if he needs them. I was down in my bunker waiting for the explosion. You know how it is when they first find out. It's either hiccups and tears and it can't be true or they go ballistic and every other word is kill or fucking fill-in-the-blank. This guy was only interested in who the man was. He was convinced it was someone he knew, either at work or a friend. He just wanted to know who it was and whether he'd been betrayed twice."

"And you said that knowing who it was really wasn't going to help anything, that he needed to decide what he wanted to do about this and if he'd have his lawyer contact you, you'd discuss the evidence you had."

"Right, but he said he couldn't decide what he wanted to do until he knew what he was dealing with and then he started asking me questions, you know the gory-detail ones that nobody needs to know. Did they do this, did they do that. I couldn't stand it, he was tearing himself apart . . ."

"So, you told him the name of the guy."

She pursed her mouth and nodded. "Yeah, I told him who the guy was. He was real grateful, it wasn't anyone he knew. He said he'd discuss it with his lawyer and get back to me."

"And?"

"And I didn't hear back from the guy or his lawyer."

"How long has it been?"

"A week. That's too long. If you've got a lawyer and you tell him what's happened and what you've got, the lawyer is going to tell you to go with it. If you act on it immediately, you've got all the leverage."

"Maybe the guy hasn't called his attorney yet. Maybe he's mulling it over, maybe he and the wife are getting into therapy instead. Maybe he wasn't such a great husband in the first place."

"I wish. No, I got antsy and I started thinking about things. The more I thought about them the less I liked what I was thinking."

"Which was?"

"That the wife and her boyfriend didn't seem at all self-conscious about their displays of affection. They met right in front of her office and kissed very openly on the sidewalk. Suppose a co-worker came out? Anyway the kicker was when I called the DMV back. I ran her plates and asked for any other cars registered at that address. None. No car. No hubby."

"Did you have his plates?"

"No. He said he was leaving his car at the airport. She'd only have the other one to use."

"Maybe his car is a company car."

"No. I went by the house yesterday, caught the mailman. He says she lives alone. He never delivers mail to anyone but her at that address."

"So your client lied to you and you're afraid that . . ."

"He's a stalker and he's going to use the information I gave him to hurt someone, probably the boyfriend."

"What can I do for you?"

"First, can I tell the boyfriend what's happened and that he might be in danger? Is that a breach of client confidentiality? Secondly, am I at any risk if this guy hurts someone?"

"First things first. Let me see your investigator's license and your driver's license."

"Why?"

"Because all the time I've been listening I haven't been able to picture you at the lecture. Oh, I remember talking to someone but I can't physically place you, so before I open my mouth and get into this mess, I want to be sure you are you."

"Oh." She took being forgotten pretty well, and pulled her licenses out of her wallet and handed them to me.

Gina Logan was licensed by the State of Virginia as a private investigator. The start date was right for the course she claimed to have taken. I looked at the back of her driver's license and memorized her address, date of birth, and Social Security number. The picture was a good likeness: large deep-set eyes ringed in shadows; pale skin contrasting with her plum red lips. Any more color on them would look like a hemorrhage. Her license said brown and brown, five five and one hundred and ten pounds. My eyes agreed, but there were pewter streaks in her hair.

"Okay. First question. You don't owe your client squat. He hired you under false pretenses and that voids the contract, explicit or implicit, that governs your services. You won't be violating a client's confidence by talking to the target because your client's behavior has waived that protection.

"Second question. Are you at risk if someone gets hurt? Yes. The vicarious liability laws would extend to you if information you gave led to an injury."

"So, I shouldn't have told him the guy's name."

"Yup."

"I guess I should contact the guy and warn him right away."

"Maybe."

"Why not?"

"Because this may be only half of the problem."

She frowned for a moment. Then she said, "I don't understand. What's the rest of the problem?"

"I've been doing this work for almost twenty years and this has happened to me two maybe three times. Your first case and you get set up this well. I don't think so. How did this guy find you?"

"He said he looked me up in the yellow pages."

"Nobody referred him to you?"

"No."

"Think about that for a second. What does your listing say."

"My name and number."

"Address?"

"No. I work out of—"

"Your home and you're a single woman, no ring on your left hand, and don't want clients to have that information. Just the way I recommended in the lecture.

"Without a referral, people go through the phone book and find an agency by location. Then they compare rates over the phone and go to the nearest and cheapest. If they feel comfortable after the first interview, you've got a client. Did you talk money over the phone with him?"

"No, I was so excited to have a client, I forgot. I made sure that we talked about it first thing when we met."

"And he had no problem with your fees, right?"

"That's right."

"What's your client's name?"

"Todd Berman."

"I'll tell you what else your client didn't do. He didn't go through the yellow pages alphabetically. Franklin Investigations would be before you and we didn't get a call like this in the last week. If we had, we'd have taken the case and it wouldn't have gotten to you. So it wasn't a referral, it wasn't your ad, and it wasn't alphabetical. Only one other way this guy found you."

"And that is?"

"Somebody sent him to you. Somebody who doesn't like you. Not one bit. If I was you, I'd like to know who that is. Then figure out what I want to do about it."

"Yeah, I'd like to know that. Do you have any ideas?"

"First, let's keep you away from the target. Your client knows what you look like. If he sees you near the guy, he'll know his story was blown. That's okay as far as him not hurting anyone but once he backs off it'll be twice as hard to find out who set you up. Why don't I contact the guy? I can warn him without your client wising up. That way we may still be able to flush out whoever has it in for you."

"Okay. What can I do?"

"Right now, nothing. I'm going to call some other people in town tomorrow. See if any of them had contact with this Berman guy before you. Try to trace his steps looking for a P.I. If that turns anything up, you can do the legwork on it."

"Okay. How much do you charge?"

"I'm a hundred dollars an hour. This thing we just did here is on the house. I don't charge people to find out if I can help them. If we're agreed I can help you, my meter starts."

Gina Logan gave me her hand. As we shook hands, she said, "Start your meter, Mr. Haggerty."

"Do you have the case file with you?"

"Yes, it's in my bag."

"Why don't you leave it with me. I'll get on this right after I finish eating. You can come by the office tomorrow, we'll do a fee-for-services agreement, and that'll make it official."

"Great. Thanks very much, Mr. Haggerty. I feel a lot better now that we've talked."

We shook hands again and smiled. This rush of optimism would recede after a while and her doubts, like roaches, would return, scurrying about in the dark recesses of her mind when she was alone, waiting for news. Optimism is just a by-product of activity, just another metabolite.

Gina Logan slipped into her coat, placed the case file on the table, fumbled around for some money for the coffee until I waved her off saying I'd pay for it, smiled again and left.

John came over. "Are you staying for dinner tonight?"

"Yeah, let me have the mixed grill and another cup of coffee. And I'm done working. Thanks, again."

"No problem."

I opened the case file on Todd Berman. Gina had his name, address, and phone number. Berman paid his retainer in cash. The information was probably all phony, but that was okay. The woman would know who he was and where to find him.

I flipped over the contact sheet and services agreement, to the information on her subjects. The woman's name was Tara McKinney. She worked as a secretary at a small trade association. Her work address and phone number were listed, so was a description of her car and tags. Gina's notes said Tara McKinney was five-seven, one hundred and twenty pounds. She had blond hair worn straight, long, green eyes, and pierced ears—all of her earrings dangled or were big hoops. She wore nonprescription sunglasses when out.

The next page was her surveillance notes and a Ziploc bag of photographs. I took them out and fanned them in my hand. There was a good one of Tara and her boyfriend. I stood that up against my water glass and filed the rest.

After she'd made her case, Gina listed the DMV information on the boyfriend: Stanley Calloway, address and phone and Social Security number.

The rest of her notes confirmed her story. After I finished eating, I tucked the file into my briefcase and left Artie's. I called Mr. Calloway from my car.

"Hello."

"Yes, is this Mr. Calloway?"

"Yes, this is Stan Calloway."

"My name is Leo Haggerty. I'm a private investigator and I have reason to believe that you are being watched by someone who may intend to do you and your girlfriend, Tara McKinney, some harm. I'd like to meet with you so we can discuss this further."

"Just who is it that's supposed to be watching me?"

"I'm not sure of his name. He calls himself Todd Berman. I have reason to believe that he's an ex-boyfriend of Ms. McKinney's."

"Jesus Christ, not him again. I thought we were finished with all this."

"What do you mean, 'finished with all this'?"

"Tara had him arrested the last time he harassed her. He got a suspended sentence and a fine. He was supposed to be in some kind of counseling. If he ever harassed her again he was going to jail."

"Maybe he's decided that the way to keep her for himself is to keep everyone else away from her. If no one else will go out with her because of his harassment, maybe he thinks he'll win her back. Did that judgment cover you?"

"No. How did you find out about this? Are you watching me, too?"

"No, Mr. Calloway. This information came to me through another investigation." Technically true. "And I felt it was important to alert you right away. I have some ideas on how to respond to this Mr. Berman."

"Don't bother calling him that. His name is Joel Silverman."

When Calloway didn't address my invitation, I repeated it.

"Can we talk about Mr. Silverman?"

"Why? I'm going to do what we did the last time, call the police and have him arrested, or get a lawyer to charge him with harassment."

"It's not that simple. He hasn't done anything to you yet. The police won't pick him up. Your lawyer might be more successful. He might get a restraining order issued, but you see what he's doing even with jail time hanging over him. He hasn't quit. He's just changed his approach. Besides, I believe that someone pointed Silverman at you for their own ends. They don't care what trouble he causes you if it helps them."

"Who is that?"

"I don't know yet. That's the other investigation I mentioned." Technical truth #2. "I'm hoping to nail both Mr. Silverman and the person who is using him. I need your help to do that."

"How do I know that you aren't working with Silverman, that this whole story isn't a scheme to get me alone somewhere and kill me? That's what he threatened Tara with. That he'd kill her and anyone who went out with her."

"You don't know, Mr. Calloway. I'm willing to meet with you anywhere, anytime, under any conditions you choose. I only ask one thing in terms of helping me understand and predict what Mr. Silverman might do. I'd like to meet with you and Tara McKinney. If not together this first time, that's fine. Do whatever you want to convince yourself that I'm who I say I am. But I think her input would be very helpful."

"Let me think about this. How can I get in touch with you?"

I gave him my office number and beeper, and got a dial tone in return.

Home was just where I'd left it. I tossed my mail, cleared the machine on the business line, and turned on the TV. I did laps around the dial until I found a movie.

I settled into my chair and watched a young couple attempt to flee a mob of the undead, lurching forward with decayed features, carrying torches to find their prey. The young couple were not successful. Trapped in their car, they were pulled out through the shattered windows and devoured by the cannibals, who gorged themselves even as their own entrails followed behind.

Oh, for the good old days, when we were the mob, and Frankenstein the monster, the only one of his kind.

I fell asleep to an unhappy ending and the threat of a sequel.

Paula Zahn woke me up. I wish. Her broadcast image was bringing me up to date on the latest in human folly. The Duke of Cornhole had just been arrested for molesting his three daughters. Good-bye incestral home. I cut the sound off, started the coffee and went to shower and dress. With coffee and reheated pizza in hand, I just liked to watch her talk. She was so expressive, so obviously intelligent, so beautiful. The fact that she looked so much like my ex-something had nothing to do with it.

In the office, I flipped open to detectives in the yellow pages and began calling. Todd Berman had done just that. His first story wasn't nearly as slick as the one he gave Gina Logan. In fact, he was turned down cold by the first three agencies he talked to. They all told the same story. The guy had no right to information about an ex-girlfriend, so they passed on it. Nobody tried to wise him up so they just said they were booked up. And nobody admitted to referring him to anyone else.

The next agency on the list was Excalibur Investigations, run by Rick Stone.

Rick was an encyclopedia of bad habits, moral turpitude, and unpunished felonies. A routine sideswiping by Rick, on a female client, would include a padded expense sheet, an offer to forgive the balance in the horizontal plane, a hold back on the photos for later blackmail, and leaking confidences like a shotgunned intestine. A woman under surveillance got the same treatment only in a different order.

His greatest talent was a nose for shame. That was probably what kept him in business. If he could smell it on a woman he went right after her. Win or lose, she'd never tell. While Rick had read way too many paperbacks, apparently so had his clients. He was macho cliché all the way up to his snow-white pompadour. To me he looked like a Q-Tip. Enough people bought the pebbled glass door, the bourbon in the desk, the shoulder holster in plain sight, and the "trouble is my business" motto to keep the lights on and the phone ringing.

Franklin Investigations followed Excalibur in the directory. Rick had fine-tuned "Todd Berman" and pointed him at Gina Logan. Why?

I picked up the phone to get an answer when Kelly announced over the intercom that a Ms. Logan was here to see me and there was a call from a Mr. Calloway. I asked Kelly to show Ms. Logan in and tell Calloway I'd return his call shortly.

Kelly pushed open the door and Gina Logan walked in. I motioned for her to sit, and pulled her case file out of my briefcase.

"Here is your file. I've talked to Mr. Calloway. That was him on the phone just now. We might be able to do something there, but first, do you know Rick Stone?"

"God, that slug. Yeah, I did some free-lance work for him. I quit when he cornered me in his records room to discuss my taking advantage of some career opportunities. Apparently he thought I'd lost one up my skirt and he was gonna find it for me."

"That it?"

"No. I filed a grievance against Stone with the state licensing board. They found against him and suspended his license for three months."

"Well, guess what, Todd Berman was your thank-you note from Rick. Berman went through detectives alphabetically until he got to Rick. Rick didn't send him on to me, we're next on the list. He sent him on to you. And he gave Berman a much better cover story than the one he started out with."

"What can I do about that?"

"Unless we can get Berman to roll over on Rick, not much. You can bet there's nothing on paper. One meeting, no witnesses. Berman is frustrated. He tells Rick about his problems with the other detectives. Rick sees a way to sandbag you. So he tells Berman how to sell himself to you, gives you a good recommendation, then declines the case on account of he's booked up. The initial consultation, hey that's on the house, sorry, I couldn't help you more. Rick's cracking open the *Post* everyday, hoping there's a disaster with your name on it. That I think we can avoid. Personally I'd like to play pin-the-tail-on-the-Ricky with this one. You interested?"

I watched her mull it over. What was Rick thinking when he put the moves on her? He must have had a head cold that day. I couldn't get a whiff of shame or even embarrassment off her. She seemed to have a good sense of who she was. But then I had no nose for women to start with.

"Yeah, I'm interested. What do you have in mind?"

"I'm going to call Calloway now. We'll need his help on this."

I got Calloway's number from Kelly and dialed it.

"Stan Calloway."

"Mr. Calloway, Leo Haggerty returning your call."

"Yes, thank you. I talked it over with Tara and we decided I should meet with you first. I'd prefer it to be someplace public."

"Fine. Where do you work?"

"In town, right near the zoo."

"Okay, how about the zoo, say forty-five minutes?"

"That's fine. Where should we meet?"

"How about the polar bears. The bench closest to the railing."

"What do you look like?"

"I'll be wearing a leather jacket, sunglasses, and a brown suede cap. I've got a beard and I'll be talking to the bears."

"I'll see you there, Mr. Haggerty."

I hung up the phone and Gina asked, "You want me there?"

"Yeah. I'd have preferred to meet someplace private where 'Berman' wouldn't see us together, but as a sign of good faith, I said I'd go any-place Calloway was comfortable, so the zoo it is. Why don't you take a position where you can keep us in view and scan the area to see if 'Berman' is following him already. If he's there, come down, lean over the railing, and drop your purse on the ground. I'll bend over to help you and you let me know what he's wearing and where he is."

"Okay."

I got my jacket and cap and motioned for Gina to lead the way. When she asked, "What about a fee agreement? I thought you . . ."

"Yeah, well that was before this turned into an opportunity to put Stone out of business. I'd pay for a shot at that. We're both doing the profession a favor."

*   *   *

I took a seat above the bear pit. One of the older males immediately stood up and began sniffing the air. Once he realized I was where he couldn't get at me he lost interest and lay back down on the rocks in the spread-eagle position, like a boned chicken that they use to sneak up on seals.

I walked over to the railing and leaned on it. The male saw me and made eye contact. I met his eyes. I stood up with my arms down at my sides. He did the same thing. I kept my head up and stuck out my lower lip as a sign of submission. The next crazy step would be for me to vault the railing and play with the bear. Except that I'd be face-down, peeled, and eaten like a banana in minutes.

"Uh . . . Mr. Haggerty?"

I snapped out of my reverie and turned to face a young man, late twenties or early thirties, wearing a long top coat, with his hands in his pockets. He had wavy reddish-brown hair, pale freckles, and a tight-lipped, serious look on his face.

"Mr. Calloway?"

"Yes."

"Why don't we sit and talk? My friends won't mind."

"I was going to apologize for meeting like this," he said, "but you seem to be very comfortable here."

"I am. I come here—oh two, three times a year—to see the bears. You like polar bears?"

"No, not really. Can't say I think too much about animals at all. The reason I was going to apologize was that Tara got back to me after we'd spoken and said that she'd talked to some attorneys about you and they'd all said the same thing. That you were a straight-shooter and honest. So I guess we didn't need to meet like this."

"No problem. As you can see, I'd as soon meet here as anywhere."

"You said you wanted my help in dealing with Joel Silverman and somebody else you felt was using him, is that right?"

"Yes. I believe Silverman was assisted in finding you by a private detective named Rick Stone. Stone showed Silverman how to dupe another detective into locating you by lying to that detective. He did this as revenge for her filing a grievance for sexual harassment against him. I'd like to put Stone out of business. This is just the latest stunt of his. He's bad news for all of us and for his clients and innocent people like you."

"Okay, obviously I'd like to get rid of Joel Silverman and you want to get rid of this Stone fella. How can I help?"

"Well, that depends on how you want to deal with Silverman. I have my own approach to stalkers, but it's not for everyone. How have you dealt with him?"

"I haven't had to deal with him, not directly. I helped Tara deal with him. You know—unlisted phone number, better security at her home and work, keeping neighbors notified, taking a lot of precautions when she's out, prosecuting as soon as he did anything threatening . . ."

"And anxious all the time. Right?"

"Yeah. But that's getting better. At least it was until this happened. Now, she's a wreck again. She's thinking about moving and starting over someplace else."

"How much does she mean to you? You willing to move with her?"

"I don't know. I mean we're not engaged or anything. It might turn out that way, but it's too soon to tell."

"So, you don't know how much of your life you're willing to get messed up for this girl." I went on, imagining Calloway's thoughts out loud. "If you get scared off, then it's proof to her that she's either Silverman's or no one's. And you already told her that wasn't true, that you wouldn't let him run you off, right?"

I turned to look at him. He wouldn't meet my eyes, but stared down at his lap. Bingo. Gotcha. Man or Mouse to the woman you love? What a trap.

"But this has scared you big time. If you don't stand up to this guy, you lose the girl. Maybe that's okay," I paused, "and you lose a little self-respect. That'll gnaw at you whether she's here or not. Is that okay?"

I had to be careful not to use Calloway for my own ends. I wanted Stone bad, but shaming Calloway into being a target wasn't right. My life didn't mean much to me these days so I could advocate recklessness. Maybe his did. Maybe he had things to lose. Cowardice is an easy call from the sidelines.

What'll it be, Mr. Calloway? We're waiting. You look like a kid who got run off a lot of playgrounds. Is this one too many or not enough yet?

I let Calloway take his time and walked over to the railing. A young male streamed up out of the pool onto the rocks, and then shook himself dry, his fur rippling and sliding like it was borrowed from a bigger bear.

"Ah, Mr. Haggerty, what do you have in mind?"

Was there an answer buried in that question?

"Stalking puts you on the defensive. Where is he? What does he want? When will he show up again? He has all the control, you have all the anxiety. I recommend to people that they take the control from the stalkers. Provoke a confrontation. But a well-planned one. Keep the risk to a minimum and maximize the chances that they'll be caught in the act and get some good jail time."

"What if it doesn't work?"

"What do you mean, doesn't work? He doesn't make a play, you try again. He does and doesn't get convicted?"

"Yeah and now he's angrier than before. Then what?"

Then you have him killed, that's what. "I don't know. You try again. You stalk him. Set him up in other ways. Keep him under scrutiny all the time."

"There goes your life. You're still chained to their obsession. How do you get free from that?"

"The same way every slave has ever gotten free. You turn on your masters and free yourselves. No master ever gave up slavery out of the goodness of his heart."

"I don't know. I need to think. If we did try to set Silverman up, you'd arrange it so we wouldn't get hurt, is that it?"

"Almost. I'd arrange it so there'd be only a small chance of you getting hurt. No guarantees."

"I have to talk with Tara about this. I'll call you back when we make a decision."

"Take your time, Mr. Calloway, this is serious business. I want you to be sure."

"No, I don't think sure will be possible. Willing, maybe."

"That's all you need. I'll wait to hear from you."

We stood up and shook hands. Calloway looked over his shoulder as he left and turned back up the path toward Connecticut Avenue.

I sat back on the bench and waited for Gina Logan to return. The snow began to fall before she sat down. Large, soft flakes that melted on your tongue.

Gina shivered. "I hate snow," she informed me.

"Well?" I asked.

"Couldn't see anybody following him. But I'm not the best in the world at surveillance. He could have been there. What did you two talk about?"

"About how to turn things around on Mr. Silverman. He's thinking it over. If he agrees, the next step is yours. You'll be setting your client up. You ready for that?"

"It's like you said, once he lied to me, and used me, all bets were off. How will I set him up?"

"You'll call him back, ask if he's talked to his attorney yet. You were concerned because you hadn't heard. He'll give you some line of shit. Then you tell him that if he wants to establish a pattern of infidelity that you know where they'll be this Friday night."

"And where is that?"

"I don't know yet. If Calloway goes for it, I'll ask the woman if she and Silverman had any special spot, someplace meaningful to him, or an activity they did together, anything that'll yank his chain. You'll tell him that's where they'll be."

"And how do I know this? I'm off the case, remember?"

"Yeah, but you overheard them talking about it in the restaurant last week when you were sitting behind them at the bar."

"Isn't this getting a bit risky, provoking him like that?"

"Yeah, but it's the only way to make sure he comes out of his hole. I want to be calling the shots, not him. That's the best way to get him off the streets for a while. We'll give him a reason to want to violate his restraining order and the opportunity, then we'll drop a net over him."

"How do we do that?"

"That's where Rick Stone comes in." I looked down at the snow starting to cover the sidewalk. The zoo was emptying out rapidly.

"And?"

"Oh, uh don't worry about that. If we get that far, I'll tell you all about it." The bears were up shuffling from one side of the cage to the other, their heads bobbing to pick out scents of interest.

"You know, you're doing a lot more than just helping me fix a mistake. You're trying to help put Silverman away and Stone, too. Why?"

"Just tying up loose ends. Old business. Rick Stone's needed fixing for a long time. This may be my one chance to do it. I want to make the most of it." I drifted away on an ice floe of memory, until her voice harpooned me.

"Listen, I'm going to go, okay. It's getting worse by the minute here. You'll call if anything comes up?"

"Sure. I want to thank you."

"What for?" she said, standing up and stamping her feet.

"Your problem has given me an opportunity to set some things right. I've waited a long time for this chance. I'm grateful."

Gina shook her head. "I'm not sure I like the way this is going. Do I want to know what's with you and Rick Stone?"

"No. You don't. Go on home. It's snowing. I'll call you."

Gina brushed her graying hair and hunched into the wind, moved carefully across the slick sidewalk, testing each step before taking another.

Well, Rick, this might just be my lucky day. The sun was going down and the light was seeping out of the slate sky. The air got colder and the snow fell faster. Do you ever think about Helen Burroughs? I think about her a lot, Rick. Especially that last night. I'd watched her in the bar, plenty of nights, just like you did. That was the job. Just watch her. Keep a log of how much she drank, how long she sat there. God, she was sad. All dressed up, hoping she was still pretty, and afraid to find out. How many guys did she turn down? Three, four a night.

That last night she had what, sixteen beers. No, that wasn't pretty at all. No way I could let her drive like that. I didn't have to pick her up, just hold her up. So there I am, at her front door, one arm around her waist, trying to hold her up while one of her breasts pops out of her top and I'm missing the keyhole like the porch is a North Sea oil rig.

When did you get the bright idea to call Mr. Burroughs? When I told you I was going to make sure she got home alive or after I left?

There you were, video rolling, lights, action, camera. Shouting at Mr. Burroughs. He was a welcome addition, going on like a thesaurus with one entry: *whore, see the following*. And then I hear you over it all. "I told you he couldn't be trusted, Mr. Burroughs. He lied about how much she drank and this is why."

You couldn't stop there though. No, why settle for a banality like winning a case when you can reach the sublime like ruining a life? I don't know whose face was more awful, hers when she saw him there, or his watching her collapse in a heap, clutching at my pants leg with one hand, trying to tuck her breast back in its mooring and throwing up in long yellow threads.

He was eight years old, Rick. A little young for such a complicated lesson, don't you think? That clinched it though. Divorce and custody hammered through without a whimper, much less a fight, from Helen Burroughs. The boy was too angry and she too ashamed to make the few visits work. You got a nice bonus, I got the boot, and seven months later Helen Burroughs, blood alcohol level .19, got a physics lesson in the rapid deceleration of deformable bodies at the base of the Springfield offramp. She did not pass.

I don't know about you, Rick, but I think about Helen Burroughs a lot. And about how you used to say we were friends.

I stood up, shook the snow loose, and shuffled off.

* * *

At the subway, an old man talking to himself invited me to referee. I listened for a minute and declared it a draw. This pleased him so much he asked if I could help him get something warm inside him to keep the cold away. He had the fuel located and held for him. All he needed was the money to liberate it.

His face was so lined and creased and seamed that if he had to blow his nose you thought he'd just wad up his face, do it, and then pat his features back into place.

There was a time I'd have brushed the old man off like a tick, thinking to myself, get a job, get a life, get away from me. Now that I've come to expect less of myself, I've extended the courtesy to others. Not compassion, just an allergy to hypocrisy.

I gave the old man five bucks to ransom himself for a night. Perhaps tomorrow he could aim higher.

I stopped off at Skyline and swam enough laps to leave me defenseless against sleep, then drove home to see if I could find it.

My answering machine had one message on it. Calloway had talked to Tara McKinney. Tara was interested in my plan, would I give them a call tonight or tomorrow to discuss it in detail. Women can stiffen a man up in more ways than one. Tonight was too much, tomorrow would do. I scribbled down the number and went to bed.

I called Calloway around eight.

"So, you've decided to take me up on my offer."

"I don't see how we have any choice. You're right, he won't go away, he won't abide by the law. It's really crazy, you know. You start out trying to decide if you even want a relationship and the next thing you know, you're imprisoned by their lunacy for life."

"Can you give me Tara McKinney's phone number?"

"Don't need to. She's right here. Hold on."

"Hello, this is Tara."

"Ms. McKinney, my name is Leo Haggerty. I'm the man who spoke to Stanley Calloway about Silverman."

"Yes. We talked about it last night. I think you're right. He won't leave me alone and I'm tired of being afraid all the time. If your plan will get him out of my life, I'm all for it."

"I think it will. The new stalking laws in Virginia call for a minimum sentence of a year and a twenty-five-hundred-dollar fine since he's already got a judgment against him. Once that lapses the sentence is six months. Now is as good a time as any to go after him."

"What are you proposing that we do?"

"Very simply, provoke him into making contact with you. Then have him arrested. The important thing is to provoke him into an attempt to harm you or Mr. Calloway but not let him be successful."

"How do you plan to do that?"

"First off, we'd have a bodyguard with you to intervene. Second, we'd set up the place and control the location so the ways that Mr. Silverman can approach you are limited, the ways he can do harm are limited. Third, we'd probably have you wearing body armor as a precaution."

"Can't you use a stand-in for us?"

"No. The stalking would hold only if you're there. That just requires his acting in a way that leaves you fearing for your safety. I don't want him to try to harm you. I'd like to intervene before then."

"Okay. So how do we provoke him?"

"Did you and he have any place special you went, anything you did together that would be especially infuriating if you did it with someone else?"

"You know, I've avoided every place we ever went together because all it does is bring back painful memories."

"That was probably a wise decision."

"I guess the first place he ever took me out. He said it was his favorite restaurant because of how well they treated him there. 'Like a king,' he said. He went there to celebrate all his successes, he said."

"What was the name?"

"Simon's."

A pretender to Morton's crown as the king of steak houses. However, the meat wasn't as good and the service, unlike Morton's, was intrusive and humorless.

"That's a good place to go. The parking lot is large, open, and well lit. I doubt that he'd try anything inside the restaurant. Too hard to get away without being seen, especially if he's known to them. No. I'd guess he'd do something to you or your car in the lot. What has he done to you already?"

"You mean before we broke up or after?"

"Both."

"Well, when we first went out, there were calls and hang-ups at all hours of the night, driving by to see if I was home. At first he said it was because he couldn't believe that a girl like me would go out with him or fall for him. I tried to reassure him that I liked him, that I was sincere."

"But it didn't work." It never does.

"No, it didn't. Pretty soon I got tired of it. The jealousy when we were out, looking at other men to see if they were looking at me . . . Then it got plain crazy, not letting me go to the bathroom without waiting outside. I said that was it. I quit, thanks but no thanks. Joel wouldn't hear of it. I couldn't leave him. He wouldn't let me. He loved me. The farther away I tried to get, the more he distorted the relationship. That was what really scared me. The less he meant to me, the more I meant to him. His phone calls got more threatening. He sent me hate letters. I changed my phone number. He went to my work and harassed my co-workers about me. That was when I went to the police. My trash was dumped all over my lawn. A dead squirrel was put in my mailbox, so I got a post office box. My car had all the tires punctured and acid poured all over the body. I had to buy a new car. My heat pump was ruined when he poured cement into the fan housing. He ran the garden hose into my dryer vent and flooded the basement. My telephone lines were cut twice, my outside lights had the bulbs removed. I had security cameras installed. That's what caught him when he came up and sprayed graffiti on my house. I tried to sell the house but the agents said no one would buy for fear that Joel wouldn't quit and no one wanted to deal with him. I felt cursed, absolutely cursed. I was afraid to leave my house. I was afraid of what I'd find when I got home. He parked in the neighborhood and followed me to work. He'd drive up alongside and get almost to where he'd sideswipe me, then he'd pull in front of me and hit the brakes. I had to stop driving to work for a while and get picked up by a car pool. Then he started leaving messages and mail for me at work. He ordered pizzas for everyone in my name. Magazine subscriptions. Anything you can order without paying for it came to the office. He was relentless. Thank God my employer was on my side. He filed complaints with the police, too. I was a basket case. I couldn't sleep. I was taking antidepressants and antianxiety pills. My job performance fell off. I lost a raise I should have gotten; I almost lost my job.

"I got the police to keep an eye out for him in my neighborhood. Then I told all my neighbors about him and what he was doing. That helped cut down on the vandalism. People yelled at him when they saw him a couple of times.

"I wasn't able to do anything. I couldn't relax. I just went to work and then went home. I had girlfriends come by to visit or I'd go to their houses, but they were scared, too.

"There was a time when things quieted down for a while. I don't know why. I thought he'd gotten it out of his system. It was quiet for months. I started going out a little bit, I met Stan. We started going out together. Then wham he's back. Now I wonder if he was out of town on a job."

"What does he do?"

"You'll love this. What better place for a paranoid. He does security work. He's a private consultant designing secure communications systems for industry and government. He told me that he got jobs out of the country that take months to do."

"He's threatened you and done a lot of damage to your property. Did he ever hurt you physically?"

"No. Joel never hit me when we were together. He hasn't really had an opportunity since then."

"Does he own a gun, or did he ever talk about having used one?"

"No. I never saw one. And he never talked about guns with me."

The guy had no history of direct physical confrontation or violence, at least not with this woman. Plenty of damage to her property, but he hadn't broken in yet.

"Other than the squirrel, anything else killed? A pet?"

"No. I don't have any pets."

The guy likes to destroy things, when no one's looking. A bomb under the car would be his style. Poison in the food? Better not let them eat in the restaurant. If he doesn't make his play in the parking lot, have them come out of the restaurant after fifteen minutes and go home. Try again another day.

"Here's what I propose." I ran through my plans for Silverman and Rick Stone, covering all of my goals, most of my doubts, and some of my motives.

Tara McKinney and Stan Calloway agreed to my plan and I asked them to meet me at my office at ten o'clock. I called Gina Logan and asked her to join us to complete our preparations.

Kelly showed Stanley and Tara in. I introduced them to Gina Logan. Gina apologized to them. They dismissed it saying they knew how easily Silverman could fool people. They sat around my desk. I motioned to the coffeepot on the sideboard but they declined. I had two phones on my desk. Speaker phones change the sound of your voice and would alert Rick and Silverman.

"First, I want you, Tara, to call Rick Stone. Let's get him committed to this case, then we'll call Joel Silverman. Do you remember the scenario we outlined last night?"

"Yes."

"Okay. I'll keep listening in on this other phone. If he asks you a question you can't answer or wants to change the plan, I'll write you a note with what to say to him. Ready?"

"Let's go." She picked up the phone and dialed. I already had the receiver to my ear.

"Excalibur Investigations. Rick Stone speaking."

"Yes, Mr. Stone, my name is Sarah Maginnes and you were referred to me by a friend, actually a friend of a friend. She said you did a great job for her and that you were the man I needed . . ."

Gina stuck her finger down her throat.

"What's your friend's name?"

"Oh, her name is CeCe, that's short for Cecilia Rodriguez, but it was a friend of hers that gave me your name."

"And what can I do for you?"

"I, well, my husband and I are going out for our anniversary dinner tomorrow and I've been getting some obscene phone calls at my home and office. This guy says he's been watching me and following me. They've got me really frightened. My husband suggested some security so that when we went out I'd be able to relax. I don't want the evening to be ruined. I don't know . . . do you think we're overreacting, Mr. Stone?"

"No, no. You know what I always say, better to be safe than sorry. I'd take care of something like this personally, ma'am. Invisible protection, you'd never know I was there. Satisfaction guaranteed. You and your husband would have the time of your lives. Afterward we could talk about installing some security devices to catch this creep and prosecute him."

Tara looked at me. I mouthed "Good idea."

"That sounds like a good idea to me, Mr. Stone. You know I feel better just talking to you. You sound so confident."

"Ma'am, I don't believe in false modesty. Let me assure you, I'm the best there is, at what I do."

My head slumped onto my chest.

"Now where is this anniversary party and what time?"

"Simon's Restaurant at 7 P.M. this Friday."

"All right, when can you and your husband—or you yourself, if he's not available—come by my office to discuss my ideas for security for the evening?"

"I could come by this morning, if that's okay with you?"

"That would be perfect. Do you know where my office is?"

"Yes, CeCe gave me the address. I know the area. How about eleven-thirty today?"

"Fine, I'm looking forward to meeting you, Sarah."

"And I'm looking forward to meeting you, Mr. Stone."

"Rick. Call me Rick."

"Okay, Rick, see you then."

Tara put down the phone. "Do you have any mouthwash I could use? Just talking to him felt sleazy."

Gina laughed. "To know him is to loathe him."

"What do I do at the appointment?"

"Pay him his retainer. Keep it to a minimum for the night. Leave anything else for later. Go along with his plans. Tell him you want to use your car. That's what Silverman will be looking for. As much as it nauseates me to say it, Rick does know how to do personal protection. It's not his competence that's in question, it's his ethics. Whatever he wants you to do will be good procedure. If you're really uncomfortable call me afterward and tell me what he said. I'll tell you if it's sound or not."

I turned to Gina. "Ready?" She nodded. I put the phone to my ear. Stanley reached over and took Tara's hand.

"Hello," a flat voice said.

"Uh, Mr. Berman, this is Gina Logan calling."

"Why?"

"Uh, well, I didn't hear from your attorney, so I thought I'd check back with you, see if you'd decided what you wanted to do."

"Well, I haven't decided yet . . ."

"I understand. I just thought your attorney would want to know that I can establish a pattern of infidelity, not just one incident."

"I don't understand. I didn't ask you to work on this case anymore."

"Well, I haven't. It's just that when I was following your wife last week, I overheard her talking about how much she is looking forward to going out this Friday to celebrate something with her, uh, friend."

"Where were they going, did she say?"

"Yes, uh, let me look it up. I think I have it here. Yes. Simon's. She said something else about it but that's the name."

"What else did she say?"

"Look, Mr. Berman, like you said, I'm off the case. I don't think that information would be useful to anyone. I just thought I'd call to let you know we can make an airtight case against your wife. If you and your lawyer want to."

"Right, you just thought you'd drum up a little business for yourself, Ms. Logan. You don't fool me with that solicitous crap. Let me make it clear to you, you are no longer in my employ. I do not want you sticking your nose into my business. If I want any other work done I'll call you. Got that?"

"Loud and clear, Mr. Berman. I'm sorry you feel this way, I was only trying to help."

"Good-bye." He hung up.

"And fuck you too, you asshole." Gina's jaw muscles rolled back and forth under her ears. "I'll take a double on the mouthwash. You know, I really hate working for assholes."

"Well, I think we're in business. Friday night you'll go out to Simon's with Rick Stone. I expect Mr. Silverman to show up and try something in the parking lot. If it all goes well, you'll have a witness to your harassment by Silverman and Stone will be forced to clean up his own mess." And a whole lot more, if I get my way.

Tara checked her watch. "I'd better be going. I'll call you after my meeting with Mr. Stone."

"Fine, I'll be here in the office until one."

Stan Calloway stood up. We shook hands and they left.

Gina was staring into space when I sat down. "What's bothering you?"

"I hate taking shit like that from anybody, even if it's the smart thing to do."

"That's why it's important to get paid and paid well for this work. With the assholes, it's the only satisfaction you get."

Friday night arrived as promised. Gina and I were sitting in my car opposite Simon's lot at six-thirty watching to see if Silverman would show up.

"What do you think he'll do?" she asked anxiously.

"I really don't know. He may want to keep her out of Simon's so it won't be ruined by her eating there, or he may consider it ruined already. This is her first assault on him. I expect he'll be pretty angry and he'll make a direct confrontation this time. He's been pretty careful so far in avoiding consequences for his behavior so I expect he'll do something he hopes he can get away with. Up to now that's been his pattern. That's your best predictor of future behavior. Not a great predictor, but the best we've got. We're changing some important parameters here and he could go off in an entirely new direction."

"Okay, but what do you think he'll do? Your best guess?"

"A direct confrontation outside the restaurant. That's what I'm counting on."

"Isn't that risky?"

"Yes, but it offers great rewards, too."

I spent the next fifteen minutes scanning the lot for running cars, occupied cars, cars parked facing the exit. If Silverman made his move he'd need to see them come in and ideally be able to make a quick getaway. I pushed away the thought of him hiring someone to do a professional job. The consequences of that response would be disastrous.

Parking lots leave plenty of room for people to approach unseen between the cars and getting out of a car is a slow, awkward movement, providing that moment of vulnerability so necessary for a successful attempt at harm.

"He either does it in the lot or he runs them down on the street, going to the restaurant. That's a longer shot. I'm still going for the lot," I said, reassuring myself.

"Rick will lose any tails he picks up and sweep the car, so I don't think it'll happen on the road. No, it's the lot. Car stopped, open, poor visibility. If he's going to preserve the sanctity of Simon's he'll deny her admission. That's my bet." My tongue was tossing verbal Valium all over the car. It dissolved on contact but had no effect.

At five minutes to seven, I pointed to a car parked just down from Simon's. "Gina, walk over to the restaurant and see what that car's plates are, also if it looks like Silverman. I'm going to call the restaurant and make sure Silverman or Berman doesn't have a reservation and isn't inside already."

"Good idea." Gina got out and walked briskly across the lot. I made two calls while she was gone.

Gina got back in the car. "It's not him." In fact, the car was easing away from the curb. "What about the restaurant?"

"No reservation for Silverman or Berman. Nor do they have one for people he's been known to dine with."

Tara's car was pulling into the lot.

"Showtime." I picked up the binoculars and scanned the lot again. "Look, over there." I pointed to a shadow moving low between a row of cars. "Here he comes."

Gina reached over and grabbed my arm. We were watching a shark attack coalescing. Each element moving into position, meaningless until the final conjunction. The bait dangling, one leg in the car, one leg out. The shark, a dark shape cutting through the night, picking up speed.

"Shouldn't we do something, warn them?" Gina gasped.

"Too late for that now. Hold on. Here comes the collision." We braced ourselves as if Silverman was running right at us.

Silverman sprinted across the aisle toward Tara McKinney. His arm was low and extended. Tara was screaming, her hands to her face. Then she was gone. A black shape rolled across the trunk of the car and slammed into Silverman. He disappeared. Columns of smoke drifted up by the car accompanied by shrill screams.

"My God, what's that?" Gina asked.

My wildest dreams, I thought, but didn't answer.

Sirens grew in the distance and two Fairfax County police cruisers pulled into view. One closed off the lot's exit, the other ventured in toward the screaming. They blocked Tara's car and turned their searchlights toward the ground. One officer crouched behind the hood, gun extended; the other spoke into a microphone.

"You on the ground. Put your hands up and come on out of there. Anyone in the car, put your hands up and come out one at a time."

I motioned to Gina. "Let's get out and see what happened." She scooted out of the car, closed the door quietly, and dashed across the street to the corner of the lot. I caught up with her and motioned to the shadows at the foot of the wall. Gina followed me, scuttling sideways between bumpers and bricks to a vantage point directly behind the police cruiser.

Stan Calloway and then Tara McKinney emerged slowly from the car, their hands overhead. Stan started to speak but was cut off.

"Hands on the roof and spread 'em. Then you can talk."

The other officer came around the cruiser and approached them from the rear.

First one pair of hands, then another appeared, rising up from the ground. The second pair was still smoking.

"Jesus Christ," the cop said and stepped out of the cruiser. "Put em on the roof, easy does it, and spread 'em. Get away from each other."

Tara and Stan had backed away from the car. The other cop was talking to them.

Rick was patted down, then Silverman.

He held up his ruined hands as he was turned away from the car. He was moaning over and over, like a scratched record from hell.

"John, we can't cuff this guy. I think he's burned his hand with acid or somethin'. You better call for an ambulance."

The officer speaking to Tara got back into the cruiser.

"What happened here?" the other cop asked.

"Look, Officer, my name is Rick Stone, I've got ID in my coat. I was hired by—"

"Stone, Stone. Yeah, you were the guy called in the report."

Silverman turned slowly and looked at Rick. He stopped moaning. The dawn of recognition in their faces was beautiful indeed, like someone had opened an umbrella up their asses.

"You, you set me up. All along. You did this to me!" Silverman waved his hands at Rick. "I'll kill you, you bastard!"

The cop pointed his nightstick at Silverman and backed him away from Rick.

"I don't know what you're talking about," Rick said. "I've never seen you in my life, you psycho!"

"Liar! Liar! Liar!" Silverman shrieked.

Rick's natural aversion to taking responsibility for anything was an easy match for Silverman's paranoia, especially without two burned hands to distract him. The more Stone did his backstroke in front of the cops, the more it fueled Silverman's rage.

Two minutes later, an ambulance pulled into the lot. Two paramedics jumped out and approached Silverman. They gave him an injection and ran an I.V. into him.

The cop and Rick followed Silverman into the ambulance.

"Listen," the cop said. "We appreciate your calling us in on this. A lot of you guys, you get headlines in your eyes, forget that we have to clean up your messes."

"Hey, I don't know what you're talking about. I never called you guys." Stone's face was white with anger.

"Liar!" Silverman bellowed from the ambulance. One of the paramedics was kneeling on him, trying unsuccessfully to get him to lie down. "Like you never saw me in your life. I'll get you, you son of a bitch! Just as soon as I get out of here. You'll wish you'd never seen me. I'll fix you. You'll—"

A closed door interrupted Silverman's recitation of things to come. The siren wailed.

"Honest, I don't know what you're talking about," Rick reiterated.

"All I know, your name was on the call-in. We need you and your clients to come over to the station, make statements. Then you can be on your way."

"Okay, we'll be right over," Rick said, shaking his head even as he agreed.

The two cruisers pulled away and after a brief conference, Tara, Stan, and Stone got into their car and followed.

When their taillights blurred in the distance, I stepped out of the shadows. Gina Logan joined me.

"Well, what do you think?" she said.

"I think you should savor this moment. It doesn't get any better than this."

Gina shivered. "Is that the good news or the bad?"

I smiled. "They're one and the same."

ACKNOWLEDGMENTS

I'd like to thank Mike Jackson for all his help on this one. He's the real McCoy and welcome in Leo's shop any day.

Writers are writers, regardless of how long they have been doing it. In the case of Christine Matthews and Carolyn Hart, the former is a newcomer—in fact, this is her first mystery short story—while the latter might be called the "old pro."

In "Gentle Insanities" Christine Matthews tackles the same theme as Carolyn Hart in "An Almost Perfect Murder." In fact, to quote a line out of Carolyn's story, they both write about "nice people in deep pain." When you deal with mysteries, and murder, isn't that always the way?

CHRISTINE MATTHEWS

Christine Matthews has published extensively in the horror field. She has published poetry and has had a play produced in the Midwest. Here she turns her impressive talent and range to the P.I. genre, which she attacks with both a fresh and frightening outlook.

"Gentle Insanities" features Omaha P.I. Roberta "Robbie" Stanton, who discovers that a private investigator's professional life is not always more interesting—or challenging—than her private life.

GENTLE INSANITIES

"They hired me because I'm a crazy lady." I squinted into the camera. Was my eye shadow smeared? Please, don't let me sweat through this new blouse—it's silk. God, I was enjoying my fifteen minutes of fame.

"A crazy lady? Is that what it takes to be a private investigator in Omaha?"

"It can't hurt."

The audience laughed.

The topic of today's "Donahue" was: *Daring People—Exciting Occupations.* I do admit I'm more exciting than the fire-eater sitting stage-left. What does it take to douse a flame? Lots of practice and some sort of protective coating gargled inside your mouth. But I don't think I'm as daring as the eighty-seven-year-old sky-diving great-grandmother. Now that takes real guts.

"Have you ever had to use that?" He pointed to the .32. I didn't have the heart to tell him I'd worn it because the leather shoulder holster matched my skirt.

"Once." I hung my head, as though the memory was too sad to discuss.

Questions from the audience were coming in spurts: "I've read that being a private investigator is boring, lots of routine, paperwork, photographs of cracks in sidewalks . . . you know."

"The agency I work for specializes in people, not pavement. We track down deadbeats who owe child support, runaway kids . . . that kind of thing. And I've only been licensed a year; guess I haven't had enough time to get bored."

The next question dealt with the great-grandmother's sex life and I zoned off wondering if it was true that the camera would add an additional ten pounds to my hips.

When I got to the office the day after the show ran on TV, Jan and Ken stood beside their desks and applauded.

I smiled, took a slow bow, and blew them each a kiss. "Please, be seated. I'll walk among you common folk and sign autographs later."

"Roberta," Harry called from his office.

"Robbie," I shouted. I hate the name Roberta, especially the way my boss, Harry Winsted, says it.

I sat across from Harry, eased into the leather chair, crossed my legs, and waited for him to tell me how lousy I was on "Donahue." The more shit Harry gives me, the better I know I'm doing.

"Saw you on 'Donahue.' That number about your little ole .32. Great stuff. Makes us look like big time."

"Just doin' my job, boss."

"Yeah, well it's back to the real world, kid. I got a job that needs your special touch." He picked up a folder from the table behind him.

"Name's James Tanner. Seems the bastard skipped town with his three-year-old son and the wife's not getting enough help from the police to suit her." He tossed the file at me.

I reached out, caught it without looking away from Harry's beady little eyes. "Anything else?"

"Yeah. You look fat on TV."

"Love you, too." I made a point to slam the glass door as I exited Harry's office. The glass rumbles; he always flinches. With my back turned, I waved over my shoulder.

After reading through the file, I found that James Lucias Tanner was all of twenty years old. He'd gotten married when he was seventeen, to a pregnant sixteen-year-old from the right side of the tracks. It was that family money paying for this investigation. After a series of bad career moves, James finally landed work as a manager at the Touchless Car Wash over on Dodge.

I made a note to check out Kevin Tanner's preschool.

The next day I drove out to La Petite Academy, in Millard. I expected to see rows of toddlers all dressed in red uniforms. Good little soldiers with teeny, tiny swords tucked inside Pampers and baggy coveralls. Instead, I found a neat room full of partitioned activities. The smell of paste and warm milk reminded me of my own kindergarten class. I'd called ahead for an appointment with Kevin's teacher and made my way to her office, located in the back of the main room.

"Ms. Kelly?" I extended my hand.

"Ms. Stanton. I saw you yesterday on 'Donahue.' "

A fan. "That was taped weeks ago." I assumed a modest smile.

"Well, I enjoyed it a lot. Is being a private investigator really exciting?"

I shrugged, surveyed the room cluttered with Nerf balls and blocks. "I do get to go to some very exotic locales."

She laughed.

But her smile curved downward into a sad pout when I asked about Kevin Tanner.

"Oh, Kevin's such a sweetie. All the children and teachers miss him. But that father of his . . . what a creep. Always came in here dirty and mean. He had such a mouth on him. Tattoos all over his arms and a green and black snake on one hand spelled out the name 'Donna.' Kevin's mother is Lynn. The man's a pig."

Good, she was a real talker. All I had to do was sit back, nod, and wait for recess.

Ms. Kelly told me, down to the rip in his seams, what James Tanner had been wearing the day he kidnapped Kevin. She described how the backseat of Tanner's car was littered with Burger King and Taco Bell wrappers. But best of all, Ms. Kelly's anal-retentive memory recalled a bumper sticker. A Mary Kay pink design telling every tailgater that inside was a representative. And the pink coffee mug Ms. Kelly saw stuck to the dashboard was stenciled with the name AMY.

By the time I got back to my apartment it was eight o'clock. The red light winked at me from the answering machine. I punched the gray button. The tape rewound, then replayed. My father's voice shouted from inside the machine, frantic.

"It's your mother. Jesus, she almost died! We're at the hospital. What am I going to . . ." His sobs were cut off by the infernal beep.

The next message started. It was Dad again. "For God's sake, it's five. Your mother's in radiation. I'm at Christ Community; they've assigned a specialist. I don't know what . . ."

The beep disconnected his agony and before I could call information for the number in Chicago, the phone rang.

I grabbed the receiver, startled. "Hello?"

"Thank God! Where the hell have you been? I've called twice . . ."

"Dad, I just got home."

"We were having lunch; all of a sudden she couldn't breathe, she grabbed her chest, turned an awful color, and just crumpled.

"I got her in the car and rushed to the Emergency Room. She almost died." He choked on his fear. "I can't lose her."

I maintained an artificial calm, not even allowing the idea of my mother's death to seep into my brain. "Could it be pneumonia?"

"Haven't you understood a word I've said? She's in radiation. The X-rays show there's a spot on her lung. But the technician said we caught it in time and your mother's so strong. You know how strong she is. Robbie?"

Cancer.

"Yes, Dad. I know." Thirty-five years had taught me well. Agree and listen. That's all Dad ever required of me. Nod, smile, be Daddy's little girl. I played the part so well that sometimes I lost my adult self in the charade.

"Oh God, what am I going to do?"

"I'll come up and . . ."

"No, we'll be fine. We're fine."

"Have you called Delia?"

"I'll do that now, while I'm waiting. Talk to you later." The connection broke.

Tears welled behind my eyes refusing to roll down my cheeks. Mother always said she'd live to be one hundred.

"I'm holding you to that promise," I whispered to her from five hundred miles away.

After staring at my scuffed floor tiles for half an hour I couldn't wait any longer. I called my sister.

She sniffed. "Dad just called."

"Well, what should we do?"

"I couldn't go up there even if I wanted to. The shop's busy. With Halloween coming, I'm swamped with fittings and special orders. Then there's Homecoming gowns."

"And I just started a new case but if I can wrap it up, I'll go see what's happening."

"That'd be great. You know how Daddy gets. He blows everything out of proportion. Maybe it's not that bad."

"Maybe." I hoped, but deep inside I knew the truth.

The leaves seemed particularly vivid as I walked to my car. The apartment complex I live in offers covered parking, for an additional fee, of course. While my car is protected from the rain and ice, birds love to poop on it as they huddle above on steel beams supporting the ceiling. I cursed the black and white blobs covering my blue paint job and crunched dried leaves beneath my feet. The morning was mild and I could smell burning leaves. Someone dared defy the law and I applauded them. What was autumn without that toasty aroma clinging to orange and yellow leaves?

Ken was using the computer when I entered the office. He glanced up and grinned. "Get any last night?"

"Why do you ask me that stupid question every single morning?"

"Because I want to know if you got any."

"Sleazeball." I punched his arm as I walked to my desk.

"If you call me names, I won't show you a new program we just got in."

I admit it, I'm computer unfriendly. I admit, too, I've depended upon the knowledge of others when accessing or exiting a screen. I still needed to pick Ken's brain.

"I'm sorry. You're not a sleazeball. You're just scum. Better?"

"I knew you'd come around. Take a look. This is great."

Reluctantly, I stood behind him as he pushed keys with the artistry of Liberace. "All we have to do is punch in a last name and we practically get a pint of blood."

"Could you try 'Tanner' and see what comes up?"

Before I could turn for the file, the screen displayed twelve Tanners in the Omaha metropolitan area.

"First name?" Ken asked.

"James L."

"Bingo! We got your credit ratings, places of employment, marital status, number of children, pets, even a ring size from a recent purchase at Zales."

"Can you print it out for me?"

"No," he scolded. "I showed you how to print something. So do it yourself."

"Kenny," I pulled his ear. He loves it when I pull his ear. "Kenny, sweetheart, you're right there, in front of the thing. Please?"

"Just this once. This is the last time." He pushed some more keys and the printer started to life.

"Thank you very much," I said in my best Shirley Temple voice. He also loves it when I talk like a little girl. Hell, if it'll get the computer work done, I'll talk like Donald Duck.

I sat up straight behind my cheap desk and studied the printout. In between reviewing blue and white lines of tedious, boring statistics, I suddenly remembered Amy and let my feet do the walking to the yellow pages. I flipped to "Cosmetics." There were four "Independent Sales Directors" listed. One of them was named Amy Schaefer. I jotted down her number and address and stood to return the book to its shelf. Passing Ken's desk, I poked his shoulder. "I bet I crack this case and don't even have to use a computer. Brains, ole bean. Human brains beat your computer friend any day."

"God, you're the most bullheaded broa—"

"Careful," I warned.

"—woman I've ever known. You belong back in the dark age."

"Where men were men . . ."

"Careful," he warned right back.

Omaha has a small-town feel to it. Tractors frequent busy streets, cowboys visit from out west when there's a cattle auction or rodeo. People are friendly and move in second gear instead of third. But with a population of half a million, a symphony, ballet company, museums, and great shopping, it also has a big-city mix.

I turned onto "L" Street and took it to Seventy-second. Making a right onto Grover, I found the apartment complex where Amy Schaefer lived. I backtracked to the Holiday Inn and dialed her number from a phone in the lobby.

After three rings a timid voice answered.

"Amy Schaefer?"

"Yes. Who's calling?" She was a regular church mouse.

"Let's just say I'm a special friend of James."

"Oh? Where do you know Jimmy from?"

"We've been friends a long time, met at . . ." Think, think. I looked across the street and saw a sign for a lounge named Jodhpurs. ". . . Jodhpurs. It was twofer night, ladies were free. You know how cheap he is." Was she buying any of this? From all the fast-food wrappers in his car, I figured the guy was not a big spender.

"Why are you telling me all this?"

"Well, Jimmy's been begging me to come back to him but after he told me about you . . ."

"You know so much about me and I don't even know your name." She waited.

"Oh, I'm sorry. It's Donna."

Suddenly her schoolmarm act exploded across the phone line. "That son of a bitch!"

"Now, calm down. The way I figure it, us wome . . . broads should stick together."

My head felt as though it had been fired at, close range, when she slammed down the receiver. She was hot! Hell hath no fury and all that jazz.

I dashed to my car and swung back onto Grover. Parking across from the Grover Square Apartments, I saw a woman come stamping across the lot toward a pink Cadillac. I followed as she screeched into traffic, flooring the accelerator as the light turned yellow. I raced after her.

Then a Trailways bus pulled out of the McDonald's parking lot. Amy swerved, the car between us rammed into her rear bumper, and I jerked my steering wheel to the right, hoping no cars were in that lane or riding my tail. Last thing I saw as I passed the accident was one screaming woman, a busload of Japanese tourists snapping pictures, and a salesman-type man calling the police from his car phone. I hate those things.

"Damn," I hissed, rubbernecking as I passed the scene. I was hungry, frustrated, and had a headache that wouldn't quit.

While I hate the plastic trappings of twentieth-century life, I do love the simple pleasures. Like mail for instance. And as I poked through my mailbox and found only an ad for a new beauty salon, I felt cheated.

The apartment seemed cold; I hiked up the heat. Rummaging through the refrigerator, I looked for the chili left over from last night. The bowl had worked itself to the back of the middle shelf. I scooped a heaping portion into a smaller bowl and put my lunch into the microwave.

The microwave is another of those simple pleasures I referred to. I know, it also fits under the category of "twentieth-century conveniences." Oh well, I use it anyway but each time give thanks that I don't get contaminated from the radiation or whatever flies around in there to produce heat. And, if I should one day wake up to find all microwaves have disappeared, I'd survive. See, I don't depend on the convenience. That's the difference: the mind-set. I enjoy the convenience while knowing full well that one power outage will not upset my life. Dad taught us that. Don't depend on anything or anyone and you'll never be disappointed.

Dad.

I looked across the room. The answering machine was blinking. As I programmed the time into the oven, I realized my headache was fierce and went for some aspirin before listening to messages.

After gulping the last swig of water, I reluctantly pressed the gray button.

Beep.

"This is Mrs. Calhoun from American Express. Your account is now two months' past due and we were wondering if a payment had been made. Please call me at 800-555-9100."

Beep.

"Ro-ber-ta," Harry whined. "Some guy, says he's your father. He's been calling every fifteen minutes. Sounds weird. Give me a call, okay? Roberta?"

Beep.

"Just got a frantic call from Dad." It was Delia. "He's kidnapping Mother from the hospital. Call me!"

Beep. Rewind.

I pulled the phone over to the table, set my place for lunch, then poured a Coke over lots of ice. I dialed Delia's number. She answered on the first ring.

"Are you okay?" I asked.

"Oh, Robbie, thank God. I don't know what's going on. I talked with Mother's nurse—the doctor wasn't available. She said when Dad brought Mother in, she was barely breathing. They thought they'd lose her right there. What the hell have they been doing all this time? I've called and called and no one's home. I'm scared."

"Calm down," I advised with my mouth full. "If the doctor let her go home, she wasn't kidnapped. I'll talk to him and call you back."

"I think one of us should go up there." She was suddenly the frightened little sister and I knew which one of us would be going to Chicago.

* * *

"Your father needs help, Miss Stanton." That's the first thing Dr. Blair said after I'd identified myself.

"I've known that for a long time." I bet he thought I was kidding. "But right now I'm more concerned about my mother."

"I can appreciate your position. Well, your mother's a heavy smoker. Maybe if she'd come in sooner." He took a breath then dove right in. "Your mother has cancer . . . lung cancer."

"Should she be home now?"

"She responded very well to treatment and your father understands how important it is she come in twice a week for it. When she regains some of her strength, we can start her on chemotherapy."

"And then? After the chemo?" I really didn't want to hear his answer.

"Six months, a year. A year and a half—tops."

I had to hang up, quickly. "Thank you."

I ran to the bathroom unsure if I was going to cry or collapse but feeling the bathroom was the direction to head. I ended up sitting on the edge of the tub, holding my head in my hands, rocking back and forth until the panic passed. I thought I was going to die.

Delia took the news better than I had, or maybe she just pretended. It's hard to figure her out sometimes. While she stands five feet seven, I barely reach five feet four inches. She has dark hair—I'm light. She explodes over situations I find amusing and laughs when I want to scream.

We had agreed that I would fly to Chicago; I'd have to be the eyes and ears for both of us now.

I called Harry and told him about my near-miss with Amy Schaefer. He grumbled until I added in the news about my mother.

"Geez, kid," he sighed. "You just do what has to be done. Family comes first, that's what I always say. I'll sit on this Tanner case until you get back."

"Thanks, Harry. Thanks a lot."

"Hey, no skin off my ass."

I couldn't tell if Dad was happy to see me. He'd always made me feel as though I was intruding. Most times he looked annoyed.

"What are you doing here?" He stood behind the storm door, talked through the screen.

"Can I come in?"

347

"Well, sure." He held the door open. "It's just this is such a surprise."

I set my suitcase down and wrapped my arms around him. He felt thinner, bony. I whispered into his ear, "How's Mother?"

Tears welled in his eyes. "Not too good today."

I held him at arm's length, surprised at how old he looked.

"Let me go tell her you're here."

He walked away from me, went down the hall, and I stood waiting, feeling like a salesman calling on the lady of the house. Then I followed him.

"Hi," I said softly. She lay on her side, on top of the bedspread. She was wearing a pink sweat suit, her feet tucked inside a pair of white cotton socks. She didn't turn to look at me. I walked to her side of the bed and knelt down.

And then she whimpered.

I threw myself on top of her and we hugged.

When my eyes adjusted to the light, I saw how swollen and misshapen her face was. She reminded me of one of those Betty Boop dolls.

"Why didn't you call me? Or Delia?"

"What could you do?" she asked, puzzled.

What could I do? Love you. Comfort you. What does a family do for one another? I knew then that she hadn't the slightest idea.

I couldn't get any information out of them and for two days watched my father dole out vitamins, steroids, and antibiotics. He cooked; he helped her up; he helped her down. I was in the way most of the time.

When I asked about Dr. Blair, I received mixed reviews. So I decided to check out Blair for myself. Telling my folks I was going shopping, I headed for Christ Community Hospital and the two o'clock meeting I'd set up the day before.

He looked like Elton John. Dark hair cut in bangs across his forehead, a toothy grin and oversized glasses. I agreed with Mother; I liked him.

"Her mental attitude is wonderful. And your father takes excellent care of her." His compassion assured me he wanted Mother to be well as much as I did. But doctors can't guarantee miracles.

I called Delia from a pay phone in the hospital lobby. She seemed relieved and encouraged. I felt better about the relieved part but cautious about the encouragement.

I packed my suitcase as my father trailed behind me. He walked in a clipped step and waved his arms as his voice rose. "How dare you."

I folded a blouse, keeping my back to him. "I'm her daughter. I have the right."

Words came in slow, deliberate syllables. "You're trying to turn your mother against me. We were doing fine until you came."

Hot, angry tears dripped down my face. I bent over the suitcase, quickly fastened the clasps, and turned to get my coat.

"Now what are you crying about? I can't say two words to you without you bawling. You're too goddamned sensitive, Robbie. Always have been. We're just having a conversation and you get hysterical."

"I gotta go." My eyes scanned the carpet as I walked toward Mother's room. I crept in and kissed her cheek. She breathed slowly, never acknowledging my presence. Confrontations were not her forte.

My father followed me to the front door, all the time telling me how I didn't understand, how selfish I'd always been.

I called a cab from the store across the street and waited, staring out the window.

It was worth one more try. I dialed Amy Schaefer's number. Timid as ever she asked, "Hello?"

"Amy. Just thought you'd like to know we're taking Kevin and going to Disneyland for Christmas." That seemed like the kind of thing Tanner would do. At least I hoped it was. "Sorry if that screws up your holiday, doll."

"You're full of shit! Jimmy ain't going nowhere."

"Jingle bells, jingle bells, jingle all the . . ."

Slam.

I dashed out of the Holiday Inn and got in my car. Sure enough, after a ten-minute wait, Amy Schaefer came out of her apartment and this time she carried two shirt boxes wrapped in Christmas paper, tied with red ribbons.

I giggled. "Oh, goody, someone's gonna get their Christmas presents early."

Once again we headed up 72nd Street. Turning west on Dodge, we passed the Touchless Car Wash. She made a right on 120th and turned into an apartment complex. Amy got out of her pink car, and opened the door of apartment number forty-nine with her own key.

I knew I'd have to sit and wait. And I admit, okay, it would have been nice to have a phone in the car.

I checked my watch against the bank's huge read-out. My watch showed two-ten; the bank displayed two-twenty. I decided to compromise. It was two-fifteen.

Around three o'clock the door of number forty-nine burst open and I saw those two Christmas packages come flying across the parking lot. Amy Schaefer dashed for her car, followed by a short guy with dirty hair. I'd seen his driver's license photo and recognized James Tanner.

I called the police from the Taco Bell across the street, identified myself, and gave them the address where they could pick up James Tanner.

Within ten minutes a squad car pulled in behind me. They'd kept the siren off as I'd advised, but Tanner spotted the car just the same. He ran for the apartment while Amy stood screaming after him, "Run! You lying son of a bitch. I wish I would have called the cops myself. Coward!"

The police knocked at number forty-nine until Tanner answered. By that time several neighbors had gathered and traffic slowed to catch a glimpse of the action. I waited while an officer escorted James out. A female officer went inside and after a few minutes came out holding a frightened little boy in her arms. She patted his back, talking softly into his ear. The boy clung to her.

I opened my car door. I just couldn't resist.

"Amy?"

She spun around, relieved to see I wasn't wearing a uniform. "What? How'd you know my name?"

"Santa told me, said you'd been a real good girl. Jingle bells, jingle bells, jingle all the way." I kept singing as I returned to my car. "Thanks for all your help. We couldn't have done it without you."

"You bitch!" the timid church mouse screamed. "You fuckin' bitch!"

Some days are like that . . . you get no appreciation.

"Here you go." I dropped the papers onto Harry's desk. "All wrapped up, neat and tidy. Tanner's in custody, Kevin's being reunited with his mother as we speak, and Amy Schaefer is selling Passionate Pink blusher with a heavy, yet cheerful heart. Life just keeps—"

"Your mother died this morning."

It took me a minute. "What did you say?"

He stood as I fell into the chair. Coming around his desk he bent to touch my shoulder. "Roberta . . . Robbie, I'm so sorry."

"But I just saw her." I was angry. No, I was upset. I was going to cry. No, I was going to faint. Don't let go. Hang on.

"Your sister's been trying to get you all day. She broke down, couldn't

say another word after she told me. I offered to break the news . . . I
didn't want you to feel, you know . . . alone."

My grief started slowly and built into deep gulping sobs. Harry knelt
in front of me, hugging me against his chest.

As the funeral procession wove down the street my parents had lived
on for the past eighteen years, I noticed the Christmas decorations. A
brick house on the end of the block had a life-sized wooden Santa,
painted a hideous red and white. I hated it. The tree lights twinkling
around doorways and windows seemed to accentuate our sadness.

Dad stood by himself at the cemetery. Bitter. He told anyone who
would listen that now he had no family. Friends reminded him he had
two lovely daughters. But he didn't hear. He repeatedly told Delia and
me that he was alone and no one had ever loved him but my mother. I
was too empty to fill him with reassurance.

"We've gotten through Easter, Mother's Day, Father's Day. I really
don't think he should be alone for his birthday." Delia worried. "We'll
make a cake, bring some presents."

It was August, and once again I found myself back in Chicago. The
birthday party had been a good idea. But the pressure of having a normal
celebration had tired us all. Delia had gone to bed early. I sat in the
living room, rocking and watched a "Fawlty Towers" rerun. John Cleese
always made me laugh.

Dad walked into the room, grunting.

"What's so funny?" Before I could answer, he attacked. "How can
you laugh? Your mother's dead! You know, come to think of it, I haven't
seen you or your sister cry."

"We've cried a lot." My agony was all that would comfort him now.

"Well, I've never seen it."

I stared at the TV.

When he realized he wasn't going to get me to play, he changed
tactics. Reclining in his chair, he sighed. I glanced sideways at him and
he smiled. When I turned to look him full on, he smirked.

"I've got to tell you something." He leaned forward, confiding. "This
is just between us."

"What?"

"I hired someone . . . to kill the doctor."

This had to be one of his lies. The kind he took back later claiming he had only been kidding.

"Your mother's doctor. That cocksucker, Blair."

"A hit man?"

"Yes." He sat back, satisfied his announcement had knocked the laughter out of me. "Money can buy anything, Robbie. That bastard is to die on the anniversary of your mother's death. At exactly eleven-ten in the morning. And if he's not alone, his wife or children, whoever's with him, are to die, too. Slowly, in agony. I want them to suffer like I have—like your mother did."

"Mother told me she was never in any pain."

"That's beside the point," he almost shouted.

"But what about Delia? And me? You could ruin our lives—our futures. There'd be headlines, reporters, we'd be humiliated. You'd end up in prison."

"It'll be done right."

"Don't you care about any of us?"

"He killed your mother. You expect me to let him get away with that?"

I walked over to him. Softly I tried to reason. "No one killed Mother. She had cancer . . . and she died."

"She didn't have cancer. She was getting better. You heard what they said. It was that doctor; he killed her. And I'm going to kill him."

"I can't talk to you now." I walked down the hall and went to the room I shared with Delia. In the morning I'd tell my sister that our father was crazy. She'd laugh and say, "So tell me something I don't already know."

By the time I returned to Omaha, it was late. The nine-hour car ride had allowed time for lots of thinking. I called Delia.

"I really think we should take Dad's threat seriously."

"Me too." She offered no resistance.

"Before we do anything, I've got to be sure. I'll try to trip him up or get him to admit he lied."

"Do it now. Please," Delia asked. "I can't sleep until you do."

"Right now."

I made a cup of tea to warm my hands, spirit, and mood. All the time wondering when things would get back to normal. But as Delia had said at the funeral, "Normal will never be normal again."

Finally I placed the call.

Dad spoke in a calm and serious tone. "I meant every word. Everything's been taken care of; there's nothing you can do now."

Then I lost it. All of it: my composure, my logic, my last shred of loyalty. "How can you do this?" I screamed hysterically. "How can you do this to us?"

Slowly, he explained, "Nothing will go wrong. No one will ever know. Just forget about it; it doesn't concern you."

"Please," I was crying now, "please . . ."

"You don't owe this man anything. He's a murderer."

"No . . ." I stopped. And that proverbial straw, the one that broke the camel's back, had finally been hoisted upon my own. I hung up the phone.

"From here on out," I later told Delia, "we're taking care of ourselves because no one else will. I'll go see a guy I know—a criminal lawyer. I'll pick his brain."

"You're the mother now," she said. "Please. Don't let Daddy hurt us."

"I won't," I said, and swore silently to protect us both.

Our lives had suddenly taken on a soap opera quality and I did not like being cast in the role of victim.

Bradley Johnson has this great office located in the Old Market area. A bricked passageway, flanked on one side by restaurants and on the other by shops, is illuminated by large skylights. Bradley's office is at the top of four flights of wooden stairs.

His secretary, Lucy, sits behind a small desk and greets clients with a cup of coffee.

"I heard your mother died. Harry told me. I'm so sorry." She buzzed Bradley.

"Thanks."

Brad escorted me into the large room that serves as his office, meeting room, and lounge. We sat next to the tall windows he prefers to keep free from draperies. He shifted his legs and leaned back in an overstuffed chair.

I confided everything. Bradley reacted with a raised eyebrow.

"Legally, there isn't a thing you can do, Robbie. It's your word against his."

"What I wanted, I guess, was more of a favor. I thought maybe you could contact my father, tell him we've talked. That might scare him enough to call everything off—if there really is a hit man. This way I'd be covered, the doctor would be safe, and my father would have to forget about all this."

"My advice is to call Dr. Blair yourself. Explain the situation, see what he suggests. That's the best you can do. But, Robbie?"

"Yeah?"

"None of this is your fault. You know that, don't you?"

"I guess. It's just that I feel so . . . dirty. It's hard to explain."

The hospital receptionist said Dr. Blair was with a patient and would get back to me. I knew he kept late hours and told her I'd wait up for his call, no matter what the time.

Around ten o'clock he called.

He was kind and my hands immediately started to shake. I finally worked the conversation around to where it should have started.

"My father told me he holds you responsible for my mother's death."

"Your father has been through a lot. Your mother and he were married forty-some years. It's only natural he misses her."

"I know. But . . . Doctor?" Nothing would ever be as difficult as this moment. "My father told me he's hired someone to have you killed."

Silence.

"Let me take this call on my private line, Ms. Stanton. Hold on a minute."

When he came back, his tone was hushed. "You don't really think he's serious?"

"Yes I do. It's to be done in four months, on the anniversary of my mother's death." My voice trembled. I felt sorrier for all of us having to go through this than I ever could for my father.

Dr. Blair said he wanted to think about things. He'd get back to me.

Sergeant Danta of the Oak Lawn Police Department contacted me two days later. Dr. Blair had filed a complaint.

I'd talked with police before. Lots of times. But this was about me . . . my life. I repeated my story for what seemed like the hundredth time and for the hundredth time I didn't believe it myself.

"We'll have to proceed with this as if it were truth. But tell me, Ms. Stanton . . . would you be willing to testify against your father in a court of law?"

I thought about all the years I'd worked for Dad's approval. I thought about all the agony Delia and I were going through so soon after losing our mother. And I answered.

"No."

"Call on line two. Pick it up, Roberta," Harry barked.

"Miss Stanton? I'm Detective Carter, with the Chicago Police Department. A report has been filed with us concerning your father."

"I've already been through this with Sergeant Danta."

"Danta's out of Oak Lawn, where the hospital is located. We need something filed in your father's precinct."

"Oh." I repeated my story from the day before.

"I have to tell you, Miss Stanton, when he first opened the door—"

"Wait a minute. You spoke to my father? You confronted him? In person? What did he say about Dr. Blair?"

"We had to get his statement. He said he thought the doctor killed your mother."

I suddenly felt as though I'd been strapped into a roller-coaster and was slowly being hauled up to the top of Anxiety Mountain. I could hear the gears clicking. And I prayed I wouldn't crack before Christmas reared its holy head.

"Your father's in bad shape."

"We all are."

"There's nothing else we can do."

"I know."

Detective Carter apologized and promised there would be no need to disturb my father again.

"Get any last night?" Ken asked as I walked through the door.

I punched him on the shoulder. "Scum."

"You may think I like it when you call me that, but I don't," he complained.

"Sorry. I had an awful night, didn't sleep at all."

He waited for the punch line and when none came, he shrugged and sat down at the computer.

Harry came banging in from outside and a frigid gust slammed the door. "Roberta. In my office. Now."

I followed behind, a little spaniel, and watched as his boots tracked wet black prints along the dirty carpet.

"Close the door." Harry pulled his gloves off and stuffed them into his pockets. Without removing the snowflaked overcoat, he abruptly turned.

"The body of one Dr. Blair, practicing out of Christ Community Hospital, in Oak Lawn, Illinois, was found this morning in the trunk of his car. The car was parked in the doctor's reserved space in the hospital lot. He had been beaten to death. They think it was one of those aluminum baseball bats. Very sloppy. I spoke with Sergeant Danta. He said it definitely was not a professional hit."

Click . . . click . . . hang on.

"Your father's in custody."

"Was anyone else with the doctor?"

"No."

I turned and we just looked at each other for a minute.

"What do I do?"

"Go home. The police will be calling you."

"Don't tell anyone. I feel so ashamed."

"It'll be all over the news soon enough." Harry shook his head in disbelief. "Go on, get your butt out of here."

After talking with the police, I booked a flight into St. Louis.

Delia was in shock when I told her. "Oh God, oh God, oh God," she repeated. "He really did it. Oh God."

"Will you meet me at the St. Louis airport at ten-five tonight?" Springfield was only a few hours away and I knew the distraction would be good for her.

"I guess. But why St. Louis?"

I didn't want to scare her, to tell her that soon reporters and television crews would be camped out on her front lawn.

"We need to be together now," I said.

When my flight finally landed, I spotted Delia standing by a fat man in a blue sweat suit. I could tell she'd been crying. I smiled a hello.

We walked silently to the baggage claim and then she said, "Oh, I almost forgot. Your office called. Ken somebody. He wants you to call him tonight. Here's his number."

After we registered and fought over who got which bed, I called Ken from the hotel.

"You lose our bet."

"What bet? What are you talking about?"

"Computers versus brains." He sounded so sad.

"That was months ago. The Tanner case."

"No, now . . . the Stanton case."

"I'm tired and . . ."

"The computer. I was playing around with it today and punched in your name, Robbie. It showed all your credit card charges for the past year."

"And?"

"There was this code number that looked familiar. When I cross-referenced with the police computer, we came up with 'Freedom, Inc.' They offer a very unique personal service. Geez, you can buy anything with a Visa card. It's really disgusting."

Click . . . click . . . click . . .

"We plugged into the airline computer and know you're in St. Louis. Even the phone number you're calling from is being recorded. . . . Why'd you do it, Robbie? Your own father?"

"Ken . . . Kenny." I know he loves it when I talk in my little girl voice. Daddy always did. "I had to protect all of us. Delia and I don't want Daddy to bully us anymore. And this way, he won't be alone. Maybe the doctors can help him now."

It's those gentle insanities that bring such clear insight. The huge problems only come once in a while. They're easy to fix. But the small, everyday, constant, infuriating irritations drop you over the edge.

Click . . . click . . . click.

CAROLYN G. HART

Carolyn Hart describes her Annie Laurence–Max Darling series as primarily exploring the exercise of power in personal relationships, and doing it, she might have added, in an endearingly lighthearted and amusing way. Her novels have won Anthony, Agatha, and Macavity Awards.

A past-president of Sisters in Crime, Carolyn Hart has also worked as a journalist. It is this last experience she uses in creating her new sleuth, Henrie O (Henrietta O'Dwyer Collins), a retired newspaper woman with a sharp wit and a sharp tongue, who made her novel debut in *Dead Man's Island*, followed by *Scandal in Fair Haven*.

In "An Almost Perfect Murder," Henrie O finds that old friends are not necessarily best friends, and memories can be deceiving.

AN ALMOST PERFECT
MURDER

A young friend of mine—Homicide Lieutenant Don Brown, Derry Hills (Missouri) Police
Department—insists I can smell murder.

That's extravagant, of course.

But I do like for facts to add up.

When they don't, I ask questions.

On the surface, the facts of Sylvia Fulton's
unexpected death appeared reasonable, even if
sad and ironic.

Sad because the death of an old friend
brings memories, and memories are always, ul-
timately, sad. Faded lives, faded days forever
gone, the ghosts of laughter and vigor.

Ironic because I had not thought of Sylvia in
years, and we had only a few seconds to talk
before she met her last deadline.

It began with her phone call. I always reach
for a ringing phone with a flicker of anticipation, the legacy of almost fifty years as a reporter. Those days were over, yet the swift
flutter of eagerness remains. The new, the unknown, the unexpected, delight me.

"Hello?" I can no more quench the questioning lift to my voice than I can suppress a
curiosity stronger than any cat's.

"Henrietta O'Dwyer Collins? Henrie O?"

I didn't recognize the voice. "Yes."

"Oh God, that's great. This is Sylvia Montague. Sylvia Fulton now."

I knew the name, of course. She'd done a couple of very successful books on famous criminal trials. And there was one trial in particular . . .

"The Hammonds case," I said immediately.

"You remember."

"How could anyone ever forget?" Sylvia Montague and I both covered that trial. I remembered her well. Tall. Blond. Deep, brisk voice. Oh yes, I remembered. South Carolina summer heat. A sweltering courtroom. And the strangest corkscrew of a mystery I ever encountered. Sylvia and I'd struck up a quick, cheerful friendship and exchanged Christmas cards for a while, but our paths didn't cross again and we'd lost track of each other years ago.

"Sylvia." I suppose my response was pleasure mixed with surprise.

"Actually, I live around here. Saw in the paper where you were in town to speak to the Women's Caucus. I know the program chair so she gave me your number. Understand you gave 'em hell."

I'm not big on buzz words. But empowerment is no joke. I consider myself a foot soldier in a battle that isn't over. Not so long as women still earn seventy cents to a man's dollar. Not so long as glass ceilings keep females and minorities in second-tier roles. Not so long as the power in the U.S. Senate resides in the plump hands of privileged white men who haven't the imagination to understand why sexually harassed women keep their mouths shut. That, or the Honorables don't give a damn.

"You rattled some cages." A hearty laugh.

The laughter brought her so clearly to mind. A big bony face like an intelligent horse, light blue eyes with a sardonic gleam, a wide mouth that smiled easily.

"Good," I said. "One of my specialties." That and never, never, never taking no for an answer. I haven't changed much over the years, in attitude or appearance. I could see my reflection in the motel room mirror, dark hair, a Roman coin profile, dark brown eyes that have seen much and remembered much, and an angular body with a lean and hungry appearance of forward motion even when at rest. No one's ever called me restful. And I still take pride and delight in the nickname given me by my late husband Richard. He called me Henrie O, saying I packed more surprises into a single day than O. Henry ever put in a short story. Dear Richard.

"Henrie O." Sylvia's tone changed. It marked the end of social pleasantries; time for business. "When I saw your name—God, it seemed like an answer to a prayer. It would be god-awful if I were wrong! Listen, if you've got a few minutes this morning, I . . ." Her voice broke off. I heard, faintly, a scraping, rattly sound. "Oh . . . there's Gordon's car." Surprise lifted her voice. "I'll call you right back."

I was left holding a disconnected phone, listening to the flat, mindless buzz. I slapped down the receiver irritably. When the phone rang, I'd been walking toward the door, suitcase in hand, ready to check out of the pistachio-colored cottage and drive down the spectacular coast road to Sausalito. Actually, it was sheer fortuity Sylvia had caught me at all. I'd been unable to resist the temptation of one last slow jog along the road with the gorgeous view of waves crashing against the jagged cliffs. Otherwise, I would have checked out two hours sooner.

I've never waited patiently. I gave it fifteen minutes, then flipped through the phone book and found the Gordon Fulton residence on the winding coastal road just north of Sequoia Cliffs. I dialed the home number. Four rings and the ubiquitous answering machine: "You have reached . . ." I hung up, waited ten minutes, tried again. The same result.

I shrugged it away. I had no reason to hang about, snarling my plans, to see a woman I'd once known for a brief period.

I checked out, left word—for Sylvia should she call again—that I was en route to Sausalito and the hotel where I could be reached.

But on the outskirts of town, I swung the rental car into a gas station. I used the outside phone and once again heard the recorded voice. I called the inn I'd just left. No messages for me.

Maybe wealth and age had made Sylvia inconsiderate.

I didn't remember her that way.

That's why, twenty minutes later, following the directions of the station attendant, I pulled up at a barred gate. There was just room to park. I tried the intercom attached to the gate, above the electronic number pad.

No one answered the intercom. I looked at the gate.

That was another topic I could have discussed at the Women's Caucus —the withdrawal of rich Americans into barred and walled enclaves. Us. And Them. The Rich and the Fearful; the Poor and the Dangerous.

Beyond the gate, the graveled road curved out of sight amid eucalyptus and gnarled cypress.

I looked at the keypad. Members of the household would have devices in their cars to activate the gate. Still, they all would need to remember the number. I glanced up at the bronze numbers adorning the gate, 69.

People are mentally lazy.

I punched in 96. Nothing happened.

I keyed 96 twice in succession. No luck.

I tried 15, then 15 twice. No luck. Okay, how about 30? Nope. Then 45. The gate on its well-oiled hinges swung inward.

That's the trick to managing numbers in our increasingly arithmetically defined society (SS #, PIN #, FAX #, Voice Mail #), pick a number you can't forget. To make it easy, use a familiar number like the address, add the digits, then multiply. To outfox burglars, do times three.

Only problem is, the forces of evil can think, too. I wasn't including myself, of course, in that category as the car bucketed past the open gate and sped up the winding road. When the car swept into the circular bricked drive, I caught my breath. Not even the French Riviera is as gorgeous and compelling as the rocky, wild northern California coast. Sunlight glinted on the red-tiled roof of the Mission-style mansion.

I grinned. Was Sylvia going to be surprised to see me.

But there was no answer when I rang the bell. I even walked around the house, tried the back door, and took a moment to gaze out at the vivid blue water. Sunlight danced on the white caps. The surf crashing below boomed like holiday cannons. I almost followed the path out onto the headland, but I was beginning to feel like a trespasser. Definitely, no one was at home. I retraced my steps and climbed into the car. Obviously, I'd imagined the stress I'd thought I'd heard in Sylvia's voice. In any event, the matter hadn't been important enough for her to call me back.

That's as much consideration as I gave it until I was drinking Kona coffee and eating a brioche on the hotel balcony in Sausalito the next morning and, of course, reading the local newspaper. The story rated a two-col. head in the lower left of the first page:

FORMER NEWS REPORTER, SYLVIA FULTON, DIES IN CLIFF ACCIDENT

Longtime AP reporter Sylvia Montague Fulton died Thursday when her wheelchair plunged over the side of the cliff behind the mansion where she lived with her husband, Gordon Fulton, a prominent Sequoia Cliffs attorney.

Fulton suffered massive head and trunk injuries in the fall. Police today theorized that Fulton lost control of the motorized wheelchair. There are no guardrails on the path where the accident occurred and a sheer hundred-foot drop to a boulder-strewn bay. Fulton had been confined to a wheelchair since a car accident two years ago in which she suffered injuries resulting in partial paralysis.

No one was at the home when the accident occurred but police report that the victim's watch apparently shattered during the fall down the rugged cliffside and had stopped at 11:22. The battered body, half-submerged in the surf, was found upon her husband's return from his office at shortly after 5 P.M.

There was a good deal more, of course. A summary of Sylvia's career, titles of her two books on famous trials, and personal information. She was Gordon Fulton's second wife. He was a widower when they met. Sylvia's stepchildren were Mark and Delores Fulton. Mark and his wife, Emma, lived in Thousand Oaks. Delores lived with her father and stepmother.

The time of Sylvia's death was the most important fact I gleaned from the news report. I'd talked to her at a quarter past eleven. She ended our call—because her husband had come home. Very shortly thereafter, she fell to her death. She was already dead when I arrived at the house and found no one there.

The question jumped out, of course.

What happened between the time Gordon Fulton arrived and shortly after noon when I reached the house?

Was Sylvia's husband there for a few moments only? Had the accident occurred after he left?

That had to be the explanation if, indeed, Fulton didn't find Sylvia's body until "his return from his office" late in the afternoon.

The answer was perhaps so obvious that the question didn't need to be asked.

But I've learned over time never to trust the obvious.

Police officers come in all the sizes and varieties common to the rest of humankind—bright or stupid, diligent or lazy, honest or venal, dispassionate or prejudiced. . . . And the combinations are as endless. What kind of havoc can result when the detective is bright, diligent—and corrupt? Imagine the failures of the stupid but honest cop.

But there is a common veneer, a stolid, dogged watchfulness, a cultivated, protective stolidity. Only the eyes seem to be alive in those faces, eyes tainted with despair, dulled by weariness, imprinted with harsh memories, resistant to emotion.

Lieutenant Laura MacKay of the Sequoia Cliffs Police Department was no exception. Her smooth face might have been cast in Plexiglas. But her icy gray eyes probed mine.

"Her husband's car?"

"To be precise, Sylvia said, 'Oh, there's Gordon's car. I'll call you right back.' Did Fulton tell you he'd been home at almost the moment his wife is presumed to have died?"

MacKay tapped a closed folder with her pen. "No." She stared at me without warmth. "What's in it for you?"

"I don't like murder."

"There's no indication it was murder."

"Funny she's got a problem so pressing she calls on a woman she hasn't seen in years, gets off the phone to see her husband, and next thing we know she's dead on the rocks."

MacKay flipped open the folder. "Accident. That's the official conclusion. Could be suicide." Those cold eyes studied me. "Could be murder. Nothing wrong with the chair mechanically. No evidence she blacked out before she fell. We'll never know."

I was ready to plunge into speech, but the lieutenant held up her hand. "We'll check with Mr. Fulton."

My memory of Sylvia's funeral will always be of dark and twisted cypress and a lowering sky and a chill wind that rattled the green canopy over the open gravesite.

There were almost a hundred mourners present. Sylvia would have liked that.

A memory popped into my mind: the two of us seeking a patch of shade beneath a magnolia on the South Carolina courthouse lawn, the sweet sharp burn of cold Coke down a dry throat. Sylvia had thrown back that mane of blond hair and exploded, "Jesus, it's too frigging hot to live! These goddam people must be salamanders."

She would never be hot again.

Her family, looking stiff and forlorn as families always do, sat on the metal folding chairs, eye level with the bronze casket.

The priest spoke too softly to be heard where I stood.

Leaves crackled behind me.

"Fulton says somebody's mistaken." MacKay's voice was as matter-of-fact as a clerk making change. "Says he never left his office that day." The homicide detective hunched her shoulders, jammed her hands deep into the pockets of her gray all-weather coat. She faced the gravesite, her face as devoid of expression as her mirrored sunglasses. "Fulton drives a red '92 Mercedes sedan. Vanity plates: Cheerio." She nudged a clump of springy grass with the toe of her shoe. "Understand she was a sharp woman. Don't suppose she imagined that car." The shiny sunglasses turned toward me. "Of course, I don't have anybody's word for that conversation but yours."

Cars were parked at odd angles all the way up the road to the Fulton mansion. The turnaround was jammed. Two young men in navy blue suits handled the parking, giving tickets to the visitors.

The house was jammed, too. I was behind a group of leggy middle-aged women. One of them said, "Sylvia always did say to hold her over till a rainy Monday."

"That's what she hated the most. About the car wreck," a breathy blonde murmured. "Not being able to play anymore."

It wasn't hard to guess golf was the game from their weathered faces and rangy stride.

But I wasn't interested in meeting Sylvia's friends. I made a beeline for the family, clustered in the center of a living room large enough to house an Olympic team.

Such a nice-looking family. A voice echoed in my mind. "Such nice people." That was one of my aunt Martha's favorite phrases. It reflected, of course, how nonjudgmental Aunt Martha was. She always saw everyone as good. It certainly would have been her call about the Fultons.

Nice people in deep pain. Gordon Fulton's face looked desolate, like bombed-out ruins. His son, Mark, kept shaking his head mournfully. Sylvia's stepdaughter, Delores, had red and puffy eyes. As the line of comforters edged closer, I heard her say, "Oh, it's so awful. I still can't believe it. Sylvia was the most alive person I ever knew—even after the accident." She rubbed her eyes with a sodden handkerchief.

I was armed, when I reached them, not only with chutzpah but with enough information to do full-length stories on each of them. It's amazing how much you can find out about people if you have the electronic savvy: credit records, property transfers, moving vehicle violations (and any other criminal charges), media coverage, educational backgrounds, hospital records, insurance policies, class attendance records, sales transactions, hotel reservations.

I knew that Mark Fulton, a computer science professor, was teaching his regular eleven o'clock class the day Sylvia died, which spotted him four hundred miles south of the cliffs. His wife was playing doubles at a

Thousand Oaks tennis club. Delores was at work at a gift shop in Sequoia Cliffs. Her clerk's number was on a Visa charge logged in at eleven-twelve. Inez and Ernesto, the Filipino couple who worked for the Fultons, were in the waiting room of an oculist at eleven-fifteen.

So I focused on Gordon Fulton. The attorney was, according to his secretary, in his office all morning and had lunch delivered to his desk at twelve-fifteen. I had a plan of the building. There was a private exit from his office that he could have used. The time would have been close, but it was possible. The parking garage was unattended. Building residents used electronic cards to enter and leave.

So, yes, he could have shoved Sylvia's wheelchair over the side of the cliff. But why? I'd dug deep. If Fulton had been carrying on an affair, he was a master of discretion. I hadn't, despite heroic efforts, uncovered any evidence to indicate he was anything other than a model husband, totally devoted to his second wife, both before and after her confinement to a wheelchair. As for money, the second greatest incitement to murder after lust, the bulk of it belonged to him. Sylvia's books had earned tidy sums, but nothing to tempt a man with assets of more than three million.

I would continue to dig.

I came face to face with Gordon Fulton. He was tall and lean, sharp-featured, his nose a beak, his deep-set eyes hooded beneath thick gray eyebrows. But today he looked shrunken in his gray pinstripe, deep hollows beneath his reddened eyes, his hands hanging limply at his sides.

He tried to focus on me. "Good of you to . . ."

Delores was talking to the woman behind me. ". . . been home just a week. God, we had such a great time. I'm so glad now that . . ."

I held out my hand, gripped Gordon's firmly. "I'm Henrietta O'Dwyer Collins, an old friend of Sylvia's. I was on the phone with her that morning."

"That morning?" Suddenly he really looked at me, his green eyes—remarkably vivid eyes—coming alive.

"I'm doing a book on top women reporters. Sylvia'd agreed to let me poke through her papers."

He still held my hand, clung to my hand. "She was a wonderful reporter. She's worth a book all by herself." A faint flush stained his pale cheeks. "Maybe . . . maybe that's what you might consider."

I've seen a lot of anguish. I've known anguish. And I had no doubt that I was seeing a man who was heartsick, a man suffering a grievous, almost unbearable loss.

But, dammit, Sylvia saw his car! And he'd denied leaving his office.

Fulton was still talking, introducing me to Mark and Emma and Delores, then sweeping me out of the room and into a short hall. He flung open the door to a study at the corner of the house with three walls of windows, encompassing the front drive, the headland, and the open Pacific.

How the hell Sylvia'd ever concentrated in here I couldn't imagine. As we stood there, the morning's heavy mist rolled away. Brilliant shafts of sunlight spilled through the windows. The view was breathtaking and, even through the closed windows, there was the constant, dull boom of the surf crashing into the rocky cliff.

The rapid eager voice stopped. He awkwardly brushed his arm against his eyes. "Everything's here. You're welcome to come any time. I . . . ." His shoulders slumped. "I've got to get back—but we'll do everything we can to help." He stared at the untenanted desk for a long moment, then turned abruptly and headed back toward the houseful of mourners.

The one non-window wall, the one with the door through which we'd entered, was covered with framed clips, the big stories she'd covered. A faded news photo of Sylvia with Maggie Higgins near Inchon. The bombing of the Casbah in Algiers. The presidential inauguration of De Gaulle. The Bay of Pigs. The Freedom Walk from Selma to Montgomery. The famous—and infamous—trials. The kidnapping and murder of little Bobby Greenlease. The Manson horror. And more, so much more.

I swung around, moved toward the desk, and stopped dead still. I was looking out onto the drive, packed now with the cars of mourners. This must have been Sylvia's view as we talked on Thursday morning. It was almost the same time, just after eleven. And the brilliant sunlight, diamond-bright, glittered off the hoods and windshields and chrome of the cars.

Eyes squeezed almost shut against the harsh reflections, I could see the automobiles, yes, but I couldn't see through the windshields.

Sweet Jesus.

That changed everything.

"Dammit, Henrie O, think!" I'll admit to occasional vocal self-exhortations. Maybe it's just what I needed because suddenly I understood. I'd gone at it all wrong.

The key fact wasn't what Sylvia said during that brief call—it was that she'd called at all.

Why call me?

There could be only one reason.

I swung around. I spent fifteen minutes making a careful, thorough survey of Sylvia's trophy wall and felt a sudden cold certainty at what I *didn't* find, the Hammonds trial. When I looked very close, I could see how some frames had been shifted to cover an empty patch. In her bookcase, I spotted copies of both her books. I picked up the second, *Killing Days,* and checked the Index. Yes, there was the chapter on the Hammonds trial, "Murder Down in Dixie." I could imagine how urgently the murderer wanted to take this book, how painful it was to leave it behind. I slipped it into my purse. My purse, always a leather shoulder bag, is large enough to carry a book or two, a gun, a folded umbrella. Whatever the day demands.

I found the butler in the kitchen.

"Pardon me, Ernesto. Mr. Fulton's asked me to look in his car pocket for a list he needs." I nodded toward a door. "Does that lead to the garage?"

"Yes, ma'am." He held the door for me.

One's actions are rarely questioned if sufficient authority is exuded.

I stepped down into the garage.

I saw the Mercedes immediately. Yes, a crimson 1992 Mercedes sedan with vanity plates. But that wasn't what I sought.

Instead, I stared at the pegboard with its neatly labeled row of hooks. Car keys dangled from each hook. I nodded in satisfaction. Then I opened the driver's door to the Mercedes and looked at the visor and the little leather folder clipped there. I unclipped it and pulled out the entrance card to the Lincoln's Inn Parking garage that served the building where Gordon Fulton officed.

Back in the kitchen, I waited until Ernesto returned, bearing a tray of used glasses.

"Ernesto, if you have a moment, please."

He looked at me patiently.

"Mr. Fulton's car keys, the extra set. How long were they missing?"

"I'm not certain, madam."

I had the same feeling—pure pleasure—that you get when the horseshoe drops neatly around the stake on the very first throw. Because, if my theory was right, the car keys had to have been missing just before Sylvia died.

"When were they found?"

He was at the drainboard now, transferring the soiled glasses from the tray. "I don't know, madam. They weren't on the board Thursday morning when I needed to move a car. Then, with Mrs. Fulton's accident, I didn't notice. But they were there this morning." He began to fill the tray with fresh cups and glasses.

"So you first missed them Thursday morning?"

He frowned, trying to remember. "Yes, madam, I think so."

I persisted. This was important. Ernesto finally tied the disappearance to Thursday because "I know the keys were there Wednesday night. I moved the car to get ready for the party."

Have you ever drawn a royal flush? That's how I felt. Because the party was the final necessary component to my equation.

"What was the occasion for the party, Ernesto?"

For the first time, the manservant's composure wavered. His eyes filled. "It was a welcome-home party for Mrs. Fulton and Miss Delores. They'd been gone for six months on a trip around the world. They got home on Saturday and the party was Wednesday night and on Thursday—" He busied himself with the glasses.

So, Sylvia and her stepdaughter were out of town for six months. They returned home on a Saturday. The following Thursday Sylvia's wheelchair went over the side of the cliff. The keys to the red Mercedes were not in their usual place on Thursday morning.

Someone at the party . . .

"The party," Ernesto said mournfully. "Oh, madam, it was such a wonderful party. Everyone was so happy to welcome them home. The house was full of laughter and cheer—and to think Mrs. Fulton only came home to die."

Because, and I knew it had to be true, at that party Sylvia saw a face she thought she recognized, but, more than that, Sylvia must have learned some fact at the party that moved her to call me the next morning.

I was remembering Sylvia more and more clearly now, her good humor, her intensity, her capacity for hard work—and her lack of subtlety. There was no guile in her nature.

Had she been less open, less frank, less easily read, she might be alive now.

I surprised myself by going back to the cemetery. But why not? That's where the dead reside and I had a lot of thinking to do about death, present and past.

A particular death, that of Elbert Hammonds of the famous Hammonds case, the case with no clips on Sylvia's wall, the case that was the only link between me and Sylvia.

I settled on a fairly comfortable bench near Sylvia's fresh grave. I opened my purse, pulled out Sylvia's second book, the one containing the chapter on the murder of Elbert Hammonds, and flipped to page forty-six.

As I started to read, I could smell that courtroom, the sourness of spittoons and the sweaty, talcumed scent of too many bodies pressed too close together in cloying heat.

THE HAMMONDS CASE

Tobacco money made the Hammondses rich. Some said tobacco money stained their souls. Certainly tragedy and scandal were forever linked to the name. Tobacco wealth made it easy for earlier generations to indulge whims, including the construction of Hammonds Castle, a huge, grotesque limestone castle with battlements, corner towers, and a drawbridge over a moat filled with sluggish, algae-scummed water from a nearby swamp. The castle stood on a ridge five miles from the nearest tiny town and through time many stories were whispered about the Hammonds, about the bloody cockfights and worse, about the ghost of a slave girl who screamed for help when the moon was high, about the drunken revelry when Elbert was young, about his wife who ran away (he said) when their daughter was a little girl (but some believed his wife's bones rotted in a nearby swamp), about Elbert's daughter, Lily Belle, who made a loveless marriage, then came home to bear a twin son and daughter before dying.

Oddly, the beautiful grandchildren appeared to work a change in Elbert's soul. He married a local schoolteacher and decorum settled over Hammonds Castle. Elbert doted on Billy and Chloe. Their every wish was his command. And he would never hear a word of criticism about his beloved grandchildren, both slim and graceful creatures with golden hair and sapphire eyes in elegantly boned faces. When the twins were home from college, parties and balls again were held and sometimes there were whispers of drugs and wild nights, especially when their grandfather, now widowed again, was gone on one of his yearly journeys abroad.

The little town was surprised when Elbert returned home in the early spring of 1973 with a new bride, Louise, a young American woman he met in Cannes. Not much to look at, they said in the town. Short straight black hair and red lips bright as a Jezebel's. And unfriendly, keeping to herself and to the castle. Women snickered over morning coffee at the airs the new Mrs. Hammonds put on, with her tulle-swathed picture hats, and, worse than that, always wearing gloves, at home or away, day and night, some said even at meals. Who did she think she was? Everyone wondered how Billy and Chloe would react, but no one expected the stories that began to seep into town, about hot quarrels and slammed doors and threats from Elbert to turn the twins out.

It was on the clear, still morning of April 22 that Elbert was found dead at the foot of the stone stairs leading from the second-floor gallery to the flagstoned central hall.

A dreadful accident.

But a dowdily dressed maid, who had come to Hammonds Castle with the new wife, walked into the police station the next morning with her damning accusation: she saw Billy Hammonds and his grandfather on the gallery just after midnight and they were quarreling bitterly. She hurried past them and was starting up to the third floor and her room when she heard the old man scream, "Don't! No, no, don't!" and she'd run faster to get away from the ugly scene.

Billy denied it utterly. He swore he didn't come in until after 2 A.M. He said he was with a woman. But he refused to reveal her name.

A married woman, of course, that was what they whispered in town.

Chloe insisted her brother was innocent. And she claimed not to have heard a sound that night, though she'd slept restlessly.

It was the young widow who found the new will, the new unsigned will disinheriting Billy and Chloe.

The police arrested Billy. The trial began in late summer.

Sob sisters had a heyday writing about the trial with snide comments about the widow's refusal to attend, about Chloe's desperate face and tear-filled eyes, about Billy, his exquisite handsomeness, his grace and elegance, his charm. There were several grainy photographs in the book, showing a young man with, admittedly, a handsome face but it was almost too delicate, too fawnlike for a man.

I tried to imagine him twenty years later.

The face would still be narrow, fine-boned, aristocratic. That much he couldn't change.

There were several photographs, too, of Chloe. The delicacy better became her. With maturity, she might be today a strikingly beautiful woman.

Chloe needn't, of course, still be blond. That was also true of Billy. Surely I would recognize them if I saw them.

I put the book down on my lap and stared out over the cypress-and gravestone-studded hill.

I didn't need to read further. I'd been at the trial the remarkable, unforgettable day the defense brought Billy Hammonds to the stand. He told his story persuasively, his face appealing, his distress evident.

The maid was called. She told her story with relish, her identification of Billy decisive.

The defense attorney rose for cross-examination. I glanced down at the book, skimmed some pages. Oh yes, Mary Trent.

The defense attorney—a big redhead from Columbia, Stewart Warner —led her through the events of the fateful evening.

I found the passage in Sylvia's book:

"So there is no doubt in your mind, Miss Trent, that it was Billy Hammonds you saw that day?"

"I'm sure." She peered through thick-lensed glasses at Billy.

"How close were you to the defendant?"

"I walked right by him. I saw him, all right." She hunched forward in the witness box, her long frizzy blond hair lying lank on her shoulders.

"Despite your evident weak eyes, Miss Trent? Those glasses appear to be very strong. But you say you saw him clearly. Will you please describe the man—Oh, you're sure it was a man?"

"Yes. Yes." A vindictive glare at Billy.

"Will you describe that man?"

The maid lifted her hand—I remembered so well that accusing gesture and the maid's hand, her outstretched forefinger in such sharp contrast to her stubby, foreshortened, deformed middle finger—and pointed at the defense table and the elegantly handsome Billy Hammonds.

"There he is. He's sitting right there."

But her words were almost lost in a growing swell of sound. Exclamations broke out. Some people stood.

The defense attorney, as if surprised, swung around to look toward the spectators.

A young man walked down the aisle.

Gasps now. And cries of, "Look at him. Look!"

The judge rattled the bench with his gavel. "Silence. Silence in—" His voice broke off.

It was the shock of the doppelganger.

Warner shouted at the witness. "Or is this the young man you saw? Quickly now, Miss Trent. Who did you see that night? The defendant? Or this young man?"

Before the witness could answer, Billy's double whirled and ran from the courtroom.

Oh yes, I'd been there.

As gorgeous a Perry Mason twist as I'd ever seen in a courtroom.

It gave it away, of course, when Chloe ran. She could cut her hair like Billy's and wear his clothes—both were slim and their height and coloring the same—but no woman runs like a man.

However, for the prosecution's case, the damage was done.

It went to the jury. The prosecution denounced the "play-acting," but the jurors took their oath seriously. Certainly no one could ever be certain of the truth. Did Billy kill his grandfather and Chloe's clever ruse save him? Or had the maid perhaps seen Chloe in the darkness of the gallery and mistaken her for her brother Billy? Was Billy lying about his whereabouts that night—to protect Chloe? Were they co-murderers?

The verdict came back Not Guilty. The Scots' Not Proven would have been much closer to the mark.

I put the book back in my purse and pushed up from the bench. I still had much to do.

Want to know a small-town's secrets? Find the old, retired soc (journalese for society, now they dub it women's news) editor.

I tracked down Elvira Murchison the next morning. Her voice over the telephone was reedy but strong. "I always said there was a world we never knew about that murder. I don't know what was strangest, the way Billy and Chloe left town the day after the trial was over or the way we all woke up one morning to find the castle empty with the windows boarded over. Of course, there was talk. Turned out Elbert'd made a new will after he got back to town with his new wife. She got half the estate, Billy and Chloe the other half. The property was sold to a developer a few years later. He turned it into a country club and a subdivision. The castle's the clubhouse, wouldn't you know. But nobody who was there

the night of old Elbert's murder's ever set foot in this town again and
nobody knows where they went or what they're doing now."

I hung up the phone and looked at the doodles on the pad, Billy's and
Chloe's names, intertwined. They would be in their early forties now.

I felt sure I knew where one of them was, sitting pretty in northern
California.

It didn't take long in the local newspaper morgue to find the story I
was looking for.

PROMINENT ARCHITECT SUFFERS FATAL FALL

Arthur Robbins was found dead this morning by his wife, Elsa, at
the foot of the stairs in the hallway of their home, one of the coast's
most famous mansions.

A retired member of the architectural firm of Robbins, Poston,
and Berryhill, Robbins was one of California's most celebrated architects . . .

It was the final paragraph that convinced me I'd found my missing
Hammonds:

Robbins's first wife, Marian Whaley, died of cancer in 1990. He is
survived by three children from his first marriage, Diane Olcutt of
Northridge, Matthew of Sequoia Cliffs, and Anthony of Paterson,
New Jersey, and his second wife, the former Elsa Froman, whom he
married three months ago in St. Thomas.

There was a good deal in the story about Arthur's tennis prowess.
He'd won the Men's Senior Division just the week before.

Damn clumsy of such a talented athlete to fall down his own stairs.

Elbert fell down and died. Arthur fell down and died. Sylvia fell down
and died.

Not a lot of originality there, but who can quarrel with success? Ah,
Elsa. You must be feeling quite safe and satisfied. But not, I hoped, for
much longer.

"Art Robbins? Oh, sure, we were great friends." Gordon's voice held a
smile and sadness. "I called Sylvia in Rome when it happened but I told

her not to come home. It was too far and would have been too hard on her. Hell of a thing. He'd married this young woman and was really full of bounce."

"A young woman?"

Now the laughter was wry. "Oh, I suppose only in my eyes. Early forties. Seemed nice enough. Never had much to say. But Art had been damned lonely after he lost Marian."

To say I was discouraged was to put it mildly. Still I kept the binoculars trained on Elsa Robbins as she clipped flowers from her garden.

For a lovely fresh bouquet, no doubt. Such an appropriate task for a lady of the manor.

Dammit, she wasn't tall enough to be Chloe Hammonds. Much could be accounted for. The dark hair could be dyed. And even a slim woman can add pounds with years. But age doesn't lop three to four inches of height. And the face wasn't right. The fine elegant bone structure wasn't there. This wasn't exactly a coarse face, but those full lips and rounded cheeks could never belong to Chloe Hammonds.

While I watched the new widow, my mind buzzed with questions. Had I missed another accident among the people in the Fultons' circle?

I didn't think so.

Was I off the mark in every respect? Had a car similar to Gordon Fulton's arrived? No.

I held tight to the binoculars.

No.

The only way into the Fulton compound was through that electronic gate. Sylvia's murderer wanted Gordon's car just in case someone saw it arrive just before Sylvia's fatal plunge. Any questions would be asked of Arthur.

And I knew Sylvia had seen her husband's car. She told me so. But there was indirect proof Arthur's car was used. The missing keys. The party the night before when the keys could have been taken. The return of the keys. No doubt the murderer had an extra set made and, once Sylvia was over the cliff, the original set was silently hung on the pegboard, the duplicates used to drive the car back to Fulton's office garage.

It all fitted together beautifully—except the woman I was watching could not be Chloe Hammonds so my hypothesis broke down at its most critical juncture. I'd been so certain that Sylvia called me because of our connection with the Hammonds case.

The plump woman put the last flower in her basket. She stood and stripped off her gloves.

And the whole picture came clear.

Once again, I could see that long-ago courtroom and the "maid" pointing at Billy Hammonds, pointing with a forefinger that made her oddly foreshortened middle finger quite noticeable. Sylvia Montague was sitting beside me that day. It was a scene neither of us ever forgot.

Everything I'd ever read or known about the Hammonds case came together and I knew now, though it might be hell to prove, that there had never been a "maid," that she was the creation of Elbert Hammonds's new wife, Louise, that she was the way that bored young wife slipped out of the shadowed castle for freedom, that Billy and Chloe in their youth and beauty and arrogance didn't pay enough attention to realize the maid was never present at the same time as Louise, that the maid's long frizzy blond hair was a wig and her thick wire-framed glasses a disguise, that Louise wore gloves to hide her deformity, not in a twisted attempt to be a Southern belle. Had Billy perhaps noticed the maid's shortened finger and made a callous remark? Was that as much a reason for the "maid's" accusation as the hope of getting more of the estate if Billy were convicted? How Louise must have laughed and enjoyed using her clever creation as a witness to try and convict her stepson of a crime he hadn't committed.

Now, all I had to do was prove it.

The rest of the day I waged a full-scale assault by telephone. There were setbacks: the courthouse in South Carolina had burned to ashes eight years ago. "Files? Why, honey, we didn't save nothin'. I think the devil himself stoked that fire, it burned so hot and so fast." And nothing came of my efforts to trace Elsa Froman before St. Thomas.

When the phone rang, I grabbed it. Maybe this would be the call that would make a difference.

Her voice still had little inflection, but Lieutenant MacKay spoke with unusual urgency. "A gardener working on an oleander hedge saw Fulton's Mercedes Thursday morning. He knew the time. He was hungry and his lunch break would start in fifteen minutes. We're sure of the ID because he saw the plates, Cheerio."

"The driver?"

"Didn't notice."

"Damn."

"Ms. Collins, time we had a talk."

Obviously, Lieutenant MacKay was ready to pursue an investigation now that the substance of my conversation with Sylvia had been confirmed. The presence of Gordon Fulton's red car had to be accounted for before she was going to mark this case closed.

A police investigation . . . Oh yes. That I would like—as soon as I attended to a few matters. "Great. I'll be at your office at nine in the morning, Lieutenant." I hung up.

I was walking out the door when the phone rang. This time, I ignored it.

Strange cars stick out in rich folks' neighborhoods, but it wasn't hard to find a household on holiday. I picked a house two blocks from Elsa's, one with walls screening the parking area from the street.

I settled myself comfortably to wait for total darkness. Elsa/Louise was a great girl for planning ahead. Probably it wouldn't have helped even if the gardener had glimpsed the driver. No doubt she'd bunched her dark hair beneath a cap and worn sunglasses. Planning ahead all the way.

That's what I was counting on, Elsa/Louise's penchant for planning and her desire always to have a scapegoat handy. She'd taken Gordon's car, which could implicate him if questions ever arose about Sylvia's death. But what else might she have done to make Gordon an even likelier suspect? I had an idea. If I was guessing right, Elsa/Louise was going to be very surprised indeed at the final turn of events—assuming I succeeded in my quest tonight.

I reconnoitered around the house three times. She was sitting in a downstairs den, watching television. No servants were there.

The house, I was certain, was well locked, a sophisticated alarm system in place.

But I'd spotted a balcony on the back of the house and open french doors and the flutter of bedroom curtains.

I climbed up the trellis with no problem. Jogging doesn't do much for arm muscles, but weight training's very effective. I don't consider myself an exercise fiend, but keeping in shape has lots of nice rewards. In addition to climbing trellises.

Bingo. The lady's room, silken sheets already turned down for night.

It took me two minutes to speed across the room to the adjoining bath. Her hairbrush was nicely clogged with black hairs silver at the roots. In her closet, I thumbed through the sporting apparel and snagged threads from the right sleeve of a navy-blue warm-up.

My other stop that night took a few more minutes. I ran lightfooted up the Fulton's dark drive, cautiously working with the lock on a side door to the garage until it clicked open. I grabbed the Mercedes' keys from the pegboard and opened the trunk.

When I swept the trunk with my pencil flash, I knew I'd guessed right. The tire tool was shoved roughly beneath the carpet. I eased up the carpet. In the cone of light, the discoloration along the end of the tire tool was evident. And a wisp of blond hair. I dropped the carpet down and hoped Sylvia hadn't seen that blow coming.

I pulled an envelope out of my pocket and used tweezers to shake strands of hair—dark hair—onto the carpet.

I took more pains with the threads, making certain a clump wedged into the locking mechanism of the Mercedes.

When I shut the trunk, I paused for an instant, then moved swiftly to the driver's door. The car was unlocked. More dark hair, a few threads, and I was done.

Lieutenant MacKay sent me a clipping several months later.

POLICE OFFICER COMMENDED FOR BRILLIANT DETECTION

The Sequoia Cliffs City Council unanimously passed a proclamation today praising Homicide Detective Lieutenant Laura MacKay for her brilliance in using the most modern methods of detection to apprehend a cold-blooded and clever murderer.

Through sophisticated chemical analysis, cloth fibers and hair follicles successfully linked Mrs. Elsa Robbins to the bloodstained tire tool accounted responsible for the death of Sequoia Cliffs resident Sylvia Fulton last summer, resulting in Mrs. Robbins's conviction yesterday for Mrs. Fulton's murder. Furthermore, through diligent and far-ranging investigation, Lieutenant MacKay proved the second Mrs. Robbins to be the widow of a South Carolina murder victim twenty years ago, Elbert Hammonds, and suggests that she, not Hammonds's grandson, who was accused of the crime at the time and subsequently acquitted, was guilty of the murder. Police theorize now that the death of Mrs. Robbins's second husband, Arthur, was not an accident as was believed at the time. Instead, police suggest . . .

I nodded in satisfaction when I finished the article. As the reporter made clear, Elsa/Louise was quite a dandy little planner.

But then, so am I.

A contract between people who live
in the same house, be it between a writer and
her secretary, or a husband and wife, implies a
great deal more than what is written on paper.
The people involved assume they have similar
goals, or at least they *want* to believe that. But
things change, and when one of the parties to
these oh-so-personal relationships changes it
can spell disaster for the other.

Though Joan Hess and Michael Collins have
dealt with the same issue there is nothing similar in Hess's wry "Paper Trail" and Collins's
disturbing "Angel Eyes."

JOAN HESS

Creator of Claire Malloy, "a bookseller and mild-mannered amateur sleuth," and the town of Maggody, "a rowdy town where murder is downright crazy," fifth-generation Arkansan Joan Hess burst into the mystery scene with novels that leave readers laughing out loud. She has been awarded the *Druid Review* Readers Poll for best first novel *(Strangled Prose)*, the American Mystery Award for best traditional novel *(A Diet to Die For)*, and both the Agatha and Macavity for her short story "Too Much to Bare."

Of "Paper Trail," a tale of the joys and pitfalls of the writer's life, she says, "this story stalked into my mind at midnight and wrote itself the next day. I was but a vehicle. Creepy, huh?"

PAPER TRAIL

Wellington House
#1 Wellington Road
Hampser, NC 27444
November 13, 1972

The Hampser Hero
c/o Hampser High School
Hampser, NC 27444

To the faculty adviser:

Congratulations on your ranking in the national contest for high school journals. How exceedingly proud of your young men and women you must be! All I can say is "Bravo!" These days so many young people are obsessed with athletics, politics, and other less admirable pursuits. To have such a dedicated and talented group must bring you vast satisfaction.

I shall assume that you are aware of my novels published under the pseudonyms of Alisha Wells and Alexandra Worthington. I would be delighted to speak to your classes. Wellington House can be rather lonely at times, and I truly look forward to each and every opportunity to visit with my fans and discuss my work. I cannot begin to count the number of times I've presented talks at luncheons—and loved every bite of it!

Perhaps I take advantage of my position in the literary community when I make this modest proposal, but I think you will agree it offers a splendid opportunity for one of your students. My filing has simply gotten away from me, as if it were a freight train barreling through the door each and every day. I put away one paper, and three more arrive in the post! If it weren't so aggravating, it would be amusing. But what with my editors calling, the publicity demands, and the necessity of responding to an increasing amount of fan mail, I can hardly find the time to write.

I would be so deeply grateful if you could recommend a student to come in for an hour or two a week and help me conquer this quagmire of paperwork. I regret that I can pay only minimum wage, but I hope one of your students who aspires to become an author might find it interesting to deal with my busy work. I would prefer a young woman, especially one who needs financial help and will appreciate any guidance I can give her in her future career. Please call me at your convenience.

Yours truly,
Aurora Wellington

T'was the night before Christmas
or the week before, anyway

Dear Heather,

You are going to die when I tell you this! I mean, you'd better sit down before you read one more word! I am working for Aurora Wellington, who just happens to be Alisha Wells *and* Alexandra Worthington. Are you dead??? I was so excited when you sent me *The Willow Lake Legacy* for my birthday that I finished it that very night. Then last month Miss Hayes gets this letter from her, and she wants somebody to file papers for her, and Miss Hayes asks me if I want to, and I just about faint! Do I want to work for Aurora Wellington? That's like asking me if I wanna marry Paul McCartney—right?

Hayes is waiting, so I say I might if the hours are right, and she says well, if you're not interested I'll speak to Rebecca Lawson, and I say maybe I'll ask my mother and it might be okay (Ma's the same and no, Dad hasn't written, but I figure it's hard to find stamps in prison). Anyway, I say yeah, and she gives me a letter that's *actually* from Aurora Wellington and tells me to go to her house (!!!) Saturday morning at ten.

I put on my blue jumper and the super shirt you gave me for Christmas last year, but I'm about to wet my pants when I ring the bell.

She's written—what? forty books?—and I'm standing on her porch, ringing her bell like I'm a Girl Scout selling cookies. Finally, she answers the door, and is she beautiful! Think about it—how would you expect her to look? She's old, sure, but she has ash blond hair to her shoulders, deep lavender eyes like Elizabeth Taylor, and she's wearing—get this— a peignoir that's the exact same shade as her eyes. She's got to be at least fifty, but her complexion's right off the cover of *Seventeen*. She wouldn't make cheerleader—but who wants to be a dumb cheerleader when you can make zillions of dollars writing steamy novels?

My knees are knocking, but I manage to stammer my name and before I know it, we're sitting in the "parlor," as she calls it, me with a Coke and her with gin, and she's telling me (your humble second cousin!) her problems. Since I doubt Paul McCartney's going to call (for the record, Charlie and I broke up, so he's not calling either), I figure I've been snatched straight up to heaven. She tells me how she cannot concentrate on her "work" with all the paperwork lying around to depress her, and she wants me to come in for three hours on Saturday mornings and help out.

So for the last three Saturdays your cousin, the one and only greatest soon-to-be world-famous novelist, drops by the home of Aurora Wellington and reads her mail. Officially, I'm getting paid for three hours, but she comes in to chat and somehow it turns into four or five. Last week she had me do her grocery shopping on top of everything else, and I was so hungry I ate one of her apples on the way back from the store. If you'd like further details, you owe me a letter.

Eat your heart out,
Kristy

Wellington House
#1 Wellington Road
Hampser, NC 27444
March 15, 1973

Friends of the Barport Library
101 Swinton Lane
Barport, NC 27031

Dear Miss Chart,

Miss Wellington is dreadfully sorry that she will be unable to speak at your luncheon next month, and has asked me to pass along her regrets.

As you know, Miss Wellington has always felt nothing but the deepest respect for the public library system's dedication to literacy. Only her frantic writing schedule could deter her from the opportunity to express her gratitude for your good works in the community. She dearly hopes you will forgive her when you read *Devilish Delights* (by Alexandra Worthington) a year from now.

Yours truly,
Kristen Childers

March 23, 1973

Dear Miss Hayes,

I'm really sorry that I didn't have time to do the interview with the head of the creative writing department at the college. I know it's too late for excuses, but Miss Wellington is having me work all day on Saturdays and sometimes on Sundays, and my mother's in the hospital again. I promise that I'll do better and won't miss any deadlines.

Sorry,
Kristy C.

Wellington House
#1 Wellington Road
Hampser, NC 27444
May 3, 1973

Dear Tommie,

Your idea was absolutely brilliant! The girl isn't especially brilliant, but she is ever so diligent and such a perfectionist that at times I want to throw my hands in the air and give up the ghost. The child can be dictatorial, if you can believe it—I'm almost afraid to open my mail, read it, and lay it down somewhere in my office, because along will come grim little Kristy, the incriminating evidence clutched in her sweaty hand, demanding to know if I've lost the envelope with the return address or gone completely batty and responded without consulting her! Consulting her, mind you! I'm old enough to be . . . her big sister, not to mention being a best-selling author (did you see the divine review in *Heartbeat Digest* last week?), and I'm being ordered about by a sweet young snippet who's not yet graduated from high school.

I know, I'm being utterly absurd. Now that I've trained her, why shouldn't I allow her to take complete control of the tedium so that I can take advantage of all the lovely free time to write, write, write—and meet the next nasty deadline? Yes, Tommie darling, I'm well aware that the book's due in less than a month and that daft young adolescent in publicity is putting together the tour. If you were more of a friend and less of a slave driver, you'd absolutely insist they put me up at the Plaza this year.

Huggies,
Aurora Borealis

A midsummer night's eve (maybe)

Dear Cuz,

I am absolutely pea green jealous about you going to Chapel Hill! There'll be so many gorgeous men that you won't have time to study, much less to "pursue a degree in political history." Try to think fondly of me as you take a toke (just joking!!!).

The junior college will have to do until I find a bag of money on the street. Ma's back at the butterfly farm (aka the rehab center), as I'm sure Aunt Sissie has told you, and her health insurance has run out. Miss W. is letting me work every day for a few hours, but I'm barely scraping by. I'd ask Dad, but I think he earns about ten cents an hour making license plates. He sent me a box of stationery for graduation. I hear you got a car, you lucky dog. Want a personalized plate? I know where to get one —ha ha.

Yeah, I'd like to hit up Miss W. for a raise, but writers don't make as much money as you'd think and she has a pretty quiet life. Nobody ever comes by, as far as I can tell, and she doesn't do anything except write all day and brood all night. She got mad at her agent because of some silly thing, and changed her telephone number, so now it's unlisted. I may be the only person on the planet who can call her. And, boy, did I learn my lesson last week! On the way to her house, I had a flat tire, and by the time I got it changed, I was two hours late. She about had a kitten, and made me promise to call whenever I'm going to be five minutes late. Remember that crazy lady who lived next door to us the summer you came? Miss W. makes *her* look like a Junior League president!!!

Okay, I'm exaggerating—Miss W. doesn't own three dozen cats. Just one, and it's a mangy, motheaten old thing named Lady Amberline after the heroine in *Sweet Surrender* (or vice versa). I wish the darn thing would surrender itself to a garbage truck! Every time I look at her, I get itchy, and I spray myself for fleas once a week.

Charlie joined the army and shipped out to some base in Texas. The night before he left, we went out to dinner at a fancy restaurant and had this really serious talk, but basically he wants me to stay home and knit socks for two years. I would have laughed in his face—had I not been so tired that it sounded like a super idea.

To answer your nosy questions: I snooped through Miss W.'s papers and she is fifty-seven years old! Can you believe it? In person she looks every bit as sleek as she does on her cover shot, even if it was taken at least twenty years ago. She's never been married, although she does drop dark hints about a lost love, and her only relative is some cousin in Tallahassee who occasionally calls or writes. No, she doesn't read anyone else's books, but she absolutely despises Veronica St. James and is forever making hysterically funny comments about her. The house is about a hundred years old, and not in great shape, but it's "the ancestral home" that she inherited from dear departed "Papa" back in the days of the dinosaurs. The living room's a shrine to her awards (lots of them!) and yes, her bed has pink satin sheets and a ruffly canopy.

So, days with Miss W. and nights without Charlie. Life's a bowl of cherries, and I'm in the pits!!

Love,
Kristy

Wellington House
#1 Wellington Road
Hampser, NC 27444
February 27, 1974

Darling Tommie,

I shall arrive at the Plaza around five in the afternoon on Friday. I would adore to allow you to take me to dinner, but the train does take quite a long time and I'm afraid I'll be utterly exhausted. Tell Natalie that I shall call upon her at eleven the next morning to discuss this latest travesty of a cover. No reader in her right mind would give it a second glance—much less buy it!

Kristy will stay at the house during my tour to feed Lady Amberline, collect the mail, water the plants, and fend off burglars. The girl is a dear thing and ever so courageous about her family situation, which has all the makings of a gothic horror story. I've told you about her mother, a pathetic alcoholic, and her father, a contemporary blackguard if ever there were one. He's currently in prison for burglary, assault, attempted homicide, and a host of other barbaric charges.

Several weeks ago I drove by her house, simply out of curiosity, and it's one of those quaint tract houses with a weedy yellow lawn, at least one broken window, a cluttered carport, a roof within minutes of collapsing, and located in a development called, of all things, Clover Creek. Dandelion Dump would be more fitting!

Kristy dropped out of college this semester, saying she was unable to pay her tuition. She mentioned that she'd applied at a local restaurant for the night shift, but I told her in no uncertain terms that I should not be comfortable employing someone who, if I may lapse into colloquialisms, slings hash. No greasy fingers on my correspondence, thank you! Although my budget is already stretched to its meager limit, I told her to plan to put in a full day's work five days a week until she is able to return to school.

I must tell you this, Tommie dear, but never ever breathe a word of it to her! She's been dating a local boy for several months, and with her mother unavailable, I felt that someone should take a maternal interest in the matter and assess the boy. She arranged for him to come to the house to pick her up one evening last week, and brought him into the parlor to meet me. For the occasion, he chose blue jeans, white socks, sneakers, and the sort of blue cotton shirt one associates with factory workers (and why not? It seems he works at a poultry processing establishment!). I said nothing, of course, but the next day I did tell Kristy that he seemed curiously inarticulate, unintelligent, and we laughed until we cried as I painted a vivid picture of his dreary, beery future as a line foreman of a merry little band of chicken pluckers. I do believe we'll see no more of that young man, thank God. Kristy's indispensable, and I'm not about to allow her to elope with a moon-faced factory worker!

Anyway, darling, lunch at the Russian Tea Room on Saturday!

Your obedient servant,
Aurora

Wellington House
#1 Wellington Road
Hampser, NC 27444
March 15, 1974

Dear Mrs. Cathwright,

I regret to inform you that your services are no longer desired at Wellington House. I have reviewed the household accounts, and was tempted to bring to Miss Wellington's attention numerous questionable purchases from Maclay's Market, an establishment owned, I understand, by your brother-in-law.

However, I feel it best not to disturb Miss Wellington. Should you desire references, please contact me directly. Miss Wellington is much too preoccupied with her work to speak to you in person or to communicate with you in any fashion whatsoever, but if you insist, I cannot promise that she will not file charges. Enclosed is severance pay of two weeks.

Yours truly,
Kristen Childers

From the desk of Aurora Wellington
March 28, 1974

Dear Mrs. C.,

Kristy has told me of your sudden decision to retire and move to Earlsville to be near your son and grandchildren. Although I am devastated by the loss of your invaluable services after all these years, I do understand your feelings. I don't know how I shall survive without your chicken salad and flaky, sinfully rich cream pies. You've spoiled me rotten for twenty years, you wicked woman! Lady Amberline sends her fondest regards, and does hope you'll send photographs of those darling babies.

Warmly,
Miss W.

Wellington House
#1 Wellington Road
Hampser, NC 27444
September 2, 1975

Dear Mrs. Harold Maron,

I still giggle every time I think of you being married! Doesn't it feel totally weird to have a new name after all these years? Harold looks divine in the photographs, you are radiant, and even our bratty little cousin Wendy is sweet (did she put thistles in the flower basket?). I'm sick I missed the wedding.

Miss W. still hasn't recovered completely, and is doing most of her writing in bed these days. You'd think the doctors could figure out what's wrong after all those tests, but no one has any ideas and poor Miss W. often feels faint if she ventures downstairs. I helped her out to the garden yesterday and we sat in the gazebo all afternoon, her dictating (and drinking gin, of course) and me scribbling until I thought my fingers would bleed. *The Scarlet Sand*, for your information, a Worthington book. It's going to be super—and after the disappointing sales figures for *The Passages of Pleasure*, it'd better be.

Did Mrs. Harold Maron come out of her honeymoon daze long enough to notice the return address? After the funeral, I went back to the house and found the sheriff howling on the doorstep. It seems my mother forgot to pay property taxes, and with the cost of the funeral and all the bills from the butterfly farm, there was no way I could catch up on the taxes and at the same time have electricity! Apparently, someone's already offered to buy it for back taxes.

I rented an okay apartment, but when Miss W. discovered it was on the wrong side of the tracks—in every sense of the word—she insisted that I move into the house. I figured I might as well, since she was keeping me until eight or nine o'clock every night, although my paycheck sure hasn't been reflecting the extra hours. Now at least I get room and board out of the deal. No satin sheets, alas. Just cat hairs on my pillow, Lady Amberline's cute way of reminding me of my allergies.

Love,
Sneezy

Wellington House
#1 Wellington Road
Hampser, NC 27444
May 29, 1976

Penman Publishing, Inc.
375 Hudson Street
New York, NY 10014
Miss Natalie Burlitzer, editor

Dear Miss Burlitzer,

Miss W. asked me to let you know that the manuscript of *Lady Amberline's Revenge* is within a few days of completion and should reach you by the end of next week. She's been working on it around the clock, and is sure you will be as delighted with it as she is.

Should you wish to discuss the manuscript, we will be at the lake house for the summer. There is no telephone, but the proprietor of the general store will convey messages, and I've been told you have his number. I look forward to meeting you this fall when we're in New York for the release of *The Sins of the Whittiers*.

Yours truly,
Kristen Childers

Banbury Cottage
RFD 1, Box 18
Willow Lake, NC 27019
July 25, 1976

Veronica, my dearest cohort,

I was so incredibly pleased for you when I saw that effervescent review in *Romantic Times!* If only the gal could have gotten the plot synopsis a bit less muddled—but we old hacks know how clumsy reviewers can be. I'm sure you laughed at that banal and ever so tacky line in paragraph four about "St. James's passion for convoluted prose," and also at the "stale predictability of the story." Then again, she did get the title right, and what else matters?

Although I'd intended to stay here until the end of August, we're heading back home tomorrow. Usually I can rely on total solitude at this end of the lake, but this year the cabin just down the road was rented to a trio of college boys . . . from Yale, I believe. There's certainly nothing Ivy League about them, let me tell you! They're forever thrashing and bellowing in the lake as if they were ungainly bears, and playing loud music until all hours of the night. One of them has cozied up to Kristy and lured her to their squalid parties, which no doubt degenerate into orgies of the most primitive and repulsive sort.

So I'm virtually getting no work done. Yesterday afternoon I ran out of typewriter paper, but Kristy was out in a battered rowboat with "her beau" and failed to return until after sunset. The beer on her breath was enough to make me quite ill to my stomach. She apologized as best she could, but I told her to start packing at that very hour and not to leave the house under any circumstances. I can only hope they've failed to exchange addresses. What on earth will I do if he begins showing up at Wellington House?

> Your number-one fan,
> Aurora

> Wellington House
> #1 Wellington Road
> Hampser, NC 27444
> October 1, 1976

Wee Care Animal Clinic
454 Pathway Road
Hampser, NC 27444

Dear Dr. Wallsby,

Miss Wellington has asked me to express her gratitude for all the loving care you and your staff bestowed on Lady Amberline on that tragic day. We have searched the house from top to bottom, and can only conclude that Lady Amberline must have slipped out and chanced upon the poison in a neighbor's garden shed. After some consideration, Miss Wellington has decided that a new kitten would only cause her to grieve more deeply over Lady Amberline's untimely demise.

> Sincerely,
> Kristy Childers

Wellington House
#1 Wellington Road
Hampser, NC 27444
September 16, 1977

Dearest Tommie,

Kristy and I had a lovely summer at the lake house. This year there was no one to disturb us, and I was able to sit on the porch all day while Kristy tended to the chores and brought me trays at mealtime, always with a little vase of wildflowers. Once a tendril of poison ivy crept in, but I spotted it and Kristy nearly cried when she apologized, and so of course I forgave her. I know you think it's appallingly bucolic, but I get more writing done there in three months than I do the rest of the year. Whenever I need inspiration, I gaze out at the rippling azure water—and *voilà!* "Monica turned her azure eyes toward Dr. Bodley and the faintest hint of a smile rippled across her pale, worried face."

The visit was timely, I must admit. I had Kristy volunteer at the hospital last spring in order to glean some insights into the dynamics of the place. She became quite adept at sneaking into the emergency room to observe the gory casualties, and came home each evening with stories both charmingly lurid and screechingly funny. All I can say is I do not intend to be placed in one—ever.

The problems began with some shaggy young intern whom she took to meeting for coffee after his shift, and occasionally on his free days. One night she came home well after midnight, and it was obvious they had behaved indiscreetly. I said nothing, of course, but took it upon myself to have a word with the head of the program, one of Papa's old friends who should have retired decades ago! He was quite stuffy in his refusal to take action until I mentioned the possibility of an endowment for cancer research. Our young "Dr. Kildaire" has decided to complete his internship at a hospital in California.

Don't think for an instant that I deserve to be scolded for interfering in Kristy's personal life. For one thing, the poor girl is technically an orphan and someone really and truly must watch out for her. If I allowed her to roam the streets when we're in New York, I have no doubt whatsoever she'd come back with someone sleazier than that convict father of hers. Her taste in men is atrocious, and without my constant supervision, she might well become the proverbial good time that was had by all!

I've encouraged her to attempt some writing of her own, but I fear it was an egregious error on my part. Only last week, she showed me the first chapter of a novel. I did my best not to laugh as I pointed out the weaknesses in her little story and the shallow characterizations.

I'm sending a snapshot of Pittypat, who simply appeared at the back door of the lake house one morning and refused to leave. I took one look at those big blue eyes and silky whiskers, and told Kristy to fetch a saucer of milk!

Your silly, softhearted author,
Aurora

Wellington House
#1 Wellington Road
Hampser, NC 27444
November 2, 1977

Wee Care Animal Clinic
454 Pathway Road
Hampser, NC 27444

Dear Dr. Wallsby,

Once again Miss Wellington has asked me to express her gratitude for your concern during the tragedy. I'm sure all of us are horrified that anyone could be so vicious as to strangle an innocent kitten and leave its poor little body in the gazebo. Miss Wellington was overwhelmed with shock when she found it, but she has finally recovered and is able to work.

Yours truly,
Kristen Childers

From the desk of Aurora Wellington
12-13-77

Dearest Veronica,

Yes, I think I will accept your kind invitation to spend a few days in Atlanta. The weather's as dreary as my thoughts (I did tell you about Pittypat, didn't I?), but I cherish the supposition that elegant luncheons, lavish dinner parties, and dedicated late night bouts of drinking and gossip will be my salvation.

It's so kind of you to consider Kristy. I must offer her regrets, alas. The deadline for the next Wells manuscript is coming up, and I've made so many revisions that she'll have to retype all six hundred pages during the holiday season.

See you in a week!

Wellington House
#1 Wellington Road
Hampser, NC 27444
January 6, 1978

Mrs. Janice O'Leod
1477 Lakeside Road
Tallahassee, FL 32304

Dear Mrs. O'Leod,

Miss Wellington apologizes for not writing herself, but the holiday season has thrown her off schedule and she is working frantically on her newest book. She asked me to let you know that she was delighted with the gloves and umbrella you sent her for Christmas, and hopes you enjoy the autographed copy of *The Sins of the Whittiers.*

I regret that I cannot give you our new unlisted telephone number, as per your request, but once it's been given to someone, it seems to spread like a virus until we're literally inundated with calls. I am under order to guard it as if it were a Vatican treasure.

As much as Miss Wellington would love to see you this spring, her dubious health dictates that she must decline your invitation to meet at your hotel for lunch. Due to time restraints, she is unable to entertain guests here at Wellington House.

Yours truly,
Kristen Childers

Wellington House
#1 Wellington Road
Hampser, NC 27444
September 18, 1983

Dear Traci,

I was thrilled to get your letter after all these years. I would have sold my soul to go to our tenth reunion, but Miss W. was so sick that there was no way to leave her for even an hour. She's had this problem for years, on and off, and it flares up at the most inopportune times. Did you hear why I wasn't at the fifth reunion? While I was getting dressed, I heard a noise and discovered Miss W. lying at the bottom of the stairs. It wasn't until the next day that I finally persuaded her to go to the emergency room for X-rays. Nothing broken, thank God, but she hobbled around with a cane for months.

My glamorous life? Get real—your carpools and baby-sitting crises and burned pot roasts sound a lot more exciting than what I do. You would not believe the amount of paperwork involved in being an author. It takes me all morning to sort through requests for personal appearances, send photographs to fans, respond to queries from the editorial and publicity departments, answer sweet little letters from junior high girls, and fend off supplications from "wannabee" writers who'd like Miss W. to critique their thousand-page manuscripts. Miss W. ordered me to fire the cook after an heirloom ring vanished, so I fix lunch and when the weather is nice, we eat in the gazebo. She dictates until it's too dark for me to see, and after I fix dinner, we spend our really "glamorous" evenings in the parlor. Miss W. can be somewhat funny when she's talking about some of her rivals, especially after she's been cooing on the telephone with them for hours.

I'm glad Heather saved the postcard from the Plaza, but the inside of the room's about all I see when we're there. Miss W. insists that I bring the portable typewriter and do revisions or work on the newsletter. Want to be on the mailing list so you'll know what Miss W. has for breakfast and what inspired her to write *Vanessa's Folly?**

Enough of this dazzling lifestyle. So Charlie's getting bald, and his wife resembles a tugboat? Three children can do that. I almost threw up when I heard Sam Longspur's a dentist—I went out with him our junior year, and he spent so much time poking his tongue down my throat that I still get queasy just thinking about it. I knew Heather was pregnant, but I agree that I wouldn't have dared put on a bathing suit if I were such a blimp (don't you dare repeat that!).

I must stop. Miss W. wants me to pack for our annual jaunt to New York, where she will wine and dine with her editor and agent, and I will merely whine. Thanks so much for all the luscious gossip from the reunion. Maybe I'll make the next one and Charlie will be as bald as a persimmon.

Love,
Kristy

*An English muffin and tea, and have you ever read *The Roses in Eden* by Veronica St. James?

Wellington House
#1 Wellington Road
Hampser, NC 27444
November 10, 1984

Thomas Domingo Literary Agency
188 W. 79th Street
New York, NY 10122

Dear Mr. Domingo,

I have reviewed the royalty statements of 10/31/84 and have found serious discrepancies either in the publisher's computations or in yours. Please note return figures for *Summer of the Shadows* and the lack of information regarding foreign sales of same. Also, in that *Cape Serenity* has gone into a third printing, I find it curious that no sales are reported for the six-month period prior to the statement.

I am hesitant to bring this to Miss W.'s attention. For the last five years she has relied on me to handle all of her business affairs, and trusts me to do so with meticulous care. Frankly, she is unable to work more than three or four hours a day as it is. I cannot allow her to lose that precious time by concerning herself with financial matters.

Please respond to this within ten days.

Yours truly,
Kristen Childers

From the desk of Aurora Wellington

Tommie, dearest:

I am at a loss for words—after having written millions of them over the last twenty years! Apparently you are, too, in that you've failed to answer my last two letters. But if what Kristy has shown me proves to be true, then I can never forgive you. How many years have I trusted you? Now Kristy has told me that you have systematically stolen thousands and thousands of dollars from me. Tommie, dear Tommie, you must come down immediately after the holidays and review all this over a civilized glass of gin, not in the gazebo at this time of year, but surely in the parlor.

Yours in bewilderment,
Aurora

Wellington House
#1 Wellington Road
Hampser, NC 27444
December 10, 1984

NC State Correctional Facility
Raleigh, NC 27603
#1987-431-1

Dear Dad,

So they're letting you out after all these years, are they? I'm sure their rehabilitation efforts have taken effect and you will enter society determined to lead a blameless life. It must be hard to imagine yourself living on the outside, but let's hope you've had enough vocational training to find a job—even in these economically depressed days. I realize there's still a lot of discrimination against convicted felons, and it's really not fair to send you out onto the streets with only a few dollars and a new suit. Anyway, good luck job hunting and don't faint when you see how expensive everything is out here!

As you know, I live with an incredibly rich old woman who's written best-selling novels for thirty years. I hate to say it, but she'd be utterly helpless without me. She's small and frail and her hearing seems to get worse every year, but thank God her mind is quite sharp and she has a fantastic memory for details. She never forgets a face and can describe it with astonishing preciseness—as can all writers. On the other hand, she can't remember to put away her jewelry in the box on the dresser in her bedroom, and last week on her way to bed, she left the kitchen door ajar and the house was freezing by morning. We're lucky that she's too miserly to install decent locks; she's misplaced the keys so often that I've become quite adept with a hairpin. I guess that's one talent I inherited from you—ha, ha.

Anyway, I think I would like to see you, if only for old time's sake. The only two days I will not be available are December 24 and 25, when I'm visiting Cousin Heather for the first time in years. She has four kids now, and Harold is some kind of manager at his office. This time I've warned Miss W. that I am definitely going, even if she objects or claims to be sick. I'm hoping to be at Heather's by dark, and will be home the next evening. I feel terribly guilty about leaving Miss W. all alone in the house for two days, but our cleaning woman insists on being with her own family and no one else ever comes by to see Miss W. I don't really blame them; the house is so isolated at the end of the road, and you can't have neighbors if you own all the land for several miles. It's the only drawback I can think of to being rich!

Write me a note once you're settled. I'd tell you to call, but the squirrels have been gnawing on the telephone lines again and it usually takes several weeks for a repairman to come.

Your daughter,
Kristy

Wellington House
#1 Wellington Road
Hampser, NC 27444
April 11, 1985

Shady Oaks Realty, Inc.
3168 Katherine Avenue
Hampser, NC 27444

Dear Ms. Rowan,

Please address all future correspondence concerning the sale of Wellington House and the adjoining property to me, c/o Thomas Domingo Literary Agency, 188 West Seventy-ninth Street, New York, NY 10122. I'm sure you're aware of how lengthy a process probate can be, but I believe that we can entertain offers and perhaps work out a lease-purchase agreement until a sale can be finalized.

As for the house Miss Wellington owned in the Clover Creek addition, I have rented it to a distant member of my family and will allow him to occupy it at least until the estate is settled.

Should an emergency arise, I am staying at the Plaza and you may leave a message at the desk. If the remodeling proceeds on schedule, as of the first of June I will be in permanent residence at the house on Willow Lake.

Yours truly,
Kristen Childers

Dear Suzanne,

I'm sorry it's taken so long for me to respond to your charming letter, but I must say I'm impressed with the dedication you've shown in discovering my real name and tracking me down at this address. I'm delighted that you enjoyed *Lady Amberline's Fortune*, and I agree that she's a feisty young woman with a strong sense of ambition. You might watch for *Shadows and Smoke*, a more contemporary novel about a girl just a few years older than you!

As for your generous offer, I fear I must demur. Although there are days that I feel as if I'm drowning in papers, I simply wouldn't be comfortable having someone come in to assist with the filing and correspondence. You sound like a sensible girl, perhaps as ambitious as Amberline, and I'm confident that you'll find a way to have a successful career in literature, just as I did.

Warm wishes,
Kristy Childers

MICHAEL COLLINS

Michael Collins is yet another past-president of PWA. We swear that this was not a prerequisite to appear in this collection.

Michael Collins and Dan Fortune have been around *forever*—well, okay, since 1969. Recently a collection of Fortune stories was published under the title *Crime, Punishment and Resurrection*. With the first Dan Fortune novel, *Act of Fear*, Michael Collins won the Mystery Writers of America's Edgar Award for best first novel—and he has been getting better and better ever since. His most recent Fortune novel is *Cassandra in Red*.

In "Angel Eyes" Fortune investigates the death of a child. The police say it's an accident. The child's father says that she was killed by her mother. A sensitive subject handled by Mr. Collins with his usual compassion and attention to detail.

ANGEL EYES

"When her child falls into a pond, what kind of mother waits half an hour to go to the police?" Sid Parker said.

We were in Elbert Walsh's law office in Placerville, California, in the foothills of the Sierra Nevada. Walsh sat behind his desk. I stood against a wall near the high windows. Sid Parker sat in a big armchair between us. The office was a second-floor walkup in one of those old two-story brick buildings from the Gold Rush days, carefully restored for the new gold rush of tourism across a rich and restless nation. I looked down at the main street, imagined the rough, violent miners and gamblers, thieves and brothel girls, when they crowded these streets. The town had another name then: Hangtown.

"Motive, means, and opportunity," Sid Parker said. "What more do you need?"

I had never been to Placerville or the Sierras, had taken the long way through the Mother Lode wine country. It was green after the winter rains; the odor of spring grass was on the rolling hills. The High Sierras were off to the right, the farms and barns like a wilder New England. They haven't been here as long, the land is less tamed. A land of harsh weather for vineyards, hard-nosed people, and a wine grape, the zinfandel, that is an immigrant like everyone else, but no one knows from where.

I said, "When the police say it was an accident, you need a lot more."

It all began with a telephone call to my office in our Summerland house from Elbert Walsh. I'd worked for Walsh a few times in New York before I moved out to Santa Barbara. He'd left his New York law firm, relocated to Placerville, gone into single practice.

"They don't have investigators up there, El?"

"Not as good as you." When a lawyer cites my abilities as his reason for hiring me, I file it under real-reason-to-be-determined-later and let him talk.

He had a client who accused his wife of murder. "Karen Watt came up from L.A. in the early eighties, opened a woodworking shop, makes the most beautiful cutting boards you've ever seen. She married Sid Parker the second year. He's from a local old-money family, works at the family winery. One child, a girl."

"Who did the wife murder?"

"The police say she didn't murder anyone."

That was when the stump of my long-lost arm started to tingle. Even for a lawyer it was a heavy evasion.

"What do the police say it was?"

"Accidental death."

"Who was it, Elbert?"

"Their daughter."

I knew why Walsh had called me. If he were going to try to prove that a local woman killed her own daughter, an outside detective was a wise move. It's an accusation that can inflame and divide a small community, and always clouds its judgment.

"What does the wife say?"

"The girl's death was a tragic accident. She feels guilty as hell, it was her fault, but it was an accident."

"No witnesses or evidence, but the wife could have done it. That the situation?"

"We'll talk when you get here."

"What about motive?"

"We'll talk."

That had been Walsh's second evasion, and after the long, all-day drive that didn't get me to Placerville and his old-fashioned office until after dark, he continued to evade the point while we waited for his client.

"Karen's a reserved woman, Dan. A war protestor in L.A., an environmental activist. Usually soft-spoken, but can get angry. Private and even melancholy. Maybe because her militancy failed to change people."

"Come on, El, why does her husband say she killed their daughter?"

A tall man, Walsh wore the same blue three-piece pinstripe suits he had in his New York office. A reserved Stetson on an old-fashioned hat stand in the corner and a pair of Western high-heeled boots propped on his desk were his concession to The West. A craggy face and gray hair going to white. Independent and stubborn, Walsh. That was Hangtown too.

"The Parkers live out on Grizzly Pond. A week ago Monday, April 17, Sid was at Debbie Burke's, Karen and Annie were alone in the house. At 6:35 P.M., Karen walked into the sheriff's office. She was scared Annie had fallen into the pond, wanted them to search the whole area in the hope the girl had only wandered away. They got up a rescue team, finally found Annie in the pond up against the dam. From where they found her, and the condition of the body, she'd been in the water perhaps half an hour."

"Annie couldn't swim?"

"The pond is a damned creek that runs into the South Fork. It's high in spring, the pond spills and has a nasty current."

"How old was she?"

"Nine."

"Nine?" What nine-year-old can't swim today?

He looked out his window. "She was retarded, Dan. Severely, with physical handicaps."

The voice spoke in the office behind me. "You wanted to know what Karen's motive was, Fortune. Now you know. She got rid of her problem."

Sid Parker walked past me and sat in a big armchair between both of us. Walsh's client was a well-built man in his mid-forties. Not tall, with dark hair long but neat above his collar, and a thin face with sharp features and prominent bones and hollows. A dark gray suit hung baggy, the collar of his dress shirt was loose.

"Your daughter was a problem for her, Mr. Parker?"

He found a package of cigarettes in his shirt pocket, lit one. "I didn't think she was." He made an angry gesture with his empty hand. "Annie was getting better. Dr. Grasselli was sure. The angel was a sign, I could feel that. Now . . ."

"Angel?" I said.

Walsh said, "A spiritual happening. Sid went there that night. That's why he wasn't at home."

"Annie knew she was getting better all the time, but Karen never believed Annie would get better. She . . ." He brushed angrily at his pale brown eyes, which had a hard shine like amber. "The first few years she wanted to put Annie away in some home where she wouldn't bother *us*. I thought she'd stopped thinking that, but she never had. What she stopped thinking about was *us*. Only she couldn't leave a husband *and* a retarded daughter for another man. Not even today."

I said, "She has another man?"

"Without a doubt."

Walsh and I said nothing. That was when Sid Parker looked at me, said, "When her child falls into a pond, what kind of mother waits half an hour to go to the police?"

Now, in the quiet office above the Hangtown main street, Sid Parker said, "She waited to get help to be sure Annie was dead, and the police won't even try to investigate. The whole town wants it to go away, to forget it."

"The police need real evidence, Sid," Walsh said.

"What about the teddy bear?"

I said, "Teddy bear?"

"Annie never went anywhere without it. If she'd fallen into the pond, the teddy bear would have been in the pond with her, or at the edge. Not on the picnic table inside the gate."

"What else?"

"Find something else! You're the detective!"

Loss, rage, another man, and a teddy bear. It didn't seem enough for Walsh to have agreed to help Sid Parker. I looked over at Walsh, the question in my eyes. He frowned into his hands as he talked.

"Karen says she fed Annie about 5 P.M. that night. Annie wanted to go outside to watch the sunset colors. There's a fence and a gate between the yard and the pond, but she says they both sometimes got careless about locking the gate, right, Sid?"

Sid Parker glared at Walsh from the hard shine of his eyes.

"Karen stood out in the yard watching Annie," Walsh went on, "then went inside to get a drink. She admits she was drinking. There was a phone call, she won't say from whom. She—"

I said, "Why not say who called?"

"That's one of my questions," Walsh said. "She was inside about fifteen minutes. When she went out it was nearly dark, and Annie was gone. She ran out to the pond but saw no Annie. She searched around the pond from the dam to the creek before she went to the police. That's the half an hour."

"No one saw Annie fall in? No one saw anything?"

Walsh shook his head. "The neighbors aren't all that close. Those on their side of the pond can see only the front of the house through the trees. There are two houses on the far side of the pond where someone could see the Parkers' backyard, but they were watching TV and saw nothing."

I said, "No witnesses, no weapon, no physical evidence. Nothing except a possible motive and a block of time when only Karen knows what happened."

"A block of time filled with too many small things that were unusual. An open gate that's usually locked. A phone call she won't identify. A woman who doesn't drink much, then only beer and not at home, drinking that night. A woman who lives by a pond, but searches the land instead of the water for at least twenty minutes before she goes for help."

Sid Parker said, "She murdered Annie, Fortune."

El Dorado is a rural county, the sheriff's department doesn't have many detectives. The one more or less handling the Parker case was named Randy Cansino.

"I can feel for Sid, Fortune. I hope I can feel for the kid too. But we have nothing to make us doubt Karen's story."

"The teddy bear?"

"Annie was retarded, for God's sake. She forgot it."

"Sid Parker says it was the one thing she wouldn't forget."

"She was distracted."

"By what?"

"How do I know? I wasn't there. No one was."

"Karen Parker was."

He swore. "I hate this case, you know?"

"I know. Where do I find Karen Parker?"

"In her shop, I guess."

* * *

Karen Parker's woodworking shop was a few doors off Main Street, with a hand-carved hanging sign so the tourists would know it was there. She worked on a wood lathe behind a cluttered counter, stopped when I came in.

"Mrs. Parker?"

She was a big woman whose short red hair was cut like a man's but more ragged. Round-faced, she wore little makeup, had deep creases of sun and wind. Her bones didn't show, and she had definite hips under tight jeans. The dark blue eyes that glanced up at me were full of pain. And something else.

"You're the detective." She didn't smile. "It's a small town. Word gets around."

Her voice was strong and clear, even musical, like the voices of women I'd heard once in Wales.

"I wasn't trying to hide."

She operated the lathe with steady hands. "You plan to prove that I murdered my daughter? For Sid?"

"Did you?" I had to shout over the noise of the lathe.

She shut it off, sat back on the stool, her back against the wall. "I was surprised a good lawyer like Walsh even listened to Sid."

"So was I."

"But you're here."

The shop was small and dark. The workshop of a solitary craftsman. There were bowls and racks, and the cutting boards Walsh had praised. They were beautiful, made of many strips of different-colored woods matched in a linear or geometric pattern and oiled.

"Walsh thinks there were too many small things that night that were sort of unusual."

"What does he know about that night?"

"He knows your story."

"So do the police!" Anger flared like a quick flame behind her eyes, the stool fell over backward as she stood. "Maybe you better get out of here."

"You're a little on edge."

"My daughter just died!"

There was violence in her anger and clenched hands, but it was pushed far back. I felt no threat from her, only a kind of deep frustration and despair that this world would ever be what she wanted it to be.

"Who called you that night? The call that kept you inside?"

"None of your damned business."

"The other man," I said. "You didn't want Sid to know his daughter died because you were talking to your sweetie. You didn't want the whole town to get down on you. But Sid can't get any angrier, and the town knows by now."

She picked up the fallen stool, set it on its legs, sat down again. "Brian feels bad enough about the call without having the whole town talking about us."

"That's his name? Brian?"

"Brian Engels. He's divorced. Owns the smallest bed-and-breakfast in town. It's all he got out of a bad marriage. He does his own cooking and tends bar. He's younger than I am. He likes the mountains and rivers and forests. That enough?"

"For now," I said. "You mind if I come to your house to look around?"

"The police closed it off until after the inquiry. Maybe it still is closed. I haven't gone back, I think Sid's with his parents." She looked at my empty sleeve. "Does the missing arm limit you?"

"I live with it."

She looked around her cluttered shop. "I know of a retarded boy who's seventeen now. He can sing some songs, read on first-grade level, sort and package nuts, bolts, and pegs by size and color. That's what they call a wonderful success."

She was bent over her lathe again when I left.

The rustic house was five miles out of town in the rocky, wooded valley of a large creek. A rambling one-story, it had been added onto over many years by many different owners with different concepts. Warm and more than pleasant in its diversity, it sat some fifty feet back from the long, narrow pond.

I walked the grounds aware of eyes that watched me through the trees from the neighboring houses. They had seen nothing on the one night they should have, were not going to make the same mistake again. The large backyard had two picnic tables, some benches, lawn chairs, and a brick outdoor barbecue. In the pond I could see a strong current that flowed toward the dam. Across the pond I saw two houses in the spring afternoon sun. The closest showed flickering colors of a television set through a picture window. For many people in late-twentieth-century United States, television is the only world they know and relate to.

The back gate was still unlocked. A worn path to the pond revealed nothing. The water of the pond was clear and shallow close to shore, dropped off sharply to a vague bottom undulating far below in the sunlight and current. From the end of a narrow spit that jutted out into the pond, the moving figures on the distant TV were visible. Both houses across the pond were close enough for anyone to have heard loud cries or calls for help. They would certainly have turned to look out at the pond.

Off the path, the patch of torn grass and dirt with deep gouges in the rain-softened ground was a few feet from the edge of the pond. The depth and length of the gouges, the marks of what had to be rubber soles, suggested two people in some kind of struggle. The shoes seemed about the same small size, one with the deep grid pattern of a hiking boot, the other the smoother swirls of a running shoe.

Inside the house, the living room had a low ceiling with dark beams, a brick fireplace, and comfortable old furniture. A section was set off by bookcases as the dining room. Three bedrooms were down a crooked hallway to the right. I checked all three bedrooms, found no muddy boots or running shoes. In the living room, dinner dishes and cutlery were still dirty on the dining table. A bottle of Johnnie Walker Black Label and a not-quite-empty glass stood on a coffee table. The telephone had a long cord, had been moved to the coffee table.

The kitchen was to the right. Pots and pans were still on the stove, the blood-red water of beets in one pot. Some kind of rice casserole hardened in a baking dish, the red debris where the beets had been skinned was still in the sink, and a single glass drained in the plastic drain basket. It was the only dish or glass in the basket. There were water spots and an oily film inside. The outside was clean. The glass had been rinsed, not washed, and dried only on the outside. I smelled a faint odor that could be scotch whisky.

It was dark by the time Elbert Walsh met me at the sheriff's office. Detective Cansino didn't want to see either of us.

"Don't you think we should maybe give Karen Parker a break, counselor? Christ, her kid's dead, she feels guilty enough."

"We owe Sid something, Randy. And Annie."

I said, "When you went over the house and yard, how many glasses were on the coffee table with the scotch?"

"Shit, I don't remember. I'd have to get out the file." He didn't want to get out the file. "I've known Karen since she came here. The woman's suffering. What does Sid want?"

"The truth," Walsh said.

Cansino got the file. "Glasses? Okay, there was one glass, still some scotch in it. Karen's prints, no one else's."

"What about the glass in the drain basket in the kitchen?"

"It's noted here along with the rest of the dirty stuff in the kitchen. Clear as hell Karen forgot all about everything. Wouldn't you, Fortune? When you find your kid missing, you don't remember the dishes."

"The glass was rinsed," I said.

Walsh said, "One glass? Only that?"

"Someone carefully wiped and dried only the outside."

Cansino shrugged. "So Karen, or Annie, or someone used the glass earlier. It could have been any time."

"What about that torn-up ground out in the backyard? Did you check the sole marks, try to match them to what Karen and Annie were wearing?"

He read his file. "Nothing here about any torn-up ground. Sure don't remember seeing that myself."

"Maybe you better go and take a look."

"Torn-up ground could have happened anytime since the rain started in January."

"Anything could have happened anytime," I said.

"I'll take a look. At the glass too."

Outside, Walsh suggested some drinks and dinner. In the Sierra Tavern we sat in a booth. I had two quick Red Tail Ales, it had been a long day. Walsh had a martini, watched me.

"You think someone else was there that night?"

"That's what I think."

"And you think Karen struggled with Annie in the yard?"

"I think someone struggled with someone in the yard."

Walsh thought about that. "She's protecting someone?"

"Or afraid of someone."

After dinner I went to my motel bar, had more Red Tails, thought long about Sid and Karen Parker before I went to bed.

Sid Parker's parents lived in a large house on a hill that overlooked the South Fork of the American River. He was a short, broad man in a Western shirt and bola tie, had a strong face as craggy as his land. She was small, with short, matronly hair.

"The original house dates from 1860, Mr. Fortune," Ethel Parker informed me with the same voice a French count would have used to announce that his château and lineage dated from the time of Charlemagne. "It's still our master bedroom."

"Sam Parker came around the Horn in 1847. He was sixteen," William Parker said. "Jumped ship in San Francisco, was on the spot when they found the gold. Sold his claim the day before it ran out, went into business right here. When too many murderers and troublemakers filled the town, he led the vigilantes that gave it the old name: Hangtown. We don't like troublemakers here."

"Actually," I said, "I came to talk to Sid."

"He's over in Napa. Winery business."

"I'm sure we can tell you anything he could." The mother smiled. "Would you like some tea, Mr. Fortune?"

"Tea would be nice, thank you."

Ethel Parker went into the kitchen. I sat on a brocade love seat that matched a larger couch and armchair set around a fine mahogany English coffee table. One of three sitting areas in the giant living room, all with fine antique couches and tables and occasional chairs. Mrs. Parker returned with a three-tiered plate of small sandwiches, muffins, and petit fours. We all sat around it and drank tea.

"Does your daughter-in-law have any special friends? A relative, maybe?"

"We wouldn't know," Mr. Parker said. "She's irresponsible, and a troublemaker. We have as little to do with her as we can."

"We never liked that Sidney married her," the mother said. "It would seem that we were right. Tragically."

"What do you know about the 'angel' Sid had gone to see that night?"

Ethel Parker smoothed her skirt. "It's a religious event in the town. At Deborah Burke's house. Thousands of people came from all over the country. I read about it in the newspaper."

"What did Sid want with this 'angel'?"

"You'll have to ask him," Mrs. Parker said.

She knew, but didn't want to tell me before Sid Parker told me his version of whatever it was.

"How did you feel about your granddaughter?"

She went on smoothing her skirt and looked somewhere out the windows. His craggy face was stone.

"We loved Annie," she said, "despite everything. She should probably have never been born. But she was here, we wanted her to be as happy as she could be."

"When she was born we took her to the best specialists, gave her everything we could."

"We wanted her to have all the special treatment she needed to get better. Someone to be with her all day."

"Karen only wanted her to die, get her off her back."

"Now she has."

They were like a Greek chorus, their voices interchangeable. A chorus that sang Sid Parker's song.

"Is Dr. Grasselli one of your specialists?"

"No," Mr. Parker said.

"He's a friend of Sid's," Mrs. Parker said. "Some kind of psychologist, I believe."

"Does Dr. Grasselli have an address?"

"I'm sure it's in the telephone book. Joseph Grasselli."

I left them there in their giant living room, side by side and holding hands.

Dr. Joseph J. Grasselli, M.D., Ph.D., Psychologist and Radiologist in Family Therapy and Advanced Spectral Treatment, had his office in a house outside Placerville. His shingle hung from a post in the front yard, but the office was in the rear.

"Sit down, Mr. Fortune." A small man with a narrow face and a neatly trimmed beard, Grasselli sat behind his desk and smiled. "Feel free to tell me as much or as little of your problem as you want. We won't rush you, we'll both learn as we go. All right?"

"Well, maybe you can sort of show me, like, I mean, what I can sort of expect?"

"Fine, fine. Why don't we take a brief tour of my office and facilities? As you can see, I have both a medical degree and a doctorate of philosophy in psychology."

Grasselli motioned toward the largest of the many framed documents on his walls. The medical degree was in German from St. Ignatius Hospital Medical School in Zurich. Certificates of internship from a hospital in Grand Forks, North Dakota, and residency from another hospital in Rolla, Missouri, were on either side. The Ph.D. in psychology was from Union University in Los Angeles. My missing arm started to throb like an abscessed tooth. Grasselli walked to a door on the right.

"In here is my spectral radiology room."

There were a lot of machines, one that looked like a fluoroscope, and others I recognized as autoclaves and an EKG. The largest had a chair and what looked like an X-ray head mounted on a heavy arm. Grasselli patted this machine.

"This is my own development: a spectral radiochrome."

"What does it do?"

"How much do you know of spectral radiology?"

"Well, I heard of it," I lied. "Does it help family stuff?"

He almost rubbed his hands together. "That depends on the nature of the problem. If your problem is physical—impotence or infertility, say— then we use one setting and bathe the area in blue or yellow light from the radiochrome. If, however, the trouble is mental, then we must use an entirely different setting and beam the brain with red light. Of course, the spectral rays are not simple light, but complex photon-neutron waves of vast therapeutic finesse."

I tried to look impressed. "What kind of mental problems? I mean, like, can it help if you see things that aren't there? Make you smarter? Stop you, like, maybe from beating your wife?"

Grasselli smiled. "Nothing comes easily, you understand. All cures take time, progress can be slow. But all of those problems can be helped with sound counseling and the spectral radiochrome, yes. Are one of those your problem, Mr. Fortune?"

I hesitated, looked nervous. "How about a sort of retarded kid? A friend of mine says you can make them better."

"Yes. There are no guarantees, but I have made special progress with the raising of intelligence levels. What friend told you—?"

"Sid Parker," I said. "He says you made Annie better before Karen went and—"

He looked at my missing arm. "Who are you, Mr. Fortune?"

"Was Annie Parker getting better? Did you tell Sid that?"

He walked to the door. "You didn't come to consult me. I think you better leave."

"Was she getting better, Grasselli?"

He crossed his office, held the outside door open, and smiled again. "Yes, and no one can say she wasn't."

"Oh, I'll bet a lot of people can say she wasn't. Like real doctors. You mean they can't prove she wasn't, especially now, right? The evidence is dead."

"Good-bye, Mr. Fortune."

"Are any of those diplomas and certificates real?"

He closed the door in my face.

The South Fork of the American River runs northwest a few miles north of Placerville. Brian Engels had his bed and breakfast on a bank of the river. The South Fork Inn, five rooms and a small café and bar. In the early afternoon the bar was open, three men sat at a table in a noisy group. A solitary woman drank at the bar in silence. Brian Engels tended bar, didn't think we needed to go anywhere else to talk.

"Not even about Karen Parker?"

"Especially about Karen," he said, and smiled. "Half the town always knew, now I guess the other half will."

He was a big man, his darkening blond hair cut as ragged as Karen Parker's hair. In his late thirties, slender and bony for his size. The same deep creases of sun and wind, the same tight jeans behind the bar. He had a nice smile. I couldn't remember that Sid Parker had ever smiled.

"How long have you known each other, Mr. Engels?"

"Brian, okay?" He shook his head. "Do all you detectives pussyfoot around trying to fool people, Fortune? Karen and I've known each other since two days after she came to town and walked in here for a Sierra Nevada. But that's not what you want to know, is it? We've been in bed maybe two years, give or take a month or so. I never wrote down the big moment."

"Is it serious?"

"What the hell is serious? It's serious loving. It's serious friendship. It's serious human beings."

His voice had risen in the small, low-ceilinged barroom. The solitary woman at the bar turned to stare at us.

I said, "Is it serious, Brian?"

He washed dirty glasses in the sinks under the bar. "I hope it is. Maybe for my sake more than hers."

"Who do you doubt, you or her?"

He stacked clean glasses on the bar. "When a woman comes to you because she's lonely, because she needs a smile, because she needs some peace, you're never sure. Is it only comfort she needs? If the problem goes away, does she still love you? Does she still want you?"

"Does she still want you?"

"I don't know. She's upset, depressed, guilty."

"Annie's dead," I said. "Annie sent her to you, Annie could take her away. The problem is solved. She—"

The lone woman at the bar who had been staring at us, stood up. Sturdy, in her late thirties, she wore a plaid flannel shirt, battered cowboy hat, baggy chinos, and running shoes.

Brian Engels said, "Annie? It wasn't Annie that sent her to me, for Christ sake, it was Sid. Her problem's Sid, not Annie. His goddamn obsession with Annie. Every waking minute put into believing the poor kid could get better, be normal. His quacks, witches, gurus, holy rollers, goddamn angels."

I said, "What about angels?"

The woman at the bar walked to us. "You want to know about our angel, Fortune? I'll tell you about our miraculous angel."

For believers in galactic harmonic convergence, the weekend of Saturday, April 15, is one of the moments that will signal either a new age of peace, or the doom of mankind.

The Friday before, April 14, Deborah Burke, a believer, switches on the television set in her living room to enjoy her favorite soap opera. It isn't quite time, she changes channels to find the latest news of the harmonic convergence. A bright light seems to swell from the TV, and the angel appears on the screen. Deborah is transfixed, stares at the image that shimmers in all the colors of the rainbow.

She is beautiful, the angel. She smiles out at Deborah with a soft, gentle smile and eyes full of love. Deborah sits alone with the glowing image until her son and daughter find her.

Teenagers, they are even more dazzled by the image, must go at once to tell their friends, make them come and see the angel too. Their friends tell their parents, who also come to look. Word spreads all through town. The local newspaper sends a reporter. Its story of the angel on Deborah Burke's television is fed into the wire service.

By Sunday, six thousand people have made the pilgrimage to Placerville. They gather in meadows on the outskirts of the town and in the yard of Deborah Burke's house to meditate and watch the sun rise over the towering Sierras. Over five thousand of them come to Deborah's house to see the wonder of the angel on the TV screen. Psychics from across the country sit before the image and speak to the angel. The sick and the lame come from everywhere to look, wonder, and pray that the miraculous angel will make them well.

"It's the harmonic convergence sign," one of the leaders of the movement declares. "The sign we've been expecting. It means peace for the world, survival. We're going to be all right."

Deborah Burke agrees. "The angel came to tell us we'd be okay. She's wonderful."

The police chief isn't so sure. He calls in a TV repairman to look at the angel. The repairman, Tom Whitney, identifies the source of the image at once: a bad capacitor and the set's low-voltage power supply.

At first, at Deborah Burke's house, he doesn't say anything. "There were so many people praying in front of the set, out in the yard. I didn't know how to tell them."

But Whitney goes to his shop and easily duplicates the image for anyone who wants to see it. He tells the chief, who tells the town and everyone at Deborah Burke's house.

"Anyone who wants the truth, go on down to Tom Whitney's shop and see for yourself."

None of the six thousand who came to pray and meditate do.

The woman in the cowboy hat said, "Sid took Annie to that TV set the moment he heard about the 'angel.' Took her over to Debbie Burke's that Sunday and sat with Annie in front of the set and talked to the 'angel.' He made Annie kneel in front of that 'angel' Tom Whitney could show anyone who had any grip on reality was nothing but an electronic malfunction. A glitch on a TV screen would make Annie better, make her normal."

The woman's eyes held the same anger and something else I'd seen in Karen Parker's eyes. It wasn't fear, not exactly. More like a dark shadow. "When they didn't come home for dinner, Karen found them there. It was way past Annie's bedtime, no one had fed her. Her diaper was dirty, she was almost hysterical. Crying and moaning and trying to get closer to the screen to find the angel inside. Karen had to drag them out of there, clean Annie up at home, feed her, and put her to bed. The next day Sid wanted to take her back to that phony 'angel'!" Karen said no, but he said he damn well would if Deborah Burke would let him and went over alone to ask her if Annie could come back.

Brian Engels said, "He grabbed at anything, even believed a couple who told him Annie was bewitched. They could free her from the witch, cure her, by putting a blessing on her while she stood naked on a hill when the moon was full and faced north."

The woman said, "The same couple killed a woman in San Francisco because she'd been a witch draining the wife of her beauty and religious powers. In court they described themselves as 'religious warriors in a holy war against witches.' Their religion authorized them to kill witches, they had acted reasonably against the imminent danger of attack by lethal supernatural powers."

Brian Engels said, "Outside of his work, it's all Sid thought about the last seven years. Karen watched him hurting that poor kid, and the rest of us watched him hurting Karen."

"Is that why she killed Annie? Because she decided Annie and her and even Sid would be better off?"

"Maybe they all are, Fortune," the woman said.

"Karen didn't kill Annie," Engels said. "If Karen was going to kill someone, it would have been Sid."

"How do you know what she did?" I said. "Were you there?"

The woman said, "Annie went out into the yard, the gate was open, Karen was in the house, Annie drowned."

I looked at Engels. "Who is this lady?"

"Sandra Gavin. Karen's best friend."

The sturdy woman wasn't my best friend. She didn't like me at all, and wasn't trying particularly hard to hide it. I looked down at her running shoes.

"Maybe you were there that night, Ms. Gavin?"

"No one was there except Karen and Annie."

I shook my head. "No, someone else was there. I don't know who or why, but Karen Parker wasn't alone with Annie. Two people drank scotch in the living room that night. That's why she was drinking at home: she had company. Whisky when she usually drank only beer, because she was upset by Sid, the 'angel,' and Annie."

"She was upset," Brian Engels said. "That's why I called her, and why she was drinking. But she was alone."

"There were two glasses. She rinsed one so no one would see she hadn't been alone. But she forgot to put it away."

"She could have washed that glass anytime."

"It was an accident," Sandra Gavin said.

Deborah Burke lived in a big white frame house on a back street. A native sycamore and two eastern maples shaded it from the late afternoon sun. Spiritual slogans and paintings hung all along the porch. When I rang, an ethereal woman in a flowing white robe opened the door and smiled up at me.

"Are you spiritual? A believer?"

She had big blue eyes that stared brightly with a beatific expression. One of those people who move in a world of their own, on some interior planet. Most of Placerville had to know by now a one-armed detective was in town trying to prove that Karen Parker murdered her child to be free of all her trouble.

"I doubt it," I said.

"You didn't come to see the angel?"

"No. I'd like to talk to you about Sid Parker."

"So spiritual, Sidney."

"And Annie."

"Poor child. No one understood."

"Understood what, Ms. Burke?"

"Why, that she was getting better all the time. Anyone with sensitivity could see that."

"How could you see that?"

"In her eyes, of course. They are the windows of the spirit. Annie's spirit was perfectly normal. A pure spirit trapped in that poor body. The spirit would triumph, we all knew that. We could see she was getting better all the time."

"Who's we?"

"Our spiritual group. We meet every week."

"Sid and Annie came to your meetings?"

"Sydney is a wonderful searcher."

"He brought Annie to see the angel?"

"Oh yes. We knew at once there was something special between them, Annie and the angel. In their eyes, you see? She had the same eyes, Annie. Angel eyes. The way she looked at the angel. It was as if the angel came just to help Annie."

"They were here a long time?"

"Oh yes. It was wonderful. Our spirits communing."

"Karen and her friends say she found Annie dirty, hungry, and almost hysterical, moaning and trying to get closer to the television screen to find the angel inside. Karen had to drag them home. Next day Sid was here again, while Karen was home alone with Annie."

The change was instantaneous. It could have been another person where she had stood in a kind of ecstasy seconds before. Her bright eyes clouded, her beatific smile became a scowl.

"Karen Parker is a woman without sensitivity! People say she is a sensitive artist, but they're wrong. She has no feeling for the Eastern wisdoms, for the world's holy places, for the harmonic convergence. She is afraid to feel the spirit. She rejects the pure foods, the mantras, and karma. She wears clothes that bind the flesh and the spirit. She has no sensitivity."

"Was Annie crying, hungry, and hysterical that Sunday?"

The beatific vision came into her eyes again. "What does the physical matter? Annie was joining her spirit to the angel."

The woodworking shop on the downtown side street showed light; Karen Parker worked on a cutting board this time. She didn't look like she'd left the shop since yesterday.

"Living in the shop now?"

"I don't have rich parents to move in with." She put down her tools. "What do you want this time, Fortune?"

I leaned over the counter to look at her feet. She wore heavy hiking boots. The kind with thick lug soles.

"Someone else was there that night."

"No one else was there."

"There was a scuffle, an encounter. Outside near the pond."

"When Randy Cansino came around today, I figured that was your work."

"What did you tell Detective Cansino?"

"I used the other glass the day before. Sid and I horsed around out by the pond a week before. I drink scotch when I'm depressed."

"Alone?"

She went back to work. "Annie and I were alone. I was careless. She fell into the pond."

Her big hands moved delicately, quick and soft. The hands of an artist in wood.

"Depressed about your marriage? Sid's obsession with Annie? Cures, miracles, quacks? Not much of a marriage, I'd guess. A woman has to change something sooner or later."

"Not much of a marriage. Not for a long time. I did change something. I found Brian."

"That didn't help Annie."

She didn't look up. "I was drinking, talking on the telephone. I was careless. Annie drowned."

After a chicken barbecue sandwich and milkshake at the local Carl's Jr., I drove out of town along the dark rural highway to the Parker house. There were lights in the neighbors' houses and in the two across the pond.

Outside the backyard fence, I looked again at the torn-up grass and soft earth with the marks of the running shoe and the boot. The marks weren't clear enough, or distinctive enough, to give identification. Across the dark pond the large television set in the nearest house was remarkably clear. From the edge of the pond, the faces and figures on the TV seemed almost real.

Out on the road I knocked at the closest house. A muscular man in work clothes looked at my arm.

"You're the detective Sid got to go after Karen."

"Dan Fortune," I said.

"Max Gerber. This is my wife."

The woman stood beside him in the doorway.

"You told the police you saw nothing unusual over there that night, didn't hear any cries. But did you hear anything? Maybe something brief, not loud. Voices, footsteps, a scuffle—"

"Scuffle?" Max Gerber looked at his wife. "You know, that's just what it could of been. A scuffle. I—"

"Start at the beginning."

They both looked off toward the shadow of the Parker house through the night trees. Mrs. Gerber said, "We was sitting out on the side porch. I mean, it was a nice night, we always have a drink before dinner, so—"

"We had drinks on the screen porch. Just about when it was dark there was this noise from somewhere. Hell, it wasn't much, didn't last more'n a couple of seconds, if that long. It—"

"Was like someone breathing hard, maybe a grunt, you know?"

"Maybe someone sort of jumping and sliding around. I mean, it couldn't of lasted more'n a second or so like my wife says."

"We figured a couple of kids somewhere around."

I said, "Could it have been Annie? Struggling?"

"Hell no," Gerber said. "When that kid made noise you could hear it to Sacramento."

"Especially if she was scared."

"Just getting dark? About five-thirty, six o'clock?"

"Closer to six, I'd say," Gerber said.

"Anything else?"

They looked at each other, shook their heads.

"No matter how small, unimportant, even routine."

The wife said, "Well, there was a car. I mean, just a car starting somewhere."

"Hell, there's always a goddamn car," Max Gerber said.

"This car was close?"

"Yeah, pretty close."

"Before, or after you heard the noise?"

"After," the wife said.

Gerber nodded. "Maybe ten, fifteen minutes. We was just goin' inside to eat. We always eat around six-fifteen, six-thirty. 'Star Trek' reruns come on the TV at seven, right?"

At the house on the far side of the Parkers, a tall, spare, angular woman answered my rings. She saw my arm, and half-closed the door.

"Sorry to bother you." I smiled my polite and reassuring smile, flashed my photostat. "Dan Fortune. Private investigator working for attorney Elbert Walsh on behalf of Sid Parker. I'd like to ask you a few questions if it isn't inconvenient?"

She studied the photostat in front of her face. "He thinks she killed the child, doesn't he? Wouldn't put it past her. Kind of thing those hippies do."

The second woman was as tall, but neither spare nor angular. Forty pounds heavier, she had a round, pleasant face that smiled at me. "If anyone killed that poor child, May, it was him. Dragging the little thing everywhere and anywhere, never letting her alone, trying to make her what she could never be."

"The Parkers are a fine family! You wouldn't know anything about that, Maggie."

They faced each other across the gap of the open doorway like two lions on an African veldt. The glare of the thin one, the smile of the second, clashed in a struggle that had probably been going on a long time. I coughed, got their attention.

"You told the police you saw nothing, heard nothing. But was there anything at all unusual? Say between five-thirty and six? Something you barely noticed?"

The heavier, Maggie, looked past me. "There *was* this . . ."

The skinny one, May, said, "This . . . sound. I was in the kitchen peeling potatoes. Sort of low grunts, a bump—"

"I was outside," Maggie said. "I remember thinking they were perhaps tussling, Sid and Karen. You know, fun in their backyard. They used to do that a lot when they first moved in."

"Could it have been Annie?"

"Oh no." In unison.

"What time would you estimate?"

Maggie always seemed to speak first. "Six o'clock?"

"Give or take ten, fifteen minutes."

I said, "What about the car?"

"Car?" Maggie said. "I don't remember—"

May said, "It went right past. Looked like a Ford Bronco. An old one. Red or dark brown. Six-fifteen or so."

"You heard it start next door? Looked out?"

"Heard some car start up, don't know if it was the same car," May said. "I had some garbage, took it out to the cans, saw the Bronco go past. Looked like Sandra Gavin's. She lives up the road that way."

At the South Fork Inn, Sandra Gavin had known my name before she joined us. Could she have heard Brian Engels say it from where she had been sitting, or had she already known who I was?

On my way to the sheriff's office, I picked up Elbert Walsh. Cansino was off-duty, wasn't pleased to see us at his home.

"I think I know who else was there that night," I said.

"We already went through all that, Fortune."

"I talked to the neighbors. They remember a brief noise about six o'clock. Hard breathing, some grunts and sliding in the dirt. They heard a car start somewhere close, one saw an old red Ford Bronco go past her house."

"They didn't tell me any of that."

"They didn't think of it again until I asked. They never thought it was important enough to talk about."

"Or they remembered what never happened when you put words in their mouths."

"Fortune didn't suggest anything specific, Randy," Walsh said. "Taken together with the glass and the scuffed ground, it at least opens the possibility Karen is lying when she says she was alone with Annie, and that makes me wonder what else she might be lying about."

"Why would Karen want to hide someone else being there?"

I said, "Why don't we find out?"

The glass-and-redwood house looked like a wing of a modern art museum about to fall into the rushing water of the South Fork that surged white in the night. Sandra Gavin answered the door.

"Randy? What's up?"

I said, "Karen Parker wasn't alone that night. You were with her. At least until six-fifteen or so."

She ignored me. "Randy?"

"They want to ask some questions, Sandra," Cansino said.

Sandra Gavin walked inside her house. The living room ran the width of the small house. Skylights showed the stars clear above in the rural night, and a wall of glass stood between the room and the dark river with its bursts of white only ten feet below. Abstract paintings hung on all the walls, nonobjective sculpture stood on the floor and most surfaces. Open double doors to the right showed an artist's studio and an unfinished sculpture. Sandra Gavin sat on a low leather-and-rosewood couch.

"All I know about that night is what Karen says."

I sat in a soft-leather Mies chair. "Two different sets of neighbors heard a brief scuffle about six o'clock, saw your car leave about fifteen minutes later."

"They couldn't have. I wasn't there."

Detective Cansino said, "Where were you, Sandy? From five-thirty to six-thirty? That's your drink time. Downtown at Matty's or the Sierra, out at South Fork Inn. Which one was it that night? Will they cover for you?"

"I worked late. On a roll."

"That'd be the first time in five years. What do you always say? Take a break no matter how good it's going, or you'll lose your edge?" Cansino was in an old butterfly chair near me. "The other place you drink is with a friend. Usually Karen Parker."

Cansino heard her come in before Walsh or I did. Rural ears. She walked across the wide room to the glass wall that overlooked the rushing river, watched the night and the river.

"Funny, I always loved water," Karen Parker said. "Fast water, remote water. Rivers and lakes. Maybe because I grew up on the ocean."

Sandra Gavin said, "They don't know—"

"Yes they do, Sandy. Fortune'll keep digging, hammering at you, until it gets in the way of your work. He'll work on Randy until none of us has any peace."

Walsh said, "She was there that night, Mrs. Parker?"

Karen Parker still looked out and down at the rushing water that was like a giant moving shadow in the night. "It wasn't her problem. I didn't want her to be involved."

"Involved in what?" I said.

Cansino said, "You were covering for Sandra? It was—"

Karen Parker spoke into the window, into the night outside above the white-edged river. "I'm not covering for her, she's covering for me. I didn't want her to be part of it. To lie, or tell the truth and feel bad, or maybe even feel guilty."

Detective Cansino said, "If there's something you didn't want Sandy to tell us, I—"

I put my lone hand on his shoulder. Karen Parker wasn't listening. She didn't hear us, wasn't talking to us, wasn't even thinking of us. She was talking to the night and to herself. "I'd had to drag them home from that television set and its 'angel.' An electronic glitch, and Sid was off on his miracle chase again. First the doctors: pediatricians, psychologists, neurologists, brain surgeons, he did them all. Then the herbal healers, and faith healers, and the layers-on of hands. The priests and witch doctors, the star-gazers and the quacks."

Sandra Gavin walked toward her. "Karen—"

At the wide picture window, her face reflected in it against the darkness outside, Karen shook her head. "He never stopped to see what it was doing to us and to Annie. We had no marriage. Annie had no stability, no peace or rest. Dragged to one empty hope after the other. Prodded and poked and studied and dieted and analyzed. Annie didn't matter. Only the obsession—Annie could be, would be, a normal child. He never asked me, and he never asked Annie."

I said, "That Sunday night was the last straw. Annie was exhausted, hungry, in her own dirt. The next night, when Sid had gone to ask Deborah Burke to let Annie come back, you—"

She watched something large and black float down the dark river with its white teeth. "I fed my daughter dinner. I'd been upset by the night before. Sandra came over. I was still upset, we had a drink or two. Whisky, beer wasn't enough. Annie was restless, wanted to go out. I had left the back gate unlocked, I don't know how or why. We had another drink. Brian called. He asked how Annie was, if she'd recovered. I realized I hadn't heard a sound in ten, twenty minutes from out in the yard. I dropped the phone and ran outside. Sandra came behind me."

She turned, looked through and beyond the glass-and-redwood living room. "She was out on the little spit of land staring across the pond. I couldn't see why. There was still plenty of twilight, but there was no one and nothing on the pond or across it." Her eyes searched for whatever was on the far side of the pond miles away behind her house. "Before I could even open my mouth to call her, or yell, she walked straight out into the pond. It's shallow for a few feet, and then—"

Sandra Gavin said, "We were nowhere near her. She just stepped off into the damned water!"

"—it drops sharply. As I ran across the yard she went down. By the time I was near the pond she came up, sputtering and thrashing in the current. Then she stopped, lay back in the water, her eyes clear and very bright. She looked straight up at the last light in the night sky." Karen Parker turned again to the wall of glass above the fast-moving river, looked up at the night sky. "She was smiling. She floated in the water, and she smiled." She turned once more, looked at us this time. "She smiled and lay back and just slipped under the water."

The long silence in that sleek room with its giant abstract paintings and sculptures must have stretched a full minute before Detective Randy Cansino finally spoke.

"Could you have reached her?"

"I don't know. I'm a good swimmer, she wasn't far out."

I said, "You didn't try, and you stopped Sandra from trying. That was the scuffle."

"It was too late," Sandra Gavin said. "The current was too strong."

Karen Parker said, "Sandra was behind me. She tried to go past, jump into the pond. I stopped her. We fought for a second or two. I told Sandra to look at her eyes, at her face. She—"

"I saw her smiling like she was just lying in bed," Sandra Gavin said. "We both saw her smile."

"As if she knew it was all okay, she was okay," Karen Parker said. "In that moment she let go. And I let go."

"Perhaps it was you who was okay, Mrs. Parker?" Walsh said.

She left the window, sat on the couch beside Sandra Gavin. "I don't know what I was thinking at that moment, Mr. Walsh. I know she was a pawn between me and Sid. I know she suffered being dragged around like an animal on show to fill her father's need for a miracle. Maybe I did decide she would be better off. Or maybe she decided she would be better off, and I let her go. There aren't any miracles."

I said, "What did she see across the pond?"

"I don't know. After she was . . . gone, Sandra and I stood there on the shore for a while, holding hands and looking out, but there was nothing to see."

"Except the television set."

"Television?"

"In the first house across the pond. A big TV. You can even see the people on it. Was it on?"

"It sure as hell was," Sandra Gavin said. "Karen—"

"That's what Annie saw," I said. "A face or a figure on the TV. Like the angel. She walked out to get close to the angel the way she'd tried to at Deborah Burke's. So eager to reach the angel she even forgot her teddy bear. Maybe, in the water, she still saw the angel. Her father's miracle."

This silence was shorter, a few seconds before Karen Parker stood up again.

"Sandra and I went back into the house. She wanted to tell the police exactly what had happened. I said no, I didn't want her to be part of it. We argued, but I made her go home, rinsed and dried her glass, then went downtown."

Detective Cansino stood up too. "Let's go down there now, get it all on the record."

* * *

The sun was too bright in Elbert Walsh's office, he'd drawn the shades.

"What will they charge her with?" Sid Parker said.

"Probably nothing," Walsh said. "She didn't kill her, Sid."

"She could have saved her. She let her die."

I said, "You don't know that, Parker. No one knows that."

"She stopped Sandra Gavin from saving her. She killed Annie as sure as if she'd pushed her in and held her under."

I said, "Annie walked into the pond toward the miracle you had offered her. Maybe she found her miracle."

"The most they can do," Walsh said, "is child endangerment, child neglect. I don't think they will."

"Annie was getting better. She would have been normal. Karen murdered my daughter. Nothing will change that."

When Sid Parker had gone, Walsh and I talked for a time about wine and fishing. He paid me, and I left. I drove out of Placerville. Sid and Karen Parker will divorce. Karen will go on with her work, Sid will always say she murdered their daughter, who had been getting better every day. The town will split, different people will judge and condemn him or her. That is the nature of towns and people. Me? I drove home down the edge of the great Sierra Nevada, through the wonderful land toward the sea, and thought about Annie.

Old friends, you think you know them. Seeing them again opens up memories of things that never seemed important before. You let your guard down, you take chances you know you shouldn't, and you end up deeper in the hole than you ever would for a stranger.

How can P.I. Nick Delvecchio refuse to help the friends he's just seen at a high school reunion, even if he knows he will discover things so disturbing that part of himself will be "Laying Down to Die"?

In "Bad Review" the old friends are writers. But when they agree to best-seller Kay Washburn's pact one of the friends discovers that forgoing normal caution is a disastrous mistake.

ROBERT J. RANDISI

Bob Randisi is the creator of two New York–based P.I.'s. Miles Jacoby works out of Manhattan, while Nick Delvecchio's bailiwick is the streets of Brooklyn. The most recent Delvecchio novel was 1991's *The Dead of Brooklyn*. Jacoby appeared in 1993 in *Hard Look*.

Randisi is also the founder of the Private Eye Writers of America, creator of the SHAMUS Award, and co-founder of *Mystery Scene Magazine*. He is a three-time SHAMUS nominee but—as befits the award's creator—he has never come close to winning one.

In "Laying Down to Die," Delvecchio attends a high school reunion—his first, and last.

LAYING DOWN TO DIE

A "NICK DELVECCHIO" STORY

ONE

All death is tragic. Particularly when it's accidental. After all, someone dying as the result of a fluke, or an act of carelessness? Tragic, to say the least. Now natural causes, that's probably the least tragic of all. I mean, what can you possibly do about that? A man goes to the doctor one week and is given a clean bill of health, and the very next week he clutches his head and drops to the floor, dead. Happens every day, right?

So where does murder fit into this equation? Well, in my opinion, murder is just a step below accident. What keeps murder from being at the top of the list is that it is a deliberate act. One person sets out to take the life of another person. There's nothing "tragic" about that—it's just a damned shame!

And where does suicide fit in?

Who the hell knows?

I stared at the casket from my seat in the back of the chapel. I chose to sit there alone because I was not a family member. In fact, I was not even a close friend. I was someone who had known the deceased in high school, and met her again eighteen years later for one evening—and then she was dead.

High school was not the favorite time of my life. I know people of varying ages who claim that, given the chance, they'd go back in time to their high school days. In my opinion, people like that just can't deal with being grown up. Given the opportunity to go back to the happiest time of my life, I'd stay right where I am. I guess that means I haven't had the happiest time of my life yet. So what? I think that's good. Gives me something to look forward to—and to me, looking forward is miles better than looking back.

Last week, however, I *did* step back in time, sort of. It was the evening of my eighteenth high school reunion. I had been invited to reunions before—the tenth, and the fifteenth—and had not gone. Why I decided to go to this one is still a mystery to me. (Why they even had an eighteenth reunion is a mystery to me. Don't they usually have them at ten, fifteen, and twenty, like that?) Well, it wasn't a *total* mystery to me why I was there. Sam had something to do with it.

Samantha Karson is my neighbor. She lives in the apartment across from me. We're friends—*just* friends, although why that situation hasn't . . . progressed after living across from each other for a few years *is* a mystery. Sam's a beautiful blonde with the body of Bardot, the hair and eyelashes of Sissy Spacek, and a face that's all her own.

The day that I received the invitation to the reunion was an afternoon that we had decided to have lunch together at a nearby diner.

"That's when you graduated?" she asked, looking at the invitation.

"You *know* how old I am, Sam."

"I know." Her smile was teasing. "It just looks so . . . archaic in print."

She put the invitation down and looked at me across her turkey club. Sam was on another diet. She was a full-bodied young woman who, as far as I could see, was proud of that fact. Why then was she constantly trying to lose five pounds?

"I think you should go."

"Why?"

"Why shouldn't you go. Didn't you have some friends in high school?"

"Sure, I had *some* . . ."

"But not a lot?"

"A few."

"Any girlfriends?"

"A few."

"Aren't you curious about what's happened to them? What kind of adults they've become?"

"No."

"Why not?"

"I might be disappointed."

She stared at me then. "Or maybe you think they'll be disappointed in you?"

Okay, so I decided to go to the damned thing . . .

The reunion was held in Marine Park, at a hall on Avenue N called the Something-or-other Château. I admit to some degree of nervousness as I entered through the front door. That disappeared, however, when I saw this huge apparition from the past advancing on me. He had his arms spread wide, a wingspread I readily recognized as belonging to Tony "Mitts" Bologna.

"Nicky-D, you sonofabitch!" he shouted, and crushed me in a bear hug that took me to within an inch of my life. As it was, I didn't think I'd ever be able to have kids.

"Tony Mitts!" I surprised myself because I was shouting back at him with almost as much enthusiasm.

It was then that I silently thanked Sam for talking me into going.

It was much later when I cursed her for it . . .

From my vantage point in the back of the chapel I could see Tony Bologna's back. His shoulders were shaking. Sitting to his right was his mother. Her shoulders were ramrod straight. On his left was the mother of the deceased. She was alternately patting and rubbing his back, the way I thought his own mother should have been doing.

I looked up toward the casket again, where Mary Ann Grosso was lying, all dressed and made up to look "good" in death. God, I hated when people said of the dead, "They look *good!*"

Mary Ann Grosso simply looked dead, which was a far cry from the way she had looked the night of the reunion . . .

Tony Mitts was just the start of it at the reunion. In rapid order I met up with Sammy Carter, Joey "the Nose" Bagaletti, and Vito "the Ace" Pricci. The four of us used to hang out together in high school, which a lot of people found odd, because while three of us were Italian, Sammy was black. We were fond of telling people he was "Black" Italian. Among ourselves, we also said that if anybody didn't like it, "Fuck 'em."

We staked out a place at the bar, watching the girls go by.

"Boy," Vito said, "most of these girls have really porked up, huh?"

"Especially the Italian ones," Sammy said, nodding his head in agreement.

"What are you complainin' about?" Tony said to Sammy. "I thought skinny black guys like you liked your women big and fat."

Sammy fixed Tony with a hard stare. "You gonna start that 'fat-assed black girl' stuff again, Tony Mitts? You were always doin' that in high school and I didn't like it then!"

"Yeah, yeah . . ." Tony said.

Eighteen years ago Tony was always teasing Sammy about his girl-friends having big asses. It was true, but Sammy had always acted like he didn't like it.

I examined my three high school friends critically. Tony had always been big, well over six feet, but he'd never been fat, and he still wasn't. He'd kept himself in remarkable shape, but then as an athlete he would. We called him Tony "Mitts" because he had hands the size of catcher's mitts. It was better, he said, than what they used to call him in grammar school—Tony "Baloney." Ah, grammar school kids had no imagination.

Sammy was as skinny as ever, and his hair had receded to the halfway point on his head. The bald part of his head, though, gleamed, the way Lou Gossett's and George Foreman's heads do. I wondered why he didn't just shave it.

Vito had gone to fat, which he was always threatening to do in high school. His arms, though, still threatened to burst the seams of his clothes. We would have nicknamed him "the Arm" except Tony was called "Mitts" and we didn't want another body part in the group. So, because of his affinity for cards—poker mostly—he had become Vito "the Ace."

"Anybody seen Mary Ann?" I asked.

Suddenly, Tony smiled. "She's here."

"Yeah," Vito said, slapping Tony on the back, "she came in with Tony, the lucky dog."

"Man," Sammy said, "she looks good, even if she ain't got an ass on her."

"You want to see her?" Tony's tone was anxious.

"Sure."

I agreed not only because he was so anxious to show her off. I was curious about what Mary Ann looked like after eighteen years.

"Come on." Tony took my arm in a grip of iron.

"See you guys . . ." I barely had time to say before he dragged me off.

I really had never gotten to know Mary Ann Grosso well in high school. I'd never gone out with her, although I knew a lot of guys who claimed they had. They all claimed to have scored, too, except for Tony. He said he never had, and no one else had, either.

He pulled me over to a table where a bunch of people were sitting. As we approached I was able to pick Mary Ann out with no problem. If anything, she was even more beautiful at thirty-six than she had been at eighteen. She had long dark hair that hung to her shoulders. Her eyebrows and eyelashes were very dark, and her eyes brown. I remembered that she had always had beautiful skin without a trace of acne, and she still did, smooth and pale.

She had been a lovely young girl, but she had grown up to become a truly beautiful woman.

"Mary Ann, here's Nick," Tony said. When she frowned he said, "Come on, you remember Nicky-D!"

"Of course. Nicky." I knew that she wasn't lying, she did remember me. She held out both hands and I took them. "It's good to see you."

"And you, Mary Ann. You look . . . wonderful."

"Don't she, though?" Tony blustered right over her soft "Thank you." He was obviously very proud of her, and when he told me that they were to be married, I realized why.

That was last week, when they were truly happy.

This week Mary Ann was dead.

TWO

After the service I decided not to accompany the family and friends to the cemetery. I stopped to tell Tony that and he grabbed my arm tightly.

"Come to Mary Ann's mother's house, Nick."

"Tony," I said, "I don't want to intrude . . ."

"Her mother wants you there, Nick. She wants to talk to you."

"I didn't think she'd even remember me."

"She doesn't. I told her you were a detective."

"Tony—"

"Please, Nick." His eyes were as pleading as his tone of voice.

"All right, Tony."

"Thanks, buddy." He was relieved. "We should be back at the house by two. Okay? There'll be lots of food."

"I'll be there."

He finally let go of my arm and I felt the blood starting to flow again.

I stood out in front of the funeral home and watched the procession of cars leave. I became aware then that someone was standing next to me.

"It's a damn shame, ain't it?" Vito asked. I hadn't seen him since the reunion, and hadn't noticed him inside.

"Yeah, it is." I looked at him. "I didn't see you inside."

"I didn't go in." He shook his head. "Couldn't. I didn't want to see her like that."

"Are you going to the house?"

"Nah." He shook his head again. "You?"

I nodded. "Tony asked me to."

"They're gonna hire you, ain't they?"

"I'm afraid they're going to try."

"Why afraid?"

"It's going to be hard turning them down."

"Why turn them down?"

"I don't investigate suicides, Vito."

"Then there's no problem, Nick." He slapped me on the back. "She didn't kill herself."

"How do you know?"

"I knew her—I knew her as long and as well as Tony did. She'd never kill herself."

"Are you saying she was murdered?"

"I'm sayin' she didn't kill herself, Nick. That's *all* I'm sayin'."

"Vito—"

"Gotta go." He moved away from me abruptly. I watched him walk to the parking lot and get into a new Chevy. I realized that I didn't know what he did for a living. I don't think we ever talked about it at the reunion. I recalled talking to everyone else about what they were doing for a living, but now that I thought of it, Vito always seemed to avoid the subject. He seemed more willing to talk about the past, not the present.

I wondered if he'd meant to imply what I thought he'd been implying when he said he knew Mary Ann as well as Tony did?

*   *   *

I got to the house at two-thirty. It was in Bensonhurst, on Sixty-third Street. Actually, it was walking distance from my father's house, where I grew up.

"Nick," Tony Mitts said as I entered, "God." He came at me in the hall and clamped down on my arm again. "I'm glad you came."

"Take it easy, Tony—"

"I been trying to take it easy, Nick, but it ain't that simple. You don't *know* . . ."

"Don't know what, Tony?"

"Look, lemme tell Mary Ann's mother you're here, all right? Get somethin' to eat and I'll find you. Get a beer, 'kay?"

He was talking a mile a minute and he was gone before I could respond. I went looking for a beer and found one in the kitchen. I also found a girl crying. It took me a minute, but I recognized her as Grace, Mary Ann's sister. If I remembered correctly, Grace was about two years behind us in high school. She wasn't as pretty as her sister, but there was a resemblance, and she had the same smooth, pale skin.

She was sitting at the kitchen table, clutching a handkerchief and crying softly. I took a St. Paulie Girl from the refrigerator and turned to her.

"Grace?"

She looked up at me, hastily wiping away the moisture from her eyes. She frowned, trying to remember who I was.

"Grace, I'm Nick—"

"Delvecchio," she finished. "I remember. I had a terrible crush on you in high school." She blurted it out, and then clasped her hand over her mouth.

"Did you?" I asked. "I never knew that."

She took her hand away from her mouth and said, "Nobody did—only Mary Ann."

There was an awkward silence, which she broke.

"It's nice of you to come, Nick," she said. "I didn't think you'd remember . . . us."

"Well," I said, "I was at the reunion. I saw Mary Ann—"

"Wasn't she beautiful?" she asked, her eyes shining either from tears, or from pride. "Even more lovely than she was in high school?"

"Well, yes, she was," I said, not really knowing how to answer. I mean, what did she want me to say? She seemed to really mean it, but I had two older brothers, and I wasn't always so happy about that fact. Were there times, I wondered, when she didn't idolize her sister so much?

"I can't believe she's gone," Grace said, starting to sob into her hanky. "Not . . . not like that."

It occurred to me then that I still didn't know exactly how Mary Ann had died.

"Nick, there you are," Tony said, bursting into the room. He didn't even seem to notice Grace. "Come on, Mary Ann's mother wants to talk to you."

"Grace," I said, "are you all right?"

"I'm fine, Nick," she said, waving her hand. "Go ahead, Mother wants you."

"Why don't we talk later? Huh?"

"Sure," she said with a little smile, "why not?"

"Come *on,* Nick!" Tony said, grabbing my arm.

Old friend or not, I was tired of having my arm mangled.

"Tony, take it *easy,* all right? I'm coming."

He released me like my flesh was hot and said, "Sorry."

"Lead the way."

I followed him down the hall.

THREE

Tony took me down a hallway past a couple of bedrooms to a room at the end. Inside, Mrs. Grosso was sitting on a bed, staring out the window. What was she seeing that no one else could see, I wondered.

From the looks of the room it was a girl's—most probably Mary Ann's. That was confirmed when I saw a framed photo on the dresser. It was Mary Ann and Tony, arms around each other, laughing. From the looks of the scene behind them it had been taken at Coney Island—certainly during happier times. It also looked to be an older photo, not when they were in high school, but certainly not much later.

"Mrs. Grosso?" Tony said.

For a moment she didn't seem to hear him, and then she turned her head and looked at us. I wondered how old she was. Sixty? Sixty-five? She was still an attractive woman, obviously Mary Ann's and Grace's mother. She had the same skin. I remembered Tony telling me she had lost her husband about five years ago. And now Mary Ann. All she had left was her daughter Grace. No, check that. Let's say she *still* had Grace. That was something, wasn't it?

"Tony."

"This is Nick Delvecchio, Mrs. Grosso," Tony said, awkwardly. Obviously, even though he was going to marry her daughter, he hadn't gotten around to calling her anything more personal. "He went to school with us—"

"Yes," she said, "I know, Tony. I remember Nick. How's your father, Nick?"

"He's fine, Mrs. Grosso," I said.

"I see him at the store sometimes," she said. "He's gone through a lot, with the death of your brother and your sister being on that hijacked plane."

"He's come through it all with flying colors, Mrs. Grosso."

"Good, that's good," she said. "I came through my husband's death five years ago . . . but this . . . I don't know if I can come through this."

"You still have Grace, Mrs. Grosso."

"Yes," she said, "I still have Grace."

"Tell him about Mary Ann, Mrs. Grosso," Tony said, anxiously. "Tell him she didn't—"

"Tony," she said, interrupting him, "can I talk to Nick alone, please?"

He looked as if she had slapped him in the face.

"But—I thought—"

"Please, Tony?"

"Uh, well sure, Mrs. Grosso, sure . . ."

Tony gave me a puzzled glance, and then backed out of the room.

"Would you close the door, Nick?"

"Sure."

"And come and sit here by me," she said as I closed it. She patted the bed next to her and the folder, and when I sat the papers were between us.

"Please," she said, "call me Angela—it's actually Angelina, but that's too long, don't you think?"

"It's a pretty name."

"Yes. When I was in school—high school—they called me 'Angel.' Isn't that silly?"

"Mrs.—uh, Angela, can we talk about Mary Ann?"

"Of course. My Mary Ann," she said, "they say she killed herself."

"Who says so, Angela?"

"The police."

"Can you tell me how she died?"

"She died here," she said, touching the bed, "on this bed."

"But how did she die?"

"Pills," Angela Grosso said, "she took pills, that's what they say."

"Suicide."

Angela Grosso nodded.

"But Tony doesn't believe it."

"Tony was very much in love with Mary Ann, Nick. He refuses to believe it."

"And you?"

"Mary Ann was . . . troubled."

"Angela—"

"Here." She picked up the folder of papers and handed it to me.

"What are these?"

"Poems," she said, "my Mary Ann's poems."

"Poems," I said, puzzled.

"How well did you know my daughter, Nick?"

"Not well," I admitted. "We went to school together, but after we graduated I sort of lost touch—"

"Mary Ann wrote these poems," she said, patting the folder. "All these years since high school, she's written these poems. She even had some published in magazines."

"Really?" I said. "That's nice." I wasn't sure how to react. What did this have to do with anything?

"You don't understand," she said. "You have to read these poems to understand. The girl who wrote these poems—the *woman*—was . . . troubled."

"Mrs. Grosso, Tony said you wanted to talk to me—"

"I told him I didn't, Nick. He wants me to hire you to prove Mary Ann didn't commit suicide . . . but I believe she did. Read the poems, Nick, and you'll see."

"All right, Mrs. Grosso. I'll read them."

Tony was waiting when I came back down the hall.

"Did she hire you?"

"No, Tony, she didn't."

He firmed his jaw and said, "Then I want to, Nick. I want you to prove she didn't do it. Mary Ann wouldn't commit suicide. Those are her poems. They're beautiful. You read them and you'll see."

"I'll read them, Tony, and then I'll get back to you."

Angela Grosso thought the poems meant Mary Ann would commit suicide, and Tony thought they meant she couldn't. I was real curious about them now.

FOUR

"So what did you tell him?" Sam asked.

We were in my apartment sharing a pizza which she had sprung for. It was her way of paying for information. She'd been waiting with the pizza when I got home from the Grosso house.

"What could I tell him?" I asked. "I took the poems and told him *and* her I'd read them."

She looked at the folder full of papers on the table, and then looked at me.

"Can I read them, too?"

Sam was a writer, mostly of romances as "Kit" Karson, but of late she had started writing mysteries, as well.

"Sure," I said. "After the pizza we'll start reading them."

"What did she say about them?"

"She said that once I read the poems I'd know that Mary Ann did kill herself."

"Her poems are supposed to tell you that?" Sam asked. "They must be pretty depressing poems."

"We'll find out," I said, picking up another slice of pizza, "after we eat."

There were dozens and dozens of poems—eighteen years' worth, according to Mary Ann's mother, but after reading half a dozen each Sam and I looked at each other, and then traded.

"Well?" I asked.

"God," she said, "these *are* depressing. The girl who wrote these was so . . . sad!"

I hated to admit it, but I agreed. Anyone who could write "Angel of Death," "Last Request," and "Midnight Crisis," not to mention something called "Laying Down to Die," *was* more than just sad.

"I mean listen to this line from 'Midnight Crisis,' " Sam said, and then read aloud, " 'Raindrops kiss my black lapels, then weep into my chest.' " She looked at me and said, "It's so . . . beautiful, yet sad."

"You're a writer," I said. "Are these good?"

We were seated across from each other on the floor with the poems strewn out on the floor between us.

"These are . . . wonderful! I'm no poet, of course, but I think they're . . . well, wonderful."

"But sad," I said, "so sad."

"Maybe not all sad. Listen to this line from 'Laying Down to Die.' 'She's blind to the jelly bean colors, of balloons on a turquoise sky.' "

"That's great, but does it mean she did or did not kill herself?"

"I don't know, but try this. What if writing it down, writing down all of the sadness she felt, was her way of dealing with it, of getting it out. What if she *wrote* it to keep from committing suicide. It could have been some sort of rite of expiation on her part."

"If you're gonna flaunt something can you make it something other than your writer's vocabulary? Like maybe your body?"

She made a face at me. "All that means is what I just said."

"That writing it down would prevent her from having to commit suicide—uh, in her own mind, I mean."

"Right."

I looked down at the poems on the floor, moved them around some, and then heaved a big sigh.

"What?" Sam asked.

"I don't buy it, Sam," I said. "I think she took her own life."

"So what are you going to do?"

"Ask some questions," I said. "Maybe if I can find out why, I can put her mother's mind to rest."

"But you're not going to treat it like a murder?"

"I can't," I said. "I just don't see it that way."

"Well . . . it's not as if you couldn't investigate it that way. I mean, as far as the police are concerned it's a closed case, so you wouldn't be stepping on their toes."

I looked at her and asked, "You think somebody killed her? By making her take pills?"

She shrugged. "Maybe somebody poisoned her."

I shook my head.

"You're getting too involved in this mystery-writing thing," I said. "You're seeing conspiracies where there just ain't any."

"All right," she said, getting to her feet. She was wearing a big floppy sweatshirt and a pair of jeans. Her feet were bare, since she'd only had to walk over from across the hall. I noticed—and not for the first time—that she had pretty feet. Her toes weren't all gnarly like some women's were.

"All right what?"

"Look into it any way you want," she said. "As long as you look into it."

"I'm only going to look into it at all because I couldn't tell Tony no," I said.

"Isn't he still your friend?"

"I don't know," I said, honestly. "Before the reunion I hadn't seen him in years."

"I have to go," Sam said, "I have to do twenty pages tonight."

"Has all of this talk about murder inspired you?" I asked.

On the way to the door she said, "As a matter of fact, it has. I'll be up past midnight, in case you want to talk, or get a snack."

"I'll let you know," I said, staring down at the poems on the floor.

"Read some more, Nicky," she said from the door. "Maybe you'll find one that will tell you something definite."

She went out the door, closing it behind her. I already knew something definite. Mary Ann Grosso was one depressed person for a long time.

What I wanted to find out was why?

I read some more, but at one point I just had to stop. Jesus, *I* was getting depressed, and I'm normally a real happy fella. Ask anybody.

I put the poems away and went to bed before midnight. Let Sam get her own snack.

FIVE

The next morning I got up—late—and leafed through the poems again, but I didn't have the heart to start reading. I left them in my desk and decided to talk to people who knew Mary Ann Grosso a lot better than I did.

I started with Grace. I called her at home, caught her there and asked her to have lunch with me. She agreed, but told me to come to the house at noon and she'd make something. That left me an hour to work with. I decided to check in with the police and see what they had on Mary Ann Grosso. I made some phone calls, invoked the name of a friend, and managed to pry this out of the detective who caught the case: there were no signs of violence on the body. That meant that no one had held her down and forced her to swallow the pills. She seemed to have simply taken the pills and laid down to die, the detective said. There was no question about it in anyone's mind but that she committed suicide.

"Did they find a pill container?"

"Yes. There was one in the downstairs bathroom on the sink. It was the mother's. The daughter must have taken the pills, left it there, and walked to the bed. And then there was the note."

"What note?" I was about a second away from hanging up when he said this.

"The one they found clutched in her hand."

"Which one?"

"I don't know," the man said, "it had something to do with suicide."

"Wait a minute," I said, and pulled out the folder. I went through the poems one by one and then found one with suicide in the title.

"That's the one," the detective said when I read the title to him. "She had it in her hand."

Her mother hadn't told me that.

"Thanks," I said, and hung up.

There was a knock on the door and I opened it to find Sam standing in the hall.

"What are you doing up?" I asked. "I thought you did twenty pages last night."

"I did, but I wanted to see if you'd read any more of the poems."

"I'm reading one now," I said, waving it. "Listen to this. 'Eyelids covering forever her pain, Beating heart eternally resting.' She had it in her hand when she died."

"Which one is it?"

"It's called 'Suicidal Daydreams,' " I said. "Whataya think of that?"

When I got to the Grosso house Grace had soup and sandwiches waiting. She also looked as if she had dressed for a date. I hoped I hadn't given her the wrong idea. Actually, she looked very pretty . . .

"Nick," she said, "Tony told me he . . . he hired you."

"He thinks he hired me," I said, and she looked puzzled. "I'm not going to bill him, Grace."

"Well . . . that's nice of you . . . but what can you do for him . . . us?"

"I don't know," I said. "Do you feel the way he does about Mary Ann's death, or do you agree with your mother?"

She opened her mouth to answer, but her voice failed her. There were two glasses of water on the table. She took a sip from one, either because her mouth was dry, or because she was buying time to think.

"I don't know how I feel, Nick," she said, finally. "I mean, sometimes I'm just absolutely numb."

"Do you feel that someone might have killed your sister?"

"My God," she said, shaking her head. She held her hands up, as if to cup her head between them, but instead she just held them there. "It sounds ludicrous when you say it out loud. Who'd want to kill Mary Ann? And why?"

She reached out suddenly and grabbed my hand.

"Nick, do you think someone killed my sister?"

"No, Grace, I don't," I said. "I'm sorry, but I believe she committed suicide."

I took "Suicidal Daydreams" from my pocket and held it out to her.

"What's this?"

"This is the poem they found in her hand. The police consider it a suicide note."

She unfolded the page and read it, then let her right hand drop to the table, holding the poem loosely.

"Do you know when she wrote that?"

Her face reddened.

"Grace . . ."

"Yes."

"When?"

She touched her forehead with her left hand, as if she had a headache.

"Grace?" I made my voice firmer.

"A couple of years ago," she said, finally.

"Did she talk about suicide then?"

She lifted her eyes then to look at me. They were shining with tears.

"It's not about suicide, Nick."

"Come on," I said, "look at the title. What else could it be about?"

"Look at the last line of the first stanza." She spread the poem out on the table.

" 'Damaged goods denied final blessing,' " I read.

"And the second stanza."

I looked at the last line of the second stanza and read, " 'Remains of a deadly assault.' "

"Don't you see?" she asked. " 'Damaged goods'? 'Deadly assault'?"

"What are you telling me, Grace?"

"Nick . . ."

Suddenly it came to me. I realized what she was talking about.

"Grace . . . are you telling me Mary Ann was raped? That's what this is about?"

She nodded, the tears now streaming down her face.

"When? By who?"

"She never told anyone," she said, "anyone but me."

"Why not?" I asked. "Why didn't she tell your mother?"

Her eyes widened. "Oh God, Nick, she could never have told Mother. She would have thought . . . Mary Ann was dirty."

"No," I said, "your mother would have helped her—"

"You don't know my mother, Nick," Grace said. "If she ever found out about this it would have disgraced her. She would have . . . would have . . ."

Have what? I wondered. Whatever she was thinking she couldn't say out loud.

"Nick, haven't you wondered why Tony and Mary Ann are just getting—*were* just getting married now? After all these years?"

"Well . . . yeah, I wondered . . . a little . . ."

"Mary Ann's led a kind of wild life, Nick," Grace said. "She's not—wasn't—the nice little Catholic girl that . . . well, she's not . . ."

She was going to say, ". . . the nice little Catholic girl that I am."

"She's been . . . promiscuous in the past, but now she was ready to settle down, and Tony—he's loved her all these years, and he was ready to take her."

"Who was it?" I asked. "Did she tell you that?"

She nodded.

"She told me," Grace said, "but . . . do you think he killed her? I mean, that was two years ago and she . . . she forgave him, Nick. Can you imagine? So why would he kill her now?"

"I don't know, Grace." I said. "Why don't you let me go and ask him."

SIX

Vito Pricci lived in the old neighborhood, not far from where Mary Ann lived, and where my father now lives. From there I walked to Vito's house.

Actually, it was Vito's father's house, but Vito lived there now, since both his parents had passed away. He had no brothers and sisters, which was unusual for someone of our generation. When I was a kid I didn't have many friends who were only children. That's what happens when you grow up Catholic and Italian.

I didn't know if Vito would be there or not, but I hoped he would, because I wanted to be able to wrap this case up quickly. I just found the whole thing too . . . depressing.

So I was hopeful when I rang his doorbell.

"Nick," he said, showing surprise. "What are you— It's good to see you."

"Can I talk to you, Vito?"

"Well . . . well, sure, come on in." He backed away to let me enter.

He closed the door behind us and led me into the living room. The house was very much like Mary Ann's, and very much like my father's. It's funny, I grew up in my father's house. It was my home for almost twenty years, and yet I always thought of it as my father's house.

"Can I get you a beer?" he asked. "Or something?"

"No, nothing, Vito. I just want to talk."

"About what?"

"About Mary Ann."

He frowned. "What about her? Did you find out that she didn't commit suicide?"

"No," I said, "I didn't find that out, but I found out other things."

He shuffled his feet uncomfortably and asked, "Uh, what other things?"

"Come on, Vito," I said. "I think you know what other things."

He shook his head slightly and said, "Uh, Nick, I don't know—"

"I know about the rape, Vito."

"What?" he said, his eyes widening. "No, whoa, wait a minute, there wasn't no rape, Nicky. I don't know who you been talking to—"

"I've been talking to someone Mary Ann confided in, Vito."

"Jesus," he said, touching his face, "she didn't tell Tony that, did she?"

"I think if she had told Tony you'd know it, Vito—you would have known it two years ago, when it happened. He would have killed you."

"Nick," he said, "wait, let me show you something. All right? Before you say anything else."

Vito went into the dining room. He went to a hutch and opened a drawer. Just for a moment I wondered if he was going to come out with a gun, but instead he took a folded-up piece of paper and carried it back to me, leaving the drawer open.

"Here."

"What's this?"

"A poem," he said. "Mary Ann wrote it . . . for me. Read it."

I unfolded the paper and read the title, "You." I read the first stanza and saw that it was Mary Ann's, all right. I mean, I was starting to recognize her style.

"Disappointments in life are many." It was three stanzas, and the third finished with the lines, "Now I will be forever changed, refreshed, from loving you."

I looked at him. "Did she write this before the rape, or after, Vito?"

Vito stared at me for a few seconds, and his eyes widened again. He said, horrified—and if he was acting he was damned good!—"Jesus, you think I killed her!"

"Tell me what happened, Vito."

"Nick . . . look . . . I've loved Mary Ann for years, man. Ever since high school. You know those stories we used to hear, about guys who scored with her?"

"Tony said they weren't true," I remembered.

"Well, they were. I mean, I loved her, too, but I wasn't blind like he was. He refused to believe the stories, but I knew they were true."

I didn't know what to say. If what Grace said was true about Mary Ann's promiscuity, then it probably *had* started in high school.

"So, what does that mean, that she deserved—"

"No, you don't understand," he said, "just listen." There was a look of desperation on his face, and in his eyes. "Tony wanted to marry her right out of high school, but she wasn't ready for that. She wanted to live her life, you know? Sow her wild oats and all that? She traveled, she had affairs, but she always came back home. Tony and her mother, they kept treating her like she was a saint, but I knew different.

"I was always here, too, Nick, and always in love with her. Then, about three years ago, she came home and she was different. It was like she found God, or something, you know? After all these years? Like all of a sudden she *was* the saint Tony and her mother thought she was—but not quite. Even though she started to see Tony regularly, and they talked about marriage, all of a sudden she noticed me, you know? It was like a high school dream come true for me. We talked, we went places together, we did things . . . but she'd never have sex with me. I couldn't understand that. She always told me I was the one who was keeping her sane, who knew her for what she was and still loved her. Tony, she said, loved who he thought she was, and her mother—well, Angelina would never believe anything bad about her little Mary Ann."

"But she wouldn't come across, huh?"

"It wasn't like that." He wiped away the sweat on his forehead with his palm. "I didn't want a quick fuck, I wanted to love her, marry her. I couldn't understand why she wouldn't make love to me."

"So you got tired of waiting?"

"Damn it, you don't understand!" he shouted. "She came over one day and she gave me that poem, said she'd written it for me. I was overwhelmed. Nobody'd ever done anything like that for me before. She . . . she let me kiss her, and then . . . then when things started to heat up, she pushed me away . . . but she didn't push very hard, you know? I felt if I pressed her, if I insisted . . . and before you knew it we were on the floor . . . okay, so I tore her clothes a little, but . . . but I wouldn't call it rape, Nick. I'd *never* call it rape!"

"But she did, right?"

"Yeah," he said. Suddenly, it was as if he lost all the strength in his legs. He sank into a chair and said, "Yeah, she did . . . but you know what? She said she forgave me. She understood."

"And?"

"And she said she never wanted to see me again . . . not like that. She said we were finished, even as friends."

"And you took that?"

"Sure, I took it," he said. "I loved her, I'd never hurt her."

I stared at him. I didn't know what had happened between them that day. She called it rape, and he didn't. Who knew? She told her sister Grace it was rape, and she was too ashamed to ever tell her mother.

He looked up at me with anguished eyes. "I didn't kill her, Nicky. I loved her. I always loved her. Why would I kill her two years later, huh? Tell me that?"

I couldn't. It didn't make sense. He wouldn't wait two years and then become angry enough to kill her. So then the question became who *would* become angry enough to kill her if they found this out?

Vito hung his head and said, "I didn't kill her, Nick . . . I didn't . . . I didn't . . ."

I believed him.

SEVEN

From Vito's house I went back to Mary Ann's mother's house to close the whole thing out.

Grace answered the door and looked at me with surprise.

"Is there something you forgot to ask me?"

"No, Grace," I said, stepping inside, "I'm here to talk to your mother."

"She's in Mary Ann's room," she said, closing the door.

"Tell me something, Grace. Did Mary Ann use sleeping pills?"

"Mary Ann?" Grace shook her head. "Mary Ann slept like a top, Nick. She slept like . . . oh . . ."

She'd been about to say, "Like the dead."

"Is there a medicine cabinet in the downstairs bathroom?"

"No, only in the upstairs. Why, Nick?"

"We'll talk before I leave, okay?"

"Sure."

I went down the hall and found Angela Grosso sitting on Mary Ann's bed, just the way I had left her the day before.

"Angela?"

For a moment it seemed as if she didn't hear me, like the day before, then she turned her head and looked at me.

"Nick," she said, "what is it?"

"I want to talk."

"Come in," she said, "sit."

"No," I said, shying away from the bed, "I'd rather stand, Angela."

She frowned. "Well, all right."

"Tell me about Mary Ann, Angela."

"What about her?"

"What kind of child was she?"

She got a faraway look in her eyes and said, "She was a beautiful child, beautiful. So obedient . . . when she was younger . . ."

"And then what happened? When did she change? Was it in junior high school? Or high school? When did she change exactly, Angela?"

"Change?"

"You know what I mean," I said. "When did she start . . . going boy crazy."

"Boy crazy? Nick, who have you been talking to?"

"Not that many people, Angela," I said. "I've read her poetry, and I talked to Grace . . . and to Vito."

"Vito . . ."

"You know about Vito, don't you, Angela? You know about a lot of things."

She remained silent.

I moved closer and said, "Tell me about Mary Ann, Angelina. Tell what she was like."

She waited a long time to answer, and I waited with her. I didn't want to hear any more of that "beautiful child" stuff, and if the truth was going to come out, I was willing to wait for it.

Finally she looked at me and her expression was different. No longer was she the mother in mourning, now she wore the expression of a dissatisfied mother, a long-suffering mother.

"She was disrespectful," she said, slowly, "she was . . . bad . . . a trial, Nick, believe me. She was . . . wild. Everyone thought she was such a saint."

"Who's everyone, Angelina?"

"My friends, who else?" she said. "They all told me what a good daughter I had, how lucky I was. They didn't know how she *really* was. When she discovered boys and . . . sex!" She said "sex" as if it had four letters, not three. "She had sex for the first time in junior high school. Did you know that?"

I didn't know that, but what could I say?

"She was . . . uncontrollable," she went on, "and she was smart, so smart. I mean, she fooled my friends, and she fooled a lot of her own friends. She fooled Tony . . . oh, she fooled him completely."

"But not you, huh?" I asked. "And not Vito."

"Vito," she said, shaking her head. "What she did to that poor boy."

"What she did to him?" I asked.

She looked at me. "You have found out a lot of things, haven't you?"

"Yes, ma'am, I have."

"You know about the . . . the rape?"

"Yes, I do."

She shook her head and made a disgusted sound with her mouth.

"There was no rape," she said, staring back out the window. "Vito was probably the only man who gave her what she really wanted."

"Why was she marrying Tony, then?"

"Why? Because she said she changed, that's why. She came back from . . . wherever she was and claimed she had changed. She'd seen the light. She actually said that." She looked at me again. "After making my life miserable for years, *she* saw the light. She was going to marry Tony and settle down. Poor Tony, he waited years for her."

"Angelina," I said, "when did she tell you about the rape?"

"The night she died," she answered without hesitation, "she said she had some things to tell me, to get off her chest. That's what she said. She told me things I knew already, things she didn't think I knew. Things she did that . . . that no Catholic girl should ever hear, let alone do."

She averted her eyes. She didn't look at me, or out the window; she looked instead at a crucifix that was hanging on the wall.

"I knew what she was like, Nick. In junior high school, in high school and . . . and after, as an adult. Did you know that she wasn't at her father's funeral? Couldn't be bothered to come back for it. What kind of daughter is that? Tell me."

"That was then, Angelina," I said, wanting to keep her on the track. "What about now?"

"She thought she could change, but I knew better," she said, as if she hadn't heard me. "I knew she'd never change. She'd make my life miserable again, and she'd do the same to Tony. She'd hurt both of us."

"So you killed her?"

Her head whipped around and she glared at me.

"I did not!" she snapped. "She was my daughter, for God's sake."

"Angela, the police found a pill container in the downstairs bathroom. They were yours."

"She must have taken them."

"Your girls never went into your bathroom, Angela, remember?" I asked. "Even as adults they thought of it as your bathroom." The way I thought of my father's house as "his" house.

"She could have gone in, and taken them, when no one was home," she said, lamely.

"Why would she take them from the upstairs bathroom, and then go downstairs to ingest them? And then leave the container on the sink instead of doing it all in her room?"

"I . . . I don't know. She must have taken them."

"Did she, Angela?" I asked. "Did she do that? Or did you give them to her?"

She hesitated, then said, "I did not *make* her take them."

"But you gave them to her, right?"

She looked at me, then away, back at the crucifix.

"I didn't know what to do," she said. "I . . . prayed for guidance. If she stayed here, if she got married and stayed here, eventually people would find out . . . what kind of person she was."

"What if she really had changed, though?" I asked. "What about that? What if she just wanted to marry Tony and live a normal life as his wife?"

"She wouldn't . . ." She shook her head. "She couldn't . . ."

"Maybe not, Angela, maybe not, but she deserved the chance to try, don't you think? Or was it more important that your friends didn't find out what a . . . a trial she was, that your oldest daughter was not the saint they thought she was?"

"She couldn't change," she said. "She just couldn't. I had to convince her of that."

"Is that what you did, then?" I asked. "You convinced her that she couldn't change, and that she might as well die?"

There was no answer.

"You went and got the pills, and you gave them to her," I said. "Did you sit and watch while she took them, Angela? Did you wait for your daughter to die, and then arrange her on the bed with the poems?"

She glared at me. "What kind of a mother do you think I am?"

I stared at her, unsure what she was talking about. Was I being criti-

cized for thinking she'd kill Mary Ann, or that she'd sit there and watch
her daughter die?

"I think you're a selfish mother, Angelina."

"You don't understand. Your father, he'd understand. He's gone
through a lot—"

"He's gone through plenty," I said, interrupting her, "but he'd never
take away the chance any of his children had for happiness. You did that
to Mary Ann, didn't you, Angelina? You took away the one chance she
did have to change."

"She couldn't have changed," she insisted, shaking her head violently. Now who was she trying to convince, me or herself?

"Well, we'll never know, will we, Angela? You saw to that."

I moved close and bent over. "Did you actually tell your own daughter she'd be better off dead than trying to change?"

"I did what I thought . . . was right . . ."

"Well, what will people think now, Angela?" I asked. "What will they
think if this gets out?"

She looked at me again then, with fear in her eyes for the first time.
"You'll tell—"

"I won't tell," I said. "I can't tell the police. Even if you did convince
her to take the pills, you're right, you didn't *force* her. Besides, I can't
prove it. Only you and I know about it, right? How could I prove it?"

"I did the right thing," she said, more to herself than me—or was it to
God. "I did the right thing, I know it!"

"She was your daughter, Angelina," I said. "No matter what she did
to you—or what you imagine she did—the right thing would have been
to help her."

I started to leave, then turned. "Did it ever occur to you that by
actually taking the pills that you gave her, by doing what you wanted her
to do, she demonstrated that she *had* changed?"

She looked at me then and there was no fear or puzzlement in her
eyes. What I saw there was horror.

What if I was right, she must have been thinking. What then?

I left her there, sitting on her dead daughter's bed, and went down the
hall. I wondered if I would have done that, left her there like that, if the
container she was holding was full instead of empty.

There was nothing else I could do. Mary Ann Grosso had killed herself, she had taken the pills by her own hand and committed suicide.
That was a fact I couldn't change. If she'd been stronger—maybe if
she'd been the person she used to be—she wouldn't have done it, but
maybe in one last-ditch effort to please her mother she had downed

those pills and laid down on the bed with her poems, laid down to die . . .

"Nick?" Grace said as I came down the stairs. She was staring at me with a million questions in her eyes. Why, I thought then, why should Angelina and I be the only two to know?

"Grace," I said, putting my hand out to her, "let's talk . . ."

ACKNOWLEDGMENT

Every title and line of poetry used in this story were written by Marthayn Pelegrimas. The story is that much better for it. My thanks to her for allowing me to use them.

SUSAN DUNLAP

Susan Dunlap's characters deal with the rules. Former forensic pathologist-turned-private-detective Kiernan O'Shaughnessy is a woman who thrives on breaking the rules. Homicide Detective Jill Smith tackles crime in Berkeley, California, a city where breaking the rule *is* the rule, and the crimes in question range from murder to capers aimed at the city's much-maligned meter maids. Vejay Haskell, meter reader for PG & E, uses the rules of the gas and electric company to lead her to larger villains. And in Dunlap's Anthony Award–winning short story "A Celestial Buffet," a woman learns the post-mortem results of breaking the rules.

In "Bad Review" a group of writers discovers the consequences of agreeing to a pact that supersedes all other rules.

BAD REVIEW

The darker the clouds, the more silvery the lining, or at least so writers believe. Every situation has the potential to drop the story of a lifetime into your waiting computer. That is such a tenet of the craft that we never discussed it. And when we should have focused clearly, when Kay Washburn suggested her pact, she dazzled us with its boldness, and blinded us with her logic. Kay never left a loose end.

I've asked myself whether she had a window to the future, perhaps a leaded-glass affair that let in colors but blurred crisp outlines of events to come. Or was the pact merely a more macabre than normal whim of hers? None of us voiced those speculations. The question everyone has asked over and over, that *I*'ve searched my mind for every day for the past two years is this: What possessed Louisa, Cyn, and me—ostensibly three normal middle-aged women—to join in Kay's pact?

I've come up with plenty of explanations, some with more of a ring of truth than others. But whatever our underlying motivation, the fact is that we all did agree on the plan. That was twenty years ago when none of us could have imagined that we'd be famous, rich, or dead, much less that conditions of the pact would come to pass. Admittedly, Kay had unveiled it after several bottles of Chardonnay at a Monday afternoon lunch. But we were used to the Chardonnay, too. It was as much a ritual as having the lunch on a Monday to celebrate the writer's freedom from the nine to five. What stunned us as much as the pact itself was Kay suggesting aloud that one of us might actually become a literary light. (At that time, affording dental insurance seemed an unattainable goal.)

We rolled the idea of renown and riches around in our mouths as deliciously as we might a black olive before biting into the meat. And being writers we soon narrowed the speculation to a more professional theme—if one of us became really famous, what wonderful book idea would trickle down to the rest? Of course we all had different ideas of what that best-seller would be: *Exposé of Famous Writer? Self-aggrandizing Autobiography (ghost-written, of course)? Her and Me?*

Had we been willing to speculate on who might hit number one on the best-seller list, we wouldn't have guessed Kay. My choice would have been Louisa.

Louisa Hammond's novels deal with the loving befuddlement between mothers and daughters. There's a kindness to Louisa's perceptions. It's as if her own body—which now looks like throw pillows sticking to a surprisingly strong frame—took literary form. Like her fictional mothers, she gives and takes, settles and resettles, she reshapes herself, and then just at the point when it appears she'll lose any semblance of herself she stands firm, strong, unyielding, and able to support everyone else.

People tend to underestimate Louisa, to see the pillows and forget the steel frame. I remember the first time I really talked to her about Kay. Louisa was sitting on an old floral couch in her living room, by no means a spectacular room but certainly better than where she's living now. Then her dark brown hair—parted in the middle, held back by clips, flopping in loose waves over her shoulders—was just beginning to gray. She never fingered that hair or played with it as so many women do; she wasn't that self-conscious. That day she sat, feet drawn up under her, drinking not tea as I might have expected but espresso she'd made with a machine she'd brought back from Grenoble well before gourmet coffees became a fad. A huge vase of gladiolus, purple hydrangea flowers (the gauzy ones, not the pompons), and Queen Anne's lace stood on the hearth, almost overpowering the small room. Lifting the espresso cup for a sip, she moved as if both the temperature and humidity were near one hundred, though, in fact it was cool that spring. But she kept her gaze on me as if my ruminations were ice cubes.

"It seems like nothing ever bothers Kay," I began. "I can't recall anything she couldn't handle with that half-smile of hers and an offhand comment that most often leaves us laughing. Does anything frighten her?"

"Do you mean does Kay confide in me about her fears? No, Vivian, not Kay. The Cabots may talk only to the Lodges, and the Lodges only to God. But I'm sure Kay Washburn wouldn't put herself at the mercy of any of the three."

I laughed, but her choice of phrase—*put herself at the mercy*—is one I haven't forgotten over the years. It didn't enlighten me about Kay, but it made me a lot less trusting of Louisa Hammond.

"It says something for Kay," Louisa went on that day, "that even with that brittle reserve she gives us something we wouldn't want to do without."

"Us and her readers," I said.

Louisa nodded, half-smiling, her eyes half-closed, as if she were sifting all this into herself. "Her readers and us." And in the corrected order of that phrase she summed up what mattered to Kay. Later I decided that wasn't quite accurate. For Kay, it was her work that was important, and the fact that people read it allowed her to keep writing it. If I had said that to Louisa she would have taken another sip of espresso and said, "Well, we all feel that way about our writing." But Louisa, as perceptive as she is about characters and relationships, would have been wrong there. Louisa is committed to the people who people her fiction, those mothers and daughters of hers. At times I know she sees them as more real than we, her friends, are. But with Kay, her characters are just one part of the whole mystique of her books, and it's that mystique that grips her. What Kay truly loves is returning to the manuscript she's had in the works for years. She never talks about it. The rest of us question whether she will ever finish, or if she will polish and repolish it year after year till she's rubbed it entirely away.

Still, if I'd been asked to guess who would make it big, I wouldn't have chosen Kay. I never once pictured myself writing magazine articles entitled "A Trip Through Kay Washburn's Psyche," or "Travels with Kay," or penning the best-seller, *The Fateful Journey to Kay Washburn's Pact.*

Had I been forced to predict startling success, I would have picked Cyn Ciorrarula. Her heroines were great adventurers, braver than brave, cleverer than even their faithful readers expected, like high jumpers who clear the bar with so many inches to spare we're left wondering how we could possibly have assumed the challenge was worthy of them. Cyn created heroines with long sinewy muscles, control that allowed them to trot across broken rope bridges over Himalayan gulches, and coordination worthy of .400 hitters. They were the women we all wanted to be: women who took no shit.

Cyn wasn't young but she was still all angles, and too narrow for her height. It was as if she and Louisa had split two persons' physiques: Louisa'd gotten the softness, Cyn the hard. And she worked at staying in superb shape. It was her heroines' fault, she'd insisted, laughing in that matter-of-fact way of hers—no edge of undelved fear like Kay had. "Each year it means one more hour in the gym just to keep close enough to imagine how they might feel. Some people write till they die. That won't be what stops me. There'll just come a point when I won't be out of the gym long enough."

I can still picture her lifting weights or running around a track. But it was a sad moment when I realized she'd never again lope easily along the pine-edged country road where I bicycled beside her a decade ago. I remember how the branches hung over the road, turning the macadam from shining denim blue to black, shifting the temperature ten degrees in a second. Cyn was panting softly with each breath and the wind rustled her short reddish-blond hair like it would a dog's. Sweat coated her tanned skin, her aquiline nose, and under the awning of the pines she was still steamy and glowing, while I, riding beside her, felt the residual chill even in the sun.

A couple of days before, Kay had given us copies of her latest manuscript before she sent it off to her editor. As Cyn started down an incline I said, "What do you think possessed Kay to ask for our opinions of her book? It's not like she thinks that my travel articles are on a par with her novels."

"Or my adventures," Cyn said in that gravelly voice of hers. "I'm sure she thinks I write for overaged adolescents."

"So why does she want our opinions?"

Cyn laughed. "Maybe she thinks we have the common touch."

"But 'art' is above the common touch. Why does she care?"

"Because," Cyn said, taking a longer breath as we started up the rise toward the lake where she would end the run, dive in, and swim to the raft. I'll bet she misses that now. I'll bet she's thought of that irony every day for the past two years—if she hadn't kept in such good shape, she could still be swimming in that lake. "Because," she repeated then, "Kay is fanatic about tying up every loose end. She probably wouldn't make a change based on your opinion, but she'd want to be prepared for that criticism. She wouldn't take the chance of your saying it when it was too late for her to do anything about it."

It occurred to me then that Cyn was not the simple, straightforward, best-way-to-the-goal woman I had assumed. And later when Kay announced that fateful pact, I'll bet Cyn was less shocked than I was.

If the spotlight had shone on Cyn I wouldn't have been surprised. But I doubt any of them ever considered me a possibility for fame. I certainly didn't, which was just as well. You don't become a celebrity writing travel books. Not unless you elect to go places where your roommates have more legs than you do, and the humans' vision of you is in several pieces and ready for the rotisserie. Not for me. I had endured a sepulchralish half-hour in a mud bath wondering just who had been in there before me and how much of their skin was still here touching mine; I'd spent a week in a nunnery in Bali where instead of blessings I'd gotten diarrhea, fleas, and ringworm. The sufferings of a travel writer are legion. Indications of sympathy, respect, and adulation are not. I don't go out of my way for adventure like Cyn. My idea of risk is trying kiwi syrup in my mai tai. Bicycling along that country road beside Cyn was as bare bones as I hoped to get.

My dream of fame was that it would befall Cyn, and I would describe the journey through her life to its happy conclusion. For me it would be the chance to translate the micro-novels that make up travel writing to full-blown form, the chance for respect and maybe a soupçon of adulation. My vision ended with me accepting praise and glory in a penthouse suite atop the Four Seasons Hotel.

But if either Cyn or I had had real visions of hitting it big I can't imagine we'd have come up with the idea of the pact like Kay did.

And Kay was the least likely of any of us to really "make it." She wasn't tough like Cyn, or earthy like Louisa, and she certainly didn't have the unpleasantly garnered ability to adjust to the unpalatable situations that I had acquired eating raw worms that didn't quite pass for squid at one hotel on the Pacific.

Kay was a tiny, dark woman with sharp features and a patrician nose down which she observed the world. Only occasionally did I look at her and focus on her pale hazel eyes, which seemed to lurk in the sockets and shift back and forth nervously. Then she reminded me of a chipmunk peering out of its hole into a world of predators, always poised to make a dash to the next safe spot. Kay's novels were seemingly without form, books that demanded all your concentration and still left you feeling like you might be asked to repeat the grade, books that left you laughing so hard you wondered what kind of mind created them. And when you thought about them afterward you realized that, in fact, there was a form supporting the flights of fancy and fear much like the steel bars under the pillows that made up Louisa. When you turned the last page every question was answered, every thread tied up.

If it couldn't have been me who stepped into the spotlight, in one way I'm glad it was Kay. I wouldn't have wanted to live with the thought of Kay, with her biting humor, writing a tell-all about me.

Still, even knowing that side of her, I wouldn't have wanted to do without her at lunch. She was too entertaining. She'd sit there on the deck, silent for long periods, then slice in one soft comment that would ricochet for the next five minutes. Kay was like her books in that sense; they, too, had a final twist, an irony that left you laughing, or gasping, or both.

Besides, Kay's houses, particularly the last one at the top of the mountain, were too magnificent to be missed. And, the unfortunate pact was, in fact, fair and right, and uniquely suited to our foursome.

That's what makes the events of her death so ironic.

We were sitting on her deck that afternoon. This was years before she had the sauna put in and the deck enlarged and edged with lacy trees that filtered the sunlight. Years before the light of fame shone on her and she moved to the top of the mountain. This deck was a few ramshackle square yards of redwood, the table one of those old metal ones with the hole for the beach umbrella. A clear bowl held the remains of shrimp salad, and the knobby end of a baguette lay next to a shapeless mound of butter on a gold-rimmed saucer Kay'd gotten as a gift at her first wedding. Both bottles of Chardonnay stood in the middle of the table, one empty, the other with its wine line hidden behind the label. Kay sat across from me, the shade from the umbrella thrusting half her face into relief, sharpening her cheekbones, darkening the sloughs in the sides of her nose. As she spoke I had the sense that I was seeing her flipping ahead to her last chapter. "Ladies," she said, lifting the glass she'd just refilled. "I propose a pact. A modified tontine. You recall the tontines." She'd paused here and waited for Louisa to fulfill her responsibility and ask for the working definition. Secure in the cocoon of love and warmth she'd woven around her, Louisa had no qualms about admitting she was hazy on dictionary skills.

"In a tontine the members bequeath their worldly goods to the last surviving member."

"So that would mean one of us would inherit enough to enable her to continue living indoors?" Cyn laughed. Of course, that was before Kay's film deal and the hilltop villa.

"But what about our children?"

"*Your* children, Louisa," Kay reminded her. "We haven't all planned to bequeath to them. As for husbands, Cyn will outlive Jeffrey and anyone she chooses to take on after that."

"So much for my prospects," I muttered, but Kay was too engrossed in her presentation to be distracted.

"What I'm suggesting is not a tontine but the reverse of it."

"An enitnot?" I'm still embarrassed to have said that, as I was then when I saw Kay's nostrils draw inward.

"Despite that," she persevered, "I consider you three my dearest friends and the only people I truly trust."

I was both taken aback and flattered by that designation. For an instant Louisa's face revealed pity, and Cyn's showed nothing so much as a lack of surprise.

Acknowledging none of our reactions, Kay went on. "My suggestion is that you become my literary conservators."

"*If* you die before we do, and, Kay . . ."

"I know, Louisa, you wouldn't want to think that. But that's not exactly what I mean." Kay plucked the butter knife from the yellow mound and tapped her delicate forefinger against it. "We've all seen women who've lived too long, who are formless shades held up by too-bright rouge, too-yellow hair, who look with watery eyes through holes edged thickly in black." I remember thinking then that her words didn't sound natural but as if she were reading them off an invisible computer screen, one on which she'd been writing and rewriting. "They've become parodies of themselves, crones they once would have laughed at." The butter knife slipped out of her hand and clanked against the metal table. Kay looked down, surprised. It was clear she'd forgotten she was holding it. Picking up her napkin, she wiped the yellow smudge off the table, then put the knife in the salad bowl so carefully it made no sound.

There were no other sounds—no birds, no traffic noises, no hum of distant conversations. It was as if the moment and we in it were frozen, no longer alive. At the time I thought it was in reaction to the painted women clutching their decaying pasts.

Kay waited a moment to let the tension ease. "Dreadful as it is for those women, they at least are just making spectacles of themselves to their family and friends, the people—as you say, Louisa—who love them." She paused and looked at each one of us. Her face was deadwhite, and it was the first time I noticed wrinkles crowding in on her eyes. "Think what they would do if they wrote books. They could turn out ninety thousand words that would stamp their memories in purple, or whatever color humiliation and ridicule wear. They would mock themselves all across the country, day after day, year after year, as long as libraries last." She swallowed, and then had to swallow again before she could go on. "And all that because no one cared enough to stop them."

She drained her wineglass slowly, letting her eyelids close as she drank. No mascara, no shrieking aquamarine eye shadow. I glanced at Cyn in time to see her shiver in the sun. Louisa, sitting on a soft deck chair with her feet under her, totally in shade, moved her hands as if to draw an imagined shawl tighter around her. The first afternoon breeze blew across my back; or maybe I've just painted that onto my memory of the scene.

When Kay opened her eyes she looked at each one of us and said in that crisp, so logical voice of hers, "What I propose is an agreement that if any of us should be in that position the others, her dearest friends, the people she trusts the most, would save her."

"Critique the manuscript? We already do that." Louisa rubbed her fingers over an African leather bracelet her second daughter had sent her from wherever it was that that one lived. "If you mean we should tell her the manuscript is a stinker, that's tough, but, well, okay. It's one of those things that has to be done."

"But what if she doesn't believe you?" I'd asked. "What if she decides *you're* the one who's lost her judgment?"

"We're talking group decision, right?" Cyn was sitting up so straight, thighs so tensed that it was fifty-fifty whether she was touching the chair at all. She hated limits and discussions of limits. And criticism.

Kay leaned forward, her face now totally in the shade. Maybe it was that darkness, or maybe I'm painting over the memory, but her pale eyes seemed to be drawn back more than usual, as if she'd seen the snout of a predator halfway down her hole. "Let's say it's my novel. You three read it. It's trash. Vivian says, 'Gee, if Kay weren't so out of it she'd be humiliated to have anyone read this.' Cyn agrees, 'Suppose someone were willing to publish it. Unlikely, but still . . .' And, Louisa, you say in that sad way you have, 'Well, we did tell her.' You all agree, 'But poor Kay, she can barely remember what she says from one minute to the next; she's dribbling her food down her cleavage. She's past the point of accepting sense. And you know her work is the only thing that matters to her—' "

Louisa gasped, then forced a shrug. As much as she would like to have believed Kay valued friendship—*our* friendship—more than painting a

masterpiece with words, even she didn't delude herself enough to pro-
test.

"So?" Cyn or I asked.

"So what I'm asking is that before I commit to a mistake that I—the
me you now know and love—should have been sorry for, that would scar
my name through eternity, or however long they might mention me in
parodies of literature, you stop me. Permanently."

Again the world seemed silent. I remember thinking that I was
stunned, not so much that Kay would ask us to decide if she needed to
be killed, much less to commit murder, but that she would even consider having us pass that kind of judgment on her work. It drove home to
me how essential her work was to Kay—more essential than she herself.

It was a ridiculous scene—four law-abiding middle-aged women sitting at a table discussing the fine points of a pact to kill one, or more, of
us. Sometimes I can hardly believe we went on with the discussion. How
many times have I replayed that scene with a different end, a sensible,
happy end? But at the time, with the sun and the wine, and the repartee,
Kay's pact didn't seem too odd to consider. Just a little literary insurance
policy.

Before any of us could speak, Kay reached into the straw bag she
always carried, pulled out a green velvet box, and laid it on the table.
The velvet was a dark green, the color you might find in an English
gentleman's library. It looked wildly out of place on the white metal
deck table. Kay caught her closely clipped thumbnail under one of the
edges and opened the lid.

I don't know what I expected, a poison pen? A switchblade knife?
Certainly not baby spoons. Four silver baby spoons lay in a row, their
handles widening from the neck up so that near the top there was room
for one letter to be monogrammed. L K C V (Louisa, Kay, Cyn, Vivian).
Cyn laughed. It was the type of elaborate, prickly joke that was not out
of character for Kay.

Kay picked up the spoon marked K and laid it down apart from the
others. "It's clear there is no other way to stop me. I've lost my marbles.
My elevator no longer goes to the top floor."

"You're paying sixty cents on the dollar," Cyn said, in that gravelly
voice. "Your thermometer stops short of boil."

Unconsciously Louisa sank back away from them and her brow tightened. She looked at neither Kay nor Cyn, but her expression was what
one of her fictional mothers would have had hearing the exploits of an
immature offspring. Then, as if to reaffirm the rules of behavior, she

proffered the wine bottle around, and ended up filling only her own glass.

Kay stared at her and then Cyn and me, much as she might control a trio of dogs. When we were still, she said, "If, in fact, I become hopeless, I am asking you, my friends, to kill me." Seemingly, as an afterthought, she added, "I assume you would want me to do the same for you."

This was the penultimate Kay, the master of tying up all the ends.

It took another bottle of wine before we all—albeit uncomfortably— agreed to the pact. Death or doddering humiliation? If they were the only two options then what were friends for? Besides, we weren't talking about murdering a friend just because she was senile, she had to be so out of it she'd lost her judgment, yet organized enough to write a one-hundred-thousand-word book.

I had misgivings, to put it mildly, but under the circumstances, it was hard to make a case for producing drivel. And after Kay's total commitment, how embarrassing would it have been to proclaim myself happy as a clam to publish anything that would allow me to spend my declining years on the veranda of the Ruggles Hotel in Rangoon or a suite at the Top of the Mark in San Francisco, or even some fine nursing home that caters to your every—ever vaguer—whim. Besides, if I started to mix up the Top of the Mark with Motel 6 my friends wouldn't have to kill me to keep me out of print.

"So the question becomes how and who?" Kay went on. "It's one thing to do your friend a favor, it's another to fry for it." We'd all laughed then. Clearly, Kay intended to leave no thread hanging. I remember smiling to myself, thinking how ridiculous to imagine that Kay would ever need someone else to make her decisions. I wondered which of us she was really eyeing as the likely incompetent. But I couldn't imagine her deciding a diminution of anyone's work but her own would really matter much.

Louisa drained her wineglass. Cyn perched on her chair, arms clasped around knees like a kid. I leaned back in the half-shade. Life was beginning to take on that open-ended feeling that an afternoon of sun and wine brings. The pact began to look like a diverting puzzle.

"So we have a little ceremony," Kay continued. "We've always liked ceremonies. By this time the recipient—shall we go on saying it is I?— knows she has created dreck."

"You mean she knows her *friends* think she's created it," Cyn reminded her.

"Right. At that point I'll know you all scorn my penultimate novel. You'll all have discussed it with me, doubtless at much greater length than I'll want. I'll be appalled. But in the end I'll trust you. If I trust you with this pact, I'll certainly trust you to show literary judgment. So I'll come to lunch, and when we've finished the last shrimp in the salad, polished off the heel of the french bread, when we're sitting here drinking wine just as we are now, one of you—say, you, Vivian—will take out the box. You'll open it. Inside all three of your spoons will be lying just as they are now, bowl down, monogram down. But mine will be reversed, bowl up, monogram showing. I'll look. I won't believe it." Kay pantomimed her expected horror, eyes and mouth snapping open, hands flying up. But no one laughed. "Then I remove one of your spoons—it doesn't matter which one—I mix the others, and put them back, bowl down, monogram hidden. One of those three, of course, is mine. I hand the box to each of you in turn and you pick one, keeping the monogram hidden." She paused till Cyn, Louisa, and I nodded in acknowledgment. "The one who gets my spoon kills me."

It was a moment before Louisa said, "But why the elaborate ceremony?"

"Because, my friend, this way none of you knows who the killer will be. If there's an investigation, the innocent two can't rat on the guilty."

Cyn glared. "Thanks a lot."

Kay laughed and I and then Louisa, and finally even Cyn couldn't help but laugh, too. Ratting was one of the cardinal sins in Cyn's characters' creeds of life. A rat never makes it to the top of Everest. No brass ring for the rat.

There was more discussion, of course. What if the appointed victim was in her right mind but the rest of us went crazy? Odds of that were small. It was worth the risk, Kay insisted. What if the killer tried to carry out her sworn duty, and failed? We talked "What If's" the rest of the afternoon. And in the next week we must have made sixty phone calls among the four of us. We ended up having dinner the following Monday and it was there that we did finally agree. Now, of course, our handling of the whole thing seems ridiculously cavalier, but at that time death was an unlikely possibility and the idea that anyone would be clamoring to publish an opus of ours that even we found wanting was much less conceivable.

But, in fact, three of Kay's last four books topped the best-seller lists. Critics raved. (And none of these even was her oft-returned-to so-well-polished manuscript still in her drawer.) The books went into fourth and fifth printings. They were translated into French, Spanish, German, Japanese, Norwegian, and languages spoken in places that weren't countries a few years ago. Kay was interviewed on "Oprah" twice.

Kay had changed by then. Her eyes had sunk farther into the sockets and she'd come to look more like a cornered possum. Those hollows in her cheeks had sagged, the sharp edges of her face dulled, and her observations had changed from rapier blades to gnarled kitchen knives that rasped rather than cut.

She'd moved away from interruption and people, to a house atop a mountain—not a hill but a full-size mountain. The view was great. The privacy was unparalleled, because Kay bought the entire mountain. An unpaved winding one-lane road led up to the gate. But the road washed out with the first heavy rain of winter, leaving her with a whole lot more privacy than I would have found appealing. Even now—when I find myself living with women I would never have chosen as housemates, women who are rarely quiet, and never interesting—Kay's four-month regimen of breaking her fast with dry cereal and powdered milk, closing the day with canned tuna dinners, and no company to look forward to but her own doesn't sound good. But—Cyn, Louisa, and I laughed— surely there she'd finally finish the great manuscript.

The only way up Kay's mountain in the winter was a steep, wet, treacherously slippery, two-mile climb worthy of a Sherpa. Not a prospect to attract visitors, even friends as close as we were. But as Kay said, we cherish our rituals. It was this climb that Cyn made every winter to prove to herself she was still in shape and to experience something of what her latest heroine, an Everest conqueror, might.

Laughingly, Cyn commented that *My Ascent to Kay Washburn's* was as close as she was going to come to the great book dropping in her lap.

Not to be left out of this ritual, Louisa and I created a ceremony to herald Cyn's departure. Louisa made a casserole of Kay's favorites: smoked salmon with fresh vegetables Kay hadn't tasted in weeks. She packed it in Cyn's backpack, along with chocolate bars to keep Cyn going on her climb. At the top, Kay was waiting with hot bath for Cyn, hot oven for the casserole, and plenty of brandy for after dinner. What this meant was that Cyn's descent the next day was frequently more harrowing than her climb. But at the bottom, I completed the ceremony with more brandy and a massage technique I'd learned in Bali.

The trek before last, Cyn said Kay seemed distracted, forgetful, her words out of focus. For the first time Cyn had gone to bed, not exhilarated from the climb, the dinner, and the repartee, but exhausted from her vain effort to get a clear picture of what Kay was saying.

Even so when Kay sent us that last manuscript we were shocked. After we'd all read it, it was two days before Cyn finally said in uncharacteristic understatement, "It's not top drawer." Another day and a

half and bottle of wine passed, and I admitted, "It's not even in the
dresser."

Then the question of censorship arose. Who were we to pass judgment on Kay's work? If Kay liked it, maybe her readers would, maybe
. . . If this was the great manuscript, all those years of polishing had
rubbed it down to dross. It was not merely a bad book. It was a bad
book, written in a pompous and blowzy style. In it her characters ridi-
culed all her previous work. And worse yet, ours. There was no chance it
would slip quickly into the ditch of well-deserved oblivion. By then a
grocery list with Kay's name on it would have been literary news. The
world would have gobbled it down. And then spit it back up. Kay's worst
nightmare. And, in this case, ours.

The manuscript, alas, fit perfectly into Kay's pact.

We stopped talking about the merits of the book and focused on the
pact. The three of us hashed over our decision, trying to find an escape
clause that we knew didn't exist. Kay never left loose ends. But still we
had to try. You don't decide to commit your first murder, to kill one of
your best friends, who disagrees with your decision, when you are not
going to inherit her newfound wealth, or even have access to the amenities it provided, without a lot of thought. When Kay died we would lose
not only her and her wonderful house to lunch in, but the lunches left to
the survivors were hardly a cheerful prospect, to say nothing of the
considerable tension we'd feel every time we finished a manuscript.

We suggested to Kay we quash the pact, but Kay insisted it was still
valid. There was no give in her position, no wit in her arguments. Kay
was impatient. She snapped at Cyn when she disagreed, at me when I
criticized her pact. It was Louisa, who'd been the most reluctant about
the agreement all along, who finally said to Cyn and me, "If Kay can't
stand criticism of this little ritual of hers, how will she ever live through
the reviews she'll get for this book? She'll kill herself. And that will start
another round of gossip. In the end her work will be overshadowed by
her bizarre death, speculation about it. And she'll be as dead as if we'd
gone ahead with the pact and killed her ourselves."

There was no other choice but to kill her.

It pains me to recall Kay's reaction when I presented her the green
velvet box. I don't know whether it was merely shock, or disbelief that it
should be she who ended up on the receiving end of her own pact. She
must have had suspicions, after all the discussion and reconsideration of
the pact. But, clearly, it had not occurred to her that we found her book
so awful we were invoking the pact. But once she did realize that, she
pulled herself together and for the first time that day looked like the Kay

of old. She never lowered herself to defend her book, much less herself. If there's one thing I'm certain of, it's that if Kay Washburn couldn't write her kind of novel she had nothing to live for.

We drank champagne that day. Kay must have downed a bottle by herself before she opened the green velvet case. Still, her hands shook as she removed one engraved spoon and laid the others bowl-down for us to choose. Purposely, I didn't look at Cyn or Louisa when we drew spoons. I forced myself not to sigh when I checked mine and realized it was not the one with the K, that I would not be Kay's killer.

The next day I considered my options and chose the most cowardly course. I booked a flight to Bali, and spent the following month in that appallingly flea-ridden nunnery. Tempting ringworm, I walked barefoot under the gaze of the Mother Superior, spent days scrubbing outhouses, nights sleeping on a hard pallet. Never once was I free of bugs, busy work, or penitents. After a week I stopped mourning Kay; after two weeks I gave up worrying about Cyn or Louisa. After a month I just wished whichever of them had gotten the damned spoon would get on with her job and let me get out of here. (And, being a writer, I have to admit the thought did occur to me that there wasn't even a chance of writing any kind of article on this place, unless I was doing it for *Microbiology Monthly*.) But the Mother Superior would provide me an unshakable alibi. It wasn't till I got word of Kay's obituary that I flew home.

Needless to say, my trip didn't ingratiate me with Cyn and Louisa. And when the police realized that Kay had been poisoned by eating a casserole made of salmon, corn, potatoes, and enough *amanita viroza balinii* mushrooms to kill a football team, things began to look bad for Louisa.

Amanita viroza, or destroying angel mushrooms, were the method one of those literary daughters of hers had used to dispatch her overbearing mother.

The police surrounded Louisa like blowflies on a corpse. She was terrified. And I was terrified for her. (Especially after my own show of cowardice.) But not so terrified as I soon would be when those same police discovered that the only place *amanita viroza balinii* grow is in Bali.

Blowflies are quite willing to move onto fresher meat. And it was all I could do to convince the police that my old car was hardly in any shape to make it up Kay's hillside in February. Nor, for that matter, was I.

It took them another week to discover Cyn's ritual climb to Kay's retreat, and to posit me giving the mushrooms to Louisa, Louisa adding the salmon, corn, potatoes to the ritual casserole and packing them in Cyn's backpack, and Cyn mountaineering up with her deadly load.

It did stretch credulity to imagine Kay sitting down with one of her murderesses to eat a dish she had delivered. But, of course, I couldn't tell the detective that—not without exposing the pact and making the three of us look a helluva lot more suspicious than we already did.

As it turned out more suspicious would not have been possible. I proved I was out of the country, Cyn swore she hadn't made the trek up the mountain in a year, and Louisa insisted she didn't make the casserole, adding rather charmingly I thought that she would be humiliated to cook with canned corn. It took a jury less than an hour to find us guilty of murder and conspiracy to commit same. The judge had no hesitation about incarcerating us for an unpleasant number of years.

I've been here for two already. Louisa and Cyn are at other ladies' establishments, so, presumably, we won't conspire again. I supposed this place isn't bad as prisons go. Physically, it's better than the nunnery in Bali—no fleas, or outhouses. But every day for the first year I swore I would put up with a camel-load of fleas to get revenge on Cyn or Louisa.

I spent that year alternately trying to figure out which of them was the culprit, and silently berating her selfishness. Could Cyn or Louisa have expropriated some of my Balinese mushrooms? Of course. Could Cyn have cooked the casserole? No chance. Cyn's culinary skills peaked at the can opener. Could Louisa have driven the casserole up the mountain before the snow? No way. And more to the point, Kay would never have eaten it.

The pact was supposed to be foolproof. Kay was a master at tying up loose ends.

Kay had told us that she'd given a lot of thought to the mechanics of our agreement to protect the innocent from endangering the guilty. But, in fact, it was the guilty who'd done in the innocent.

It took me almost the entire next year to realize the truth, the miserable, stinging truth of the only one who could have killed Kay.

We'd all thought of writing *Me and Kay Washburn's Murder*. I'd envisioned it as the travelogue up to Kay's body. Cyn, I'm sure, had imagined it as the trek to same. And Louisa, a sort of Last Supper, with corpse and recipes.

Louisa would never have gone to print with corn from a can.

I'd like to think it was because Kay changed her mind and saw the wisdom of our decision. But my suspicion is that what she saw was the inevitability of the pact she had instituted. She knew one of us would kill her, so she took the mushrooms, opened cans of salmon and corn, cubed the potatoes she had up there with her, cooked the casserole, and she ate it. And as she lay there dying she must have been smiling at the irony of it all.

I'd like to think that. But the truth is that from the beginning she planned her death and our conspiracy in it. How do I know? Kay's great manuscript, the one she kept polishing all those years, was just published. It is stunning. The characters are, if not flattering, definitely Louisa, Cyn, and me to a T. And none of us will have to scramble to sell our version of *Me and Kay Washburn's Death Pact*, because Kay's brilliantly written book is the final word on it.